Marcy Dermansky lives in Astoria, New York, where she is a film critic and award-winning short story author. Her fiction has been published in numerous literary journals, including McSweeneys. Marcy Dermansky is not an identical twin.

D0533677

twins

Marcy Dermansky

review

Copyright © 2005 Marcy Dermansky
Published by arrangement with William Morrow, an imprint of
HarperCollins Publishers, Inc.

The right of Marcy Dermansky to be identified as the Author of
the Work has been asserted by her in accordance with the
Copyright, Designs and Patents Act 1988.

First published in Great Britain in 2005
by REVIEW

An imprint of Headline Book Publishing

First published in paperback in 2005

10 9 8 7 6 5 4 3 2 1

ISBN 0 7553 2564 8

Typeset in Garamond by Palimpsest Book Production Limited,
Polmont, Stirlingshire
Printed and bound in Great Britain by
Clays Ltd, St Ives plc

Headline's policy is to use papers that are natural, renewable and
recyclable products and made from wood grown in sustainable
forests. The logging and manufacturing processes are expected
to conform to the environmental regulations of the country of origin.

HEADLINE BOOK PUBLISHING
A division of Hodder Headline PLC
338 Euston Road
London NW1 3BH

www.reviewbooks.co.uk
www.hodderheadline.com

twins

Sue

I wanted tattoos for our thirteenth birthday. Chloe didn't. Chloe refused. I told her I did not know what I would do if she kept saying no.

'Tattoos are dirty,' Chloe said.

Chloe was four minutes older. She was an eighth of an inch taller. She was smarter. She was prettier. We were identical twins, but Chloe had turned out better. She was the better twin, she had the better name, and I was desperate to hold on to her. Horrifying girls like Lisa Markman were inviting Chloe to their parties and offering her cigarettes and beer and birth control.

My childhood had passed in a golden bubble of happiness. I adored Chloe and Chloe adored me. We didn't need our parents; we didn't need our brother or friends or parties or separate bedrooms. Chloe and Sue. Our hair was blond, our eyes were blue. For twelve perfect years, Chloe and I lived and breathed each other. We took baths in the same bathtub, shared the same rubber bath toys. Now Chloe took constant showers, all by herself.

We needed tattoos.

'I won't,' Chloe said. 'You can't make me. No one in the eighth grade has a tattoo.'

She was right. No one did. We were from the suburbs. I hated every single person in the eighth grade. They were all morons, out to steal my sister. Chloe was much too good. She was too eager to please.

I sat on my bed, staring at Chloe, waiting for her to crack. Chloe wanted her own room, but there were no extra rooms in the house. It was a stupid idea. We were meant to share a room. We were identical twins. We had no secrets. Chloe picked up a hairbrush and started brushing her hair. She was obsessed with being clean. Chloe was always taking showers, smoothing her hair, washing her face, washing her hands, looking at herself in the mirror.

'You want to be like everybody else,' I said. 'But they're all boring.'

'Who is boring?'

'Everyone.'

'Everyone?' Chloe said.

I reached for her hand. Chloe laid down her hairbrush on the bed and squeezed my fingers.

'There is no one like us,' I told her.

'Everyone is boring?' Chloe repeated.

I picked up Chloe's brush and threw it against the wall.

Chloe bit her lip, looking down at her hands.

'Our tattoos won't be dirty,' I said.

I'd explained it to her. I had found someone who didn't care that we were underage. I had paid in advance. Everything was planned. Our tattoos would be simple. Chloe would get a SUE tattoo. Mine would say CHLOE. If Chloe ever got lost or made friends with someone who was not me or had sex with some strange, awful man, she could never forget who we were. Who we belonged with. It wasn't enough that we looked the same. Chloe could put a rhinestone barrette in her hair and she became someone else. She would get upset with me when I put a barrette in my hair too.

Chloe looked at her brush. It had left a dark mark on the pale pink wall.

'I can't get a tattoo,' she said.

'You have to,' I said.

Chloe shook her head.

'We could get our ears double-pierced,' she whispered.

'No,' I said. 'Tattoos. It's all planned. It's already paid for.'

Chloe crossed the room, picked up her brush, and started brushing her hair again. She was so beautiful. Wherever we went, people stared at Chloe, they stared at us. I knew that I looked like her. Technically I was beautiful too. But when I wasn't next to Chloe, I didn't feel right. I tripped on my shoelaces. My hair tangled easily.

'Three letters,' I said. 'To make sure we are never apart. No matter where we go. You won't do that for me?'

'It's enough to be twins,' Chloe said. 'It's practically tattooed on our faces. We look the same. Why isn't that enough?'

We had been having the same conversation for days. Chloe wanted friends, boyfriends. She wanted to blink her eyes and imagine me gone. I sat down on the floor and cried. I cried until my chest hurt and then I coughed. Snot dripped down my face and my head started to ache. Chloe sat down next to me and put her hand on her own head, like it hurt her too. For a while, she did nothing, just watched me cry. I'd blink through my tears, wipe the snot on to my sleeve, and watch her, watching me.

'Sue,' she said. 'Why do you do this?'

And then Chloe wrapped her arms around me. She rocked me like I was her little baby. I was miserable, but I felt wonderful, rocking. We rocked back and forth. Chloe and I were miserable together. It was the middle of the night. I could hear our older brother, Daniel, in his room down the hall, strumming chords on his guitar.

'We are underage,' Chloe whispered. She kissed the top of my head. Our age didn't matter. The appointments were made. The tattoo guy had taken my money and told me how to come in the back door. I had been slipping twenty-dollar bills from my father's wallet for months.

One day, Chloe would be glad. One day we would be old, we would be thirty, and Chloe would thank me.

Chloe's interest in other girls was temporary. It was adolescence. The tattoos, I knew, would keep us safe.

'We could get a computer,' Chloe said. 'Or leather boots.'

'No,' I said.

I stretched across Chloe's lap and reached over to open her schoolbag. I took out her pencil case and removed a freshly sharpened pencil. Chloe liked her pencils sharp. She loved multiple-choice tests, filling in the small circles with all the right answers.

'What are you doing?' she said.

I stuck the sharp tip of the pencil into my arm. A bubble of blood spurted from the spot. It was more brown than red. I touched the blood with my finger, smearing it over my skin.

'Why do you have to be so dramatic?' Chloe said.

If I was lucky, the lead from the pencil would make it into my bloodstream and I'd die an early death.

'Stop crying,' Chloe said. 'You make my head hurt.'

I wanted to die. Chloe was the better twin and I was not necessary. She did not need me and soon, any day now, she would pretend she did not know me.

'You should clean up your arm,' Chloe said. 'You're bleeding.'

twins

I shook my head. I hoped the lead would spread quickly. I closed my eyes. If I was dead, Chloe would no longer be an identical twin. She could cut our pictures in half, and no one would know I had ever been born.

She got up. I could hear her walk into the bathroom, hear the water running from the sink. She was washing her face, scrubbing her hands. That's what Chloe did. But then she came back to the room with tissues, a Band-Aid, antibiotic cream. She wiped the tears from my face. She put the cream on my cut. Chloe was a good nurse, but she wouldn't become a nurse. She'd be a doctor, a neurosurgeon. I prayed that she would not want to be a lawyer, like our parents. Our parents were miserable shits. Our parents were raging bores. They were divorce lawyers.

'Stop crying,' Chloe said. 'Please. Please stop crying.'

I would not stop crying.

'Are they safe?' Chloe said. 'Tattoos? Are they hygienic?'

I nodded, still crying. I was winning. I knew I had won. 'Yes,' I said. 'Yes.'

Chloe bit her lip.

'Everything is sterilized?' she said. 'Clean?'

'Of course,' I said. 'One hundred percent clean.'

I didn't know. I had no idea. For all I knew, we would get hepatitis B and die. That would be fine. We would die together.

'I want mine to be pink,' Chloe said.

'Fine,' I said. 'Pink.'

I hated the color pink. The walls of our bedroom were pink. Most of Chloe's clothes were pink. Most of mine were too. I didn't care. I reached for Chloe's hand. I squeezed it tight.

She looked sad. She shook her hand out of my grip, but I couldn't stop grinning.

'You are such a drama queen,' Chloe said.

*   *   *

Our parents had left for the office when we woke up on our birthday. No note, no presents. It was a Saturday, but it didn't matter. They were always working. Their office was in New York City, and we lived in New Jersey, so they liked to leave early to beat the traffic. They also liked to work late to miss the traffic. Even on the weekends. Maybe they were okay lawyers, but they were useless parents. My father liked to dictate idiotic rules into a tape recorder.

'They forgot?' Chloe said, staring at the empty orange juice container in the trash can.

'Wowee,' I said, thrilled. 'Not bad.'

I loved my parents' screwups. The bigger, the better. More ammunition for me. The next time my father accused me of raiding his wallet, I'd remind him about the time he forgot our thirteenth birthday. I'd never had any interest in my parents. They dressed in matching suits and never smiled or got down on the floor to wrestle with our dog, Daisy, a standard poodle who loved to be wrestled with. They were the most boring, irritating people alive and, like I was always reminding Chloe, entirely unnecessary. Chloe would do her homework without being told. She brushed her teeth and folded her clothes. She didn't need any parenting. She was already perfect. Chloe and I had each other. We were never lonely.

Our older brother, Daniel, sat at the kitchen table; he was eating chocolate pudding, reading a book about Nazi war criminals.

'You ever hear of Josef Mengele?' he said.

'No,' Chloe said. 'Who is he?'

She opened the refrigerator, shook her head, and then turned to look out the kitchen window. The driveway was empty. No matching Mercedeses, no parents. Gone. One day Chloe would learn.

I felt giddy. Today we were getting tattoos.

twins

'He performed experiments on identical twins during the Holocaust.'

'You're lying,' Chloe said. 'That's disgusting.'

She smoothed her hair.

'Nope,' Daniel said, smiling. 'It's a fact.' Daniel was a creep, always watching us. We didn't need an older brother. I wished he didn't exist. 'He did all sorts of sick shit. Instead of killing the twins like he did with the other Jewish kids, he set them aside and performed all sorts of cruel and twisted tests. He tried to change their eye color and performed surgeries just for the heck of it. He would stretch their limbs, or would take out their organs, try putting them back into the other twin.' Daniel held up his book, pointing to a photograph of a blond man in a laboratory. 'He's world famous for his experiments on twins. You can see for yourself.'

'It's our birthday,' Chloe said.

Daniel ate another spoonful of pudding.

'The Bobbsey Twins turn thirteen,' he said. 'I know. Happy birthday.'

Daniel had always hated us. We were twins. We were blond, we were movie star pretty, and he was a dark, ugly boy. Who cared about his made-up Nazi doctor? Not me. Daniel didn't matter. Chloe and I were off to get tattoos.

'This book is for you both,' he said. 'For your birthday. When I'm done reading it.'

'We have to go,' I said. 'We're going to be late.'

Chloe looked at Daniel.

'There was really a doctor who performed experiments on twins?'

Daniel grinned. 'Sick, twisted shit,' he said.

Chloe opened her purse and removed a small tortoiseshell comb. She started to comb her hair.

'Walk the dog before you go,' Daniel said.

I gave Daniel the finger.

'I'm sure as hell not going to walk her,' he said.

If Daisy went in the house, we'd clean it up later. We couldn't be late. Daisy had been part of a settlement my mother had gotten for a client, only the client hadn't actually wanted her; she had wanted to spite her husband. Daisy had always preferred me over Chloe. She was a good dog. She loved to wrestle and to chase after tennis balls.

'Fuck off and die,' I said, grabbing Chloe's hand and pulling her out the door. I wanted to get to the tattoo parlor fast, before Chloe could change her mind.

'I hate it when you curse,' Chloe said, pulling her hand away from mine, running her fingers through her hair.

'I'll never curse again,' I said.

'You will too,' she said. 'You always do.'

The air felt good, warm and cool at the same time. Like spring. Summer would come, and then there would be no more school. Just Chloe and Sue, free to do what we wanted. We were identical twins. It was us against Nazi doctors and mean older brothers and boring, rotten parents and popular girls who dressed like sluts and tried to steal my sister. We were Chloe and Sue, off to get tattoos. We loved each other best. Everything was all right.

Chloe had hers done first.

She wanted the tattoo on the small of her back. She wanted to cover it with clothes, but I didn't care. The tattoo would be there, even if no one could see it. Chloe undressed shyly, folding her T-shirt and handing it to me. Then she climbed onto the table, where the tattoo guy told her to lay flat on her stomach. She balled her hands up into fists, closed her eyes. I looked at the pretty, smooth skin on her back, the thin strap of her pink cotton bra.

'Twin number one,' the tattoo guy said. 'Ready, aim, fire.'

I wished the tattoo guy didn't have to touch Chloe. He was the ugliest man I had ever seen. He wore a black bandanna over his bald head. He had a red dragon on his arm and wore a leather vest. He had said it was illegal to work on minors and charged me double the regular price.

The tattoo gun made a loud, steady buzz; a tiny drip of blood bubbled on Chloe's back. I had no idea there would be blood. The tattoo guy wiped it off with a clean white cloth and kept working. My leg started to shake. Chloe closed her eyes.

'Does it hurt?' I said, petting Chloe's hair. 'Does it?'

She didn't say anything, just shook her head. She kept her eyes closed. There were beads of sweat on her forehead. The tattoo guy hummed to himself while he worked. He kept on wiping off her back with the cloth, now stained pink and red. As he started on the last letter of my name, I could see the S and U inside a curvy red scab.

'Done,' he said. 'I've never tattooed twins before.'

He smeared Vaseline on her back.

'Not so bad,' Chloe said with a small, fake smile. She sat up slowly, looked at me for a long time before she hopped off the table.

'It looks amazing,' I said.

Chloe shrugged. She reached for her T-shirt, but the tattoo guy told her to let the skin breathe. She crossed her arms over her chest.

The tattoo looked horrible. Chloe's skin was puffy and red, and pink dye oozed from the letters.

'It really looks amazing,' I told Chloe.

The tattoo guy snorted. 'Twin number two,' he said. 'Get your butt up here.'

I took off my pink T-shirt, the same as Chloe's, and looked at my beautiful twin sister as if it were the last time. It was crazy how much I loved looking at Chloe. It felt sort of creepy to be standing in my jeans and a bra in the back room of a tattoo parlor. A disgusting tattoo guy was about to touch my skin.

'I'm ready,' I said. I was scared. I wondered why Chloe hadn't been scared.

The tattoo guy laid his cigarette in the ashtray.

'La-di-da,' he said. He wasn't in awe of us the way most people were. I wanted Chloe to hold my hand, but she opened her book bag, pulled out her fancy comb.

'Ow,' I said. My eyes started to tear with the first prick of the gun. 'Ow, this hurts. You didn't tell me.'

I thought my spine was going to pop through my skin.

'Chloe,' I said. 'This hurts like hell.'

Chloe sat on the plastic chair, brushing her hair, while the pain kept on coming. I couldn't see her. I looked straight ahead to the sample sheets of tattoo designs pinned against the wall. Bugs Bunny, Daffy Duck, Betty Boop, a bald eagle. I couldn't see what was happening, but I knew from watching Chloe get hers done. I could picture the bubbles of blood on my back.

'What letter are you on?' I said. 'Tell me.'

'C,' the tattoo guy said. 'I just started, for fuck's sake. Stay quiet so I can concentrate on my work.'

'Drama queen,' Chloe said from her chair. 'I didn't cry. I didn't complain.'

I tried to be quiet, but my whole body started to shake. I could feel the tattoo gun jump off my back.

'Yo, identical twin,' the tattoo guy said, calling out to Chloe. 'I need your help here.'

Chloe came to me. She held my shoulders down on the table so that I would lie still and not ruin my tattoo.

twins

'I should never work on minors,' the tattoo guy said. 'Knock it off, so I can finish this damn thing.'

'Can't you suffer just a little?' Chloe said.

'No,' I said. 'This hurts too much.'

'The back is practically the worst place for this,' the tattoo guy said. 'Less body fat than any other part of the body.'

Chloe had acted like it was nothing. She'd lain on the table, quiet and calm, as if there wasn't a creepy old man with a gun shooting pain into her beautiful back. My name had only three letters. Chloe's had five.

'What letter?' I said. I was practically screaming. 'What letter?'

'O,' Chloe said. She held my shoulders. 'This was your idea,' she said. 'So stop screaming.'

My back felt like it was on fire. The tatoo guy dabbed at my skin with his cloth. He was cleaning up my blood with that dirty cloth. I leaned over the table, threw up on the floor.

I looked down at the vomit and felt bad. This was our birthday.

'God fucking damn it,' he said. 'Never again do I tattoo a freaking kid.'

Chloe stepped away from me. I couldn't see her, I was looking at the vomit, but I knew how she must feel. We were half naked, huddled in the back of a tattoo parlor at a seedy strip mall, being cursed at by a foul, ugly, disgusting, horrible man. I hated the tattoo guy. I hated him like crazy.

'If you want me to finish, one of you twins better clean up this puke.'

'It's okay,' Chloe said. 'I'll do it.'

'Twins,' the tattoo guy repeated, as if he was saying a dirty word.

I hated him.

Chloe kissed the top of my head. She found a mop and cleaned up my vomit while the tattoo guy finished up. I was grateful Chloe had kissed my head. She loved me. She did. We loved each other. Now I would be strong. I certainly would not vomit again. I had purpose; the tattoo guy could never hurt us. I'd kill him before I'd let him hurt Chloe. I'd ram his stinking tattoo gun up his ass. I'd spend my life in jail to protect my twin sister. My other half.

I suffered the next letter in perfect silence. I spelled the word *fuck* in my head. F U C K F U C K F U C K. Chloe would never even think the word *fuck*. She was a great speller. She had won spelling bees, but she never cursed.

'Done,' he said. I felt him smearing cold Vaseline on my back. 'Now get the fuck off my table.'

'Wowee,' I said, sitting up. 'Hooray.'

I felt giddy, gleeful, bursting with happiness. We had done it. Not only was Chloe in my genes, she was part of me. CHLOE and SUE, tattooed on our backs.

'This must be what shock treatment feels like,' I said. 'This must be what you feel like when they shock you in the mental hospital. The zap that wakes you up.'

'You have to be so dramatic,' Chloe said. 'Let's get dressed.'

'Let's look,' I said. 'Let's see.'

I jumped off the table. The pain was already going away, fading, something to be forgotten. The room smelled like vomit.

The tattoo guy gave us each a hand mirror. We gazed at our backs the way you would, after a haircut, look at the back of your head, using the small mirror to look into the large one. The skin was inflamed, greasy with Vaseline, and Chloe's tattoo was crusted with blood.

'It's not really pink,' Chloe said.

'It will be,' the tattoo guy said. 'Once the inflammation goes down. Make sure you don't scratch. Or let the skin get dry. You gotta keep them moist for a couple of days. Hold still, I'm going to cover them up.'

We stood, silent, as he stuck square bandages to our backs.

'I love you,' I said to Chloe.

From the mirror, I could see the tattoo guy smirk.

Chloe reached for her soft pink T-shirt, shoved it on over her head, covering her soon to be beautiful tattoo.

'We are sisters,' she said. 'Identical twins. You don't have to say that. It's an understood fact.'

'A given,' I said.

'A given.' Chloe nodded.

The tattoo guy was still smirking. I wanted to punch him, hurt him. He had no right to make fun of our feelings for each other. No one loved him the way I loved Chloe. He was nothing, nobody.

'What do you know?' I said. 'You're a creep, a pervert, the local pedophile. You give tattoos to underage girls in your back room so you can leer at them in their underwear. I could call my parents. My mother is a lawyer. My father is a lawyer. They'll put you in jail and they'll melt the key. How do like that idea? Does that make you smirk?'

His mouth dropped open. 'Hey, calm down, kid.'

Chloe thrust my T-shirt into my hand.

'Get dressed,' she said. But I didn't want to go. I felt too good. I didn't want to cover my tattoo. We had suffered, Chloe and Sue, together.

'I bet you violate health codes,' I yelled.

'Come on, Sue,' Chloe said. 'Stop screaming.'

The tattoo guy picked up his cigarette, but he didn't bring it to his lips. He stared at me, confused.

'You're all done here.'

'I'll scream rape, you ugly bastard,' I said. 'You'll get thirty years. You'll get life in the penitentiary.'

I could feel the rush of color in my cheeks. I felt great, really great. I'd get the tattoo guy. I'd ruin his life and then I'd go after his family. Chloe tugged on the loop of my jeans.

'We have to go,' she said. Sweet, good Chloe. Always avoiding a fight. She never wanted to hurt people, to break things. She was turning into a Goody Two-shoes, studying for tests and doing the laundry. I had no idea why I had turned out so badly.

I gently touched the place beneath her shirt where our new tattoo lay. My name. Chloe flinched.

I pointed my finger at that tattoo guy. 'You want to go to jail?' I said.

He had backed away from us, moving all the way to the opposite corner of the small room. His hands were shaking. I had him scared.

'The federal penitentiary,' I said.

I put on my T-shirt, grabbed Chloe's hand, and we ran out the door. Outside, it was still bright daylight. We were back in the cool spring air.

'We did it,' I said, hugging Chloe as hard as I could. 'We did it. We did it, we did it.'

Chloe pulled away.

'That hurts,' she said.

'We did it. We're marked forever. Forever and always.'

Chloe shrugged.

'We already were.'

When the scabs healed, the tattoos would be perfect. We would always be a part of each other, our names inscribed on each other's skin. But Chloe seemed sad. She kicked a pebble down the sidewalk as we walked home. Why wasn't she happy? I put my hands in my pockets and walked ahead of her. My tattoo had started to itch. I wouldn't scratch. We walked this way, one block then another, until the houses and the lawns got bigger and nicer, and we were almost home. I turned a corner, I could see our house, the house we had grown up in, and I was walking all alone, when Chloe suddenly bounded forward, wrapping her arms around me from behind.

'Okay,' she said, her breath warm on my ear. 'The tattoos are cool. Or they will be cool, after they heal.'

'They will be so cool,' I said.

'You are my sister,' Chloe said.

'I am your identical twin,' I said. 'I am part of you.'

Chloe kissed the top of my ear.

I dragged Chloe the rest of the way home, her arms around my neck, her legs heavy as mud. I loved our birthday, I loved Chloe. I didn't want anything else.

Our parents' Mercedeses were parked in the driveway when we got home, but the house was dark. I didn't like it. 'Nobody's home,' Chloe said, pulling on her hair.

We went inside. Daisy barked. The lights flashed on.

'Surprise,' yelled a room full of people. 'Surprise.'

My parents had thrown us a party. I could have killed them. There was no one I would invite to a birthday party. I didn't care about anyone besides Chloe. Other people didn't interest me, they only got in the way. The living room was decorated with colored streamers dangling from the chandelier, a birthday cake and a punch bowl on the coffee table. Presents stacked on the mantel-piece. My parents stood behind the couch, beaming, wearing polo shirts and faded khakis. Daniel glared at us from an armchair. Lisa Markman was on the couch, her horrible group huddled around her. They were the popular girls. They were not welcome in our house. They would have to leave.

'This is so wrong,' I whispered to Chloe.

But tears were streaming down Chloe's cheeks. She was smiling.

She was crying and happy at the same time. I couldn't believe it. We had gotten tattoos. That was all that we wanted, all that we needed. But there was Chloe, ready to love this stupid party. Her response was exactly what was required. Chloe was right, I was wrong. Always wrong. I pressed the tips of my fingers into the bandage covering the raw flesh on my back. The pain felt good. Tears sprang to my eyes.

It was as if I had entered a slow-motion universe. They were all there, in the living room, waiting, watching. Chloe gasped for breath. Daisy raced toward us.

I reached for Chloe's hand, but she was already gone, rushing to the couch, to Lisa Markman. Daisy jumped on me, licking my face. I stood in the doorway, patting Daisy's fluffy poodle head, watching as Chloe hugged Lisa and then, one by one, hugged the other girls from school. As if she *liked* them.

'Thank you. Thank you so much for this party,' she said to everyone in the room.

My parents held up their glasses of punch. They looked pleased with themselves.

Lisa Markman whispered something into Chloe's ear. Chloe giggled, then she shrugged. They walked together to the punch bowl. She looked at Lisa Markman and said, 'I can't believe you're here.'

Lisa Markman's skin was the color of coffee ice cream. Her father was a professional basketball player. Tall, black, and handsome, he used to play for the New York Knicks. He did TV commercials for Nestlé Crunch bars and multivitamins, so Lisa was popular even though she had a big, ugly nose like her father. Her mother was white, dead, killed in a car accident when we were in the fourth grade. Chloe thought that Lisa was pretty.

I wanted Lisa to get her hands off my sister. I looked at my brother in the corner. Daniel was staring back at me. He seemed to understand what had happened. He stuffed a baby carrot up his nose. The scabby tattoo on my back had started to itch. It itched like crazy. Daisy stood next to me waiting.

'Hey, Daisy,' I said. 'Hey, good girl.'

Daisy jumped back up on me, wagging her tail, licking my face. Chloe and I were identical twins, the same in almost every way, but the dog, I knew, loved me more.

Chloe

I had trouble sleeping after we got our tattoos. The skin on my back itched, and my mind couldn't stop racing. At our thirteenth birthday party, Lisa Markman had whispered in my ear that she liked me better than Sue. I knew that I should have defended Sue, my other half, but instead I was pleased. I took Lisa up to our bedroom, where she laughed at all the pictures of us: identical twins wearing matching clothes.

'I'd go insane,' she said. 'Having another person who looked exactly like me, following me around all day.'

I shrugged.

'It's not that bad.'

I looked down at my shoes, trying not to let her see how thrilled I was. Somehow Lisa was able to recognize what no one else ever could. She was the richest, most popular girl in the eighth grade, and she understood me.

'Is that you?' Lisa said, picking me out from our second-grade class picture. Sue and I were standing next to each other, wearing matching green corduroy overalls. Sue had loved those ugly overalls. She wanted us to wear them everywhere.

'Yes,' I said shyly, looking at Lisa sideways. 'Guess again.'

With every picture, Lisa was able to tell us apart.

My entire life, no one had ever singled me out in this way. When we were younger, my parents used to call our names so fast it sounded like one word: Chloeandsue. Strangers would point to us and whisper: *Look at the twins*. We were constantly told how pretty we were, together, but somehow on my own, it wasn't the same. I wasn't interesting. At school, Sue and I were in all the same classes, and she always sat next to me. Everyone took for granted that Sue was my best friend and that I was hers. We were considered the same person, undistinguishable, even when Sue threw pens at boys or hopped through the halls like a kangaroo. But I was not Sue.

I was not Sue.

I would say this to myself over and over, lying in bed, praying that the tattoo would heal properly, that the itching was not a sign of infection. I didn't want to be ruined before I had a chance to begin my own life.

Sometimes Sue would follow me into the bathroom; she would keep on talking to me while I brushed my teeth or washed my face. She wouldn't leave, even when I had to pee. She didn't think I ever needed to be by myself. Sue said that we would never have to get married, that we'd never need to bother making friends, because we'd always have each other. She said we didn't need anybody else. She had scared me the night she convinced me to get a tattoo. She stuck a pencil into her arm, and I watched her, imagining that one day it would be a razor blade. Sue thought tattoos would prove to the world that the bond we shared went deeper than DNA.

The funny thing was, the tattoos made us different. When we died, it would be easy for a forensic scientist to tell us apart. It wouldn't be necessary to check our fingerprints or our dental records or measure our bodies from head to toe. After we got our tattoos, we were never really and truly the same.

I didn't tell this to Sue.

For a little while, at least, she'd be happy.

Sue

Not long after our birthday, Chloe got her period.

Chloe did everything first. She was the first one out of the uterus, the first to hold up her head. First to walk and talk. We were identical, but my parents could tell us apart because I was always two steps behind. I didn't stand up until a month after Chloe had started walking. Chloe learned how to read first, to scramble eggs and memorize her multiplication tables. She was the first to make the honor roll. Actually, I'd never made the honor roll. There was no point to it. Chloe's success was my success. I never got jealous of Chloe; she was my other half, my property, my identical twin. Studying her, I always knew what to expect from life. When I finally did learn to walk, I never fell.

We were in the school cafeteria sitting across from each other at an empty table when Chloe started to bleed. Even before she put her hand on her stomach, I knew what was happening. I knew. My face turned hot. Before, guys could only look at Chloe, but now they could get her pregnant and buy her earrings. Nothing had been the same since Lisa Markman had shown up at our house. Chloe had shown Lisa our room. Lisa had petted our dog. I felt numb watching Chloe walk quickly out of the cafeteria, pushing the swinging doors open wide, disappearing down the long hallway. I didn't run after her because Chloe hated when I did that. But I watched, stunned, as Lisa and her gang followed after her.

I counted to one hundred and touched my tattoo. Then I made my way to the girls' bathroom. I tried to walk slowly, but my stomach hurt and at least four minutes had passed. I was scared I might be bleeding too. We were twins, had the same DNA. I ran down the hall into the bathroom and crashed right into Lisa Markman, who was standing in front of the mirror, putting on mascara.

'You know Chloe can go to the bathroom all by herself,' she said.

I felt my face turn red. Melanie Meyer and Brittany Lopez giggled. I wanted to throw Lisa against the wall, but I didn't do it. Lisa was taller than I was. Her father was enormous.

Chloe emerged from a stall, smiling shyly.

'Are you okay?' Lisa asked my sister.

Chloe nodded. She shrugged. She must have seen me, but she walked straight over to the mirror, straight to Lisa. The metal counter above the sink was covered with products: minipads, maxis, tampons with and without applicators, a pack of condoms. The periods had started almost three years ago. Lisa Markman, already five feet ten inches, had gotten hers first, breaking all menstruation records at the age of ten.

'I feel fine,' Chloe said. She pulled a pink lip gloss from her purse and examined it. 'I feel older, somehow.'

She meant older than me. She always thought four minutes made so much difference. I reached around to touch my back, to press my fingers against my tattoo. Knowing it was there made me feel better. We had taken the bandages off. The flaking had stopped and the skin was smooth. If I stood naked in front of the mirror, held another mirror to my back, I could read Chloe's name backwards.

'You do look more mature,' Lisa said, nodding her head.

I wanted to cry.

'You look the same,' I said, but Chloe didn't look at me.

'Did you use a tampon?' Brittany Lopez asked. Chloe shook her head no. 'I would never use a tampon,' Brittany said. 'Never ever. Not until I've lost my virginity.'

Lisa Markman snorted.

'Grow up, girl,' she said.

Chloe applied her lip gloss, nodding as she listened to this rush of womanly advice from these girls who would ruin her. She seemed happy. For a second, she looked at me, we were looking at each other, but then she was gone, my twin sister, disappeared. She simply stopped seeing me. She brushed mascara onto her pale eyelashes.

'I am not going to be a slut,' Brittany said. 'I might even wait until I get married.'

Melanie Meyer moved closer to Chloe and touched her hair. 'You have such pretty hair,' she said. Melanie's hair was curly and dark. Brittany examined Chloe's hands. 'I want to give you a manicure,' she said. 'My mother taught me how to do French tips.'

They surrounded Chloe from both sides. My leg started to shake.

Lisa Markman uncapped a thick purple Magic Marker. She added Chloe's name to a long list on the door of one of the stalls. I could not believe what was happening. It wasn't right for Chloe's name to be on the wall without mine. We were a package deal.

They wanted Chloe, not me. We were identical, but it was Chloe they liked.

'You have to call your mother,' Melanie Meyer said.

Finally I spoke. 'You're going to call our mother at the office about *this*?'

We were only supposed to interrupt our parents at work in case of emergencies.

'You have to call,' Melanie said, holding out her cell phone. 'It's a mother's proudest moment.'

'Until you get married,' Brittany said.

'Or get into an Ivy League college,' Melanie said.

I pictured my mother at her desk at her midtown law office. She was always busy, shuffling papers, talking on the phone, scamming money and summer houses from cheating husbands, bargaining for custody rights, demanding outlandish amounts of child support. It made my mother giddy, the settlements she got for her clients.

'I guess I should,' Chloe said. 'She'd want to know.'

'About your period?' I said. 'You think that is important?'

Now they were all looking at me. They were morons. I did not see why Chloe would want to waste her time.

'So what?' I said. 'Big deal. Chloe's a woman now. Tenth graders can knock her up. She can have little babies that suck teenage milk from her breasts. You think that's worth disrupting a busy lawyer's day?'

Chloe narrowed her eyes at me. It was an ugly look, the way Lisa Markman stared at me when I read out loud in English class.

'She's jealous,' Lisa said. 'It's pathetic.'

Every time I had the urge to hurt Lisa Markman, I thought of her father. He was tall, taller than any person I had ever seen.

'You're such retards,' I said, staring at Lisa. She stared right back. She was also bigger than me. She looked at me like she knew how much I hated her and she didn't care. I wanted her dead. She had no right to whisper secrets into Chloe's ear and invite her to the movies. 'You make such a big deal out of something so ordinary. Biology. I got my period yesterday. Big whoop-dee-whoop. It's not broadcast news. It's no *accomplishment*. It's something mammals do.'

Chloe tilted her head to the side, looking at me the way Daisy did when something confused her. She had to know that I was lying. Because Chloe did everything first. We both knew this. But I would not be the only girl in the eighth grade who had not gotten her period. Chloe would have to back me. She would have to prove her loyalty. She would not be a giggling retard girl. I would not allow it.

I nodded at Chloe. Waiting.

'Yesterday,' I said. 'I took one of our dear mother's tampons. So what?'

'You are so telling a lie,' Lisa said. Lisa Markman thought she was beautiful like her mother, the dead fashion model. Her black T-shirt spelled out 'Hot Babe' in silver glitter.

'She's lying,' Melanie said.

'Chloe,' Lisa said. 'Your twin sister is so not cool.'

I rubbed my tattoo. Chloe and I stared at each other. Chloe's pink lip gloss slid from her hand to the floor. I watched it roll under the sink.

'I wouldn't waste my time lying to you,' I said to Lisa.

Brittany got on her hands and knees and picked up Chloe's lip gloss.

'It's okay,' Melanie said, patting Chloe's shoulder. 'We know *you* are not a liar.'

Lisa put the cap back on her purple Magic Marker.

'I can't think of anything worse than being a twin,' she said.

'An identical twin,' Brittany said. 'That's worse.'

I punched my fist against the tampon vending machine. My knuckles turned red; pain shot up through my arm to the top of my skull. I sat down on the floor. For a second all I could see was black. I could hear the drip of a leaky faucet. I looked at Chloe. She was biting her lip. I would wait, I would wait for Chloe to defend me. My hand throbbed. I didn't know what to do. I could punch Lisa Markman in her big, ugly face. I could rip off Chloe's pink, baby doll T-shirt, reveal my name, *my* name, etched into Chloe's pale white skin. I had ownership rights. Chloe was mine.

'It makes sense,' Chloe said finally. 'We are twins.'

My heart started beating fast. I was so relieved. She understood. Of course, she could only choose me.

'Identical twins,' I said. 'Same genetic material. DNA. You can't mess with DNA.'

'She didn't even tell you, your identical twin sister, when she got her period?' Lisa Markman said.

Chloe shrugged.

'Twins have this way of understanding one another,' she said. 'We don't have to always tell each other things. It's hard to explain.'

Chloe walked up to Lisa Markman and reached for the purple Magic Marker. She wrote my name on the wall. My skin flushed with pleasure. My knuckles were throbbing. I'd bang a thousand tampon machines to protect Chloe from evil forces.

Chloe had chosen me.

I nodded coolly at Lisa. *Bitch,* I thought. *Cunt, whore.* Her days were numbered. Black spots danced in front of my eyes. I passed out on the cold bathroom floor, and when I came to, Chloe was holding a warm maxipad to my forehead.

'Always a drama queen,' she said, softly, so that no one else could hear.

Chloe did call our mother. She talked to her assistant, who offered her congratulations. Our mother was taking a deposition and could not be disturbed.

twins

'Melanie's mother took her shopping,' Chloe said as we walked home from school. 'She bought her a red cocktail dress.'

'I'll take us shopping,' I said. 'I'll make Daniel take us to the mall. We can go crazy with Dad's credit card.'

I whipped one of his credit cards from my back pocket.

Chloe stared at me.

'Where did you get that?'

I put the card back in my pocket.

'Forget about it,' I said. 'You never saw it. You know nothing. Let's take Daisy to the park.'

Chloe shrugged. She never liked it when I stole from our parents. She also didn't like to play with Daisy. The dog was always running in mud, getting Chloe's clothes dirty.

My parents were doing a high-profile divorce. An actress and a rock star. They'd been together for eight years. My parents held meetings with both the stars' publicists and private detectives. My mother's assistant called to say she would be on the five o'clock news. Chloe insisted that we watch. There she was, my mother, walking down the steps of the courthouse with her client at her side. The movie star was wearing dark sunglasses. My mother said the offer on the table was insufficient.

'She looks good on TV,' Chloe said.

Chloe was wrong. Our mother looked like a nobody. She looked liked mashed potatoes next to the famous actress. The actress had adopted all three of her children to keep her figure.

By eight o'clock, we were hungry. We never learned how to make our own dinner.

'The no-food diet,' Chloe said with a shrug.

I thought of the credit card, the food we could buy. Chloe did her homework while we waited.

'Do you need protein?' I said, thinking of Chloe's period, the lost blood.

'I need food,' Chloe said, closing her math book. 'I need regular parents.'

She was wrong. She was wrong about our parents like she'd been wrong about the tattoos. Our mother and father could pay for Chloe's college and drive us places on the weekends. That was all we needed. I had the credit card. I could buy Chloe anything she wanted to eat. All Chloe needed was me.

Daniel came down the stairs into the kitchen, dark hair in his eyes, stubble on his chin. He was wearing a red T-shirt with a picture of a bomb and Japanese characters underneath it. He grabbed a Häagen-Dazs bar from the freezer.

'Can you believe them?' he said. 'Defending the rich and famous while the precious twins starve.'

Daniel got into loud screaming fights with my parents, which was a good thing, because it focused their energy on him. Chloe and I watched him eat ice cream. I would only have an ice-cream bar if Chloe had one, but Chloe wouldn't eat food that contained fat calories. She wouldn't eat ice cream. She was on a diet, which was practically as bad as liking Lisa Markman. She shoved her hands in her pockets.

Then our parents came home, rushing into the kitchen, carrying big bags full of food.

'Sorry, sorry, sorry,' my mother said, taking off her heels.

'Lasagna,' my father said. 'Salad. Belated congratulations.'

Lasagna was my favorite food. Lasagna for our periods seemed like a good deal. Daniel brought a second Häagen-Dazs bar to the table.

'None of that for me,' he said, pointing to the tray of lasagna. 'Tomato sauce reminds me of identical twin blood. Strong enough to fuel a rocket ship.'

My mother laid down her fork.

'This is an important day in a girl's life.'

twins

My mother held up her glass of wine. For some reason, she looked at me.

'To Sue,' she said.

Chloe frowned. I knew she was thinking, What about me? But I didn't like the way my mother said my name either, as if Chloe's menstrual success was not a surprise. I wondered what I would do when I actually got my period. I had no idea how to use a tampon. The idea of it was too gross.

'And to Chloe,' I said.

'Of course,' my mother answered. 'Sue and Chloe. It's an important day for you both.'

We were identical twins, but the expectations were different. Chloe got better grades, brushed her hair, expressed interest in our parents' work. And I didn't. That didn't make me less smart. I was saving my energy. School was boring, so I didn't pay attention. I didn't see why the parents couldn't bask in our achievements as a unit, instead of always making distinctions. When Chloe made the honor roll, they gave her money. I got nothing.

My father cleared his throat.

'An important day,' he said. He reached for his wallet, giving us each a one-hundred-dollar bill. This was the best part about our parents' busy careers: the constant infusions of cash. I grinned.

Daniel snorted.

My father turned to him.

'You get your period?' he said. 'What did you accomplish today?'

Daniel snapped the stick from his ice-cream bar in half.

'I cut myself shaving,' he said. There was a Band-Aid on his chin to prove it. He was so ugly, my brother. 'That's a milestone,' he said.

My mother offered him a twenty. Daniel snatched the bill. He always got less, which made sense to me.

I smiled to myself. The day had been a strain, but now Chloe and I were home, eating delicious dinner, accepting well-earned parental tokens of love. I felt safe at home. Mostly our parents weren't around, and I liked it that way. Daniel ignored us, reading books about serial killers and Nazis, practicing the guitar. Daisy had chewed all the cushions of the living-room couch. The house was a mess, but it was ours. Mine and Chloe's. The nightmare of school would slip away, and Chloe and I would play board games or watch TV. Sometimes I'd let Chloe brush the tangles out of my hair. We were happy at home.

I hummed, eating my lasagna. I loved to eat lasagna. I felt good with money in my back pocket. I'd attached a maxipad to my underwear in case my period started. I reached around my back to touch my tattoo.

'Why does Sue always rub her back?' Daniel said.

My father frowned.

'Do you have a skin condition?' he said. 'I represent an excellent dermatologist. I got him joint custody. I'm sure he'd take a look at you.'

My father pulled his cell phone from his pocket. He loved cashing in favors. He thought nothing of disturbing a doctor at home when it could wait until the next day.

'No,' I said. I put both hands around my water glass. 'There's no problem.'

Daniel grinned, watching me, knowing that he had made me squirm, even if he didn't know why. He would go off to college next year, and then Chloe and I could relax.

Chloe picked at her lasagna. I knew what she was thinking. Lasagna was *fattening*. Lisa Markman was on a diet. Melanie Meyer and Brittany Lopez were on diets. So Chloe was also on a diet. All of a sudden, we weren't thin enough. We had to give up pizza and ice cream and potato chips for no reason at all. If Chloe lost any more weight, she would be thinner than me, and we wouldn't look the same.

'Isn't this good?' I said to Chloe. 'Lasagna,' I said. 'Look.' I took a bite of lasagna, and then another. 'Look,' I said to Chloe. 'Watch me eat.'

'Stop it, Sue,' my father said. 'Let Chloe eat.'

'Sue,' my mother said. 'Leave your sister in peace. Let us enjoy our dinner.'

'Freakoid,' Daniel said.

Chloe took a sip of water.

'Look at me.' I took another bite of lasagna. 'Look.'

Chloe's face was strained. She had a choice: she could listen to my parents or she could be loyal to me. She nodded, as if to herself, and then she started to eat. I took a bite of lasagna. Chloe took a bite of lasagna. I took a bite, then Chloe took a bite. She knew we had to weigh the same to be identical.

Chloe needed me. She couldn't stand up to peer pressure on her own. I would not let her succumb to diets like the other idiot girls.

'Good,' I said to Chloe, nudging her with my elbow.

'All right,' she said, nudging me back.

That night, I woke up at three in the morning.

I had eaten too much. I stuck my stomach out, pushing it up and feeling it curve past my pelvis bones. I didn't understand how it could get so big after just one meal. Chloe had finally eaten, but still, I'd had more. I always ate more. I got out of bed and snuck into the bathroom. I knelt in front of the toilet and stuck my finger down my throat. Out came the lasagna. Tears welled in my eyes; though this was the third time I had forced myself to throw up, I still hadn't gotten used to the taste of bile in my throat. Chloe should have never gotten her period.

It seemed so unspeakably sad that we had to grow up.

Chloe was still sleeping when I snuck back into our room. Her life was easier. She didn't have anything to keep her awake. She worried about small, stupid things like her grades and friends and whether her hair was clean and shiny. My mouth tasted like vomit even after I brushed my teeth. My throat hurt. I knelt on the floor next to Chloe, watching her sleep.

She lay on her side, cradling an old teddy bear in her arms. Her pretty blond hair stretched out behind her on the pillow. If I stared hard enough, I could see her blanket rise and fall. Right now, blood was twisting down the tubes, deep inside her body. The biology was out of my control. I wanted to sleep the way Chloe slept.

Chloe opened her eyes. 'Go away, Sue,' she said.

She flipped over so that I was looking at the back of her head.

I wanted to climb into Chloe's bed. Put my mouth in her untangled hair. Instead, I got up from the floor. The only way to get rid of vomit mouth was ice cream.

Daniel was in the kitchen with the dog. He was reading a book with a picture of a black man wearing square glasses on the cover. My brother didn't like to read normal books.

'Do African Americans also like to torture twins?' I asked.

I went straight to the freezer, not bothering to wait for his answer. I got myself a chocolate chocolate-almond-covered Häagen-Dazs ice-cream bar.

'Throw up again?'

I stared at Daniel. He couldn't possibly know. I only threw up in the middle of the night, when everyone was sleeping. Daniel kept reading, but I could see him looking at me from behind his book. Daisy wagged her tail. It thumped on the floor.

'What are you talking about?' I said.

There was a plate of cold lasagna on the table. Daniel took a sip of his drink. It was whiskey. I would remember this; I would use it against him when I needed it.

'Why aren't you sleeping?' I said.

'This is my favorite time of the day,' he said. He took another sip of his drink. I bit into my ice-cream bar. 'Dark. Quiet. Everyone quiet in their beds, sleeping.'

I did not know what to think. He was supposed to be asleep. He was not supposed to hear me in the bathroom or see me sneaking ice-cream bars. I wanted him to stop noticing everything. He put down his book, looking straight at me. It was stupid as hell for me to eat more after I'd thrown up the lasagna. I could never keep up with Chloe this way.

'Do you want one?' I said to Daniel.

'Sure,' he said, and I tossed him an ice-cream bar.

I never spent this long alone with my brother. I didn't like to look at him. He was dark and we were fair. There was an uneven scattering of facial hairs, the Band-Aid on his chin.

'You didn't get your period, did you?' he said.

I frowned.

'I know you didn't.'

Somehow Daniel knew things. He knew about the throwing up, he'd guessed about my period. He watched me with Chloe. I sat down at the table. Daisy rearranged herself at my feet.

'I most certainly did get my period,' I said. 'It's not like I would talk to you about it.'

'You barely talk to me at all,' he said.

'You don't talk to me either.'

It had never occurred to me that Daniel might want to talk to me. Daniel hated us. When we were little, he used to hide our stuffed animals, and then he laughed when we cried. He made up stories about evil Nazis to upset Chloe. He spied on us.

'Do you want a drink?' Daniel said.

I was surprised. I shook my head no and regretted it immediately.

Daniel and I finished our ice-cream bars in silence. I kept sneaking looks at him. Friend or enemy? I wondered how long he had been drinking my parents' booze.

'I got my period yesterday,' I said.

Daniel nodded.

'I'm glad for you,' he said. 'Otherwise, it would probably be hard. With Chloe always being first.'

Daniel put his popsicle stick on the table. It was a kind thing to say. I hated him for it. I didn't ever want to seem less than Chloe. We were twins, identical twins. We should have been on TV, selling shampoo and Doublemint gum. Daniel shouldn't have been able to tell us apart. But when I came downstairs, he knew right away that I was Sue. Even though Chloe and I wore the same Victoria's Secret satin, pink nightshirt. He knew.

'I didn't know that you like whiskey,' I said.

Daniel held up his glass to me, like a toast. My hands were empty.

'I'm surprised you don't,' he said.

'I'm thirteen years old,' I said.

Daniel smirked.

'I don't know,' he said. 'I get the feeling you're going to get into lots of trouble.'

I shook my head. Daniel didn't understand me at all. I wasn't a bad girl. I didn't want to be a juvenile delinquent. I wanted to be in bed, asleep, like Chloe. Chloe was driving me insane. We hadn't even made it to high school.

Lisa Markman invited Chloe to a party at her house.

'No way,' I said. 'We won't go.'

Lisa Markman invited Chloe, not me. She didn't get that we

were a package deal. It was ridiculous for her to think that Chloe would pick Lisa over me. That Chloe would go anywhere without me. We were identical twins. Chloe wanted to go. 'Everybody goes to parties,' she said.

Getting ready, she put on more makeup than I had ever seen her wear before.

I told my parents we couldn't go because Lisa Markman's father, the professional basketball player, took drugs and gave them to the kids. 'Cocaine, ecstasy, speed, pot, Xanax, acid, anything you want so long as it doesn't require a needle.'

Mr Markman had been in the local newspaper that morning. He had granted some wish to a dying child. I knew it was all lies.

'Xanax?' my mother said. 'Could you bring some home for me?'

She had been putting in longer and longer days at the office; she complained that celebrity divorces were exhausting. I stared at her, confused. I couldn't tell if she was joking about the pills. She forced a laugh.

'Mr Markman puts all the pills in a big punch bowl and kids gobble them down like M&M's,' I said.

Chloe shook her head. 'No,' she said. 'He doesn't.'

My parents believed Chloe, of course. They always did.

My father looked up from a stack of file folders.

'Daniel will drive you.' He opened his briefcase and removed a new folder.

'You take us, Daddy,' Chloe said, but he shook his head.

'Work to do,' he said.

On the ride to Lisa Markman's house, Chloe and I sat in the backseat. 'Don't you have anything better to do?' I asked Daniel.

'Many, many things,' he said.

He didn't. He was lying. Daniel had no friends, no identical twin. All he did was read books and play his guitar. I could pretend, at least, that Daniel was the chauffeur, that we didn't know him.

When we got close to the house, Chloe brushed her hair one last time. Then she looked at me and sighed. She reached over to fix my hair too, but I pushed her hand away.

'This will be fun,' Chloe said.

Daniel shook his head. 'Every event I went to in the eighth grade was a swell time,' he said.

The palms of my hands were sweaty. I hated parties. I closed my eyes, imagining a terrible car accident that would stop us from making it to the party. I could see the car in flames, Chloe screaming in pain, broken legs. Blood everywhere. I shivered and put on my seat belt.

'Put on your seat belt,' I whispered to Chloe.

'We are two blocks from the house,' she said.

'Please,' I said. 'Chloe.'

Chloe put on her seat belt.

Daniel pulled in front of the Markman house. Kids at school called the place a mansion, but it wasn't. It was just a big house, a house made out of bricks that was bigger than other people's houses. Mr Markman was bigger than other people. He needed a big house. So what? I unbuckled my seat belt. Chloe begged me with her eyes. She wanted me to be good. To behave. I didn't know why she needed this, to go to other people's parties. We were identical twins. We never ever had to be alone.

'You can come home with me, Sue,' Daniel said.

I pretended not to hear this.

Together, Chloe and I walked to the front door. Before Chloe rang the bell, she took her brush out of her purse and ran it through her hair one last time. I shoved my hair back into a pony-tail. Lisa Markman opened the door. She was taller than ever. She wore purple stiletto heels, a short black dress, bright red lipstick. Hooker clothes, a Halloween outfit.

'Is this a costume party?' I said.

Lisa put her arm around Chloe's shoulder and led her into the house. Every single thing in that house was big. The potted plants were more like trees, the paintings took up entire walls, the TV was more like a movie screen, and the leather couch seated six eighth graders. The closet, because Lisa Markman decided to show us the downstairs closet, was large enough to hold a full-length mirror, two fur coats, a shoe rack full of basketball sneakers and a red-velvet chaise longue.

'I lost my virginity right there.' Lisa pointed to the velvet chair.

Chloe nodded. I felt my heart beat fast. We had to go home. Chloe would not lose her virginity. Not here, not tonight. The idea was too awful to consider.

'Is your father home?' I asked.

Lisa Markman looked at me like I was a cockroach. 'What do you care?' she said. 'He's upstairs.'

Lisa Markman had shown us the closet because that was the place for her party game: two minutes in the closet. 'Kissing games?' I said. At the party Chloe made us go to the year before, it was all girls and they smoked cigarettes crowded around an open window. 'You can do a lot in two minutes,' Lisa said, winking at Chloe. Chloe's face turned red. But she smiled at Lisa, her Goody Two-shoes, eager to please smile. Chloe would drive me crazy with that smile.

Lisa showed us the table with the refreshments. I grabbed a chocolate cupcake. Melanie Meyer and Brittany Lopez ran over to greet Chloe. Brittany had on the same stupid shoes as Chloe. 'I just bought four new pairs,' Brittany said, giggling. Melanie sneered at my high-top, canvas sneakers. I watched Chloe pop open a can of diet soda. I shoved the entire cupcake into my mouth.

'That's really disgusting,' Brittany said.

Chloe got a napkin and cleaned off the chocolate frosting from my face.

I reached for another cupcake.

Lisa Markman was on the other side of the room, on the couch with the boys. She was sitting on some guy's lap. She pointed at us. Chloe reached for the cupcake in my hand and put it back on the table. The boys, the same boys who did not talk to me at school, started chanting: 'We want twins.'

They were drinking soda, but they seemed drunk. Drunk and loud and dangerous. I shook my head. I would not be an identical twin for some boy.

'I'm not playing,' I whispered to Chloe.

I looked at Chloe, blond and soft and lovely. I didn't want her to be kissed. I felt myself shaking. Chloe reached for my hand. 'It's okay,' she said. 'They like us.'

'You're kidding?' I said.

'We want twins!'

Lisa Markman waved her hands. I saw a rum bottle being passed back and forth.

'Shut up,' she hissed at the boys. 'Will you shut up?'

The room got quiet. Lisa Markman was taller than all of them.

Mr Markman appeared at the top of the stairs. 'It's getting loud down here,' he said. The rum was stashed under a cushion in the couch.

Lisa shifted her weight on her heels.

'We'll be quiet,' she said. 'Don't worry.'

'Are the twins here yet?' he said. 'The famous twins you talk about.'

Lisa frowned. Chloe smoothed her hair. I touched my tattoo. Lisa Markman had no right to talk about us.

'Chloe and her sister are here,' she said.

twins

Mr Markman put his hands on his hips.

'I'd like to meet them,' he said. 'The famous identical twins.'

Mr Markman descended the staircase. I had seen him before at school plays and at a bake sale, but I had forgotten how ridiculously tall he was. The already enormous staircase didn't seem as large with Mr Markman on it. Even his hand, resting on the thick wooden banister, seemed enormous.

Chloe took my hand, and we stepped forward, as if he was the Wizard of Oz.

'It's nice to meet you, Mr Markman,' she said. 'Thank you for letting us come to your house.'

Mr Markman whistled.

'You certainly do look alike,' he said.

I was pleased. We had dressed in completely different clothes. Chloe's T-shirt was pink, tucked into a short skirt. I was wearing a black T-shirt, baggy black carpenter pants, and my hair was pulled back. But to a stranger, we were still the same thing. Identical twins.

'I am an eighth of an inch taller,' Chloe said quietly.

'That much closer to the hoop,' Mr Markman said.

Chloe liked to point out our differences. She did not look taller than me when I stood up extra straight.

'I am delighted to meet you both,' he said. He held out his hand. I took a step back. I had no interest in befriending Lisa's famous father. Everyone at the party had gathered around us, trying to get near him. I was not impressed. Of course he was a famous basketball player. There was nothing else a man that tall could possibly do.

Chloe put her small hand into his large one.

'That's enough, Dad,' Lisa said.

'You kids be good,' Mr Markman said. 'Or I'll have to stay down here and chaperone.'

Lisa moaned. 'You promised you would stay upstairs,' she said.
'Be good,' he said.

Chloe nodded. 'We will,' she said.

'Good clean fun,' Brittany Lopez called out, even though she
also looked like a slut in her tight, skimpy party clothes.

Mr Markman headed back up the stairs.

I hoped he'd trip and fall.

'Game time,' Lisa said.

The boys stopped chanting. The dice rolling began. Doubles got
you into the closet for two minutes. A double six meant an extra
minute. I passed when the dice came to me. Chloe rolled a double
three.

I looked at her. She shrugged.

'Todd?' she said, pointing at Lisa's brother. He was two years
younger, only in the sixth grade.

They walked off into the closet. Lisa Markman started her stopwatch.

'Go, Chloe. Go, Chloe,' she said, moving her shoulders as if
she were dancing.

'Oh, wow,' I heard one guy say. 'Chloe in the closet.'

It was a long two minutes. The boys poured rum into their
Coke cans. So did Lisa. Everyone in the circle was drinking rum
in their Coke except for me and Brittany Lopez.

'I'm a Christian,' Brittany said, puffing on her cigarette and
blowing the smoke out the window.

I didn't have a reason I could say out loud. I would not experience anything for the first time with this group of people.

'Hey, Sue. Are you jealous?' Lisa said, so that everyone looked
at me. 'Look at how she touches her back.'

I didn't realize I had been touching my tattoo. I gave Lisa a
mean look. I sat on my hands. Then the two minutes were up.

Chloe looked at the floor as she walked back into the living room. She sat down next to me on the couch and held my hand. 'It's fine,' she said, but I wasn't sure. The palm of her hand was sweaty.

Todd was beaming. He joined the group of guys. His back got slapped. He looked around and then poured some rum into his Coke.

In the next hour, Chloe was picked five times for the closet. She kissed four different boys, going in twice with the ninth-grade track star. Every time she came out of that closet, Chloe looked the same. Her hair still smooth, her lip gloss still gleaming. She giggled when the boys called her name. She practically skipped across the room.

'You are burning up,' Lisa Markman said to me. 'Mad with jealousy.'

I looked at my shoes. I couldn't attack Lisa in her own house. There wasn't a thing I could do. Guys kept on rolling doubles. Melanie Meyer and Brittany Lopez both got picked once. Lisa twice. Otherwise it was Chloe, every time. Once Chloe became the popular closet choice, she ignored me. She didn't sit next to me anymore; she didn't look at me, though I stared at her, desperate for her attention. Lisa Markman hooted. When a boy rolled a double, it was Lisa who cheered, 'Chloe, Chloe,' pumping her fists, flaring her nostrils. I found myself staring at Lisa, her made-up face and her smooth, light brown skin, her long arms and big hands. I wondered if Lisa's long arms were long enough that if I grabbed them and pulled, I could wrap them around her neck so she choked herself.

Todd, Lisa's brother, rolled a double two.

'Chloe,' he said, pointing.

Lisa laughed. 'Don't you corrupt my little brother.'

Chloe shrugged, smiling. She seemed glad. Todd practically raced toward the closet. I stared at the second hand on the enormous grandfather clock in the hallway. That clock must have been eight feet tall. The seconds passed slowly. I knew no one could see Chloe's tattoo in the dark and understand that she was mine. One of the guys who had kissed Chloe whispered into the ear of another guy who had also kissed Chloe. The second guy spit up his drink, laughing, and then they high-fived each other. It was time to go home. I slid off the couch to the floor, making my way to the closet.

I knocked on the closet door.

'We have to go home,' I said.

'Please,' Chloe said. 'Sue. Not now.'

I put my ear to the door. It was silent.

I knocked again. 'I am leaving,' I said.

'Don't forget your coat, psychopath,' Lisa Markman called.

I grabbed my coat and I left. It felt good. Opening the heavy wood front door, slamming it behind me. It was straight down-hill going home. I had gotten three blocks from the house when Chloe raced up from behind and put her arms around my neck.

'You didn't wait for me,' she said. Her cheeks were pink. She was out of breath.

I dragged Chloe for a couple of steps. I didn't understand what had happened to us. She had spent the night in a closet, getting kissed by gross boys who didn't love her, when we could be together, dragging each other through the streets.

'It's okay,' she whispered into my ear. 'Kissing. It's kind of nice.'

I dragged her some more. We would go home. We would eat ice-cream bars and watch TV. I started walking faster.

'It's fun,' Chloe said.

'Fun for you,' I said.

'They'll kiss you,' she said.

twins

'I don't want to kiss stupid boys.'

'We'll switch,' Chloe said. 'No one will ever know the difference.'

Chloe had not let me switch since forever. Chloe was the one who pointed out the differences. Who was ready to tell Mr Markman she was an eighth of an inch taller. But we were the same. Same hair, same weight. Same eyes, same face.

'Do you promise?'

Chloe touched the spot on my back where we had the tattoo. I shivered inside. Chloe tried to deny me, but she couldn't. She wrapped her arms back around my neck, and leaned her weight to the right, a signal for me to turn left, and she kept leaning, dragging her feet until I completed a U-turn. Chloe led me back up the hill, back into Lisa Markman's big, ugly brick house and into the outrageously big bathroom. The whirlpool bathtub was practically big enough for the party. The seashell soaps in the soap dish seemed extra big. Chloe and I switched shirts. She put on my black carpenter pants. I put on her short skirt. She wore my sneakers; I felt unsteady in Chloe's platform shoes, naked in her baby doll T-shirt. Chloe looked pale in my men's extra-large T-shirt. She pulled her hair back into a ponytail, and then she brushed mine. She brushed my lips with her lip gloss.

'Relax your face,' she said.

We looked at each other in the mirror. I had Chloe's hair, Chloe's eyes, Chloe's face, but I looked like Chloe only when I wore her clothes. I did not want to kiss these boys.

'Relax your face,' Chloe repeated. She smiled. I smiled back. We stared into the mirror. Chloe slumped. I stood up straight. She looked like me. I looked like Chloe.

'Let's go home,' I said.

'This is fun,' she said. 'The boys are scared in the dark. We have all the power. I swear to you.'

I went quietly into the living room and sat down on the couch next to Lisa Markman. Chloe stood in the corner, watching, like I had done before. 'Chloe in the closet, back in action,' Lisa said.

'Here I am,' I said.

Lisa Markman touched my hair. I wanted to punch her. I sat on my hands.

I watched the dice roll. Lisa went into the closet with the track star. He came back with lipstick on his teeth. My turn came. I rolled a double six. I stared at the dice.

'Chloe, you slut,' Lisa said. 'That's an extra minute.'

'Pick me,' Todd said. 'Pick me.'

I didn't look at Chloe. Chloe wouldn't look at me if the situation was turned around. I liked being Chloe, having people think that I was Chloe.

'Sure,' I said. Todd was younger. 'Why not?'

I smoothed my hair.

Lisa Markman winked at me.

'Three minutes.'

I shrugged my shoulders. Or maybe it was Chloe who shrugged her shoulders.

I followed Todd into the closet. I walked slowly, looking at my feet the whole time. Platform shoes. I wasn't comfortable walking. Todd closed the closet door behind me. I put my hand on the wall and went over to the chaise longue. I could hear Todd breathing, standing next to me. He put his hand on my waist, and I opened my mouth to be kissed. For Chloe, I would try. Only Todd didn't kiss me. He reached with his hands up under Chloe's pink shirt, slipped his fingers under Chloe's pink bra.

'Aren't we supposed to kiss?' I said.

Todd put his lips on my neck and started to suck. He pressed his pelvis into mine, put his hand on my chest. Was this what Chloe did in the closet? Four different boys. All of them pressing

and panting. She told me she had all the power. Power to do what?
I grabbed the back of Todd's head, pulled him off me.

'I love you, Chloe,' he said.

I punched him in the stomach. No one else got to fall in love
with Chloe.

Todd sat down on the chaise longue.

'That really hurt,' he said.

I sat down next to him.

'I'll hit you again.'

'It's almost time,' he said. He was breathing hard. 'Kiss me.'

'Fine,' I said. Chloe had kissed boys; I'd have to kiss one
too. I leaned over and kissed Todd. His tongue wiggled in my
mouth. My mouth was dry. His tongue was scratchy. It was
revolting.

Someone banged on the door of the closet.

'Time is up.'

I went straight to Chloe. She grinned at me, as if I had done
something important and good; I laid my head on her shoulder.
She let me do it. For just a second, I felt her rest her hand on
my head. I closed my eyes. The game seemed to have ended.
Someone turned the music up loud, and Lisa Markman started to
dance. She was the only one dancing, tall and sexy and repulsive,
swaying to the music in her purple stiletto heels.

'What is wrong with her?' I said.

Chloe shrugged.

'I like her,' she said.

It was nice, being able to sit next to Chloe at the party with
my head on her shoulder. I reached for her hand, but she pulled
it away.

One day at school, right before English class, Chloe and Lisa
Markman went to the bathroom together, and Chloe came out

45

with short bangs. She sat at the desk next to me, and she smoothed her hair. I watched, stunned, as she put her books on the table, lined up her pencil next to the books, and smiled at the teacher. It was a substitute teacher. The bell rang.

'What did you do?' I said.

The substitute told me to be quiet.

'I can't believe you,' I said to Chloe. I felt my eyes go wet. 'Look at you.'

I could hear some of the girls giggling in the back of the classroom. The substitute teacher started taking attendance. She stopped when she got to our names.

'You are identical twins?' she said.

'Obviously,' I said to the teacher. 'Are you stupid?'

Chloe bit her lip. Somebody in the back of the room laughed.

'You look terrible,' I said to Chloe. Tears started streaming down my face.

'Don't,' Chloe whispered.

The substitute continued with her roll call.

'You can't believe how bad you look,' I said.

Chloe handed me a tissue.

'Total psychopath,' Lisa Markman said. She was sitting at the desk directly behind Chloe. She was smirking, watching me cry.

I took the tissue and crumpled it into a ball.

I'd fight Lisa after school. The time had come. I didn't care about her father. He'd get jail time if he came after me. He had an unfair height advantage.

'Is there a problem?' The substitute teacher was so stupid she did not see that Chloe's bangs were the problem. She started passing out papers to people in the front row.

'What is this?' I said, scanning the paper. 'A quiz?'

Chloe took her quiz and leaned over her desk. The quizzes hadn't made it to the back of the room and she'd already started answering questions. Chloe's forehead looked much too large with short bangs. Her eyes were bigger. Her head was bigger.

'You look really stupid,' I whispered.

The substitute teacher said 'Shh.'

I looked down at the paper. I hadn't done the assigned reading. Everyone else was peering down at the stupid sheet of paper, answering questions like trained circus animals.

I stood up and walked out of the room.

When the bell rang, I was standing there at the door. We'd made it to the end of the day. We got to go home. I waited for Chloe to come out of the classroom.

'Lisa asked me to go to the mall with her,' she said.

'Not the mall.'

'I said I would go.'

I hated the mall. The mall made me dizzy, made me want to smash in window displays. The music, the stores, the people, the women at the perfume counters spraying flowery smells before you could do anything about it. I stood with Chloe at the curb. It would be okay. I rubbed my back. We could get ice-cream cones with fancy toppings at the food court.

Lisa Markman came down the steps of the school. She headed straight toward us.

'What is she doing here?' Lisa said to Chloe.

'We're going to the mall.' I shrugged the way Chloe would shrug.

Lisa looked at Chloe, and Chloe looked at Lisa.

'You hate the mall, Sue,' Chloe said.

'No,' I said. 'I love it. Shop till you drop.'

'Hey, who invited who?' Lisa Markman grinned at me. 'I asked Chloe to the mall. *Chloe.*'

'Chloe won't go anywhere without me,' I said.

Chloe didn't say anything.

Lisa Markman cut her arm through the air between us. 'You are not Siamese,' she said. She pointed down the street to a black SUV heading toward us. 'That's our ride. *You* can get lost.'

I looked at Chloe. She ran her fingers through her hair. She had those horrible short bangs.

Lisa Markman opened the car door and climbed in.

'Let's go,' I said to Chloe.

Chloe shrugged.

'Let's go home,' I said. 'Now.'

But Chloe got into the car; she closed the door behind her, and I couldn't see her face through the tinted glass window. The driver pulled away, and I was left standing alone in front of the school.

Daisy loved me best, but sometimes she was a pain in the ass.

She was waiting for me at the door with a tennis ball in her mouth.

'Go away, Daisy,' I said. She dropped the ball by my feet.

I ignored her, going into the kitchen for something to eat. Not that I could eat anything. Not since Chloe started consuming about six hundred calories a day. I took a bag of baby carrots from the fridge and threw them out the window.

'Fucking carrots,' I said.

Daisy barked for a while from the hallway, standing in front of the dropped tennis ball, but she finally picked it up and followed me into the kitchen. I looked at the big white dog. Wagging her tail, wanting to play. Chloe was at the mall with Lisa Markman. Daisy dropped the tennis ball back at my feet. I picked it up and put it in my jacket pocket. Daisy started to whine.

'Shut up,' I said. 'Shut up, you stupid, idiot dog.'

Daisy started to whimper. She put her tail behind her legs and lay down on the floor. I hated it when I was mean to Daisy. She was my love dog. My good girl. I gave her a dog biscuit. I knelt down next to her, scratching her beneath her neck, scratching hard the way she liked it.

'Better?' I said.

Daisy lay on the floor, and for a while I rubbed her belly. Then I got up and took a Häagen-Dazs bar from the freezer.

'The last thing I should do is eat this,' I said to Daisy.

She wagged her tail at me.

I knew I shouldn't eat this ice cream. I could not get any fatter. There was too much for me to lose.

I sat at the kitchen table, eyes closed, loving my ice cream. I knew what came next. I had eaten a Snickers bar for lunch.

'Upstairs,' I said to Daisy.

Daisy jumped to her feet. I walked slowly, taking my time, but Daisy bounded past me, racing through the living room to the foot of the stairs. She waited for me, panting and wagging her tail. Daniel was sitting on the couch, practicing the guitar. Instead of playing an actual song, he kept repeating the same ugly chord. He was the worst guitar player I had ever heard.

'You sound awful,' I said.

'Thanks for your support,' he said.

I headed upstairs, Daisy racing ahead of me, going back down, jumping on me as we went up the stairs.

'Jesus Christ, dog. Calm down.'

I went into the bathroom. I slammed the door in Daisy's face. She barked at the door.

I sat on the floor in front of the toilet. I leaned my head into the bowl and stared at the gleaming porcelain. Chloe had bought a new bathroom product that kept the toilet water crystal clear; she'd recently complained that my mother did not keep the bathroom clean enough. My mother said she did not have the time, promising to hire a maid, but she had never gotten around to it. Since then, Chloe cleaned the house. Sometimes, she went crazy with the cleaning products. My eyes watered. I was inhaling bleach.

Outside the door, Daisy continued to bark.

'I'll kill you, Lisa Markman,' I said. The words made a funny little echo in the bowl. Somehow, that only made me feel worse. I'd get rid of Lisa and some other monster would come along.

I sat up, away from the toilet. I hated throwing up. I had to stop eating ice cream. Chloe never gave in to ice-cream bars. Chloe ate salad without dressing. Why would she go to the mall without me? Why didn't she tell Lisa that she would never consider going anywhere without me? That she loved me more than anyone else in the world? Chloe knew how to say that. We used to tell each other every night before we went to sleep.

I leaned back against the bathroom wall. There was no hurry; I wouldn't be any fatter in ten minutes.

Daisy scratched at the gap between the floor and the door with her paws. 'Leave me alone, Daisy,' I yelled.

Even in the bathroom, I could hear Daniel's lousy guitar playing. I stuck my finger down my throat, and out came smooth, solid chunks of chocolate coating. I stared at the steaming toilet bowl. When had I ever felt sadder than this?

Daisy jumped on the door. Barking and barking.

I opened the door, and Daisy jumped on me. Her paws landed hard on my chest.

'Damn it!'

I smacked Daisy on the head, hard, pushing her down. I kicked her. Daisy cowered, her eyes open wide. I couldn't believe I had kicked my own dog. I got down on my knees and wrapped my arms around her. 'I didn't mean it,' I said, crying into her fur. 'I didn't mean it.' I petted Daisy and I hugged her. My mouth tasted like vomit. There was vomit on my chin.

'Daisy,' I said, breathing in her poodle fur.

twins

Daniel stood at the top of the stairs, staring at me and the dog.

'What the fuck is wrong with you?' he said. He knelt on the floor next to me and pulled me away from Daisy.

'My God,' he said. 'Look at you.'

'She was driving me crazy.' My leg was shaking. I wiped my face with my hand.

Daniel petted Daisy's head. He scratched her under her chin until her tail thumped on the floor. We were all okay. Daisy was fine. I would stop throwing up. I would never hit her again.

'Why don't you go wash your face?' Daniel said.

I nodded. I didn't know he could be so nice. He stayed crouched on the floor, petting Daisy. In the bathroom, I looked at myself in the mirror. It was Chloe's face. Her eyes, her nose, her straight, even teeth. Chloe was television pretty. We should have been on TV. I touched my hair. My bangs were all wrong.

'How are you in there?' Daniel said.

'Can you cut hair?'

I knew Daniel couldn't cut hair.

'I need to get my bangs cut,' I said. 'Would you drive me to the mall?'

Daniel was trying to be nice. I knew he would take me. I could feel myself starting to breathe a little easier.

'Where is Chloe?' he said.

'The mall, I think.'

Daniel stood up from the floor. Daisy jumped to her feet. She was fine. Daisy. My good girl. 'Why do you want to go, if Chloe went without you?' he said.

I shrugged. It was Chloe's shrug.

'Come here, Daisy,' I said. But Daisy didn't come. She was scared of me. I went to her, held out my hand, and she licked it.

'You are in for a world of pain,' Daniel said.

I nodded. Daniel didn't know anything. I already was in a world of pain.

Daniel held up his car keys. 'Let's go,' he said. 'I need a new shirt.'

'You need more than a shirt,' I said. I put my hand on my mouth. Daniel was going to take me to the mall and I insulted him anyway.

Daniel started downstairs, ignoring the last thing I'd said. 'Dreams come true at the shopping mall,' he said. 'Follow your dreams. Buy yourself a pair of leather pants.'

'I need to have short bangs,' I said.

Daniel jumped when the miniature volcano in front of the video arcade exploded.

'It's not real,' I said. I knew about the volcano.

'When did this place turn into Vegas?'

I pointed to the clown in front of the fountain, handing out balloons.

Daniel wiped the palms of his hands against his pants.

'Do you want to buy some shirts?' I said.

'No,' Daniel said. 'Not really. You wanted to get a haircut.'

The hairdresser at Sheer Beauty had a bad perm and frosted blond hair. She couldn't be trusted. We kept walking. Three stores later, we passed another hair salon. I shook my head. I didn't even look inside. I had never gotten my hair cut without Chloe. Either she cut it or she told the hairdresser how we were supposed to look.

'Look at that,' Daniel said, pointing to a mother with two redheaded boys in a stroller, both of them holding enormous plastic guns. One boy looked at us, held up his gun, and went 'Pow'.

I held out my arms and stuck out my index fingers as if they

were guns. I shot the little boys right back. Aimed at their fore-
heads.

'Nice kids,' Daniel said.

But mainly Daniel was quiet. I liked that. We walked by another
hair salon.

'Why are we here?' he said.

I shrugged. I knew that he knew. I wasn't going to tell him.
Chloe wasn't in the upper tier, or the lower tier. She wasn't at
the makeup counter at Macy's.

'Let's try the food court,' I said.

'You want more ice cream?'

I gave Daniel the finger. He laughed. We had never gone
anywhere together before without being forced by our parents.
Daniel was on his own, and I was an identical twin: blond, beautiful, golden. Maybe Daniel was lonely, but I couldn't worry about
him. All day long I had to watch over Chloe. I led Daniel into a
shoe store where Chloe had once bought a pair of boots. She
wasn't there. A salesgirl walked our way.

'Can I help you?' she asked.

I backed us out quickly, my hand on my tattoo.

'Why do you always rub your back?' Daniel said.

I ignored the question, even though I sort of wanted to answer
him. When I'd first thought of tattoos, I had this idea that everyone would see them. But instead the tattoos became our secret,
and I liked it that way too. Maybe I liked it better. I walked ahead
to the food court, walking faster and faster until I could hear Lisa
Markman's laugh.

'Hurry,' I said.

They were walking arm in arm on the other side of the food
court. Chloe and Lisa and Melanie and Brittany.

'Ah, shit,' Daniel said. 'I'm sorry, Sue.' He reached for my
hand. 'Why don't we go home? Before they see us.'

They were giggling. They were giggling and licking double-scoop ice-cream cones. Chloe was eating forbidden calories without me. My mouth still tasted like vomit.

'Ice cream,' I said.

They came walking toward us. I would not go home. I was on a mission. Lisa Markman might seem like an attractive, happy teenage girl, but she was worse than a drug dealer or a child molester.

Daniel had his car keys in his hand. 'Fuck, I hate the eighth grade.'

Chloe saw me. She hesitated, and then she waved. Her smile was fake. Lisa Markman saw me. She held up her arms and said loudly, so that everyone could hear over the piped-in music and the artificial waterfall: 'You are not Siamese twins.'

'I hate you,' I said.

I didn't know who I was talking to. It was Lisa Markman I hated, Lisa Markman who was ruining my world, but for some reason, I was looking straight at Chloe.

'It hurts how much I hate you,' I said.

I was going to cry. Chloe hated it when I cried. Daisy's tennis ball was in my jacket pocket; I wrapped my fingers around it. They were getting closer with every step.

'Oh my God,' Lisa Markman said, drawing out the words. 'I feel so sorry for you, Chloe. I do. Having to share your life with a psychopath.'

Chloe shook her head, looking at me.

'Just until college,' she said.

She looked so pretty and terrible and strange with her bangs cut short. She couldn't possibly mean what she said. Chloe would never go to college without me.

I drew the tennis ball from my pocket, aimed, threw. It was the best throw of my life: Lisa Markman, right between the eyes.

twins

Blood spurting from her nose. She held her hand to her face. She sat down on the floor of the food court. Now it was Lisa who was crying.

'I think you broke my nose,' she said.

I jumped up and down. I started to laugh.

Daniel sighed. 'Oh, Sue,' he said.

I could move in closer, kick in Lisa's teeth. That would feel good. She had big front teeth to match her big, ugly nose.

Chloe stared at me. She looked helpless standing there, the ice cream from her cone dripping down her fingers. Her eyes were open wide. They were so blue.

'Help,' Melanie screamed. 'We need help.'

Chloe knelt next to Lisa. She put her arm around Lisa's shoulder.

My legs were shaking.

'Can you get up?' she said.

Lisa shook her head. Her white tank top was covered in blood. I rocked back and forth on my feet. Daniel shook his head. 'I think you have problems, little sister,' he said.

Daniel was my enemy too. He'd never liked me. He'd brought me to the mall because he wanted something horrible to happen to me. Chloe was still holding Lisa. In a TV movie, Chloe would have rushed over to comfort me. I was the one she should have loved most. She should have been petting my hair and telling me that everything would be all right.

'How could you do that?' Chloe said. 'What is wrong with you?'

I turned and ran, ran out of the food court, and out of the mall, into the bright day. The faster I ran, the better I felt. My heart was racing. I lay on the hood of the car, waiting for Daniel. He would come soon, and he would take me home. Lisa Markman had gotten what she deserved. Sooner or later Chloe would have to understand. I'd make her figure it out. They were stupid girls, Lisa Markman and all of the rest of them. Chloe didn't like them. She didn't need them. She didn't want them. I closed my eyes and listened to the traffic. I could feel the sun on my face.

'Off the car, Sue,' Daniel said. 'Time to go home.'

I didn't hurry. I listened to Daniel unlock the car. Listened to the sound of the door open. I jumped off the hood of the car, stretched my arms over my head. And there was Chloe. Short bangs, shopping bags, pale face, blood on her sleeve. She got into the backseat of the car and buckled her seat belt.

'Assault,' my father said. He lay his briefcase down on the dining-room table, taking out his tape recorder, hitting the record button. He leaned forward in his chair to get a closer look at me. He believed in making eye contact with his clients. I stared right back at the cocksucker. 'You could get juvie time for this. Juvenile detention.'

My mother held a yellow legal pad on her lap. She was already taking notes.

'You committed a violent crime, daughter,' he said.

My mother bit her pen. 'First offense,' she said. 'Good family. That's absurd. Let's not scare her.'

Chloe came in from the kitchen. Always a Goody Two-shoes, she brought fresh drinks to my parents. She did not look at me.

'I'd like a drink,' Daniel said.

My father kept his gaze fixed on me. 'When you go to your overpriced alternative college, then you can act up any way you want.'

I wondered how my father spoke to his clients.

'That is terrible advice,' my mother said. She drew a large X on her notepad. My father sipped his whiskey. I watched Daniel watching him drink it. It was only six o'clock and my parents were home from the office. My mother took off her heels. She rubbed her feet, idly.

My parents thought they were big shots. They worked fourteen-hour days, drove expensive cars, and represented famous people; they had two beautiful children, identical twin daughters. They came home tired, self-satisfied.

My father started in earnest. He had a list of questions. Why did I go to the mall? Why had I carried a tennis ball? Why didn't Daniel try to stop me? What had I hoped to accomplish? My mother scribbled notes in her pad. My father sighed continuously

'Am I being sued?' I said. 'Is that why you're upset?'

'We don't know yet, baby,' my mother said.

'Who is a baby?' I said.

My mother winced. I saw her write the word *hostile*. She was right.

There was no way I was getting sued. Or arrested. Mr Markman could afford to pay his daughter's medical fees. He could send her to Switzerland, put her in boarding school if he wanted to keep her safe. Maybe I needed to talk to him directly. Someone had to do something about Lisa Markman. Someone had to tell her to stay away from Chloe or there would be consequences.

Chloe's eyes were roving all around the room. She would look anywhere other than at me. I was desperate for Chloe to forgive me. She hadn't spoken to me since we'd come home from the mall. She'd marched into our bedroom and locked herself in without me. I did not have time for this idiotic meeting.

My father cleared his throat. 'Honestly, I don't know quite how to approach this case.'

'We are not a case, Daddy,' Chloe said.

I tried smiling at Chloe. She shrugged.

'No, no,' my father said, with his small, fake lawyer laugh.

'But certainly this is a situation. Mr Markman has grounds for a lawsuit.'

We were identical twins, pretty and smart, but my father preferred Chloe. Chloe was the one with law school potential.

'Lisa is getting a nose job,' Chloe said. 'She has always wanted one. She called me from the hospital right before she went into surgery. Lisa is unbelievably happy. There won't be any lawsuit.'

I looked at Chloe. She hadn't told me. Since when did Lisa Markman call our house? My father shook his head. He spoke into the tape recorder's microphone.

'Perhaps the Markmans won't choose to press charges,' he said, with a meaningful look at his tape recorder. 'But had this case proceeded to a court of law, the judge's foremost concern before passing judgment would have been to assess the home life of the plaintiff, Sue. Your mother is right. Rather than punishment, the legal answer for this particular type of situation is rehabilitation. Why would this beautiful girl with so many of life's advantages feel the need to resort to violence?'

'It wasn't violence,' I said. 'It was a tennis ball.'

My mother wrote that down.

'Why did you take a tennis ball to the mall?' she wanted to know.

'You already asked me that.' They stared at me. Daniel was strumming a throw cushion like it was his guitar.

'I took the tennis ball to hide it from Daisy.'

My mother wrote that down. She had hidden lots of tennis balls on the top of her dresser to keep Daisy from bothering her at night. Daisy loved to play ball. There were balls all over the house.

'How can the pattern of violence be put to rest?' my father said. 'What would be the best course of action?'

'I don't think Sue meant to break Lisa's nose,' Chloe said.

'No,' Daniel said. 'She meant it. Sue was pissed off.'

I looked at him. It was none of his business what I meant to do. I wanted him to stop trying to understand me. He could go off to college, get lost.

My mother noted Daniel's opinion on her pad.

'Counseling would be the most obvious conclusion,' she said. 'I have done some research, and I've been recommended an excellent doctor who works with twins.'

'The solution is simple,' Chloe said quietly. 'Sue was upset that she wasn't invited out with us today. It was insensitive of me to go to the mall without Sue, and I am sorry.'

I bit my lip. Chloe wasn't sorry. She knew just what she was doing when she got into Lisa Markman's car. Chloe was lying to my parents. My mother reviewed her notes, shuffling through the papers in her manila folder. She had files about us: our likes and dislikes. Distinguishing characteristics.

'But Sue hates the mall,' my mother said, reading from her pad.

Chloe nodded. 'I was insensitive,' she repeated.

'That isn't true, honey,' my mother said. 'You are allowed to have your own life. You can go out with a friend and not be made to feel guilty.'

'Or persecuted,' my father said.

'I am sorry,' Chloe said again, nodding. 'I will be more sensitive.'

'I think family therapy might be a good idea,' said my mother.

My father looked alarmed. He reached into his briefcase for his date book. 'Our schedule is fairly booked,' he said, flipping through the pages.

Daniel snorted. 'I'm going to college in the fall. It's too late for me to get emotionally healthy.'

My mother also noted this down. Had she forgotten? Daniel had gotten into some college in Massachusetts where you didn't get grades and you could design your own classes. A school for morons. This meeting was not necessary. My parents' lame solutions were not worth listening to; if they would take me and Chloe out of school, we wouldn't have any problems.

'What I think,' Chloe said, laying her palms flat on her lap, sitting up straight, 'is that this was an isolated incident.'

My father smiled. He loved it when Chloe talked like a stuck-up lawyer in training.

'Speak louder, honey,' he said, gesturing toward the tape recorder.

'Daniel is going to college in the fall, and if he agrees, I would like to move into his room.'

I stared at Chloe, horrified.

'I think it would be good for me to have my own private space while I am in high school,' Chloe said. 'I think if I have my own room, it will be easier for me to be more sensitive to Sue's feelings. Otherwise, we are fine,' she said. 'We are happy.'

Chloe knew just what to say to my parents, and she knew just how to say it. She said we were happy. I wanted for us to be happy. We had our names etched into each other's skin. C H L O E. I traced the letters of the tattoo on my back. Maybe Chloe was lying about wanting her own room.

My father shook his head.

'Happy girls don't break people's noses,' he said. 'I think we need to hear from our plaintiff.'

'Sue's not on trial,' Daniel said.

He patted my hand. I shook his hand off. He would go off to college, and Chloe would take his room. He was ruining my life.

'Sue?' my mother said. 'Tell me. You didn't mean to hurt Lisa Markman, did you?'

She held her pen ready. I could see that there were two interpretations: I could have thrown the tennis ball at Lisa Markman and meant to cause her grievous harm or I could have thrown that tennis ball, aimed it right between her eyes, for no reason at all.

'No,' I said. 'I didn't.'

My father turned off his tape recorder. We were done. He nodded to my mother, finished his drink. My mother put her legal pad back in her briefcase. I realized that I wasn't going to get punished. The meeting was over. I had broken Lisa Markman's nose, and Chloe was going to get her own room. I looked from one parent to the other. They couldn't leave things like this. Chloe would put a lock on the door. She'd keep a secret diary, where she would write terrible things about me.

'You are right,' I said. 'I am trouble. I am bad news. Chloe and I could try twins' therapy. That could help us. We could talk everything through.'

Chloe shook her head.

'We are fine,' she said.

My father had a thought. He pressed the record button and spoke. 'Follow-up meeting in one month,' he said. The tape recorder went back into his briefcase. He stood up and stretched.

'We're done?' I said. 'This can't be it?'

I couldn't go on the way I was going. I would never eat a good meal again. I would never get my period. Chloe didn't love me. I had no reason to live.

'We can't be done,' I said.

I looked at Daniel.

'You were right,' I said. 'I meant to hurt Lisa. I am deeply disturbed.'

But my parents' briefcases were already closed.

'No histrionics, Sue,' my father said. 'That's enough for one day.'

Chloe got up from the couch. She reached for my hand.

'Come on, Sue,' she said.

I looked at her hand, the one she wanted me to take.

'Let's go upstairs,' she said, and because I didn't know what else to do, I let her lead us to our room. Our room. Chloe closed the door. I looked for open suitcases, empty drawers, but it was the same. The framed pictures of us on the wall. My favorite: me and Chloe, three years old, naked in a sandbox. Neither of us could tell who was who. I sat on Chloe's bed. I wanted to die.

'Look,' she said, handing me a shopping bag. 'I bought these today.'

Inside were two baseball shirts. They were my favorite colors, black, with dark gray sleeves. Extra-large.

'One for me. One for you,' she said.

'Thank you,' I said. I touched the shirts.

'Would you like me to cut your bangs?' she said.

I nodded. I had a lump in my throat. Earlier today, Chloe had tried to leave me behind. She'd cut her hair and turned into another girl. There were tears in my eyes. More than anything, I wanted Chloe to cut my bangs.

'Come sit on the chair,' she said, holding a pair of scissors.

Chloe knelt on the floor in front of me. She combed my hair straight over my eyes, and then, with a series of clean, quick cuts, she trimmed my bangs.

'Look,' she said. 'Look at yourself.'

Chloe got down on her knees, leaned her head on my shoulder. She had cut my bangs short and straight. They were identical to Chloe's short bangs. We were identical. She kissed the top of my head.

'Let's put on our new shirts,' she said.

Chloe lifted her arms, and I pulled her pink sweater over her head. She did the same for me. We stood with our backs facing the mirror, looking over our shoulders at our tattoos. Chloe put her finger on my tattoo. 'Let's get dressed,' she said.

We put on our new shirts.

'We look nice,' I said.

Chloe shrugged. 'I like pink better,' she said. 'But I knew you would like them.'

I nodded.

'You can wear this shirt whenever you want,' she said. 'Even when I don't.'

I shook my head. I would only wear this shirt when Chloe wore hers too.

'You have to stop with all the drama,' Chloe said. 'We are twins. I love you. I love you more than anybody else. I don't have a choice about that. It is a given.'

I gazed at us in the mirror. I looked right in my new shirt with my short bangs. Chloe's bangs. I looked like my identical twin sister. She looked like me. We were okay.

Chloe

The summer before we started high school, not long after our fourteenth birthday, Sue bought unicycles. She didn't ask me what I thought before stealing my father's credit card. I could feel her eyes glued to my face, watching me, as I examined her new toys. If I didn't act happy, Sue might cry or perhaps throw things. I felt my head start to ache. Until that moment, I had never known how much I did not want to ride a unicycle.

I never knew what would happen if I stood up to Sue. When we were younger, I used to know how to handle her. I could handle her crying and her pouting, and I would always forgive her if she gave Daisy one of my sweaters to chew on. We were fine until we turned thirteen and Sue decided that we needed tattoos.

'This will be the greatest thing we have ever done together,' she said, tossing me a helmet to wear when I rode the unicycle. The helmet, I dully noticed, was pink.

A few days later, my father came home from work and slapped a credit card bill on the kitchen table. If he knew about all the twenties she slipped from his wallet, he never let on, but he had already canceled two other cards.

twins

My mother sighed as my father set down the briefcase next to the bill and then reached for his tape recorder. 'I'm hungry,' she said. 'Tonight you play the bad cop.'

My mother winked at me. She took off her heels and, carrying them in one hand, went into the kitchen. Daisy followed her.

'Let's start with Chloe then,' he said, looking directly at Sue. Her hair was greasy. She hadn't washed it in six days. 'For our voice of reason.'

'Not me,' Sue said. She was grinning. 'Try again.'

'My bad.' My father laughed at himself, as if it was a simple, easy mistake to make.

My father looked very much like lawyers look on television shows. He was handsome like a television star, and home so rarely that, as I got older, he had stopped seeming real to me, and more like a TV actor who had been paid to play my father. A real father would never confuse the identities of his twin daughters after fourteen years of parenting, nor would he need a tape recorder to conduct a simple conversation. He took off his jacket and loosened his tie. I watched his thumb press down on the record button.

'It's been a long day,' he said. 'Chloe, do you know about this?'

I found myself staring at the red light on the little tape recorder. I realized that this would be the perfect moment to betray Sue. She desperately needed to be disciplined, but my parents did not want to take the time to discipline her. My parents always looked to me when there was trouble. Sue was my twin and therefore my responsibility. I could never remember it being any other way. She had started to ruin my things when I said no to her. I looked at the unicycles lined up against the wall, the metal wheels shining, the blue plastic seats.

Sue had stolen my father's credit card, and there he was, wanting to know what I thought. I noticed Sue's hand snake behind her back; she had no idea how desperate she was for someone to discover our secret. She had no idea how much I wanted to grab her arm and twist it round until it snapped.

'Let me see the bill,' I said.

I didn't know what the smartest thing to say was, and so rather than say anything, I scanned the items on my father's bill. I recognized most of the places where he spent his money: payments on the Mercedeses; Brooks Brothers, where he bought his suits; the Carlyle bar, where my parents often went for martinis after work. The two unicycles cost eleven hundred dollars. I looked at Sue, almost impressed. There were also three separate charges at Godiva.

'You like chocolate?' I said to my father.

I had never seen my father eat chocolates. I wished that he would come home from work with a box of Godiva chocolates just for me.

'Gifts for the staff,' my father said, his voice impatient. 'Please answer the question. There are two pricey, unapproved expenditures to be accounted for.'

'Ask me, ask me,' Sue said.

My father looked at Sue.

She held up her middle finger.

My father choked on his drink. I waited, excited, for his reaction. Sue had been rude to his face. Not only that but she had stolen from him a significant amount of money. If a member of his staff were to behave in such a way, my father would have that person fired and prosecuted. Finally, he would have to take action against Sue, and whatever he decided would be forever recorded. My father opened his mouth to speak, but before he had formed his sentence, Sue started to cry. Her flair for drama worked on most people, especially my parents, who were usually tired when they came home and bewildered by her intense emotions.

'Stop that, Sue,' my father said. 'We are having a conversation.'

'Bullshit,' she said. 'Fuck you.'

I bit my lip. I could see that no matter how bad Sue got, my father was not going to win. He'd been too easy on her for too long. She had no respect for the law or for lawyers either. My father looked at me, his face pleading.

'The unicycles are good,' I said. 'We need a project for the summer.'

'I thought you wanted to intern at our office.'

My face burned red. I was letting the perfect moment get away; I loved my parents' office, the floor-to-ceiling rows of silver file cabinets, the quiet, carpeted halls, and the computers on every desk.

'I would rather die,' Sue said.

'Sue and I want to have fun before school starts again,' I said. I listened to myself calmly, knowingly ruin my chance at escape. It had been a stupid idea in the first place. If I interned, Sue would intern too. She would always ruin everything.

Sue wiped her face. She stared at me, and I could see a smile begin to spread on her face. She had already stopped crying.

'We are going to have so much fun.' Sue nodded her head, vigorously. 'So much fun.'

'Expenditure approved,' my father said. 'But you should have consulted with me first.'

I shrugged. I had given him an easy way out, and I wasn't surprised that he took it. My mother emerged from the kitchen, waving an empty Häagen-Dazs box in her hand.

'Who ate the last ice-cream bar?' she wanted to know.

Sue pointed at me.

'Liar,' I said.

I was tired of Sue blaming everything on me. I had stood up

for her, protected her after she attacked my only friend, told my parents I wanted to ride a unicycle. And still she turned on me.

My mother sighed. Like my father, she wore crisp, clean, professional suits, but she did not have the glamorous aura of a television star. My mother looked tired. She didn't care if Sue betrayed me time after time. Sue was *my* identical twin to worry about.

'There is absolutely nothing in this house to eat,' she said.

Lying in bed late at night, I imagined myself in a large classroom taking standardized tests, deliberately darkening in the circles of the correct answers with my freshly sharpened pencil: antonyms and analogies, reading comprehension, geometry problems and algebra. I loved sitting in a quiet classroom, figuring out answers to questions. Math was my favorite, especially algebra: $x + y = z$. I found the process calming. The equations were easy. I always got the right answers. Even though it was summer, I counted the days until high school. I was enrolled in an honors program, classes which Sue did not qualify for. For the first time in our lives, we would have completely different schedules.

I decided I would give Sue my summer. I would give her my summer and then I would move into my own room. She wouldn't like it, but I had to pretend not to care. It pained me to hurt Sue, but there was no getting around it. I would not pierce my lip for her or go to the same college. Sue and I would grow up, and with any luck, we would grow apart.

Neither Sue nor I had any natural talent for the unicycle. We practiced one at a time, using each other to lean on until we got our balance. It was hard to get upright, let alone think about getting anywhere. I told myself that it was a good thing I had no friends around over the summer, because I would be too ashamed for anyone to see me. Lisa Markman was in Milan. She had been discovered by a talent agent soon after the bruises healed from her nose job. She was mainly doing runway work, which according to Lisa, was how most elite models started their careers.

My life wasn't so glamorous. My arms were covered in bruises from the imprint of Sue's fingers. There were more bruises on my legs from the pedals slamming into my calves when I fell. I also had scabs on my arms and legs and my knees, and most painful of all, the palms of my hands.

'Scab city,' Sue said, looking me over.

She thought that it was funny. Sometimes, when she was about to fall, she would reach out for me, wildly grabbing on to my arm. One time she got my head, pulling out a clump of my hair. All summer long, learning to ride the unicycle, I'd suppressed the urge to cry. Sue, I reminded myself, was the twin who cried.

Sue tried harder than I did, and she fell harder. I watched her go down headfirst onto the cement sidewalk. She screamed as she fell, and as Sue lay there in the street, the wheel of her unicycle still spinning, I started to imagine what would happen if she never got up. I'd pack her clothes and send them to the Salvation Army. I would have to call the funeral parlor and make the arrangements. We had never talked about it, but I was certain that Sue would want to be cremated.

'That's the hardest fall yet,' Sue said. Her voice was pleased. Her knees were bloody. She'd reopened a scab on the palm of her hand.

'Is this fun?' I asked her, pulling a twig from her ponytail.

'Let me tell you,' she said. 'These sidewalks are paved with blood.'

The mailman had just walked up to our house, and he saw Sue fall from across the street.

'I thought I was going to have to race you to the hospital myself,' he said. 'You girls should wear helmets.'

The kneepads and the pink helmets Sue had bought were on the top shelf of the hall closet. We looked freakish enough simply riding unicycles without the further burden of unflattering safety gear.

Sue wiped her bloody hands on her T-shirt.

'Not us,' she said. 'We are too cool for helmets.'

'Too cool for school,' said the mailman. 'I never imagined in a million years that I would see identical twins riding unicycles on my mail route. You'd sooner expect that in a David Lynch movie. Are you girls training for the circus?'

Sue shook her head.

'It's for the pure pleasure,' she said. 'The exult.'

Exult was a word in one of the vocabulary lists of my Princeton Review guide to the SATs. The book had disappeared from my knapsack, and when, a week later, it had mysteriously reappeared, the vocabulary pages with the words from sections D through F ripped out.

'Identical twins, pretty girls like you, could be the stars of a circus.'

'We are thinking about doing a sitcom,' Sue said. 'If the money is good enough.'

I would never be on a sitcom with Sue. More than anything, I hated the thought of the Olsen twins, who had turned themselves into a twins corporation. Daisy barked at the mailman from inside the house, jumping on the front door.

'I bet we could get at least seventy thousand dollars an episode,' Sue said.

'Nah, you've got to set your standards much higher,' the mailman said, shaking his head. He was wearing shorts. Clearly, this was a man without dignity, and I did not understand why Sue was encouraging him to hang around. He stared at us as if lost in a reverie. Older men often had that reaction seeing the two of us together.

'Why not aim for the big screen?' he said, scratching his head. 'That's where the money is.'

I could still hear Daisy, barking herself into a frenzy inside the house, and I sadly noted that Brittany Lopez was in the passenger seat of the green SUV that drove slowly past our house.

'You ride for the mailman,' Sue said, pointing at me. 'Chloe,' she explained to him, 'is the better rider.'

I shook my head.

'Why not?' Sue said 'Why? Are you ashamed? Why won't you ride?'

'I don't want to.'

Sue threw her unicycle on the ground.

'You never want to. You act like you're out here every day just for me.'

I didn't know why that wasn't enough. Sue had to know this wasn't what I wanted. I could see her gearing up toward a crying fit. I would have to console her in front of the middle-aged mailman.

'One little ride wouldn't hurt.' He looked at his watch, and then he looked at Sue, who was repeatedly kicking the trunk of a tree, breaking off chunks of bark.

Gingerly, I put the unicycle between my legs. It was still painful, balancing a hard piece of plastic in my crotch. I hated everything there was about riding a unicycle. But this time it was easy to find my balance, and I knew right away that I would be able to ride. I started to pedal, held my arms out to keep my balance, and kept on going all the way to the end of the block. I felt wonderful, competent and sure of myself, the way I did at school when I was handed a test and one look at the questions revealed that I would have no problems. Finally, I fell, speeding over a large tree branch in the street.

'You did it, Chloe.' Sue ran down the block after me. Her face was red. She was out of breath. She pulled me up from the pavement. 'You did it.'

The mailman also came over, to see that I was okay.

'I've got to finish my route,' he said. His voice was regretful. 'Congratulations on some fine riding.' He patted my head, handing Sue the mail.

'You did it!' Sue repeated, but the excitement had already faded from her voice. 'You do everything first.'

I heard what was happening.

'No,' I said. 'You don't get to cry. I am the one who fell on my head.'

I looked hopefully at the bloody pile of mail in Sue's hand. In the beginning of summer, Lisa had sent me postcards from Italy, the first a picture of a gondola in a Venice canal and another of a cathedral in Milan.

Inside the house, Daisy had peed on the floor.

'Bad dog,' Sue yelled. 'Bad girl.'

Daisy put her tail between her legs, and then she sat down in her pee. I felt a headache starting at the back of my skull.

'Let's go swimming,' I said.

The sun was too hot to be teasing Daisy, but we teased her anyway, Sue and I in the pool, tossing her yellow plastic mouse back and forth. Daisy ran up and down the length of the pool, barking. We didn't even notice Daniel approaching.

'Look at this,' he said. 'The Bobbsey Twins torture the dog.'

'We're just playing,' I said.

I tossed Daisy her mouse. She dropped it right back into the pool. I kept my eyes away from Daniel's disapproving sneer. All our lives, Daniel was the only one who could always tell us apart. For as long as I could remember, he didn't seem to like either of us. He didn't seem to like people in general. He never went out. He would be home all weekend, practicing his guitar and reading books written by anarchists. About a year ago, he got interested in Sue. He started talking to her, giving her advice. He was the one who drove Sue to the mall the day she broke Lisa Markman's nose.

'What are you home for anyway?' Sue said. For no reason at all, she started to splash Daisy with water from the pool.

Daniel sat down, rolled up his jeans, and dangled his feet into the water.

'You beg me not to go to college,' he said, 'but you hate it when I'm home.'

Sue got out of the pool and dried Daisy with her towel.

'Poor baby,' she said. 'Poor wet dog. Poor wet poodle.'

Daisy thumped her tail.

'She begged you?' I said. 'You are going, right? Orientation starts in two weeks.'

Daniel laughed. 'Both twins want me gone,' he said. 'Fantastic.'

'That's not what I meant,' I said, though it was exactly what I wanted. I was going to start high school and I would move into his bedroom. It would be the first time that I had my own room. My parents had agreed to this in a meeting. It was a documented fact.

Sue shook her head. 'You are going to stay home and work at the bookstore. Education is a waste of time.'

Daniel shook his head. 'Sorry, kiddo.'

He looked at me. 'I'm going to leave some of my things in the room if that's okay with you,' he said.

I nodded even though I didn't want any of Daniel's things in my room. I wanted my own room, clean and new. Our parents were wealthy divorce lawyers, but they had never considered buying a house big enough for all of their children. They were too busy to shop for real estate. Probably they thought that identical twins would want to share a room.

'Just some clothes,' Daniel said. 'Some books. Whatever won't fit into my car.'

I lifted my hands and placed them gently on the surface of the water, watching the tiny ripples spread from my fingers, imagining his empty room and how I would fill it. Out of nowhere, Sue kicked Daisy in the belly.

'Sue,' I said. 'Why did you do that?'

Daisy whimpered. Her tail hung between her legs, but she didn't leave Sue's side. She licked her paws as if her pride had been wounded.

'Sue,' Daniel said. 'You cannot keep hurting the dog.'

Sue didn't answer. She rubbed her back. Her tattoo, of course. She was always rubbing her tattoo. Sometimes, Sue forgot to walk Daisy or give her water, but that was nothing unusual. It was no different than Sue forgetting to do her homework or clear the table after dinner or wash her hair. Sue would never hurt Daisy intentionally.

'I'm going away to school in the fall,' Daniel said. 'I have been counting the years.'

'The years,' I said. I didn't know Daniel wanted to leave, too.

'She's your responsibility,' Daniel said to me.

His voice was cold, as if he did not trust me to take proper care of Sue. I had no idea why Daniel disliked me the way he did. Sue had always been my responsibility. When had it ever been otherwise? He'd stood at Sue's side and done nothing when she attacked my one and only friend.

'I'm no one's responsibility,' Sue said.

She picked a scab off her elbow.

twins

I hoisted myself out of the pool, walking past Daniel to get my towel.

'What is that?' Daniel said. 'What the hell is that? A tattoo?'

I was wearing a pink bikini that left my tattoo exposed. No one had ever noticed our tattoos before. For gym class, Sue and I both changed in a bathroom stall.

Daniel got up from the side of the pool and walked over to me. He pulled the towel from around my waist.

'Sue,' he read. 'How weird is that? You twins are so fucked up.'

'You're a fucking idiot,' Sue said. I put on my T-shirt.

She marched straight over to Daniel and raised her arm as if to slap him, but he grabbed her before she made contact. 'You are so fucking jealous of us, you can't even bear it,' Sue said, struggling to pull away. Daniel twisted her arm behind her back.

'Goddamnit,' Sue said. 'That hurts. I hurt my arm on the unicycle, you asshole.'

Daisy was up on her feet, barking.

'Don't try to hit me again,' Daniel said, letting go of Sue's arm, 'or I will throw you in the pool.'

Sue gave Daniel the middle finger, and Daniel grabbed Sue and threw her into the pool. Daisy crawled under a lounge chair, and from that protected position, she gave out a low, steady growl. Sue climbed out of the pool, and rushing right back in front of Daniel's face, she pulled down her one-piece bathing suit and turned around. From where I stood, she looked small and skinny and helpless. Her chest was as flat as a board, her ribs sticking out, her wet hair plastered down in straggly bunches. I didn't know that Sue was that skinny. She was always eating Häagen-Dazs bars.

'Okay. I get it,' Daniel said to Sue. He was looking down at the grass. 'Why don't you put your bathing suit back on?'

'I want you to look,' Sue snarled at him.

'Chloe,' Daniel read off of Sue's back. He started to laugh like it was funny, but really, he seemed nervous.

'You both have tattoos,' he said.

Sue turned to face Daniel. Her chest was completely exposed, but she wasn't embarrassed.

'We have tattoos,' she said. 'There is nothing funny about it. It's the most serious thing in the world. Why are you covering yourself up?' Sue screamed at me. 'Take off your shirt. Let Daniel look at your tattoo.'

I shook my head. I didn't want Daniel leering at us. We'd been having a nice day together. Why could nothing be easy with Sue? I wanted to be good to her, but she required so much from me. I would not undress for my older brother. This time, I would not give in to Sue's sick ideas. I simply wouldn't.

'Let him look at your tattoo.'

'This is perverted,' I said. 'I won't.'

'Let him,' she said.

Daniel looked nervous. But I shook my head.

Sue just stood there, half naked. Her hand balled up into a fist. 'Let Daniel look at your tattoo,' she said.

I stared at Sue's fist, spellbound. Would she actually hit me? She had broken Lisa Markman's nose. She had punched her own dog. If she ever hit me, would I let myself hit her back?

'Show Daniel your tattoo, Chloe,' Sue said. 'Let him really see.'

The sun was shining. The water in the swimming pool was a clear, crystal blue. I wanted to be a normal teenage girl. Sue was standing practically naked by the swimming pool, showing off my name, tattooed on her back. I lifted up my T-shirt.

'It's nice?' Daniel said.

He touched the tattoo on Sue's back with his finger. I felt myself shiver; it was as if Daniel had touched me. Today it was

Daniel, but someday it would be someone else, a stranger, a boyfriend. He would run his fingers across Sue's back, stroking my name.

'The tattoo is the reason you're always touching your back,' he said.

'I do not always touch my back,' Sue said.

I pulled my T-shirt back down over my bikini. I remembered the disgusting man who gave us the tattoo, his nervous breathing when we undressed. I did everything for Sue. She needed me as if I were part of the oxygen she breathed, but she didn't understand what it cost me.

'It's not just about DNA,' Sue yelled. Her nipples were pale, pink. She stuck her flat chest out proudly. 'It's the choice we made to love each other forever and foremost. More than anyone else. We don't need anybody else.'

I closed my eyes. My head started to hurt. I never chose to be an identical twin.

'Put on your bathing suit,' Daniel said.

'You'll never understand,' Sue said.

But Daniel wouldn't need to understand. There would always be Chloe and Sue, but Daniel would go to college and then he would do something else. My parents would go to work in their silver Mercedeses. They would earn large sums of money, using the rules of law to dismantle unhappy families as they ignored problems of their own. Here, at this house, for the next four years, there would always be Chloe and Sue, and I would be all alone, every day, with my obsessive twin sister. I closed my eyes, feeling the sun beat down on my eyelids. I saw a sample page of a standardized English test. I squeezed my eyes shut. I could see the questions, antonyms and analogies and reading comprehension. Whenever I didn't know an answer on a multiple-choice test, I guessed the letter D.

'I feel sorry for you,' Daniel said.

I felt grateful for his kindness, but when I looked up at his face, I realized that he was talking to Sue.

Two weeks later Daniel loaded his car and drove off for college and I moved into his room. Sue sat on her bed, glaring at me as I packed my belongings. I could feel her eyes pounding into the back of my head as I folded my clothes, and every once in a while, the pain became so intense that I had to close my eyes.

The week before school started, I went shopping for school supplies, and every night before I fell asleep, I would look over my purchases. I bought a pink three-ring binder and two thin spiral notebooks made from recycled paper, two boxes of extra-fine pens, one black, one purple, a box of number two unsharpened pencils, two pack- ages of pastel-colored index cards, file folders, a lime green stapler, three pink highlighters, and a translucent pink pencil case. I had filled this pencil case with one purple pen, one black pen, a pink highlighter, an eraser, and index cards. I had also bought an intro- duction to French book and a French-English dictionary, a *Webster's New World Dictionary,* and two SAT study guides.

I hid these supplies under my bed, but Sue found them. I had no lock for the door, and Sue found them one night when I was in the shower.

'You used to buy makeup,' Sue said, tapping a pink highlighter on top of the dictionary. 'Clothes.'

I shrugged.

I used to be interested in clothes and makeup, but all that seemed hopeless now. Lisa Markman was gone. Even though she wrote every once in a while, I knew that we would never be friends. Even if Lisa continued to like me, Sue wouldn't allow it. No one who got close to me would ever be safe. That summer it began to feel ridiculous to worry about my appearance if I could not expect to have either friends or a boyfriend, so I decided that I would be smart instead of pretty. Every night, I studied for at least an hour before I went to sleep: irregular verbs for the French class I would take in the fall, vocabulary for the SATs.

'They have nothing to teach us at school, you know.' Sue flipped through the pages of my SAT guide. She was rough with the book, purposefully ripping pages as she went. 'I say we run away, join the circus or maybe go to Alaska on a fishing boat.'

Sue put down my SAT guide and opened a new spiral notebook, uncapped a new purple pen, wrote 'Chloe and Sue's Adventures in Alaska.' The notebook was ruined.

'You can have that,' I said. 'If you want it.'

Sue looked at it, looked at me, and then tossed the spiral notebook across the room to the trash can.

'You are fucking out of your mind,' she said. 'Studying in the summer.'

My eyes stung. 'That was mean. I am never mean to you.'

Sue tossed my SAT guide into the trash too. 'I hate that you think so much about high school,' she said. 'You're going to go to all of your honors classes and forget you have a twin sister.'

'How could I possibly forget?' I said.

It came out sounding sarcastic. I wasn't surprised to see the tears streaming down Sue's cheeks. My head started to hurt like it always did when she cried, but Sue couldn't see headaches.

'That wasn't nice either,' she said.

I shrugged. Somehow I was glad to see Sue cry. I had done everything she wanted for the last two months, and still, it was not enough. I had to promise her my entire life.

'I could never forget about you, Sue,' I said.

'You couldn't?'

'I love you.'

Sue shook her head. 'You don't,' she said. 'You hate me.'

It was true. Sometimes I did hate Sue. I wished that when she fell off her unicycle, her head would crack on the hard sidewalk and she would not get up.

'Look,' I said, knowing what I had to do. I pulled my nightshirt up above my underwear to remind her. I had thought that the tattoo would always remind Sue what I would do for her. 'Look.'

I reached for Sue's hand, leading her fingers to the tattoo. She pressed the palm of her hand on my back. We sat that way quietly until Sue stopped crying. She had started to trace the letters of her name on my back, again and again and again. I knew, without looking at her, that she was fine.

My eye wandered to the trash can. Sue owned me, but it was only for the summer. I felt so sad, looking at the ruined notebook. School had not even started. I wondered if Sue would ever let me go to college. I wondered if I would let her stop me. I longed to take two aspirin, but I realized that if I were to get up, risk upsetting the peace I'd created, she might start again.

College was still four years away.

The next day, I told my mother that I needed glasses. She looked at me with concern, and before I knew it, I was crying.

'What are you?' Sue said. 'A retard?'

I already knew that I would not be popular in high school. I knew that I would not have friends, because having friends was not a safe thing to do with Sue as a twin sister. I also knew that smart girls wore glasses, and that it was my intention to be smart. Wearing glasses would make me look like an ugly smart girl, and I had never wanted to be ugly. I only hoped that glasses would stop the headaches.

'Honey,' my mother said. She looked at me for a moment before wrapping her arms around me. She planned a special day for us. She made an appointment with an ophthalmologist, took the day off work, and made lunch reservations for just the two of us. But when the day of the appointment came, I heard Sue approach my mother in the hallway upstairs and tell her that she was ready.

'Right on time,' my mother said. 'It's a shame you needed a doctor's appointment for me to take some time off.'

I was in the bathroom, brushing my hair.

I stared at myself in the mirror. I couldn't believe it. We had the same features, but Sue and I did not look alike. I was an eighth of an inch taller. I brushed my hair and tucked in my clothes. My clothes were clean. For a moment, everything went black. I stood still until my vision cleared.

I listened in disbelief as they walked down the stairs. My mother did not know that she was talking to Sue, who babbled about her progress on the unicycle. I heard the front door open and close. I listened to the ignition of the car. I knew that I had plenty of time to run after them, but I didn't. I didn't want to spend the day with my mother anymore, not if she didn't even know who I was. I could get used to the headaches. I put down my hairbrush, went into my room, and climbed back into bed.

It was quiet in the house. I realized that I never got to be alone. Sue never wanted to go anywhere without me. I pulled the blanket over my face, and it was dark. Daniel's room had proven to be a disappointment. He'd left his drawers and the closet full of clothes, a Jimi Hendrix poster on the wall, his books on the shelves. I didn't know what to do with his things, so I left them where they were.

But still, I wondered what it would have been like to eat alone in a restaurant with my mother. She once said that she liked to eat steak, but we never ate steak at home. Maybe I could have ordered a steak too. Women at lunch, I supposed, ordered salads.

Spinach salad or chicken salad or mixed greens with goat cheese. I lay in the bed with my eyes closed. My headache was slowly going away. I closed my eyes and pictured a steak on a plate, with a baked potato on the side. I put my hand on my stomach and rubbed it. I must have fallen asleep, because I didn't hear the door to the house open and I was surprised to see Sue standing over me, laughing.

'She had no fucking idea,' she said.

I blinked, confused, because I was staring at myself. Sue was wearing my clothes. She had brushed her hair and put on my lip gloss. She even smelled like me; she had put on my perfume.

'Now she is pissed,' Sue said, 'because you are going to be late for your appointment, and she just wanted to relax for a change. On her precious day off.'

'She is pissed at me?' I said.

'She is just pissed,' Sue said. 'She can't even tell her own daughters apart. She feels like a retard. She had this idea of a special mother-daughter day, only she had the wrong daughter. I would have pulled it off if I hadn't started laughing. She was asking me about the honors classes, and I told her it was all bullshit.'

'What's bullshit?'

'The idea that good grades make you smart.'

I got out of bed.

'This isn't funny,' I said, rubbing my forehead. 'I need to go to the eye doctor. I get headaches.'

'I bet you a hundred dollars there is nothing wrong with your eyes.'

'You don't have a hundred dollars.'

Sue's arm snaked around her back. She was touching her tattoo.

'Hurry up,' she said. 'The bitch in the silver Mercedes is pissed.'

I found my mother reading a legal brief while she waited.

twins

'Whoa,' she said when we got into the car. 'I better get my eyes tested, because I'm seeing double.'

The plans had changed, and my mother had invited Sue to come along with us. I got in the front and Sue hopped into the back.

'That's a terrible joke,' I said, putting on my seat belt.

My mother nodded.

'I'm sorry about the mix-up before, Chloe.'

I shrugged. Once I let myself get angry, I'd never be able to stop.

'Why aren't you sorry to me?' Sue said.

The ophthalmologist told me that I had perfect vision. I did not need glasses. My mother seemed relieved when she heard the news.

'You are perfect,' Sue said. Her voice was cold with hate.

At the Italian restaurant afterward, my mother ordered the capellini with shrimp and peas. I don't know why, but somehow, this made me feel sad. There wasn't any sort of steak on the lunch menu. I felt too tired to eat, but Sue insisted I finish my Caesar salad. She put butter on my bread and made me eat that too.

I was good at school. I sat in the front row of my classes, and I took careful notes. Lisa Markman didn't return home in the fall and the postcards stopped coming, but I assured myself that I was relieved. I told myself it was too dangerous to have friends, not with Sue always lurking around. I spent lunch periods studying in the library. The teachers praised me and called on me constantly to answer their simple questions, but no matter how well I did, I was not smart enough. I stayed up into the middle of the night studying and still got Bs on pop quizzes in French.

Always, I tried to keep my distance from Sue.

She cut her classes to stare at me through the glass windowpanes of the doors of my classrooms. One time, my history teacher stopped in the middle of a lesson to ask her to leave, and I watched, amazed, as Sue slapped the woman in the face and ran wildly down the hall. Sue was given a week's detention. Not long after that, she got put into detention again for smearing worms in Brittany Lopez's hair during biology lab. Sue was failing all of her classes.

I walked home from school alone. I hated myself for feeling lonely. My mother had started going to Pilates after work. My father was handling the divorce of the deputy governor, his stockbroker, and the masseuse at his gym. He came home late each night. For Valentine's Day, he gave us an enormous, heart-shaped box of Godiva chocolates to share, but Sue flushed them down the toilet, one by one by one.

'Look how fat you've gotten,' she said.

I looked at the chocolates sadly. I didn't know who she was talking to.

Sue came into my room and asked me to trim her bangs. Her face was wet with tears. We had not talked in weeks.

'Your bangs?' I said.

Our bangs had grown out a long time ago. I had loved the way I looked with the short bangs; coy, I thought, like a girl from a magazine. But once Sue had copied the style, I didn't want my bangs to be short anymore.

I looked at Sue, her desperate face and her greasy hair.

'Yes,' I said, slowly, unsure of what I was agreeing to. 'If you will cut mine too.'

Sue grinned at me.

Chloe and Sue. Our lives could be so simple if only I gave up on the idea of having a separate life. I knew that we could be dazzling. On the outside, we were blond and tall and thin. If I could let myself be the twin sister Sue had always wanted, we could be starring in our own sitcom.

twins

'I missed you like crazy,' Sue said. 'You cannot even imagine how much I missed you.'

'You could have talked to me any time.'

Sue wiped her face clean. She looked at me with her big blue eyes, my big blue eyes, and I smiled. It didn't make any sense for us both to be so miserable. I would make Sue take a shower. She would wash her hair. We would trim each other's bangs, and maybe tomorrow, we could go shopping at the mall. We could eat nonfat frozen yogurt in the food court. We could start again.

'Are you hungry?' I said.

Sue looked at me. 'I am always hungry,' she said.

I nodded. 'So am I.'

'Why don't we eat something?' Sue said.

'We'll have dinner,' I said.

'I have money,' Sue said. 'We can order something.'

She pulled five twenty-dollar bills and my old mascara from her back pocket. Sue always had money.

'Let's have pizza,' Sue said.

I couldn't remember the last time I had eaten pizza. Pizza was strictly off-limits. There was no such thing as low-fat pizza.

'Pizza?' I said. 'Can we really eat pizza?'

Sue nodded her head. 'Yes, absolutely. We can eat as much as we want.'

I felt my heart beating fast.

'If you eat too much,' Sue said, 'you can always throw it up.'

'You do that?' I said.

I always wondered about all the ice cream Sue ate, the chocolate Häagen-Dazs bars coated with chocolate and almonds. Sue got up and put my mascara back onto my dresser. She pulled my missing calculator from her back pocket and lay that down too. 'Sometimes,' she said. 'Almost never.'

'Let's get pizza,' I said.

Sue smiled at me. 'That is so great,' she said.

'But first I will cut your bangs,' I said.

'Hooray,' Sue said.

'Hooray,' I said.

I had forgotten how easy it was to make Sue happy.

When our parents came home later that night, we were eating pizza and watching television. I had a French test the next day, but I wasn't studying. I was watching television like a regular girl. Anything Sue wanted to watch was fine: the sitcoms, the entertainment news, a TV movie about a mother and daughter who had the same lover, only neither of them knew. I looked for Lisa Markman in the commercials. I had not heard from her in so long, it was possible she had moved to Hollywood and started an acting career.

'Junk food,' my mother said, sighing. 'Is this how my lovely twins feed themselves while we work?'

She put down her briefcase on the table, next to the pizza box, took off her heels, and sat on the couch next to me. She put her hand on my head for a moment, and then she reached for the last slice. I wanted to lean over and grab the slice from my mother's hand. I felt fiercely protective of our pizza. It was our food. Ours. The depth of my anger surprised me. I had clenched my hand into a fist. My head started to pound.

It was Sue who hated our parents.

It was Sue who had violent impulses.

I couldn't sleep. I could feel the pizza silently spreading through my body. When I closed my eyes, I saw page sixty-two of my French text: the past tense of-*ir* verbs. I was a master of English vocabulary, I could absorb lists at a glance from a SAT guide, I had no trouble with science or sine and cosine in trigonometry, but no matter how hard I studied, I could not keep straight irregular verb conjugations. I lay my hands on my stomach, my fat, bloated stomach, and I wondered why I had listened to Sue in the first place. Then I got out of bed and walked down the hall to my old room. I bent to look through the keyhole. It was three in the morning; the light was on. I heard something dull thump on the floor.

'I can hear you,' Sue said.

There was another dull thump, and then another. I was surprised that the noise hadn't ever woken me up before, or my parents, further down the hall.

'Can I come in?'

For a second, everything was quiet.

'You were never supposed to leave.'

I opened the door. The room was the same, the twin beds, the desk, the framed baby pictures over the desk, the matching beanbag chairs, the old rocking horse in the corner. But it also looked and felt like Sue's room now; the floor was covered with clothes and ice-cream-bar wrappers and tennis balls and paper bags and books. My bed was covered with dirty towels. Sue had cleared some space in the center of the room, where she stood in the middle of a circle of mess, holding three colored balls in one hand.

'You're learning to juggle?' I said.

Sue tossed the balls in the air: red, yellow, and green. She had them going for a couple of rounds, her body moving wildly to catch the balls that fell out of the arc.

'You're good,' I said.

'No,' Sue said. 'I still suck.'

One by one, the balls dropped to the floor.

'What are you doing here?'

I shrugged. I never thought that I would set foot back in my old room again. Daniel's room was not everything that I had thought it would be, but once I had left, I never considered going back.

'My stomach hurts,' I said softly. 'From the pizza.'

'You want me to show you how?' Sue whispered.

I shrugged again. 'My stomach really hurts.'

'It's worth it.' Sue smiled. 'We got to eat pizza. I'll show you how. It's no big deal.'

I followed Sue into the bathroom, and we sat down next to each other on the tile floor, next to the toilet.

'The quicker you do this,' Sue said, 'the better. You lean over, put your finger down your throat, fast, and it comes.'

Sue rubbed her back, touching her tattoo.

'That's it?'

I had always done everything first. It was not just riding the unicycle, it was everything: walking, talking, learning how to read. Now Sue was giving me vomiting lessons, and I realized I didn't trust her to explain everything properly. I wished I had looked it up on the Internet, though probably there wouldn't be any useful explanations of how to induce vomiting. There would be only advice on how to stop.

'That's it,' Sue said. 'The faster, the better. It tastes horrible, but then you brush your teeth, gargle some mouthwash. All gone. I'll go first if you want.'

'Are you sure?'

The door was closed and locked from the inside. I was afraid that our parents would wake up and find us.

'I'll show you how,' Sue said. 'I promised I would. I keep my promises.'

We looked at each other.

Sue knelt in front of the toilet seat, leaned over, stuck her finger down her throat, and just like she said, the vomit followed. I watched, revolted.

twins

'Good-bye, pizza,' she said. She rubbed her hands together.

I closed my eyes. I did not know what to say. I had made a mistake. I did not want to be throwing up in the middle of the night with my identical twin. I wanted to start the day all over again.

'We'll give you a nice, clean bowl,' Sue said. 'I know you like everything to be clean.' She flushed the toilet. 'It's really easy,' she said. 'You just have to be quick. Switch places with me.'

I got up and knelt where Sue had been kneeling. The toilet bowl gave off the chemical smell of the chlorine ball I'd bought to keep it clean.

'It's okay,' Sue said. 'Fast.'

I was embarrassed that I needed lessons from Sue. I leaned over the toilet and started to put my finger down my throat but pulled it right out. I was terrified that I would gag, that the vomit would only come up halfway and I would die gagging. Was I willing to risk my own death because of three slices of extra-cheese pizza? I leaned back on my heels. Sue rubbed my hair.

'I can't choke to death, can I?'

Sue looked at me. 'Your hair is so soft,' she said, rubbing my head. 'The faster you do this, the better.'

I took a deep breath, resumed my forward kneeling, and gently put my finger inside my mouth. I was certain that if I threw up, I would die. I pulled my finger out of my mouth and sat back up.

'I think I won't do this after all,' I said.

'You have to,' Sue said. She put her hand on my shoulder and pushed me back down toward the toilet bowl. 'You have to. I threw up tonight for you. To show you how.'

I shook my head. 'I'm sorry, I can't.'

'I threw up for you,' Sue said.

'I'm sorry. I just can't.'

And then the tears came; not mine, of course, but Sue's. 'I can't believe you would do that. That you would back out like this after I threw up for you. I hate throwing up. I threw up for you and now you won't do it.'

Her voice was getting louder. I thought of our parents asleep in their bed. They needed their six and a half hours of sleep each night. They would be unhappy if we woke them. They would set up another meeting, and they would threaten us with the therapist, again. Tears streamed down Sue's face. I ripped off a long piece of toilet paper and crumpled it in her hand.

'Sue,' I said. 'Please.'

'I wouldn't treat you this way,' Sue said. 'I would not. I do not.'

I put my hand on my stomach; it was bloated. My stomach was big and bloated as if I had swallowed a basketball.

'Fast?' I said.

Sue nodded.

'I wouldn't lie to you,' she said.

I looked at Sue, her red face, her tangled hair. This would not be a good time to accuse her of stealing my textbooks, of destroying my homework assignments. We had had a nice night together. She was my identical twin sister. I had been lonely without her.

I got back on my knees, leaned over, closed my eyes, and stuck my finger as far back down my throat as it would go. The vomit shot up through my throat and out my mouth into the toilet bowl. My throat burned. My eyes filled with tears. But the pizza was gone, it was out of my stomach, and I was glad.

'Thank you,' I whispered. 'Thank you.'

Sue rubbed my hair.

'I would do anything for you,' she said.

She flushed the toilet.

*　　　*　　　*

twins

Daniel did not come home for Thanksgiving or Christmas or spring break. My parents were on a television news show about the legal emancipation of child actors. My perfect grade point average was ruined by a B plus in French. Sue rode her unicycle to school, unconcerned about what other people thought. We had started a new, uneasy friendship.

When Sue and I threw up our pizza together, I realized that something was horribly wrong with us both. I pictured the two of us at a mental institution, standing in front of a room of student psychiatrists, a roomful of men and women wearing white jackets, taking notes on their clipboards. 'Here we have an interesting case,' a young doctor would say, reading from an index card. 'Twin bulimics.'

Sue was thrilled to eat meals with me, though she hated the fact that I served steamed vegetables and brown rice almost every night.

'Glub, glub, glub,' she said, chewing with her mouth open. 'This sure ain't lasagna.'

'You know,' Sue said, throwing her brown rice into the air and then trying to catch it in her mouth, 'it was really horrible when I was raped in detention hall.'

'What are you talking about?' I said. 'You were never raped.'

'I might have been raped,' she said.

'You also might have gotten your period.' It felt good to say this.

Sue glared at me, and I knew that she had been lying.

'You have no self-worth,' she told me. 'Zero self-esteem. You care too much about what everyone thinks. You think it is important that we *brush our hair*. You have the personality of a goldfish.'

Our new friendship was complicated. We had begun to insult each other with increasing regularity. Sue began to wash like a normal person, and in exchange, I did her homework, washed her clothes, and walked the dog. Sue had also started to behave at school, but I knew that it was on the condition of my continuous affection. She gave me massages when I got my headaches, but her hands on my back made my skin crawl. I often wondered if I was better off lonely and afraid.

I was still occasionally invited to a party by someone from Lisa's old crowd, but I never went, and as the months passed, the invitations stopped coming altogether.

We were identical twins, tall and blond and beautiful, but somehow, Sue and I had become invisible. Our birthday was coming up again. First our birthday, and then another summer. We would be fifteen. I did not know how I would bear another summer.

My father had called a meeting to discuss birthday gifts. He wanted to avoid last year's confusion. Sue wanted another unicycle. She pulled out a catalog. It was six feet high and cost twelve hundred dollars.

'Request denied,' my father said, staring at the picture. 'That looks both dangerous and unseemly.'

'You asked me what I wanted,' Sue said.

My father turned to me.

'And you, Chloe, do you also want a circus unicycle?'

I shook my head. I wanted to throw my unicycle in the Hudson River, pretend that I had never learned how to ride the thing. I could not believe how badly the year had turned out. Every day, the more time I spent with Sue, the happier she seemed, and the more tired I felt.

My father was pleased with my answer. 'With all this new technology, the circus is a dying art form,' he said, grinning at Sue. 'Riding a unicycle won't get you a job, for instance, and it certainly won't get you into Harvard Law School.'

My mother snorted. 'The last thing the world needs is more lawyers.'

I looked at her, surprised. She worked long hours every week at her practice. She loved her work more than she loved staying at home. I had always assumed that she loved her job.

'You don't want me to join the firm?' I asked. 'After I get my degree?'

'I wanted to be a poet,' my mother said.

This time, my father snorted.

'But unfortunately,' she said, 'there's no money in poetry.'

'So you're a sellout,' Sue said.

My mother pulled a nail file out of her red leather bag.

'I was a mediocre writer,' she said.

'Any other requests?' my father said, looking at Sue.

Sue did not seem surprised that he would not get her the unicycle. Maybe my father felt proud of himself for telling her no, but I knew that whatever Sue really wanted, she got for herself.

'Money,' Sue said. 'Lots of it. My own credit card. A pink cockatoo.'

My father sighed. We knew that he would give her none of these things.

'What do you want, Chloe?' my father said.

'She wants a dildo,' Sue said. 'She wants a vibrator. Chloe is a dirty girl.'

I blushed. 'No,' I said.

This had been one of the less effective meetings. My father tapped his fingers on the table. My mother smiled at me encouragingly. But I didn't know what I wanted for my birthday. Once I'd decided not to have a life, I lost interest in everything. It made me sad just to look at my makeup. Every once in a while, after I watched Sue pedal away on her unicycle from outside my window, I would put on some lipstick and then wipe it off with my hand.

In the end, my parents did what they wanted. We both received gift certificates from J. Crew, but Sue also got one hundred dollars cash, and I got a pink cell phone that I did not want or need. No one called me, and I had no one to call. I had asked my parents for a summer job at their firm, but my father had just interviewed a new batch of interns. Sue wanted to take acting classes. She believed I was hers again and that before long we would be on television, where we belonged. We spent another dull summer at home, riding our unicycles all over town.

In the fall, we went back to school. The classes were different, my teachers were new, but somehow, it felt exactly the same. I had no idea it was possible to feel so bored, so flat. My hair grew longer than it had ever been. Sue could spend hours braiding my hair into tiny little braids. I continued to study, to do well in school, but I stopped participating in class. I wouldn't be able to get into an Ivy League college without extracurricular activities, but my expectations were steadily dropping. Any accredited school would do. Anywhere I could go without Sue.

We made it that way until spring, when Sue went on a broccoli strike. She went back to eating just ice cream and candy bars. I had tried to feed her healthy food. I had told her why bingeing on fattening food was wrong, but she grinned at me, methodically licking the chocolate coating off her ice-cream bar. Her face was dirty, smeared with chocolate, and I couldn't bear to look at her.

I pretended not to hear the toilet flush in the middle of the night.

I thought of my life as a jail term, counting down the days until I started college. I kept count in my head. I did our homework in front of the TV while Sue watched sitcoms. She seemed happy, perfectly content in our nonexistence.

And then one day, not long before our sixteenth birthday, my cell phone rang.

twins

Sue and I stared at it. She turned the sound off the television.

'Wrong number,' she said.

'Probably,' I said.

'Who,' Sue said, 'would want to call you?'

I shrugged. Sue watched me as I answered the phone. She reached behind her back and touched her tattoo.

'Hello?' I said.

My heart had started to beat faster. I wanted so much for the call to be for me, though I knew that Sue was right, that disappointment lay ahead. No one ever called, not for me.

'Did ya miss me, Chloe baby?' the voice on the phone said. I had not heard from her for over two years, but it was Lisa. Lisa Markman. 'I bet you missed me like crazy.'

Sue

Chloe went to Hawaii for Christmas vacation with Lisa Markman. I said I'd kill myself if she went without me. She didn't flinch.

'I don't believe you,' she said.

'Then I'll kill your ugly friend,' I said. 'You don't know what I might do.'

I had already broken Lisa Markman's nose with a tennis ball. I didn't know why Chloe didn't understand. She should have been afraid of me. She had no idea that I had also stolen Lisa's Armani purse or that a security guard had caught me attempting to pry open a back window of the Markman house. Nothing had happened. The guard was nice to me. He gave me an autographed picture of Mr Markman and told me to get lost. It was almost impossible for me to go home every day and know that Chloe was with Lisa. It was more than feeling excluded. I worried that one day I really would have to hurt her.

When the school year started again, Chloe told me she was through doing my homework and taking care of Daisy. Lisa Markman was back from Europe. I had to watch my sister walk down the halls with that bitch, the two of them, talking and laughing like I did not exist. I felt numb, watching my world collapse. Chloe went to Lisa's house almost every day. She'd gone sailing on Mr Markman's sailboat and to a movie premiere in Manhattan, where she wore a strapless pink dress. But Hawaii was where it had to stop. Hawaii was on the other side of the planet.

'How cruel can you be?' I said. 'Don't go. I'll do drugs. I'll inject heroin into my veins.'

'It's just a short trip,' she said. 'I'll bring you back a present.'

Chloe was getting better and better at going places without me. A limousine came to the house to pick her up.

'You need to make your own friends,' she said.

I walked with her to the limo, I sat next to her on the black leather seat. Chloe stared out the window, purposefully ignoring me, and I started to cry.

'I don't like other people,' I said.

I could not think of a single person I liked. There was no one but Chloe and me.

'I can't be your whole world,' Chloe said.

'Too bad,' I said.

'I won't be.'

'Too late.'

Chloe smoothed her hair.

'Well you better not scuba dive,' I said. 'With your luck, your oxygen tank will explode, if you don't die in a plane crash first. I hope you die a painful death.'

I got out of the car, slammed the door in her face. Then I watched the limo pull away. Maybe she was looking back at me, but I couldn't see her through the tinted windows.

I didn't know. I really could kill myself, if I wanted to.

There was no point in celebrating the holidays. My parents had been busy at the end of the year. Since Daniel went to college, we'd been skipping the Christmas tree. I didn't want one; I didn't want their pathetic presents either. There was nothing my parents could give me. With Chloe in Hawaii, my mother decided to keep things simple. She ordered sushi. The wasabi came shaped like a Christmas tree.

Daniel showed up before dinner with his new girlfriend, Yumiko. We were all surprised when he called early in the morning to say he was coming home. Daniel never came home. Last summer he stayed on some weirdo farm where he took care of goats and learned to make goat cheese.

My parents were angry. They didn't like surprises. They spent their days reacting to family problems, and at work they got paid for their efforts. My mother was mortified that she had ordered Japanese food for a Japanese houseguest.

'You could have cooked a turkey,' I told her.

'I could have been a happy homemaker for that matter.' My mother frowned at me. 'How long,' she said, 'has it been since you've washed your hair?'

It had been twelve days. My hair was good and greasy. Chloe would be thoroughly disgusted.

Yumiko sat at Chloe's place at the dining-room table. She wore a white lace dress over a pair of blue jeans. I had never seen anyone do that before. Everything about Yumiko was fascinating to me. She had shiny black hair that fell to her shoulders. She was so little, she barely came up to my shoulders.

'You are staring,' Daniel said to me.

Yumiko didn't care. She stared right back.

'I love a big American holiday,' she said, looking at the Styrofoam containers filled with sushi on the table. 'Turkey, cranberry sauce, mashed potatoes. The gluttony of it all.'

'Pie?' Daniel said. 'What about the pie?'

'Dessert is the best part,' Yumiko said. 'When you are so stuffed you have to undo the top button of your jeans, that's when the dessert comes around.'

I looked at Yumiko with admiration. She looked as if she weighed ninety pounds. She looked like a little china doll.

'Have you ever gone scuba diving?' I asked her.

'No,' Yumiko said. She looked right at me. 'Have you?'

I shook my head. 'I wonder how often people die. If they are not properly trained.'

Daniel looked at his hands.

'Here we go,' he said.

'Anything could happen,' I said. 'Chloe could run out of oxygen, or she could get caught in a cave and panic. She could get eaten by a shark. There are great white sharks in Hawaii. She could get carried away by the current.'

My mother rubbed her eyes.

'Chloe won't die,' she said.

My father leaned back in his chair. 'After the holidays, you'll start seeing that therapist. This has gone on for too long.'

'What has gone on?' I said. 'This is the first time Chloe's gone scuba diving. Clearly you don't care. Maybe you're the one who needs the therapy.'

'Are we going to eat or what?' Daniel said.

Daisy growled from underneath the table. She could always tell when something was wrong. She had turned into a weird dog, peeing in corners, flinching when I tried to pet her. I slipped her a piece of California roll.

'I've never seen a poodle eat sushi,' Yumiko said.

'You do not react to situations rationally,' my father told me. 'I think we made a significant mistake the day you assaulted the Markman girl.'

'I don't give a rat's ass what you think,' I said to my father.

I smiled at Yumiko.

'Let's not talk about that now,' my mother said. 'We have other things to talk about.'

I wondered how horrible my parents must seem to Yumiko. She had a small, pretty nose. Dark eyes. Almond colored skin. She was much prettier than Chloe.

Daisy put her head on my lap. She wanted more sushi. I gave her a piece of yellowtail.

'Sue,' my father said. 'That's two dollars a pop.'

'Yep,' I said. 'It's expensive.'

My father was home for a couple of hours at night, and he thought he had the right to offer his opinion on my life. To control my behavior. He could try as hard as he wanted. He was nothing to me. I had no reason to listen to him. Chloe was gone. She was on the other side of the planet, with another girl, someone she liked better than me. The day Lisa Markman came back from Italy, Chloe had stopped brushing my hair. She refused to hold my hand or cook me dinner, the steamed vegetables and rice I pretended to hate. Chloe wanted her own life. She always wanted her own stupid life. Yumiko sat at her place at the dinner table. She was much too pretty to be my brother's girlfriend.

'Is this the first time your sister has gone away without you?' Yumiko asked.

'Hey,' Daniel said. 'Let's not pressure the kid.'

I smiled at Yumiko. 'The other side of the planet. She couldn't have gone much farther.'

'Australia is far,' Yumiko said.

I gave Daisy a piece of eel.

'Daisy will eat the weirdest things,' I told Yumiko. 'She likes sushi and celery. One time I fed her macadamia nuts.'

'I'm dead serious about the therapy,' my father said. 'These days, it feels like you are beyond my control.'

He finally got something right. I threw a piece of salmon at

him, aiming for his bald spot. My mother smiled as he swatted
the air around his head.

'I've had it with you,' my father said. 'I've really had it.'

'Goodie for you,' I said.

'Do you want some stickers?' Yumiko asked me.

I turned to look at Yumiko. Stickers. She gestured toward her
purse. Yumiko had the craziest purse I'd ever seen: a stuffed pink
rabbit with a zipper down the center.

'Please,' I said. 'I'd like some stickers.'

Yumiko leaned over and opened her stuffed rabbit purse, handing me a long, narrow strip of small green frog stickers. The frogs
had big eyes, round bellies. One frog was sick. It said 'hospital'
over the sick frog's head.

'Thank you,' I said.

I peeled off a tiny frog sticker and stuck it to my water glass.
I thought my mother might object, but she was staring off into
space.

'I wish Daniel had told me he was bringing home a friend,' she
said suddenly. 'I am afraid this is not appropriate for the occasion.'

Yumiko smiled. 'This is fine,' she said. 'I showed up unan-
nounced. Who am I to say anything? I love sushi. My uncle Haruki
is a sushi chef. A tuna roll is like Wonder bread to me.'

My mother offered Yumiko a pained smile. Her eyes were wet.

'What's wrong with you?' I said.

My mother shook her head.

Yumiko sipped her Sapporo from an orange-and-red-striped plastic straw.

'Do you want a straw?' she said.

'Please,' I said. I held out my hand.

From the same pouch that carried a sheet of frog stickers,
Yumiko's hand emerged with another straw. This one was striped
blue and green.

'Would you like a straw?' she asked Daniel.

Daniel shook his head. I wanted to spit at him. He didn't deserve Yumiko. He deserved to be miserable. For going to college, for letting Chloe move into his room.

Yumiko offered straws to my parents.

My mother declined. My father accepted.

'That's definitely a straw,' he said, dipping his straw into his glass of beer, bending the top back and forth.

My mother picked up a piece of sushi, but she didn't eat it. Daisy left me, going to my mother to beg.

'Are you going to tell them?' my mother asked.

'Shouldn't we wait until Chloe comes home?' My father played with his striped straw as he spoke, bending the top back and forth.

'Tell us what?' Daniel said. 'Anyway, I won't be here when Chloe gets back.'

'If she makes it back,' I said.

Yumiko ate a piece of ginger with her chopsticks.

'Your mother and I are getting separated,' my father said. 'I have become involved with a woman whom I hope you will meet soon. I will be moving out on the first of the new year. I have rented an apartment with a room for you and Chloe to stay in on the weekends. If you want to.'

'Fat chance,' I said.

'I did not think you would want to,' my father said.

'You're kidding?' Daniel said.

My father sipped his beer with his striped straw. 'There will be plenty of money for your college tuition. You don't need to worry.'

I looked at my parents, almost giddy that they might actually hate each other.

'I brought home a girlfriend,' Daniel said, looking at his hands.

'She wanted to meet my family. I can't believe you're talking about this now.'

'She's small,' my mother said. 'Your father's girlfriend. His client. Like Yumiko. Asian.'

Yumiko nodded. Everything seemed to make sense to her. Take-in sushi for Christmas, an AWOL twin in Hawaii, standard poodles under the table, divorce announcements. 'White men like Asian women,' she said to my mother. 'It's a domination thing. Chances are it won't last.'

Daniel blushed. 'That is not why I like you,' he said.

'That's what you think,' Yumiko said. 'It's hard to see a situation clearly from the inside. Who knows what caused your attraction to me? It is not uncommon for white men to show a preference for Asian women.'

Now, my mother really smiled at Yumiko. It was an open, friendly smile. Almost loving.

'What are you studying?' my mother asked her.

'I'm a psychology major,' Yumiko said.

'That's not why I like you,' Daniel said. 'That has nothing to do with it.'

Yumiko leaned across the table, took a piece of salmon with her chopsticks, dipped it in her dish of soy sauce, and expertly popped it into her mouth.

'That's fine,' she said. 'Motivation doesn't matter. It's action that counts.'

Daniel's mouth hung open. I didn't get how Yumiko could be his girlfriend. She was so clearly superior to him in every way. I wondered what it meant, his bringing her home to meet us. Did they have sex? I was furious with myself for thinking about it. Of course they had sex. I spent three minutes in a closet with Lisa Markman's little brother and he tried to squeeze my chest with his sweaty, grubby hands. What would Daniel do with Yumiko in her white lace dress? What were the Markmans doing to Chloe halfway around the world?

And my parents wanted to bother me with talk about their fucking divorce. My father was doing it with some client. He was repulsive.

'I'm sorry,' Yumiko said to my mother.

My mother shook her head. 'This is not your fault.'

'I am still sorry,' Yumiko said. 'This can't be easy for you.'

My mother touched Yumiko's hand.

Yumiko seemed to be having the same effect on my mother that she had on me. Daisy put her head on my lap. I gave her another piece of yellowtail.

'Stop that,' my father said.

'Two more dollars shot to hell,' I said.

'I have known about the situation for quite some time now,' my mother said.

I stared at my parents in wonder. My lawyer parents, getting dressed each day in their matching lawyer outfits, driving off to work in their silver Mercedeses. I knew nothing about them. I wondered if I was supposed to be upset about their announcement. I wanted Chloe to be home, she would know the right way to feel. Once my father left the house, it would be harder to get money. My mother never had cash in her wallet.

'This is some holiday,' Daniel said.

I looked at him in surprise. He seemed to be hurt. Even though he never came home, he was disappointed. Let down. My parents' marital status mattered to him. Maybe they meant something to him when he was growing up. He must have looked to them for answers. I had Chloe. I gave Daisy another piece of sushi. It was the only thing I could think to do.

'We thought the holidays would be a good time to tell you,' my father said. 'I thought you would all be home.'

twins

But it was Yumiko sitting in Chloe's seat. She continued to eat, unfazed. She was an expert with chopsticks. I tried to mimic her, but I dropped my sushi in the soy sauce.

'Chloe's not here,' I said.

'Of course,' my father said. 'Chloe's not here. But originally, I didn't know she would be going off for the holidays.' My father leaned back in his chair. 'You just don't look right,' he said suddenly, staring at me. 'All by yourself.'

I knew that.

I knew that.

I looked down at my Christmas sushi in the toilet, individual grains of rice, pink bits of salmon. I rinsed my mouth and went downstairs for something sweet. I was hoping to find Daniel and Yumiko in the kitchen, drinking whiskey, reading at the table. But they were in bed. Together. In Chloe's room.

The day after Christmas, Yumiko wanted to go the mall.

'I want mittens,' she said. 'White woolen mittens with pompoms at the ends.'

I'd stayed away from the mall since breaking Lisa Markman's nose. Daniel had never gone out in public with me again.

'Let's eat breakfast and go,' Yumiko said. 'We can get cute barrettes for your hair.'

If Yumiko said barrettes, I wanted barrettes. I had no idea what Daniel had told Yumiko about me. He could have used me to make himself seem interesting. Lying in bed, stroking her thigh, he could have looked at her and said, 'I have this messed up sister, Sue. She lives in her own private world of pain. I bet she will crack you up.'

'The mall will be crowded,' Daniel said slowly. 'There will be big sales and loud suburbanites. You really want to go to the mall today?'

Yumiko sipped her coffee. She didn't care that Daniel maybe didn't want to go. We were going. I bet she always got what she wanted. It was easy to see that Daniel was the one in love. He would do whatever she wanted, because if he didn't keep her happy, she would dump him. The way Chloe had dumped me. I wanted Yumiko to like me more than Daniel. She was wearing her hair in braids and had on pale yellow overalls over a white long-sleeve shirt. Nothing was more important than finding the perfect mittens for Yumiko. Chloe was in Hawaii with Lisa Markman, doing unspeakable things in dark closets. Or she might have pricked herself on a poisonous coral reef, and was being rushed to a hospital for the antidote as I tried to drink the coffee Yumiko had poured for me.

We left early to beat the crowds.

'You both look so unbelievably serious,' Yumiko said when Daniel pulled into the parking lot.

'The mall makes me a little nervous,' I said.

'I have an answer for nervous.' Yumiko opened her magic bunny bag. I wondered what I would get next. She placed a small, football-shaped pill into my hand.

'Sue,' she said, and I nodded. 'This will calm you.'

I had never taken one before, but I trusted Yumiko. She was a sophomore in college and looked more like a little girl, but she knew things. I could tell. I had the urge to tug on her long shiny braids. I swallowed the pill.

'You need one too,' she told Daniel. Yumiko dug back into her bunny bag and got a pill for Daniel. She dropped the pill onto his tongue. I watched them, jealous. Maybe they had done this before. Yumiko dropped her hand onto Daniel's knee and left it there. I clenched my hand into a fist, and then I remembered that I was getting calm. Yumiko had given me a pill.

'Your brother is always a little nervous,' Yumiko said.

twins

'Will you take one too?' I asked her.

'I love shopping,' she said, shaking her head. 'You know, your parents don't know anything about the spirit of Christmas. And your dog is a total nutcase.'

Daisy was afraid of Yumiko. She had run out of the kitchen while we ate our breakfast and growled at her from the hall.

'I'm sorry,' Daniel said. 'About them. About Christmas.'

'I invited myself,' Yumiko said. 'I love watching families. I don't expect them to get along. Tell me, what's Chloe like?'

It occurred to me that Yumiko had met me first. Without Chloe. I wasn't an identical twin to her. If Yumiko ever were to meet Chloe, she'd confuse Chloe with her idea of me.

'She's perfect.' Daniel and I said it at the same time. We looked at each other. He knew it too. I guess it was that obvious.

'And you're not?' Yumiko said. She turned around in the car to look right at me. 'I'd love to do research about twins. There are so many different ways I could approach the topic.'

'I can ride a unicycle.'

I reached around my back to touch my tattoo. I wished that we had put it somewhere I could see it, like my wrist or my shoulder. I needed something better than a unicycle to impress Yumiko.

'You can?' Yumiko said. 'A unicycle?'

She sounded excited, as if I had told her something fantastic.

'I'd love to see you ride your unicycle,' she said.

Daniel giggled.

'What?' I said.

Daniel held the steering wheel with his thumbs. 'I feel pretty good.'

We were just driving around the parking lot. I hadn't noticed. The place was full. Yumiko put her tiny feet on the dashboard. She'd taken off her shoes. There were little white rabbits on her yellow socks.

'I can't believe your sister is perfect,' she said.

'She is,' I said.

Yumiko shook her head.

'I already don't like her,' she said.

Daniel laughed.

'You would like Chloe,' I said.

'I'm not interested in perfect people,' Yumiko said.

'What is your family like?' Daniel asked. 'I don't know anything about them.'

'My parents are dead,' Yumiko said.

Daniel started to giggle. He covered his mouth with his hand.

'You're serious?' he said.

'They drowned in a riptide in Kyoto.'

'Oh, my God,' Daniel said. 'I'm sorry.'

Dead parents, I thought. It seemed like there could be advantages. Then I felt ashamed. I was always thinking sick, terrible thoughts. I'd wished Chloe dead, told her so to her face, but I would die if anything happened to her. I wasn't a normal person. I was all wrong. I didn't care how Yumiko might feel; some people loved their parents.

'That is terrible,' I said.

'I was five years old,' Yumiko said, as if it were no big deal. She opened her window, and cold air rushed into the car. I could see Yumiko wiggle her toes through her socks. Daniel had found a parking spot, but while he turned to look at Yumiko, whose parents were dead, a minivan pulled in first.

'They were nice,' she said. 'I remember once we went to the beach, in Japan, and I watched seals sleeping on the rocks.'

'I am sorry,' Daniel said.

Yumiko closed the window.

'They have been dead a long time,' she said.

I wanted to look at Yumiko. To see her face.

twins

'You know what?' Yumiko said, turning around to look at me. Her eyes were so dark they were almost black. 'I've never known anyone before who could ride a unicycle. You are the very first.'

I felt my heart beating fast, even though I had taken that pill. Maybe Daniel was too calm. He had driven right past another parking space and headed out for a more distant part of the lot.

'How long have you been going out with my brother?' I asked.

'Two weeks,' Yumiko said.

'Two weeks,' I repeated happily.

That wasn't long. Even if they'd had sex, it wasn't long enough for her to feel attached to him. Yumiko couldn't love my brother. Maybe she was with him for his family. He had told her his sisters were identical twins and she was using him for a research project. She'd come back with him to meet me. Suddenly I wanted to tell Yumiko everything.

'I broke a girl's nose,' I said. 'Right here in this mall.'

'You did?' she said. 'In this very shopping mall?'

I nodded.

I could feel myself beaming with pride.

'Look, Daniel,' Yumiko said, twisting around, 'a parking spot.'

Daniel had already driven past it. Daniel didn't want to go to the mall, but Yumiko did. She had seen the space. We couldn't let it go by. I opened my door, ran from the car, and stood in the center of the space. Another car was already there, ready to pull in. It was Brittany Lopez and her mother. I wasn't budging. They honked the horn. I shrugged, Chloe's shrug. They would have to run me over to get this parking space. I had claimed it for Yumiko. Daniel began backing in. I gave Brittany Lopez the finger. She leaned over and whispered something to her mother.

Yumiko hopped out of the car and stood next to me.

'I close my eyes and I can see the mittens I want,' she said, wrapping her arm around my shoulder.

'How are the nerves?' she asked.

I felt fine. I felt wonderful. I'd take on the shopping mall for Yumiko. We would find her mittens with pom-poms.

'Good,' Daniel said. He put his arm around Yumiko. I took her hand. We were a threesome. We walked into the mall that way, entwined. It was the day after Christmas and the place was packed with people. If I'd had my way, I'd have ridden my unicycle down the crowded hardwood floor of the mall and watched the sea of people part before me as if I was Jesus Christ.

Yumiko and I went into Banana Republic while Daniel waited for us outside. He wanted to sit on a bench and read. Daniel was an idiot. I was thrilled to be alone with Yumiko. In the store, I grabbed her hand and pushed through the shoppers until we found the mittens. Like she knew she would, Yumiko found the perfect pair. They were white and bulky, pom-poms dangling from white strings.

'Would you do something for me?' Yumiko said.

I nodded.

'Go stand over there.' She pointed to a table full of sweaters. 'Count to five, maybe, and then hold up a sweater to look at in the light, up over your head. Then put it down, count up to around ten. You got that?'

I understood perfectly. I wouldn't miss a word Yumiko said. Yumiko twirled a braid behind her ear, grinning at me. I walked over to the angora sweaters, did everything that Yumiko had told me to do. When I put the sweater down, I looked for her, but she wasn't by the mittens. There was a long line at the cash register, but Yumiko wasn't in it.

I looked at the flared jeans, counting to twenty just to be safe, and then I went looking for Yumiko. She was sitting next to Daniel on the bench, leaning her head on his shoulder.

'Hey,' I said.

I didn't like the way her body touched Daniel's.

'Sue,' Yumiko said, smiling, smiling at me. She had perfect teeth, small and glinty white, even rows. She sat up and held out her hands, and I saw she was wearing the mittens.

'Wow,' I said.

I thought they had security tags on everything.

'They look like ice-skating mittens,' Daniel said. 'Why don't we go ice skating?'

Yumiko shook her head.

'Let's shop some more.'

'More?' Daniel said. He picked up his book and sighed. 'I'll wait here, I guess.'

Me, I was thrilled. I loved the idea of it, shoplifting. In some way, I had been practicing all my life, stealing cash and credit cards and cashmere socks from my father. He could go to Hawaii too and get eaten by a great white shark for all I cared. Daniel turned the page of his book. Yumiko and I left him behind, sitting alone on the bench.

In the changing room at Macy's, Yumiko cut the plastic security tag with a pair of nail scissors. I went in with her, standing in front of the changing mirror, which Yumiko said would block the hidden camera. We slid lace dresses over our clothes, and then, for everyone to see, walked out of the changing room, through the women's section, back toward the mall.

'This is fun,' I said. I'd never gone anywhere without Chloe before. 'This is funner than anything.'

A security guard came up to us from behind as we were leaving the store.

'Party's over,' he said. He grabbed us by the wrists and led us away. Me and Yumiko, in the hands of the law. I knew I was supposed to be scared, but I couldn't stop smiling.

The guard led us to a dark, cramped room in a hidden corridor of the mall.

'You girls look cute like that,' he said before closing the door.

'Well,' Yumiko said. 'This is definitely extreme. Usually, they just let you go. It costs more for them to prosecute than to forgive and forget.'

An hour later, we were in the back of a police car. I thought about Daniel alone on his bench and I giggled. He had been left behind, my poor loser brother, while Yumiko and I were off on our own adventure. When I had woken up that morning, the day had seemed cold and ugly. Chloe was in Hawaii with Lisa Markman. But now I was going to jail with the prettiest Japanese girl in the world.

When the cop pulled out onto the highway, Yumiko slipped me another pill, giving me the thumbs-up. Then she also swallowed a pill. 'Jails are a little dirty,' she said apologetically.

'Yumiko,' I said. I loved to say her name out loud. 'Thank you.'

She laughed. 'I got you arrested.'

'It doesn't matter.'

I always knew one day I would be arrested.

At the station, we were instructed to fill out forms, then we were fingerprinted. I loved rolling my thumbs in the black ink. The police officers were all polite. I didn't have an ID card; Yumiko gave them her driver's license. She had braces on her teeth in the photo. I wanted to stare at it, but a police officer put the license into an envelope. We were led to a holding cell. It was a square room with orange and white tiles on the walls, a toilet in the corner, and big glass windows where the police officers could watch us. The room smelled like pee, just the way a holding room was supposed to smell. Yumiko looked out of place in her little-girl overalls and her long, shiny braids. I felt like I fit right in.

I sat next to Yumiko on the orange plastic bench while we waited for my parents to pick us up. I lay my head on her shoulder, like she had laid her head on Daniel's. This was the best I had felt in a long time. I never wanted to go home. Wherever Yumiko went, that was where I would go next.

'Do you feel the pill?' Yumiko said, rubbing my head.

I nodded, careful not to move my head.

'It's really not all that bad, getting arrested,' Yumiko said. 'Real-life experience is a good thing. So many psych majors read books, study case histories, but I think there has to be more than observing humanity if you want to truly understand it. You can't, for instance, truly understand a kleptomaniac unless you have stolen.'

'You should write a book,' I said.

'My friend Smita is writing a book,' she said. 'Her memoirs. Her father is a big movie star in India.'

'What kind of name is Smita?'

'Indian,' Yumiko said. 'I love her name. Smeee-ta.'

'I love your name.'

Yumiko grinned.

'What is your twin really like? Chloe?'

I looked at my shoes. Big, clunky black shoes and dirty red shoelaces. Chloe hated these shoes.

'Daniel says she isn't worth half of you,' she said.

'He said she's perfect.'

'Oh, that.' Yumiko shook her head. 'Is perfect all that interesting? Honestly, Sue.'

I lifted my head to look at her. Of course Chloe was interesting. Yumiko didn't know her or she'd understand. Yumiko wore lace dresses and had cute frog stickers, but that didn't mean she could insult my identical twin. Chloe was smart and beautiful and she was good at everything she did and I loved her more than anyone else. We had once done everything together: breathed the same air, thought the same thoughts, shared the same bed. We shared hamburgers, eating from the opposite ends until our lips met in the center. That was all I wanted. But now Chloe wouldn't even eat hamburgers; meat was full of fat and antibiotics, and the carbohydrate calories from the bun turned to sugar in the bloodstream.

'Daniel's wrong,' I said. 'Daniel is jealous. He's always been jealous.'

Yumiko put her hands in her pockets.

'I wish they hadn't taken my purse away,' she said. 'I want some lip gloss. My lips are so dry in here. Aren't yours?'

I nodded.

'I love your bag,' I said.

'I know,' Yumiko said. 'It's fantastic.'

I looked out the big, glass window. The guard, a black woman in a uniform, sat behind a desk, reading a magazine. She was wearing orange lipstick. It was the same color as the tiled walls and the plastic benches.

'You've been arrested before?' I asked.

Yumiko licked her lips.

'Oh, sure. Lots of times.'

'Shoplifting?'

She nodded. 'Shoplifting, breaking and entering, protest rallies. Mainly protest rallies.'

'What do you protest?'

'Oh, all sorts of things. Clean air. WTO rallies. Antiwar. Abortion rights. One time, I got so furious at this pro-life guy. He was carrying a fetus in a jar. I grabbed the jar from his hand, smashed it on the ground, and threw the fetus in his hair. The guy went insane. He attacked me.'

I thought of Yumiko, small and frail in her white lace dress, standing up to angry mobs.

'You didn't,' I said. 'Really?'

'The cops broke my arm, breaking up the fight.'

'They did?'

Yumiko held out her arm proudly, and I touched it.

'Big lawsuit,' she said. 'I'm five feet tall. I weigh ninety-two pounds. The settlement is going to get me through school when the inheritance runs out.'

'The inheritance?'

'It seemed enormous when I was younger. Over eight million yen. But the currency in Japan is fucked. I shouldn't have picked such an expensive college. Anyway, I've given up on protests. It's too exhausting. I'm taking a sculpture class this semester.'

The guard looked up from her magazine. We made eye contact. I tried to stare her down like I did with Daisy. I felt as if I was becoming a hardened criminal. It would drive Chloe crazy, having a twin sister in jail. The guard went back to her magazine.

'My arm still hurts sometimes,' Yumiko said. 'Mainly when it's cold.'

I didn't know what to say. I knew how to ride a unicycle, but I had never been beaten up.

'You grew up in Japan?' I asked Yumiko.

'New York,' she said. 'I moved here when I was five. After my parents drowned. My uncle has a restaurant in midtown.'

'He does?'

Yumiko nodded. 'What else is there for a Japanese person to do in this country?'

'Cameras?' I said.

Yumiko laughed.

'Poor Daniel,' she said. 'I wonder when he figured out we were hauled off.'

She stood up from the bench and stretched. Bent perfectly in half, she skimmed her fingers over the surface of the floor.

'Dirty,' she said, holding the backs of her calves, laying her head against her knees. 'You don't appreciate Daniel,' she said. 'He's got his charms, you know.'

I didn't want to know.

'But you like me better?' I said.

Chloe was in Hawaii with Lisa Markman. But maybe I didn't need Chloe. Maybe I didn't want her anymore. She could run out of oxygen and die at the bottom of the ocean. I had Yumiko.

Yumiko swung up out of her stretch, reaching her fingertips up toward the ceiling. 'Of course I do,' she said. 'You ride a unicycle.'

'Can I visit you at college?'

'Sure,' Yumiko said. 'That would be fun.'

A telephone rang in the hall. The guard answered, staring at us through the glass while she talked. I crossed my eyes and she laughed. Jail was fun.

'That's our call,' Yumiko said. 'Your parents will be upset.'

'Therapy time,' I said.

The guard had a big set of keys on her belt, just like on TV.

'You're free to go,' she said, opening the door.

We followed her down the hall.

'I believe in therapy, you know,' Yumiko said. 'I'm a psychology major after all. I have, at times, greatly benefited from talking to a trained counselor.'

Yumiko slipped her hand into mine.

'Don't admire perfect. Perfect is a mess. Who knows what kind of crap lies beneath a perfect exterior? Pus and guts.'

I had no idea what Yumiko meant. My parents were waiting

out front. Daniel had come too. Yumiko drove home with him in his car, but I was put into the backseat of one of the evil silver Mercedeses with my unhappy, divorcing parents.

'We've made you an appointment with a highly recommended therapist for next Thursday,' my father said.

Outside, it had started to snow. I rubbed my tattoo, making small circles on my back. I wanted to show my tattoo to Yumiko. I wanted to tell her everything.

'You are an idiot and a moron,' I said to my father.

Chloe

Lisa had spent two years abroad, working as a runway model in Paris and Milan. She barely resembled the person I remembered before she left. She had a smaller, more delicate nose, styled to re-create the likeness of Catherine Deneuve. She had also shaved her head, which made her look older and somehow more exotic. She looked like somebody famous. She was now six feet tall and only wore heels so that she towered above everyone at school, male and female. She wore asymmetric shirts and tight, striped pants. She had become both glamorous and frightening, and I couldn't understand why she still wanted to talk to me.

Lisa thought it was cute, how hard I studied. I sat with her in her big, gleaming kitchen while she drank espressos, smoked cigarettes, and casually told me about her sexual experiences.

'There was a Frenchman,' she said. 'A cellist. He liked to give me baths. He used to rub me all over with a loofah sponge until my skin was red and tingly.'

Lisa held out her wrist, and I leaned over to examine the piece of jewelry, a heavy gold bracelet.

'That is beautiful,' I said.

'He gave it to me,' she said. 'Men are fools when it comes to sex. You can't even believe the things you can get. Only now I'm under house arrest. My father doesn't want me to work anymore until I finish high school.'

I tried to return Lisa's intimate smile. She had singled me out when she came back from Europe. She did not have any use for any of her old friends. According to Lisa, they were not sophisticated. I didn't know why she thought I was somehow better than them. I did not approve of the idea of men giving women presents for sex. That sounded like prostitution to me, and it seemed to me that Lisa was too young to be wearing such expensive jewelry. She wore a diamond stud in the top fleshy part of her ear. Some of her stories about men sounded like lies, but I had learned to expect lies from spending so much time with Sue. Lisa Markman was my friend and she had spent time in Europe, where according to Lisa, people had different ideas about life.

Lisa wanted to quit school and get her own apartment in New York, but her father refused.

'Now that his career is shot to shit, he's worried all of a sudden that I don't have a mother,' she said. 'So I have to get an education and explore my options. My father talks like he's quoting some bullshit self-help book. I think he's remembering his Christian upbringing. He wants me to realize my full potential. He wants to teach me how to play basketball. I can't stand being near the bastard. It was his fault that my mother was drunk, driving drunk in the middle of the night. She was going to see her lover. I know, because she told me. I loved my mother.'

I nodded, nervous. Not only did I not know how to respond, but I didn't want to insult her father, whom I had liked from the first time he shook my hand. Lisa's anger reminded me of Sue's, and I wondered if she would not be better off with my sister, who seemed equally mad at the world. But no matter how little I contributed to the conversation, Lisa seemed to like me. And though I was not sure that I still liked Lisa, I loved spending time at her house. After desperately trying to assert my independence at home, I had fallen back into a routine with Sue. We had begun acting like *twins*. Sometimes, I even slept in my old room.

But Lisa's return from Europe changed everything. I had a safe place to go, a real person to escape to. Lisa had a trunkful of designer samples, and she could spend hours discussing the new designers and what was fashionable in Europe. She gave me an Armani beaded sweater and a red dress by Stella McCartney. When she invited me to go to Hawaii with her family for Christmas, I knew that I would go, and wouldn't even consider for a second how Sue might react. I knew that she would react badly. I knew that she followed us back to Lisa's house after school. The trip would be the first time I would ever travel anywhere without her. In Hawaii, halfway around the world, I would cease to be an identical twin.

Lisa started to tell me the virtues of Hawaii. Their house on Maui, right on the beach, the dolphins and the turtles and the tropical fish, the volcano we could take a helicopter ride to, the incredible bars where we could drink tropical drinks without ever getting carded.

'The sky is so blue,' Lisa said. 'The water is so blue. We'll wear killer bikinis. We'll drive men wild. You'll love it there. You have to go scuba diving.'

I listened to Lisa describing our vacation and surprised us both when I spontaneously hugged her.

'You don't know how happy I am that you are back,' I whispered.

It did not matter that Lisa had had a threesome in Milan with her hairdresser and an English model named Martha. It did not matter that she smoked a pack of cigarettes a day, and sometimes poured vodka into her orange juice at breakfast. I was grateful to have a friend.

Lisa seemed embarrassed. She pulled away and lit a cigarette.

'I am wild about your hair,' she said. 'I know it's, like, stupid, but you remind me of a princess. Martha totally reminded me of you.'

Lisa stopped talking suddenly. She leaned over closer to me and started to stroke my hair. 'Sometimes,' she said, 'I used to call her Chloe.'

'Who?' I said.

'Martha,' she said, touching my hand and looking at me with such tenderness that I felt uneasy. 'I used to call her Chloe.'

Lisa's dead mother had bought and decorated their beach house on Maui the year Mr Markman won his first NBA championship. It was a pretty white house on top of a cliff. Sun filled the rooms, and I could hear the birds sing and the sound of the waves crashing against the rocks. Mr Markman had to sleep diagonally to fit in the canopy bed in the master bedroom. His long legs did not fit under the dining-room table, and he often banged his head against the crystal chandelier in the living-room. This, according to Lisa, was all intentional. 'Mom hated him,' she whispered, the first time we heard the dangling crystals clatter across the house.

'She bought that chandelier just to spite him,' she said.

Lisa's younger brother, Todd, laughed. I thought it was cruel the way Lisa and Todd made fun of their father. He took them on vacation. He was sweet and funny and kind. But I never said anything. I would be spending ten days with them. Todd had stared at me with puppy dog eyes on the airplane, a twelve-hour flight.

Mr Markman rubbed the top of his head. No matter what time of the day, it looked as if he was just waking up.

'Got to bend those knees, Dad,' Lisa said.

'Show the old man some compassion.'

'When you let me get my own apartment,' Lisa said.

Mr Markman had gotten arthroscopic surgery on his knee in the fall. He walked with a limp. He was thirty-six years old and already retired. Though he smiled at me warmly, he did not talk much. I worried that I would be a nuisance to a man who clearly was set upon a quiet vacation, but Lisa said it wouldn't matter because we would ignore him anyway. 'You, me and Todd are going to run wild,' she said. 'I've got to teach you infants the ways of the world.'

Mr Markman had packed a suitcase full of videotapes, his whole basketball career, including games he played in high school. In the mornings, he went for a swim at the small, perfect beach not far from the house. Even in the water, he was quiet. Mr Markman floated on his back, looking into the vast sky. In the afternoon, Lisa and Todd and I would go to another beach, a bigger beach further down the road, where we rented blue lounge chairs and ordered drinks from roving waiters. We left Mr Markman alone in the house, watching his old games.

'He's so depressed,' Lisa said, her voice gleeful, 'he won't notice what we do.'

Lisa wanted to take a glass-bottom boat cruise. 'Free drinks,' she said.

'Awesome,' Todd said.

'We can't go swimming drunk,' I said. Sue had warned me about so many death scenarios that I had become overly nervous.

I was amazed by the fish that swam underneath: yellow and blue angelfish, a school of long, purple fish, hundreds of them, clustered under the glass. Through the glass bottom, I saw trumpet fish and sea turtles. I kept on pointing out amazing new fish for Lisa to look at, but she had been to Hawaii before. 'Oh, sweet, naïve Chloe,' she said. 'This is nothing. The last time I was here, I swam with a school of dolphins.'

'Bullshit,' Todd said.

The boat anchored over a large coral reef, and we were all given masks and snorkels and flippers. I swam right up to a pair of sea turtles and followed them. I could feel myself smiling underwater. It was hard to believe that this underwater paradise existed, and that somewhere, on the other side of the planet, Sue was stewing away with her filthy hair and her filthy clothes in her filthy bedroom. When the turtles finally swam away, I hovered over the coral closer to the boat. I noticed Todd hovering over one spot, and when he saw me he waved excitedly. He was swimming above a big nurse shark. A school of yellow and blue angelfish hovered above them. Underwater, we grinned at each other.

Hawaii, I thought.

Back on the boat, Lisa, Todd, and I drank rum punch. We took drinks from the trays, and no one seemed to care that we were underage.

'Aren't we having a great time?' Lisa said. She wrapped her fingers around a strand of my wet hair.

'Todd,' she said, 'has an enormous crush on you.'

I looked at Todd and smiled. I remembered kissing him in the closet at Lisa's party. He was younger and he was shy, which was the reason I had picked him first. I was surprised that Lisa wanted him to hang out with us at all on this trip.

'He's sort of cute, isn't he?'

I drank my rum punch and smiled.

'Sure.' I wondered what it would be like to have a little brother. It could be fun, I thought. He would look up to you, not the way Daniel looked down on me and Sue.

'Chloe thinks you're cute,' she told Todd.

Todd blushed.

I looked at the boat's glass bottom, wishing that I was still swimming with the fish. I did not understand what Lisa was getting at. Todd was two years younger. Back at her house in New Jersey, neither of us ever talked to him.

'I bet you would kiss Todd again if he asked you to,' Lisa said.

I shook my head. 'He showed me a nurse shark,' I said. 'That was nice.'

After the boat docked, Lisa and I rented beach chairs. Lisa ordered pina coladas and sent Todd away to bodysurf.

'Are you having a good time, Chloe?' she asked me.

I looked at the drink that had magically appeared in the sand next to my chair. I did not want to drink anymore. I thought about the sea turtles and how simple and good life had seemed swimming beside them.

'I am,' I said.

Lisa nodded.

'I knew you would,' she said. 'That's why I asked you here. You're going to burn. Let me put more lotion on you.'

I had brought only one-piece bathing suits, to cover my tattoo. Lisa wore skimpy bikinis, like she had said she would. Men stared at us wherever we went. I knew they were checking out Lisa because she was so ridiculously sexy that they could not help themselves and not because I was a freak of nature. I knelt in the sand in front of Lisa's chair and let her put lotion on my back. She slipped her fingers past the edge of my bathing suit with the lotion, reaching much further than she needed to.

'You should consider modeling,' she said, giving my ass a small squeeze. Ever since we had gotten off the plane, Lisa had been acting strangely. She watched me get dressed. She was rude to her father. 'You could get lots of work.'

I shook my head. Modeling was worse than Sue's idea of starring in a television sitcom. I would not make a career out of having people look at me. I had been stared at my entire life. Lisa leaned forward and kissed my neck. She looked at me for a second and then leaned back in, putting her lips on my neck, sucking hard. I felt myself freeze, uncertain about what was happening, but then I pushed her away.

Lisa laughed like nothing had happened.

'You taste salty,' she said.

I put my hand on my neck. Lisa had told me about kissing the English model when she was in Milan, but I never thought anything about it. She said all sorts of things about sex. It would have never occurred to me that Lisa would try to do anything sexual with me. We were both girls. She was my friend. Lisa Markman was the only friend I had ever had.

'This is Hawaii,' Lisa said. 'You have to loosen up. Look at Todd. There in the water. He's hot, right? You said so.'

Todd stood up in the water, and clutching his boogie board to his chest, he waved at us.

'He's in love with you,' Lisa said.

'He's two years younger.'

I looked at my foot in the sand. I scooped up a handful of sand and let it slide through my fingers, covering my toes. I knew that I was uptight compared to other kids my age. I knew that when I walked down the halls at school clutching my books I was taking school too seriously. I wanted to have friends and I wanted to have fun, but I did not think I was ready for the kind of fun Lisa was offering me. I closed my eyes. The blue sky was too bright. I wondered if I had remembered to pack aspirin in my beach bag.

'Let's be serious,' Lisa said. 'Two years is nothing. Todd's a little lamb and he worships you. You could do whatever you wanted with him and he would be grateful. It is so past time for you to lose your virginity, Chloe. You don't know yourself until you start having sex. There is this whole other world that you're not a part of, that you're totally excluded from. Sex is everywhere, Chloe. Do you see him, that hot guy over there?' Lisa looked across the beach and pointed at a blond guy in a pair of pink bathing trunks, who was coming from the water carrying a surfboard. He looked much too old for us, in his twenties at least. I wanted Lisa to put her arm down. He would see us. I didn't want to talk about sex. I didn't want to think about sex. I wanted to play in the waves and see more turtles. 'I could totally have him if I wanted. You want to see how it works?'

'What?' I said. 'See what?'

Lisa waved for him to come over. I watched as he jogged our way across the sandy beach, still dripping wet from the ocean. It was that simple. She had never talked to him before. She knew nothing about him. *Think*, I could hear Sue say, *of the diseases this guy could give you.*

'Why would you want to?' I whispered. 'Why would you want to sleep with him?'

Lisa laughed. 'You don't want to be a child forever, Chloe,' she said. 'This is what you do. You have fun. You screw. No one falls in love anymore. Anyway, why do you think people come to Hawaii?'

'To snorkel?' I said.

Lisa sighed, exasperated with me.

'You're definitely better off with younger men. I'll tell Todd you're interested, okay? He needs so much help, and you have to start somewhere. Unless you want the surfer. I'll let you have him if that's what you want.'

I shook my head. The surfer had already reached us. I couldn't get myself to look at him. I scooped more sand onto my toes, wishing he would go away.

twins

'Hey, girls,' he said, and Lisa pointed to the edge of her long beach chair. I watched it happen. The surfer sat down; I could see him notice Lisa's long, brown body in her tiny, red bikini.

'How are the waves?' Lisa said.

'Awesome,' he said. I saw his knee bang into hers. I watched Todd catch a wave on his boogie board, ride over the crest, and then go under the surf. I did not want to watch Lisa flirt with the surfer. I hoped that she wouldn't sleep with him. I thought we were going to hike up volcanoes in Hawaii. She had not told me she had plans for my virginity. I was staying in her house. I was her guest. I didn't want to make her angry with me. Now my head really hurt. I walked down to the water. The white sand, like the sky, was blindingly bright. The water was clear and warm. I thought about Sue, threatening to slit her wrists.

I floated on my back, staring at the blue sky. I tried to float the way Mr Markman floated in the mornings, steady and purpose-ful.

I hoped that Sue would not be dead when I came home.

Todd came into my room late that night.

Lisa had gone out with the surfer. Mr Markman was down-stairs, alone in the dark living room, watching himself play basketball on the TV. I listened for the steady thump of the ball on the TV, the squeaking of the sneakers on the wood floor and then the sound of the VCR as Mr Markman fast-forwarded through the tapes. I could not sleep. I was hurt and confused by the fight I had had with Lisa, watching her get dressed to go out.

'I expect you won't tell my father I went out,' she said. She opened the window to the room we were sharing and hopped out.

'I wouldn't,' I said.

'You might,' she said. 'It's revolting the way you look at him during dinner. "Thank you for the meal, Mr Markman." "Everything is wonderful, Mr Markman."'

I sat on the bed with my SAT study guide books open, but I was so focused on listening to the ball that I couldn't concentrate on the questions. I wondered what Mr Markman would think if I went to join him. He had cooked us a nice dinner, grilled sword-fish and vegetables, which Lisa and Todd picked at. Lisa was on a diet, and Todd said that the fish was disgusting on account of the eyes and the bones. I was also on a diet, but I ate the fish to make Mr Markman happy. He showed me how to separate the flakes of fish from the skeleton while Lisa sneered. Mr Markman smiled at me when I told him that the food was wonderful. My father had never taken me and Sue on a vacation. All of our life, I could not remember a single vacation we had been on, ever.

Now Todd was trying to look down my nightshirt.

'You like to study a lot,' he said, sitting next to me on the bed. 'I never met anyone who studied on vacation before.'

I crossed my arms over my chest. I had always thought that Sue was strange, but I wondered if maybe we were both odd.

'I never forgot what it was like at the party,' Todd said. 'You are the first girl I ever kissed. You were so soft and you smelled so good. You let me put my hands wherever I wanted. I never forgot that.'

'I did not,' I said, surprised, but then I remembered. It was only supposed to be a kissing game, but Sue had let a boy do whatever he did to her in the dark. I had let Sue pretend to be me, to keep her from making us leave the party. I had let her pretend to be me, and that was how she'd treated my body.

'I didn't even mind that you punched me in the stomach,' he said.

'That wasn't me.' I shook my head, wondering if Todd had told Lisa. 'That was Sue. We switched clothes.'

'It was you,' he said. 'We went into the closet three times together. I know how you kiss, Chloe. I've never stopped thinking about you.'

'I want to study,' I said.

Todd took the SAT guide from my hands and tossed it on the floor.

'I love you,' he said. 'I have loved you for so long, Chloe.'

I looked down. I could have stayed home to be harassed like this. Sue loved to throw my things around. She had gotten more reckless since Lisa came back from Europe. One time, she snatched a finished essay straight out of my hands and threw it into the fireplace. She cracked the spines of my textbooks as I watched, silent.

'Kiss me,' Todd said.

He leaned over and kissed the edge of my mouth. I reached down to the floor for my book. I had felt silly packing study guides for a tropical vacation, but my books had become a source of comfort. I had been stupid enough to hope that Hawaii would be a dream trip, an escape, and Sue had known better. She had predicted all kinds of misfortune. The undertow that would carry me away, the third-degree sunburn that would fry my pale skin, an oxygen tank that would turn out to be empty when I was thirty feet under the sea. Mr Markman had signed me up for a beginner scuba dive, but when the instructor tried to familiarize me with the equipment, I got an instant headache. I started to shake putting on the gear, and once we were in the pool, which was only five feet deep in the deep end, I refused to go underwater. But even Sue hadn't thought to warn me about Lisa and Todd.

'You were a different kind of girl in the closet,' Todd said, leaning over to kiss me again. 'You acted all sexy.'

'That wasn't me,' I said. 'You kissed Sue in the closet.'

'You don't have to worry,' he whispered. 'This will be special.

I won't get you pregnant. I promise.' Todd leaned over me again, but this time he put his hand directly on my chest. The room was quiet, and I could hear the sounds of Mr Markman's basketball games coming from the living room. Todd and I stared at each other. We both looked at his hand on top of my pink nightshirt. I heard the buzzer go off on the television and the broadcaster's voice talking about the game. 'You don't have to be shy. Lisa already told me you liked me,' he said. 'She said you wanted to lose your virginity. She said that's why you came to Hawaii.'

I smiled, embarrassed. I did not want to hurt Todd's feelings. Todd was a nice enough boy, and it seemed unfair that Lisa had led him on this way. But I wouldn't sleep with him just to spare his feelings. More than anything, I wanted for us both to stay very quiet. I did not want Mr Markman to know what was going on in this room, in his house. Todd lifted his hand from my nightshirt and slid it underneath. I could feel my whole body tense. I could feel the familiar pounding at the back of my head.

'I'm sorry, Todd,' I whispered, 'but Lisa should never have told you that. I don't know why she would tell you that.'

'I am totally into you, Chloe,' he said. 'I want to touch you like we did in the closet. I want to do everything with you.'

I grabbed Todd's wrist and tried to pull his hand away.

'We're in Hawaii,' he whispered, reaching for me with his other hand.

I was still trying to get Todd's first hand out from under my nightshirt when I realized that he wasn't letting go of me, and then I felt panicked. Even though he was younger, Todd was larger than me, taller and heavier and stronger. Without thinking, I bit his shoulder. Todd jumped away, fast. He fell on the floor with a loud thud.

'Shit,' he said, rubbing his shoulder. His eyes looked watery, and I was afraid he was going to start to cry. 'You didn't have to bite me.'

I could feel myself shaking all over. I had no idea why Lisa would do this to me. I wondered if she knew that Todd would come tonight while she was out with the surfer. I had thought Lisa was my friend. I had thought she was saving me from Sue. I tried to smooth out my hair.

There was a knock at the door.

'Is everything okay in there, sweetheart?'

Mr Markman came into the room before I could think of an answer. I straightened my nightshirt. Todd got up from the floor, picking up my SAT guide as if we were having a late-night study session. But the look on my face must have told Mr Markman that everything was not all right at all.

'Get out of Chloe's room, son,' he said. 'I did not raise you to show such disrespect to a guest.'

'No.' Todd snorted. 'All you ever did was play basketball.'

Mr Markman looked at his son. They did not look alike. Todd's skin was much fairer than Mr Markman's, and his eyes were almost blue. Lisa once told me that Todd had no interest in sports whatsoever.

'You're angry at me,' Mr Markman said to Todd. 'But that has nothing to do with imposing yourself on a young woman. I am suppressing the urge to whack you upside the head, but I will if you don't leave this room this instant.'

Todd opened his mouth wide, but then he said nothing, and without looking back at me, he stormed out of the room. I smiled shyly at Mr Markman. No one had ever come to my rescue before. If my father had ever come to check on me at night, if he had come into my room to wish Sue and me good night before our thirteenth birthday while I rocked my weeping twin sister in my arms, maybe he could have saved me from getting a tattoo I never wanted.

'I have to apologize to you,' he said, 'for my son.'

I had stopped shaking, but I was embarrassed to be talking to Mr Markman in the middle of the night, sitting on a bed in my nightshirt.

'This is not the kind of hospitality I meant to provide to a young girl.' He looked at Lisa's empty bed. 'Her mother was a wild woman,' he said. 'I was only twenty when we had Lisa. My career was just starting to take off.'

'That isn't your fault.'

'I know a lot more about playing basketball than raising children.'

But I knew that Mr Markman was a wonderful parent. He took us to the beach every morning and cooked us dinner every night, serving local fruit for dessert, slices of mangos and papaya, berries and star fruit. My parents had never grilled us a fish or taken us on a vacation or thought to rescue me, ever, from Sue. It broke my heart that Mr Markman was unhappy.

'Can I come sit with you?' I said. 'Can I sit with you and watch you play basketball?'

'You want to do that? You would like that?'

I nodded. I put on a pair of jeans and a T-shirt and joined Mr Markman in the living room. I sat in the armchair and he sat on the couch. Mr Markman leaned forward, his hands on his knees; on the television, he stood poised on the foul line, readying himself for a free throw.

'Swish,' he said when the ball slipped through the net. He pressed the rewind button, and we watched it again.

That is how I spent Christmas night and New Year's Eve, alone with Mr Markman, watching basketball in his living room in Hawaii. I learned about his career from beginning to end. He was more than just an excellent shooter. I was able to appreciate his strength as a rebounder and the generous way he always passed the ball to his teammates so that everyone could score baskets. I felt honored to be allowed to sit in the same room with him. I could not believe that the awesome basketball player on the TV screen was the same kind man who cooked my meals and said good morning to me when I drank my juice.

By the time we were ready to go to the airport, Lisa and Todd were outright ignoring me.

Sue was waiting for me in front of the house, riding her unicycle. It was a relief to see her, pedaling up and down the street, alive and ridiculous and unembarrassed. She was Sue. I couldn't wait until the car stopped so I could be with her; until that moment, I had no idea that I was so worried about her. But then, just as fast, I felt exasperation. Sue and I, we were nothing alike. It was a dirty trick, having been born an identical twin with someone like her. The sidewalks and lawns were covered with snow, reminding me how far away I had been. Sue had gotten amazingly good; she pedaled back and forth, staying in the same place as if she were treading water, while the limo was stopped in the middle of the empty street to let me out.

'That girl is a total psychopath,' Lisa said when she saw her. 'Welcome back, Chloe, to your own private hell.'

Mr Markman looked at Lisa, confused. There was nothing more he could do for me now that we were back. By the end of the trip, he had begun to notice our deteriorating friendship, the way Lisa and Todd would go to the beach without me and leave me out of their conversations. Lisa got worse when Mr Markman reprimanded her manners. Our friendship, my first and only friendship, was over. Lisa might have been able to tolerate the fact that I would not fool around with her brother, but she could not forgive me for getting along so well with her father.

Mr Markman patted my shoulder. 'You take good care of yourself,' he said. 'We'll see you soon.'

Todd and Lisa rolled their eyes. We all knew that Lisa would never invite me back to her house.

Mr Markman gazed out the window at my sister. She made crisp turns around the limousine. Her posture was straight, her cheeks were pink from the cold. She wore her hair in long, girlish braids.

'Will you look at her?' he said. He whistled between his teeth in admiration.

'Good-bye, Mr Markman,' I said. 'Thank you for the wonderful vacation.'

I opened the door to the car. Sue circled around me while the chauffeur opened the trunk and handed me my suitcase.

'So you didn't die,' Sue said.

'I could say the same thing to you.'

I thought we might hug each other, but we didn't. Sue was unreachable on her unicycle. The limo honked its horn twice and then pulled away. I said a silent good-bye to Mr Markman. Sue gave the car her middle finger as it drove down the block.

'You've gotten so good,' I said.

Sue turned to me. She directed her middle finger at me, and when she was sure I understood her feelings, she rode off in the direction of the limousine.

My father, I would soon find out, had left the house the day before. My mother was taking a nap. Daniel and his girlfriend, Yumiko, had gone back to college. He had left a dirty sock, some Jockey underwear, and a three-pack of condoms in my top dresser drawer. My pink silk pajamas were missing. I also found a pink lace bra in my bed. It wasn't mine, though I had one like it.

*   *   *

twins

Sue stood in the doorway, watching me unpack.

'You probably thought that I was going to miss you. But you were wrong. More and more, Chloe, you are wrong about things.' Of course I thought Sue would miss me. She'd stood in the same spot two weeks ago, threatening to kill herself if I went to Hawaii. She didn't think I could have forgotten that. I knew I had done a horrible thing, leaving the way I did. I had gotten away from Sue, but now I was back, and there she was, staring at me with hate in her eyes. 'I didn't miss you,' she repeated.

She twirled the end of a braid around her finger. She was lying. She always lied to me. Without me, Sue was all alone.

'Your hair looks nice that way,' I said.

'I know,' she said. 'I am a fascinating person.'

I nodded. I had to be careful with Sue. When I looked at her, I remembered how she hit Lisa Markman with a tennis ball, how she kicked Daisy for no reason by the swimming pool. As my father once noted in his tape recorder, Sue had the potential for violence. I felt cornered by her, sitting on the bed, following my every move. Any second, she could pounce. Her fingernails were ragged and uneven.

'I got arrested while you were gone,' Sue said.

I nodded again. I already knew. My mother had left a bulleted list in a sealed envelope on my pillow, informing me of the events that had taken place in the short time I was away. Item one was my errant father. Item two was Yumiko, Daniel's girlfriend, who 'seemed wonderful but had taken an unhealthy interest in Sue'. Item three was Sue's arrest at the shopping mall. Sue's upcoming therapy session was item four. Item five suggested that the therapist might be interested in talking to me in future sessions. Item six was Daisy, underlined and in bold, with a request that I walk and feed her, as these responsibilities were 'being neglected as of late'. Item seven explained that my mother was exhausted and offered an apology if she would not be emotionally available for the days to come.

It was a concise, impressive list that fit on one page. But the list did not answer any of the questions I would have had for my mother had she not been asleep when I got home. It was the middle of the afternoon and confusing to me that my mother should be asleep. The idea of my parents not being married also did not make much sense. They drove matching silver Mercedeses, and wore the same small wire-frame glasses. They were partners at the same firm and could finish each other's sentences. It occurred to me that my parents had seemed more like twins than Sue and I. I did not understand why I needed therapy when it was Sue who had been arrested. I did not understand why so much had to be so radically different when all I had done was go away for a vacation.

'Look,' Sue said, pulling a plastic ID bracelet out of her back pocket. 'I rode in the back of the police car, I got fingerprinted. I sat in a holding cell for two hours.'

'Why are you so happy about it?'

'You can't believe how pissed off our respectable father was. Pissed off! Lawyer's daughter arrested! Oh, the shame. Get this crazy girl off to the therapist! Cocksucker. It's fine with me. Yumiko believes in therapy. She thinks I might like it. She says that any halfway intelligent person should jump at the offer of free therapy. Yumiko thinks I'm smart.'

Yumiko explained the bra in my bed and the condoms in my dresser. In other people's families, someone would have made my bed before I came home. The sheets would have been changed.

'Yumiko doesn't love Daniel,' Sue said. 'She is much more interested in me.'

My head had started to hurt the instant I got back home. The bottles of pills were lined up beside my bed like always: generic

twins

aspirin, Advil, Excedrin, Tylenol, Bayer. They made my room look like a place for a sick person. I decided to keep them in my closet from now on.

'You don't have to worry about me bothering you anymore,' she said.

'You don't bother me,' I said. 'I'm glad to see you.'

Sue smirked at me.

'You are such a bad liar,' she said.

After two weeks of Lisa and Todd Markman, Sue seemed a little less terrible. On the flight back, as Todd caressed my hand and told me that it was not too late to change my mind, I realized I was looking forward to seeing Sue. I had not called home once. My family had Mr Markman's phone number, but no one had called to wish me a Merry Christmas or a Happy New Year or even to explain about the divorce. I felt heartbroken, though I wasn't sure why. They had never paid enough attention to me when they were married, and now, I knew, they would be busy litigating their divorce. Sue was lashing out at me, and I had no one.

'I like Yumiko better than you,' Sue said. 'She appreciates me. She says perfect is pus and guts.'

'Who,' I asked, 'is perfect? What are you talking about?'

But Sue had slammed the door in my face. The noise was sharp and loud. I heard the sound echoing in the back of my head. I was home. I didn't understand how Sue could have told anybody that I was perfect. I had gotten a B minus on my French midterm. I had lost my only friend.

My father was not, as Sue liked to say, a cocksucker. He was busy and in love with a woman who was not our mother, but that did not necessarily mean he had stopped caring about us. I could give him a chance. My mother's Mercedes had been blocked in by the snow during the holidays, so he came all the way home in his to drive her to their office. We had talked on the phone, and he had promised to arrive early so that we could talk in person.

'Angel,' he said when he got out of the car. He was late. 'Traffic,' he said. 'It's so good to see you.'

I had taken notes in anticipation of his arrival. I had learned from my parents that it was important to prepare for even the most casual encounters, and I had many concerns: the ever-increasing mess in the house, my mother's fourteen-hour-a-day sleep schedule, the empty refrigerator and the almost empty twenty-five-pound bag of dog food, and the worst thing, the sense of dread I had begun to feel whenever Sue entered a room. Not only did my head begin to ache but my entire body tensed. I tried to keep my distance in case she had the urge to lash out and hit me. My father was a lawyer, and I thought he must remain responsible for the quality of life in our house. If my mother wasn't doing well, then he had to take her to the doctor and hire a maid; he had to be a parent to Sue because she had finally stopped listening to me.

'You look so beautiful,' he said, holding my hands. 'So tan.'

I felt something in me let go. Someone in my family was glad to see me. I did not know how he could leave me alone with them. I abandoned the agenda in my head; I just wanted my father to save me.

'I want to come live with you,' I said. 'In your new apartment. Please.'

My father let go of my hands.

He looked at me.

'Honey,' he said.

It was such a wonderful idea I wondered why it hadn't occurred to me before. A new apartment, empty and clean, where I could be my father's only daughter.

twins

'That is the sweetest thing I've heard,' he said. 'But I need you to look after your mother and Sue.'

'That's your job,' I said.

My father picked up a handful of snow. Sue watched us from the living-room window.

'This will get better,' he said. 'You'll see.'

Earlier, Sue watched me get dressed and comb my hair, telling me that I should not expect shit from our father. The word she used to describe him came back to me. It had always sounded horrible. But now I was glad for the word. Cocksucker. Mr Markman would never abandon me with such complete indifference.

My father molded the snow in his hand into a ball. 'You must have liked the warm weather in Hawaii,' he said.

I shrugged. My mother came out of the house. She walked carefully down the front path, which was still covered in ice. She looked fine. She was wearing a pair of sensible shoes, holding her heels in her hand. She looked like a lawyer again, dressed in a conservative gray suit instead of her dirty bathrobe. She looked like my father's business partner. It did not seem coincidental that his suit was also gray. I could not believe that they were really getting divorced.

'Right on time,' my father said. She was, in fact, five minutes early, cutting into my meeting with my father.

'I am always punctual,' my mother said. 'Why would that change?'

'You've got a point,' my father said, looking at the snowball in his hand. 'Anyway, it's back to the old grind.'

'Who's going to handle our divorce, I wonder?' My mother smiled serenely.

My father threw the snowball against a tree. 'We can discuss that at the office,' he said.

My mother kissed me on the cheek. 'Make sure Sue gets to

school on time,' she said. She got into the car, laying her brief-case on her lap.

'We'll talk more,' my father told me. His voice, at least, was apologetic. He took my hand in his, and I felt him press a bill into my palm.

He got back in the car, closed the door, and without looking back, drove off: two lawyers on their way to work. Sue came out of the house and joined me on the sidewalk. She had her back-pack on over her winter parka, a black ski cap covering her dirty hair. She held her unicycle at her side. I looked at the fifty-dollar bill my father had given me.

'It is not even worth hating them,' she said, snatching the money.

'I don't hate them.'

'Well you should.'

'I love you,' I said.

'No, you don't.'

Sue pulled a pair of gloves from her pocket. I looked at my empty hand.

'I do. You are my twin sister.'

'Yeah, yeah. I know,' Sue said. 'It is a given.'

She hopped on her unicycle. She could get up and keep her balance effortlessly, without leaning on a tree or gripping my shoulder. She pedaled evenly, without looking back.

The thought of going to school gave me a headache.

I did not know what I wanted to wear. Someone had gone through my dresser while I was gone. My pink chenille sweater, my favorite jeans, and the red Stella McCartney dress I had never worn were missing – in addition to the silk pajamas. Maybe Sue had taken these things, the way she stole my textbooks or the cash my father had just put in my hand, or maybe it was my brother's new girlfriend, the Japanese kleptomaniac. I was shaking all over, looking for my missing things. If I confronted Sue, she would deny it. She'd laugh in my face. Now I would be late. I hated to be late to school. Being on time was something I could control, like brushing the tangles out of my hair or tucking in my clothes.

I did not want to go to school.

I went to the garage and found my unicycle hanging on the wall. I had not ridden it in over a year, but it came right back to me. I pedaled directly to the Markman house on the hill. Lisa and Todd were sure to be at school, and no one would know that I had gone there. I would not let myself hope to see Mr Markman. I just wanted to see his house, to be near him.

Mr Markman was lying on the front lawn, making snow angels. They were the biggest snow angels I had ever seen. Mr Markman seemed like the tallest person in the entire world, although he'd informed me that there were numerous players in the NBA who had several inches on him. I was surprised to see him playing in the snow. I had never seen an adult play in the snow. My parents were not playful people. I was not a playful person. I got off my unicycle and walked over to him.

'Chloe,' he said. 'Hello.'

'Hello, Mr Markman.'

'So you ride that thing too?'

I nodded.

Mr Markman laughed. He sat up from the snow, brushing the fluffy white powder from his lap.

'You are not your twin, in disguise?'

I laughed. 'No, it's me.'

'But twins do that. Fool people?'

'I don't,' I said. 'I'd rather be recognized for myself.'

'But you also ride a unicycle.' Mr Markman laughed again. He stood up from the lawn, wiping still more snow from his pants.

'Pretty twins like you could get a career going. Ride for the Ringling Brothers at the Garden during the off-season.'

'I would never do that,' I said.

'No?' Mr Markman looked at me. 'Why not?'

'It lacks dignity.'

'Dignity?' Mr Markman said. 'And here I look like a grown fool playing in the snow.'

'It looks nice,' I said.

'Do you want to come inside? Watch a basketball game?'

'Are Lisa and Todd at school?'

I did not want go inside if they were home, but Mr Markman misunderstood my question.

'You don't need to worry about being alone with me, Chloe,' he said. 'I am a father. An honorable man.'

I felt my face go red. We had spent so many nights alone in Hawaii, watching tapes of Mr Markman's games. He was six feet, ten inches tall.

'I enjoyed watching basketball with you in Hawaii. Your presence soothes me.'

'I enjoyed it too,' I said.

'But you should be in school,' Mr Markman said. 'Earning good grades.'

Mr Markman was a responsible parent; it was an admirable quality, but I was sad to be denied the morning in his house, sitting on that comfortable leather sofa watching Mr Markman play basketball. There were lots of games I hadn't seen: his high school championship on Super 8, and last year's all-star game where he had been named most valuable player.

'I practically get straight As,' I said softly, looking at my unicycle, wondering how long it would take me to ride back to the house and then walk to school. 'I could miss a day.'

It was useless, I thought. Mr Markman and I could not be friends.

He would send me to school. I belonged in school. I was the top
student in my grade.

'Have you had breakfast?' Mr Markman said.

'No,' I said.

'Would you like some?'

'Yes, please.'

Mr Markman led me into his house. We walked through the
enormous living room, past the dining room and his office, and
turned left into the kitchen.

'I'm making sausages,' he said. 'You want eggs with your
sausages?'

I shook my head. 'Whatever you're having is fine,' I said.

'Let's skip the eggs,' Mr Markman said. Mr Markman fired up
a frying pan full of sausages while I sat on the table, watching.
'These are chicken apple sausages,' he said. 'Healthy and delicious.'

Mr Markman and I watched the sixth game of a championship
series from three years ago. We had watched this one before. It
was Mr Markman's favorite: the final game of the championship
series. The Knicks were down by twelve points and Mr Markman
had the flu. He had a 102-degree fever and his doctors had told
him that he shouldn't play. During the time-outs, he draped a
towel over his head, his head sunk down to his knees.

'What were you thinking then?' I said, watching as his coach
and the players hovered anxiously around him.

'Not a thing,' Mr Markman said. 'I just closed my eyes, and
waited for the buzzer to ring so that I could get back on the court.'

I kept looking back and forth from the tall, gentle man sitting
on the couch to the awesome basketball player on the court, dripping sweat, moving the ball. The fans were going crazy. The noise
seemed deafening, even in Mr Markman's living room, coming
from the enormous television with its state-of-the-art surround

sound system. At the end of the game, with only eight seconds left on the clock, I felt myself getting nervous and excited, even though I already knew how the game would end. The other team had the ball; another player took the shot and missed. Mr Markman got the rebound. He threw the ball to a teammate halfway down the court, and he kept on running, full speed to the basket, his dark black skin shiny with sweat. Mr Markman leapt in the air to catch the pass, got fouled, and dunked the ball through the hoop. Then he took his place at the free throw line. The camera panned around the stadium, showing the court from Mr Markman's point of view. Behind the basket were thousands of fans waving colored foam rods, booing wildly, trying to distract him. I couldn't begin to imagine what it would be like, to stand so quiet in the center of a crowd like that, and shoot a ball into a small hoop from so great a distance. Mr Markman didn't blink. He just stared at the basket. His eyes did not wander. He did not look at the other players on the court or let his eyes drift to the hysterical crowd. He looked at the basket, and then he lifted his arms to take the shot. The ball rose in a high arc and came down into the basket, making that beautiful swishing sound. The crowd went wild.

'Swish,' Mr Markman said.

The TV commentators called Mr Markman a champion. They called him a legend in the game. They praised his stamina, his courage, his inspiration to other players. I felt proud to sit in the same room with him. I looked down at the empty plate on my lap. I had eaten all six chicken sausages.

'How about that?' Mr Markman said.

I stood at the free throw line with the basketball in my hand.

'What do I do?' I said.

'Look at the basket.'

twins

'And then what do I do?' The basket seemed farther away in Mr Markman's basketball court than it did on the television. My oxford shoes squeaked on the shiny floor. I had made a mistake agreeing to this lesson.

'I don't think I can,' I said.

Mr Markman nodded at me. 'You can do anything you want,' he said. 'Take a moment to reflect. You have been graced with good health and intelligence and inner beauty.'

I looked away from the basket at Mr Markman. It was so far away. I was afraid I would miss.

'Just look at the basket,' he said. 'Don't look at me. Visualize the ball going into the basket. Raise your arms high, to eye level, and when you shoot, let the ball roll off your fingertips. The ball is connected to your fingers. *You* decide where the ball will go.'

I stared at the basket. I removed one hand from the ball and smoothed back my hair.

'You don't need to make the shot, sweetheart,' he said. 'This is only your first lesson.'

I nodded. I had both hands on the ball and I was looking at the basket. I was learning something new. I felt comfortable being a student. I raised my arms, like Mr Markman instructed, and concentrating on the basket, I let the ball roll off my fingers. We watched as the basketball rose and fell through the net.

'You are a natural,' Mr Markman said, nodding his head.

It was strange to me how calm I always felt in Mr Markman's presence. He palmed the ball in his hand and started dribbling.

'Ready?' he said.

Mr Markman passed me the ball, and I instinctively stepped forward to catch it. I liked the solid feeling of the ball in my hands.

'Passing,' Mr Markman said. 'Another vital part of the game.'

I passed the ball back to Mr Markman. He caught it, and then passed it back, so that it bounced on the court, and I caught it as the ball rose.

'A bounce pass,' he said. 'Now back to me.'

I passed him back the ball, bouncing it the same way.

We practiced passing for several minutes without saying a word, and then Mr Markman introduced dribbling in between passes. I imitated Mr Markman, trying to mimic his moves. Soon we were dribbling down the court, making forward movement as we passed.

'Most young players only care about shooting,' Mr Markman said, 'but it's important to get a feeling for the ball. To feel the basketball in your hands and to learn how to control it.'

I nodded. I bounced the ball from my right hand and, when it came back up, bounced it again with my left, and then my right.

'Relax,' Mr Markman said. 'That ball is following your lead. You can trust it. Try closing your eyes.'

I closed my eyes, and like Mr Markman said, the ball went where I wanted it to, up and down, from my left hand to my right. It was quiet in his gym; the only noise was the steady sound of the ball hitting the floor, the squeak of our shoes on the floor.

'Are you enjoying yourself?' Mr Markman said.

'I am,' I said.

We had made it from one end of the court to the basket, passing and dribbling. I had not made a single mistake.

'Go ahead,' Mr Markman said. 'Take your shot.'

I looked at the basket, aimed, and shot. The ball went in. It was what Mr Markman would have called a swish shot. I found myself grinning.

'This gives me great pleasure, Chloe,' he said, moving forward to grab the ball.

'It does?'

'Try taking the shot again,' Mr Markman said. 'But this time, try to sink it using the backboard.'

twins

He passed the ball back to me. I shot, aiming for the back-board, and the ball went in again.

'How tall are you, Chloe?' he said. 'Five nine, five ten?'

'Five ten.'

'Are you still growing?'

'I don't know. Maybe.'

'Do you want to learn the game?' Mr Markman said. 'I can teach you.'

I didn't see how the same man I had watched on television would have the time or the patience to spend the day with me in his own private basketball court. I could hear the words of the broadcaster in my head, screaming with excitement when Mr Markman made the winning basket, calling him a living legend.

'I would love to teach you the game,' Mr Markman said. 'Basketball is a beautiful combination of mind and spirit. Grace in motion.'

I looked at my black oxfords.

'I will need to get sneakers,' I said.

Sue looked at me suspiciously.

'I didn't see you in school today,' she said.

'I didn't go.'

'You always go to school.'

'Today,' I said, 'I didn't.'

'You didn't miss anything.'

'You always say that.'

'It always sucks.'

'Oh, Sue,' I said.

'Oh, Chloe,' Sue said, mocking me.

Sue felt less and less like a person I knew. I used to be able to read Sue's mind, to finish her sentences, anticipate her thoughts, but now I had no idea how to talk to her. I heard her at night talking on the phone to Yumiko.

'So what did you do?' Sue said. 'When you didn't go to school?'

I looked at my hands, remembering how it felt holding a basketball. I wondered if Sue would believe me if I told her. I had never considered doing anything athletic before. I had always hated gym class. The idea of sweating, especially while I was at school, used to disturb me. I had broken a sweat on the basketball court today as Mr Markman and I went up and down the court, but I felt good, concentrating on learning the tasks he set before me.

'What did you do?' Sue repeated.

'I don't know,' I said.

'Liar,' Sue said.

My mother appeared at the top of the stairs.

'Don't fight,' she said.

Sue and I jumped. We were not used to seeing her home during the day. She was wearing her bathrobe, which I knew was a bad sign.

'What are you doing home?' Sue said.

'I didn't feel comfortable at the office.'

'That figures,' Sue said. 'I don't know why you'd pick a career that defends the law. It puts you on the side of the cops and the government. Your career makes you one of them. A dressed up pig.'

My mother smiled at Sue. She did not deserve a smile for being rude, but she was often rewarded for her bad behavior. A good daughter would have been concerned that her mother was so uncomfortable in her workplace that she came home to sleep in the middle of the day. My mother had never missed a day at the office.

'Not necessarily, Sue,' she said. 'Someone needs to stand up to the powers that be. What if the police arrested you without cause? You'd want a good lawyer to stand up for your rights.'

'I was the one shoplifting,' Sue said. 'My rights weren't violated.'

'Okay,' my mother said. 'But what if you were wrongfully accused? Wouldn't you want someone to defend you? Even now, even if you are guilty as charged, don't you think it's good to have a lawyer at your side to protect your interests? Everybody has the right to self-defense. Lawyers do a lot of good in the world.'

Sue said nothing.

I was glad my mother stood up to her.

'I believe in what you do,' I said.

My mother smiled. 'Thank you, Chloe.'

I knew, though, that it did not matter whether I offered support to my mother. It was always Sue and her rude behavior that got my parents' attention. My father had never spent time with me the way Mr Markman had today.

I looked at my mother, standing there on the steps. My conversation with Sue seemed to have died. I was relieved that I would not need to explain to her what I had done that day, because I wanted to keep my basketball lesson with Mr Markman secret. It was mine, and it was precious.

'I hope I am not intruding on your privacy,' my mother said. 'It must be strange to find me at home.'

'I don't care what you do,' Sue said.

'She doesn't mean that,' I said. 'We're both worried about you.'

My mother looked at Sue. 'I hate it that you are so angry,' she said.

Sue pointed to me. 'Blame Chloe for that.'

I was sick of Sue blaming me for everything. Everything was always my fault. I was surprised she didn't blame me when she got arrested for shoplifting.

'Come upstairs,' my mother said. 'I'm watching television in my room. Come keep me company.'

We went to my mother's room and took positions on opposite sides of the king-size bed. Daisy also jumped on the bed, curling up on the bottom, beneath my mother's feet. My mother was watching *Sesame Street*. 'There are so many new characters,' she said, 'since the last time I watched. This big elephant, for instance. Who is he?'

'Big Bird's imaginary friend,' Sue said. 'Snuffleupagus.'

I could hardly believe it when Sue curled up next to my mother, laying her head on her chest. She hated our parents, used to cringe when they tried to hug her or kiss her good night. I felt neglected, somehow, on the other side of the bed, watching my mother idly rub Sue's head. I wondered how she could bear to touch Sue's dirty hair. I wondered what I had missed in school that day and if I could fall behind after one day's absence. My mother was supposed to be a role model, a powerful woman lawyer, but as I looked at her, it seemed clear that she was unable to take care of herself, let alone the house, or Sue.

My cell phone rang from my backpack. I didn't want to answer. The Count was suffering from insomnia and was counting sheep. That would not help me with my grade point average, but the sheep floating outside his window were cute, and I was enjoying the show. This was something we never did: watch TV with my mother. It wasn't a basketball lesson, but it was nice in its own way. The phone rang again.

'We can't hear the show,' Sue said.

'Why don't you answer that?' my mother said.

'Aren't you going to answer it?' Sue said.

I looked at the phone. The caller ID displayed Lisa Markman's number. Her father must have told her I had been to the house. She would be angry with me.

twins

I shrugged. 'I'm watching *Sesame Street*.'

Sue lifted her head from my mother's stomach, looking at me curiously. It was the first time that Lisa Markman, my only friend, had tried to call me that I had not answered, and Sue knew it.

'This is wonderful,' my mother said. 'Me with my girls. Come closer, Chloe. Let's all snuggle together.'

I put the cell phone back in my backpack. My mother patted the space next to her pillow.

'Come here,' she said.

Maybe, I thought, this is what life could be like. Maybe it would be nice to have our mother home for a change. If she stayed home for a day or a week or a month, maybe she would realize that we were more important than the work she did for other people, and simply by being home, she would be able to restore some balance in the house. She would help make everything all right again between me and Sue. She would take care of the dog.

'Don't you have to study and shit?' Sue said, just as I started to scoot over closer to my mother. 'Can't you feel your GPA dropping by the second?'

'Sue,' my mother said. 'Don't say "and shit". That sounds so horrible.'

I had missed a day at school. In just one day, I had already fallen behind.

'I do have to study,' I said.

I got up from the bed and left quickly, before my mother could protest, before I even stopped to question why. When I got back to my room and closed my door, I was shaking with anger. No matter how hard I tried, I still let Sue bully me, push me around. If I fought back, I'd be reduced to her level. I didn't want to be anything like Sue, but I also didn't want to study. I wanted to lie on my mother's bed while she stroked *my* hair. My clean, soft, pretty hair. I was the better daughter, easier to love. I thought of them, my mother and Sue, Daisy sleeping, Big Bird talking to children from all over the world. I opened my French book. The letters swirled around the page. I took four extra-strength aspirin and shut my French book. When I closed my eyes, I could picture a basketball rolling off my fingers and into the hoop.

'You are a natural,' Mr Markman had said.

Sue

School was a fucking waste of time.

It had always been a disaster for me. I was in preschool the first time I got in trouble, for trying to color orange spots on the class hamster with a Magic Marker. But Chloe had always liked it. She had always been a Goody Two-shoes, climbing onto our kindergarten teacher's lap during story time. I hated school more than I hated Chloe. Kids called me queer because I liked to wear men's extra-large shirts. The kids sucked, the teachers sucked, the homework sucked.

In the weeks before Christmas, I had stopped going to school. I'd sneak back into the house every morning and spend the day at home. I'd go through my parents' drawers, see what I could find. Then I'd search through all of Chloe's stuff. I'd move her sweaters from her top drawer to the bottom one, just to piss her off. I'd ride my unicycle in the living room, or try to juggle tennis balls while taking a bath. If I felt lazy, I'd hang out on my parents' king-size bed, sleep and watch TV.

Daisy was my only problem. She followed me everywhere. She'd bring me her tennis balls, put her head in my lap, beg for food, and if I yelled at her, she'd pee. She barked when I locked her in the basement. Other times, Daisy would lie on my mother's bed next to me and I'd rub her belly. I always got back to school on time to meet Chloe at the end of the day. Chloe would see me and wave, before going off with that bitch Lisa Markman. Then they went to Hawaii.

I wished Chloe had died in Hawaii. I'd be better off. Chloe had become a stuck-up, superior bitch who didn't love me at all. She went halfway around the world to get away from me. I would never forgive her.

'Pus and guts,' Yumiko had said.

Dead would be the best thing.

So when I watched Chloe getting out of that ridiculous stretch limo, her pretty blond hair, her nervous smile, I acted like I didn't give a fuck. I knew that Chloe wasn't even perfect. She was dull, she was bland, she was boring, she studied all the time, even though I told her repeatedly that school was bullshit. She had pimples on her nose. Plus I had Yumiko. There was no one like Yumiko, and she was interested in everything I had to say. Sometimes when I called her, if I said something really good, she would make me repeat it so she could write it down in her note-book. Yumiko was writing a paper all about me for her psych class. Me, not Chloe. I sent her whatever she asked for, baby pictures, elementary school class photos, a snapshot of my tattoo that I took with a self-timer.

I could be famous without Chloe. Special without Chloe.

I had been arrested. I could break Lisa Markman's kneecaps if I wanted. I bought a pair of black leather boots with thick rubber soles. I found a baseball bat in the basement and put it under my bed. I was getting better and better on my unicycle. I could jump curbs, do 360-degree spins, I could walk Daisy two entire blocks before she pulled me off my perch.

twins

After my mother fell apart, I had no choice but to go back to school. I couldn't stay home. Some days, she would leave the house for work, but she never lasted. She'd come home around noon, and I'd have to spend the afternoon hiding in the closet.

'Go to school,' Yumiko told me. 'Take photography. Learn skills that are useful. Your high school probably has a great darkroom.'

I hated it when Yumiko was as stupid as everybody else. I couldn't get interested in any class. I told Chloe that I hated her, that she bored me, but I still couldn't think about anything at school but her, trying to picture where she was, who she was talking to, how wrong it was that we were not in the same class. But I had to go back. I would take two of my mother's Valium and weave down the hall, almost happy.

The idiot math teacher beamed at me when I took an empty seat at the front of the classroom for first-period geometry.

'Chloe,' he said. 'Precalculus meets after lunch.'

It had been so long since I had come to school, he forgot I was taking his class. He thought I was Chloe. I loved it when I passed for Chloe. I loved my mother's pills. 'Is it okay if I sit in?' I said. 'I need to brush up on my geometry for the PSATs. At least half of the math section is geometry.'

The idiot teacher believed me. I sat in the front row seat, taking notes the way Chloe would take notes – as if I actually gave a shit about isosceles triangles. I had no idea what the idiot teacher was talking about, but I grinned at him and he beamed back at me, thinking that I was the good twin, that I was Chloe. There was still hope for me. My face had not changed.

When the bell rang, I saw Lisa Markman staring at me from the back of the classroom and I knew I was back where I belonged. I had new purpose. Lisa Markman didn't get to have

Chloe without me. She'd have to put up with me, in her face, all the time.

I walked over to Lisa and touched her fake little nose.

'So delicate,' I said.

I followed Lisa Markman everywhere, sat next to her in the bench on the parking lot when she went out to smoke, walked into the bathroom with her, watching her reapply her makeup. 'You stink, you know,' she said once, puffing on her cigarette. I grinned back at her, glad that my odor bothered her.

Another time, I kicked open the bathroom door stall. Lisa sat on the toilet, red underwear bunched around her ankles.

'You are so out of your mind!' she yelled. She kicked the door shut with her pointy black shoes.

I waited for her while she finished. Lisa went to the sink and washed her hands. Then she opened her purse and took out a prescription pill bottle. 'A lot of celebrities take these,' she said, swallowing a pill without water.

I reached out and touched Lisa's new little nose. She offered me a pill and I took it. I almost thanked her, but I stopped myself. It felt strangely okay to be alone with Lisa in the bathroom. She seemed to almost accept me being around. It was more difficult with Chloe. She had started eating three meals a day. She jogged to school and did sit-ups in the living room, and said nothing when I borrowed her clothes or destroyed her schoolbooks. I didn't take a shower for a week, and Chloe didn't even notice.

'I like your hair,' I said.

Lisa Markman had started shaving her head when she was in Italy. She was almost a different person bald. I would be a different person without my hair. 'Maybe I'll shave mine too.'

'You shouldn't. Your hair is gorgeous.'

'You mean Chloe's hair.'

twins

'*Your* hair is gorgeous,' Lisa said. 'Honestly, what is your fucking problem? You have the same exact hair.'

Lisa Markman walked to the door and motioned for me to follow. We walked down the hall, out the door, down the block. When we got to the corner, Lisa leaned on me, taking off her fuck-me shoes, so that we stood almost eye to eye.

'These things are killing my feet,' she said and started walking barefoot down the street.

'Where are we going?' I said.

'My house,' she said.

We didn't have to go far. She called a cab that picked us up when we were a couple of blocks from school.

The walls of Lisa Markman's bedroom were covered with photographs of herself. We sat on her bed facing each other, and then she lay back, stretching her long legs across my lap. I looked around, trying to imagine Chloe in this room. I felt myself wanting to touch Lisa's milky brown toes.

The picture of her red underwear around her ankles flashed in my mind.

'Chloe won't be here for a while,' Lisa said, 'so we might as well chill.'

I could feel her celebrity pill working. I could hear Yumiko encouraging me, wanting to hear whatever story I could report to her. Chloe wouldn't like it that I was here with her best friend. Now it was Chloe who was left out.

'Chloe drives me crazy,' Lisa said. 'She is so fucking boring, and I know I've got to forget about her, but I can't.'

'Chloe drives you crazy?' I said.

I was surprised. I tried to look at Lisa's face, but she caught me looking so I turned my head away.

'What's it like to be a twin?' Lisa said.

I shook my head. 'Haven't you asked Chloe?'

'I want to hear what you have to say.'

'I would never tell you,' I said. 'I don't even like you.'

Lisa Markman nodded. 'Like I care,' she said. 'Do you know how many people out there worship me?'

'How many?'

Lisa looked at her fingers. 'Sixty-two,' she said.

'You made that up?'

'Eighty-two. I don't know. When I was on the runway, I could see those eyes, rows and rows of them. People worshiping me.'

Lisa suddenly rolled onto her stomach, inching her way over to me, her butt in the air. She slid her hand under my sweater. 'Why do you rub your back all the time? Do you also have a tattoo?'

I was proud of my tattoo. I lifted the back of my sweater so she could see.

'Chloe,' Lisa said, scooting over until she was right next to me. She put her finger on my back, tracing the letters. I felt a shiver go down my spine. 'I saw Chloe's in Hawaii when she was getting changed.'

Her hand was going up and down my back, softly under my sweater. I closed my eyes.

'Right now,' she said. 'I'm rubbing your back and I'm pretending you're Chloe.'

I liked that. I liked the idea of being Chloe.

'I look like Chloe,' I said.

'You are identical to Chloe. You have princess hair.'

'Is this nice?' Lisa said. She leaned forward and put her lips on my back, right on top of my tattoo. 'Do you like this?'

I wanted her hand to go further, spreading that feeling of softness all over my body.

'Call me Chloe,' I said.

twins

'Chloe,' Lisa said. 'Beautiful Chloe. Lift your arms.'

Lisa slid my sweater up over my shoulders, over my head. I was looking directly at a glossy photo of Lisa wearing red lipstick, a trench coat open to her belly button, and knee high leather boots. I liked it better when my eyes were closed. I hated Lisa Markman. I had hated her for years. I crossed my arms over my flat chest. I had never bothered to wear a bra. I didn't have anything to cover myself with.

'Don't,' Lisa said. 'You are so beautiful, Chloe.'

I closed my eyes. Lisa Markman kissed my neck.

'I've wanted to do this for so long.' She cupped her hand under my chin, tilting my face to hers. With my eyes closed, I knew what to do. Lisa Markman slid her tongue into my mouth. This was what it was like for Chloe to get kissed.

Lisa Markman and I lay back together on the bed.

'I love kissing,' she said.

Lisa rolled me over onto my side. She put her hand on my chest. She felt my nipple with her fingers. I squeezed my legs closer together. I was trembling.

'You'll let me touch you, won't you, Chloe?'

Lisa Markman's hand moved down to my stomach. A soft moan escaped me.

'I adore you, Chloe,' Lisa said.

'You do?'

I opened my mouth to be kissed some more. I felt sick with jealousy. This was how Lisa wanted to touch Chloe. She wanted to possess her. Steal her away. I did not know how I could bear it when Chloe would really leave me, pack her bags and go far away. She was still set on going to college. Lisa licked the tears as they slid down my cheeks.

I reached for her hand and put it between my legs.

*　　　*　　　*

Later, Lisa Markman showed me her indoor track. It was on the second floor of the house, above a full-size indoor gym.

'My father runs here when it rains,' she said.

I didn't understand. We had fallen asleep on her bed. I'd woken up thirsty, confused. My clothes were crumpled on the floor.

'What are we doing here?' I said.

Lisa hissed. 'Shut up, psychopath,' she said.

I balled my fingers into a fist, thinking I was going to hit her. Then, the door to the gym opened and Chloe came in. She was wearing a pair of blue sweatpants and a New York Knicks T-shirt. Her basketball sneakers. She walked to the far wall and picked a basketball from the rack.

'What's going on?' I said.

Lisa shook her head.

She pointed down to the floor.

Chloe stood at the foul line. She bounced the ball twice, staring at the basket. Her expression was almost fierce.

'Basketball?' I said.

Lisa put her hand on my mouth. 'Shut up already.'

Chloe took foul shot after foul shot. Most of them went in. In between shots, she smoothed the hair in her ponytail. For maybe ten minutes, Chloe did nothing but shoot foul shots. I couldn't get over it. What was she doing here playing basketball? Chloe came to Lisa Markman's house to hang out with Lisa. Chloe was not athletic. Chloe was an honors student.

She started taking shots from different points around the basket.

Lisa looked at me.

'It's totally fucked up,' she whispered.

Then Mr Markman came into the gym. He was a giant next to my sister, tall and solid and black. We had a perfect view of his gleaming, bald head.

Lisa shook her head at me.

twins

'Every day,' she whispered. 'They're here.'

'Good day at school?' Mr Markman said to my sister.

Chloe shrugged. She raised the ball to her chest.

'Higher,' Mr Markman said. 'So the defense can't block your shot.'

Mr Markman took two steps toward her, so she would have to shoot above him. The man was a fucking giant. But Chloe shot the ball up high, like he told her, and Lisa and I watched it sail over Mr Markman's arm and fall into the basket.

Chloe grinned.

Lisa bit her lip.

Mr Markman whistled. 'Nice shot. Very nice. It's that natural talent.'

He dribbled the ball, staring at my sister.

'You're all warmed up?'

Chloe nodded.

'Let's work on your lay-up this afternoon,' he said. 'What do you say?'

Chloe nodded at Mr Markman. 'Okay, Rodney,' she said.

She blushed saying his name. I couldn't believe it. Mr Markman tossed her the ball, and without hesitation Chloe caught it, dribbled to her right, and then drove to the basket. She had been here before, meeting with Mr Markman, playing basketball. I looked at Lisa. She was biting her lip. Nothing was the way I thought it was. Chloe had a secret life. I watched, speechless, as Chloe tripped over her sneakers when she got close to the basket. The ball hit the backboard, circled the rim, and went back out. Chloe landed on her butt.

'I missed,' she said sadly.

Mr Markman offered Chloe his arm. She grabbed it, and he pulled her up to her feet. Chloe smoothed her hair.

'Try again,' he said. 'Take your time.'

Chloe got up. She did ten layups from the right side, ten from the left. She made every single layup from the right side. She missed three from the left. She looked expectantly at Mr Markman every time a shot went in.

He grinned, passing the ball back to Chloe, saying, 'Try it again. Try it again.'

Chloe

Nothing felt as good as making a jump shot and watching Mr Markman nod his head in silent approval. Or when he hooted after I made my first reverse layup. He had dared me to do it, and remembering his moves from the videotapes, I'd taken a run at the basket. I couldn't believe it when the shot went in. There was nothing Sue could do to take that away from me. No cold glare from Lisa or Todd could stop me from returning to their house to practice basketball with their father in his gym.

Once again, I made the decision to become a new person. I gave up on the idea of being an exceptional student. I had to accept the fact that, as hard as I tried, I was not and would never be extraordinary at school. As Sue liked to say, any idiot who studied enough could get good grades. I had agonized over French and still made the same mistakes over and over.

But in just a few weeks, I had mastered both the right- and the left-handed layup. I had a killer fadeaway jump shot and what Mr Markman said was essential to any elite player: a pair of fast hands. Mr Markman said that should I choose to develop my skill, I could be a top player, because I had a natural gift. A gift. I repeated these

163

words silently to myself throughout the day – when I was at home waiting for Sue to come out of the bathroom, or watching her walk through the halls at school, following Lisa. I didn't like the two of them together. I was certain that they were conspiring to get me, but I pretended not to notice. I tried to concentrate on what was important: basketball.

Mr Markman had convinced me that I had to play on a team to fully expand my talents. He also told me that it would be selfish not to play for an audience. Gifts, he said, need to be shared. The day before the high school team tryouts, Mr Markman presented me with wonderful presents: a pair of Nike Air basketball sneakers and a stuffed animal, a soft white polar bear with a red ribbon around its neck. Mr Markman had a way of looking at me and making me feel special.

Mr Markman was proud of me when I made the varsity squad. He wanted me to play on the team, and so I would, but I hated the idea of giving up my afternoons with him. I had started playing basketball just to be near him. If he had been a skydiving teacher, I would have eagerly jumped out of an airplane. The team practices made me nervous. I was one of fifteen other girls; all of them, I was sure, would dislike me if I made too many shots or outran them during the drills. I was wary of the team coach, who called me Swiss Miss, making it clear how much I stood out on the almost all-black team. I talked to no one when I got changed in the locker room. And I missed Mr Markman. I could hear his voice while I played, always telling me to push a little harder, run a little faster. I thought about him constantly, remembering every little detail of the day's practice, the jump shot I nailed, the layups I missed, so I could report back what I learned to him.

By the end of the first week, I knew that I would be fine. Mr Markman had prepared me for all of the shooting drills and the passing drills; I understood the concept of zone defense even if I had not actually experienced it on the court. The other players seemed to accept if not actually like me. The center, Kendra, sometimes told me 'nice shot' during practice.

I had a brand-new life, centered on basketball. Mr Markman was adamant that I change the way I ate. According to him, I could not reach the peak of my form without proper nutrition and required protein and carbohydrates to keep up my energy. He insisted on three meals a day.

'No more diets,' he said. 'I look at my own beanpole daughter and I see a poster girl for malnutrition.'

Sue watched me eat with open hostility. It had never been easy eating with Sue. The day I had gotten my period, my parents had come home with lasagna, Sue's absolute favorite food, but she wouldn't eat until I had eaten, and she stared at me, her fork poised in front of her mouth, waiting until I swallowed. Now we were almost seventeen, and I worried that Sue still had not gotten her period. I remembered us throwing up together, sure that she needed help. Sue had always been furious with me for being on a diet, and now that I wasn't, she still wasn't eating. She was still furious.

'Aren't you worried about getting fat?' she said.

Of course I was terrified about getting fat. I was worried about exposing my arms and legs in the ugly team uniform: shiny blue shorts with green stripes down the sides, and a matching green-and-blue tank top. The colors made me look sickly, and I was afraid that I was becoming muscular and ugly. But I was on the varsity basketball team, and Mr Markman was proud of me. I had to trust that I burned off the calories through exercise.

Sue looked at the food I prepared with disgust. She wouldn't eat unbuttered toast or apple cinnamon oatmeal. She would not eat roast turkey sandwiches or salad without dressing, but sometimes I saw her eating at school. One time, I saw Sue and Lisa

Markman sharing a Snickers bar, chewing from opposite ends, the way we used to when we were little. I saw their tongues touch as they ate, and I decided that I would not think about them together. I remembered Lisa's fingers exploring under my bathing suit. I did not want to know.

I would not think about Lisa Markman any longer, and though it was harder, I also tried not to think about Sue. Mr Markman had told me that to be a great basketball player I needed to focus all of my energy on basketball. I discovered that I had more energy from eating, that I could run harder and play longer. Mr Markman kept close track of my progress. He said that if I wanted to I could be a star; I could play for a college team and then move on to the Summer Olympics, the WNBA.

I didn't care about stardom. I didn't want to go to college and play on a college team. I wanted only to play for Mr Markman.

Mr Markman took me to see the Knicks play at Madison Square Garden.

I had been there before, a long time ago. My parents had taken us to see the Ice Capades and the Ringling Brothers and Barnum & Bailey circus. Sue had loved the clowns in their enormous shoes, riding the unicycles. Daniel had put cotton candy in my hair. My father yelled at him, and made him cry. This was to be the first time Mr Markman had been back since his own retirement. The Knicks had offered him a coaching position that he had turned down. He had also been offered a recruiting position and a broadcasting spot and probably more jobs that I did not know about. 'I don't need money,' he explained to me. 'When a man retires, he retires.'

On the way to the game, Mr Markman warned me that there would be attention from fans and other players and perhaps even the press. He wore a dark blue suit, a crisp light blue shirt, and a matching pastel tie. I felt young and simple in my jeans and pink sweater, and the Nike Air basketball sneakers Mr Markman had given me.

'You're going to like this,' he said. He squeezed my hand as we stepped out of the limousine. A photographer took our picture. The bulb flashed in my eyes, and for a second I felt blinded.

Our seats were in a glassed-in VIP box, far from the court. The seats were soft and leather and filled with middle-aged white men, men who looked like but who were not my father. They were lawyers and executives, all of them, according to Mr Markman. They began to murmur excitedly when we took our seats, and several came over to Mr Markman, to shake his hand and welcome him back. 'How's the knee, Rodney?' they asked. 'How are the kids?'

Even I could understand what was behind the question. They wanted to know where were Lisa and Todd, and who was I, this young, blond girl at Mr Markman's side? I assumed that Mr Markman had not invited Lisa and Todd to come with us. This game was a present for all my hard work. It was also a learning experience, for in a couple of days' time, I would be on the court in my ugly green-and-blue team uniform, playing in my first competitive game. His children didn't appreciate basketball the way I did. They did not want to learn from Mr Markman. They were self-absorbed and sex-crazed and so insanely selfish that they did not understand how lucky they were to have such a splendid father.

Mr Markman had introduced me as his prodigy. I was thrilled with the word. Prodigy. I felt my heart beating fast. I played basketball because I enjoyed it. I played for the pleasure I felt when the ball went through the hoop, *swish*, and because Mr Markman believed in me.

The men in the box blinked through my introduction, staring

at me with open curiosity. I hoped that it was because I was too pretty to look like a real basketball player, that despite my newfound athleticism, it would be hard to believe I could take the ball to the hoop. 'So, you shoot hoops?' one of them said, his eyes wandering down to the round neckline of my sweater. None of these men believed Mr Markman. Suddenly, I understood that, as Mr Markman's prized student, I should have been a young, black boy from the projects instead of a white, teenage girl. They thought I was a slut. I felt my face turn red. I excused myself and went to the women's bathroom to comb my hair.

For a long time, I stared at myself in the mirror. I looked different since I had started playing basketball. My face had filled in. Despite all the exercise, I had gained weight. I was not fat, I told myself, I was healthy. I put on lipstick and then wiped it off. I wished Mr Markman had arranged for a private box.

When I got back, Mr Markman handed me a pair of binoculars.

'Look for celebrities,' he said. 'Spike Lee comes to a lot of games. So does Woody Allen.' He pointed to the center seats on the floor right behind the players' benches. I directed the binoculars until they were focused right on him, Woody Allen in a baseball cap, and next to him Soon-Yi, who had a little boy on her lap. I smiled at Mr Markman.

'Women also play at the Garden,' he said. 'The WNBA is making enormous strides in the game. The Liberty play a fine game of B-ball.'

'I won't be a professional player,' I said.

I did not want to disappoint Mr Markman, but I had seen female professional basketball players. They had beefy faces and thick arms, thick legs and ugly hair. I didn't want to look like them. I had always thought I would be a lawyer like my parents.

'Next time,' Mr Markman said. 'I'll take you to a Liberty game. You should see these women handle the ball.'

twins

I had never been to a professional sporting event. It was an entirely different thing than watching a videotape in a quiet living room in Hawaii with a gentle breeze wafting through the open window, the sounds of tropical birds in the distance. At Madison Square Garden, the game was there, directly in front of us. I could hear the basketball hitting the court, the loud squeaks of the players' sneakers on the wood floor. With only two minutes left in the game, the Knicks down by five, they scored four straight baskets to win the game, and I was cheering at the top of my lungs with the rest of the crowd. Thousands of people, strangers up on their feet, all for a basketball team. I felt that I understood finally why it was not enough for me to play alone. It was one thing to practice; I got the same quiet feeling sinking free throws that I had once experienced studying for the SAT. But a game was something else altogether.

I had no idea that it was possible to get this excited about anything.

The whole time, without actually looking at Mr Markman, I could sense him watching me.

'Not long from now,' he said, pointing to players on the floor who were hugging and slapping each other on the back, 'that will be you.'

Mr Markman helped me into my jacket.

'So I take it you enjoyed the game?' he said. He gently touched my nose, and I nodded.

'I was hoping you would feel that way,' he said.

Then Mr Markman zipped up my jacket as if I were a little girl.

I wondered where my father was. He lived in Manhattan, and there I was, also in Manhattan, but my father did not take me to basketball games. He had said that Sue and I should come visit him at his new apartment, but so far, we had not gone.

'Thank you so much,' I said. 'This was wonderful.'

Now that the game was over, the executives were back to watching us. Surely, they could not think that I was Mr Markman's girlfriend. I was sixteen years old. Mr Markman weighed more than 250 pounds. There was a camera crew waiting for us outside the VIP box.

Later that night, Mr Markman and I were on the TV news. The footage showed us walking quickly away from the cameras, Mr Markman steering me through the crowds with his hand on the small of my back. My face was not visible, only my blond hair. 'Rodney Markman, back in the public eye for the first time since his retirement from the New York Knicks, attended the game with an unidentified young woman,' the newscaster said.

Three days later, another picture—Mr Markman holding my hand as I stepped out of the limousine—was published in *People* magazine.

It did not take long for my identity to be discovered. Kids at school stopped and stared. My English teacher called me aside after class; he asked me out for coffee. The guidance counselor had me in for a talk. 'How is your life at home?' he wanted to know. 'Fine,' I told him. The man wore corduroy moccasins to work. I wouldn't talk to him.

For the first time since we'd come back from Hawaii, both Lisa and Todd had something to say to me. Todd Markman waited for me after basketball practice. I came out of the gym, tired and sweaty, and he looked me up and down. 'You are not that pretty,' he said.

Lisa also found me in the gym, where I was doing wind sprints during lunch. I went mainly to the gym during my lunch breaks instead of to the library. Mr Markman had told me that

twins

conditioning made all the difference between a good player and a great player.

'White women always like a tall, fine black man,' Lisa said. 'My mother got herself a black basketball god. She drove off the fucking road, you know.'

My mother, who had gone back to work, who had started working later and later and sometimes didn't come home at all, thought the very worst of me. She approached me nervously while we were having breakfast, her yellow legal pad and a copy of *People* on the table next to the bowl of cereal with sliced bananas I had made for her.

'Are you still a virgin?' she said.

I didn't want to blush, but I felt myself blushing.

'He teaches me basketball,' I said.

My mother sighed. I looked down at her pad. I saw her cross out the words *statutory rape*. On the next line, I saw the words *birth control*. I couldn't believe she would really think something that awful about Mr Markman.

Sue blew bubbles into her orange juice with one of her stupid striped straws, letting the cereal I had poured for her go soggy.

'Only lesbians and ugly girls play basketball,' she said.

'I know it's not the fifties.' My mother looked at me knowingly. 'But you should consider getting a boyfriend. To protect your reputation. I know that your father is concerned.'

'The cocksucker,' Sue said.

She mashed a banana with her spoon into the side of her cereal bowl. I wondered why I continued to make food for Sue that I knew she would never eat. 'Pretty soon,' she said, 'you're going to be too fat to have your picture shown anywhere.'

I had to stop myself from throwing Sue's cereal against the wall. Sue wanted to hurt me, and she did, every time. I looked to my mother to defend me, but she was done parenting for the day. My hands were shaking as I watched her finish her breakfast.

My father's paralegal called to set up a meeting. Later another paralegal called to cancel the meeting. A letter came FedEx the next day. My father had put three crisp one-hundred-dollar bills inside with a note to buy myself something pretty to wear.

A reporter from *Sports Illustrated* called the house when I was at practice. I did not return the call.

'I told him,' Sue said, 'that I can ride a unicycle, but he wasn't interested.'

Kendra, the center on my team, asked me if I liked black guys. She was tall and skinny. Her greatest skill on the court was to stand under the basket and get in everyone's way. She seemed curious, friendly, and it occurred to me that if I said yes, I did like black guys, Kendra, who was also black, might like me. I very much wanted a friend on the basketball team. 'No,' I said, shrugging my shoulders. 'I don't. I'm sorry.'

I started to blush, realizing that I had handled her question all wrong. I didn't like guys, white or black. I played basketball. I was terrified Kendra would think I was a racist, but I told myself it didn't matter what she thought. There was no way we could become friends. I was a better player, the coach gave me more attention at practice, and before long, Kendra would certainly begin to hate me.

Some guy from school called to ask me to the movies. He did not mention the magazine, but I knew that was why he called; no one had ever called before. 'I don't go to the movies,' I told him. 'I'm sorry.'

'You don't?' he said. 'What do you do?'

'I play basketball,' I said.

'I know you play basketball,' he said.

He said that his name was James Patterson. I had no idea who he was.

twins

The same reporter from *Sports Illustrated* came to a practice. He talked to my coach and other players on the team.

'You could be a real story,' he told me. 'Like it or not, Rodney Markman calls you his prodigy. If it's true, that's something the sports world takes seriously.'

Mr Markman told me not to pay attention to any of it. He called me at home to wish me luck the night before my first game.

'This silliness will all go away,' he said. His voice was as calm as ever. No matter the circumstances, Mr Markman radiated a sense of tranquillity. 'Don't pay attention to the chatter in your head. You just play your game and your mind will go quiet.'

'You'll come see me play?' I said.

'Child,' he said. 'You couldn't keep me away. You have worked so hard for this. I am proud of you.'

I scored twenty-two points in my first game. I was the top scorer of the night. During a time-out, the coach told the other players to pass the ball to me when they did not have an open shot. The center, Kendra, would scoop up all the rebounds with her long arms and pass the ball back to me.

'Our Chloe's on fire,' the coach said. He had stopped calling me Swiss Miss.

We won the game with an eighteen point lead.

'A blowout,' Kendra called it.

Mr Markman sat in the front row. He had dressed for the high school gym just like he had for the Knicks game, wearing a dark suit and a pastel tie. He sat up straight, and he clapped proudly every time I made a basket.

Sue had also come to the game. She sat by herself in the back of the stands. She was dressed all in black, her hair pulled back tight. She never clapped. One time, after I scored an easy layup, I snuck a glance at her. She was staring directly at me, but she didn't acknowledge me when I waved. I missed my next shot, flustered, angry that she had ignored me. I decided then never to look at her again when I played. I had to think about what Mr Markman had told me and shut out the chatter in my head. My parents had not come to the game, though my mother had made a point of writing down the time and location in her yellow legal pad. I had called my father's assistant and given her the information as well.

At the end of the game, Mr Markman came down on the court, and in front of everybody, he kissed me on the forehead.

'Nice game,' he said. I heard the clicking of a camera, someone taking our picture. 'Would you like to go out for some ice cream to celebrate?'

I looked up into Mr Markman's dark eyes. I nodded, pleased, too excited to say yes. And then I noticed Sue, slinking down the steps, her hands jammed in her pockets. Mr Markman turned to follow my gaze. 'Your twin,' he said.

For a second, I was surprised that he had recognized her. Lately, I had begun to feel so far removed from her I was startled by the fact that we still looked alike.

She stood next to me on the court.

'Would you like to come out for some ice cream with us?' Mr Markman asked. 'To celebrate Chloe's first game?'

Sue rocked back and forth on her heels.

I stared at her, willing her not to come. We stared at each other. The gym was beginning to empty out.

'Hot fudge sundaes,' said Mr Markman, an innocent, still believing that Sue and I could go out together and eat ice cream. I wondered if he remembered that it was Sue who had broken Lisa's nose. I looked at her, waiting, afraid she would break out into tears and Mr Markman would have no choice but to comfort her.

'Well,' I said. 'Yes or no?'

I didn't want to worry about Sue. This was supposed to be my night.

twins

'We were supposed to be on TV,' Sue said, like she was spitting the words. 'None of this basketball bullshit.'

She held up her middle finger to us both and then ran out of the gym.

Mr Markman sighed.

'You two are nothing alike, are you?' he said.

We walked to his car, and we drove to the restaurant in silence. Mr Markman shook his head when I tried to order a scoop of vanilla ice cream. 'We're celebrating,' he said, telling the waitress to bring me a hot fudge sundae with wet walnuts. It was much too big for me to finish, but I made myself eat the entire sundae, just for him.

Sue

I had taken a Percodan and finished two beers when I asked Lisa Markman to shave my head. My pretty blond hair had started to bug me. Lisa wanted to fool around, but she bugged me too.

'You want me to shave it off?' Lisa said.

'Yeah,' I said. 'Cut it all off.'

I had always liked Lisa Markman's shaved head. It was the one cool thing about her. I ran my fingers through the tangles of my hair, disgusted. It was Chloe's hair, and I hated Chloe. I did not want to be pretty or have friends. I had spent my whole life hating those boring girls at school. I didn't want to join them now. I would rather be miserable. I hated Lisa Markman. This, I decided, would be the last time I spoke to her. She could forget about touching me naked.

'Go ahead. Shave my head.'

Lisa nodded.

'I'll shave it,' she said.

'Shave it,' I said.

'I will shave it,' she said, laughing. 'And then *we* will look like twins.'

'Shave it already,' I said.

Lisa ran to her closet to get her tools.

'I'll have to use scissors to cut off the long part first.'

'Great,' I said. 'I want you to.'

Finally, I wasn't bored. While Chloe became a local basketball star, I'd been taking pills with Lisa. We had a big pool of pharmaceuticals: Lisa's celebrity pills, the anxiety pills I'd stolen from my mother, the superstrong pain pills Lisa took from her father. Sometimes, when we were high, I almost believed that I liked Lisa.

She brushed my hair back into a ponytail. I closed my eyes, feeling her hands on my hair, pretending it was Chloe, that it was Chloe about to trim my bangs. Chloe, who used to be able to make everything all right. With one sharp cut, the scissors went right through my ponytail.

'That felt so fucking cool,' Lisa said.

I kept my eyes closed, blocking out Lisa's voice, stupid, boring Lisa. She put the ponytail in my lap. There it was, my hair, laying there like a dead animal.

Chloe and Sue.

We were blond.

We used to be golden.

Identical twins.

Without even looking in the mirror, I knew it was over. Anybody could tell us apart. I'd be the one with the bald head. The freak. The outcast. The loser.

Lisa cut closer and closer to my head.

'I'm going to shave it now,' she said.

'Go ahead.'

'I'm shaving,' Lisa said.

I closed my eyes, kept them closed. When we were children, Chloe and I would go everywhere together. If I was sick, Chloe was sick. If I fell and scraped my knee, Chloe gave me a Band Aid.

While Lisa shaved, I reached around to touch my tattoo. My hair didn't matter. I had Chloe's name etched in my skin. My name was imprinted on hers.

'Holy shit,' Lisa said, laughing. She dropped the shaver on the floor. She covered her mouth with her hand, she was laughing so hard.

I made myself look. I was bald. I wasn't stylish or edgy or interesting. I looked sick. It was more than just hair. I could see my collarbones jutting from my chest. My skin was so pale that I could see the blue veins coursing beneath. I saw how my shirt fell straight down over my flat, flat chest. I looked like one of those twins that crazy Nazi doctor my brother once told me about had used for his twisted experiments. I looked like death.

Chloe

I was the star of my basketball team. I was named most valuable
player and selected for the New Jersey all-star team. College
recruiters came to watch me play. My grades were steadily slipping, but I was beginning to understand that if I had a high shooting average, my GPA would not matter to most colleges. It had
been such hard, ungratifying work, doing well in school, and if I
was honest with myself, I was not especially intelligent. It was like
Sue said. I was average at school. My looks, I had to admit, were
also average. I couldn't bear to look at myself in the mirror and
see my horsey face. I had discovered my one true talent: basketball. All the signs were pointing to a glorious future in the game,
but the only person that should have mattered to had lost interest.

Mr Markman was dropping me.

He had continued to come to my games, and made sure to
congratulate me afterward. He would compliment me on what I
did well and mention opportunities I could capitalize on in the
future, but he no longer asked about me, Chloe. Everything
slowly started to change after we were shown together on the TV

news. Mr Markman had told me not to listen to the chatter in my head, but I never questioned him about what was happening in his. Without even bothering to explain why, he had dropped me without a fight. As if the time we spent together never meant anything to him. A month ago, nothing had been more important to him than instructing me on my footwork or improving my jump shot. Mr Markman had held my knees while I did sit-ups.

On the last game of the season, the night I scored fifty-six points, Mr Markman left at halftime. I knew that he was gone, but I continued to play as if he was watching. I felt like I was on fire, like a force was running through my fingertips, carrying the ball to the hoop. I couldn't miss. I closed my eyes, and I saw an explosion of fireworks shooting off beneath my eyelids. Impossible shots fell through the basket. I could be off-balance, double-teamed, in the three-point range, and still, the shot would go in. I felt like a force of nature: like an earthquake or a tidal wave. When the game was over, the crowd got up on their feet. This was a girls' basketball game; no one got worked up about girls' basketball. But I knew all along that Mr Markman wasn't there watching. He had left without saying good-bye. I had been playing for a ghost.

Sue didn't come that night either. It was the first time she had skipped one of my games. She was probably with Lisa. I made my way home in the dark, limping on an ankle I did not remember twisting, only to find an enormous pile of dog shit in the living room, and poor Daisy, under the living-room table, nervously wagging her tail.

I was exhausted. 'Oh, Daisy,' I said.

I sank down on the couch and contemplated the dog. The house had begun to smell of piss and shit. My mother had pretty much stopped coming home. First she went back to the office, and then she started working late, and before long, she began to spend her nights at my father's midtown apartment. The client my father had left my mother for, the Asian investment banker, had reconciled with her husband.

Daisy came over and licked my hand. She had not been fed dinner. Sue was supposed to feed her. I didn't have time for Daisy anymore, and besides that, Daisy's dinner was not my responsibility. She was not my dog. Daisy had always been Sue's dog, from the day my mother brought her home from work and Sue proclaimed that the puppy loved her best. I was eleven years old. I had also wanted a dog. I wanted to pet the puppy and roll with her on the floor, but I let Sue have her. I did these things for Sue. I had ruined myself, I had gotten her name tattooed on my back. I had given up any chance of a normal adolescence to protect Sue from hurting others, from hurting herself, and I got nothing in return.

'Sue will come home soon,' I told the neglected dog. 'She will have to walk you. She will have to feed you. I can't take another step.'

Only Sue never did come home. I fell asleep on the couch, waiting for her.

I woke up, shivering, in the middle of the night. My ankle had blown up, swollen to almost double its normal size. It hurt just to walk to the bathroom. I got up in the middle of the night to pee, and then I hopped upstairs. I checked Sue's room to see if she had come in while I was sleeping. She wasn't there. The room was the same as when I had moved out. I pushed her dirty clothes off my old bed and crawled under the covers.

When I woke up again, it was morning, and she had still not come home. I did not go to school. I napped in Sue's bed, resting on top of the blanket. I was still wearing my jeans over my dirty basketball uniform. I did not have the energy to change my clothes.

I did not know anymore what Sue did while I went to school. I did not know what she did after school with Lisa Markman, or what she did at night for that matter, but she had always come home. Some nights she would juggle in the hallway, standing outside my door. The impact of the balls hitting the floor would shake the walls. No matter what, Sue always came home. She always came home.

I called the Markmans. Lisa would know where she was. Or Mr Markman might be willing to talk to me. He had left my game early, but once I told him that Sue was gone, that my ankle was sprained, everything would change. I had never been injured before. Certainly he would come over and help me ice my ankle. Maybe he would send his driver out to look for Sue. My heart beat fast as the phone rang, but no one picked up.

I waited another day, and Sue did not come home. I called Mr Markman's house again, and once more, no one answered. I called the police station but hung up when someone answered. Daisy whined at me all day long. Finally, I called my parents' office.

The receptionist put me on hold, and then my mother came to the phone.

'Chloe, honey,' she said. 'I have been horrible, haven't I? Staying out all night. Not calling to say when I'm coming home. I feel like a teenager all over again.' She started to laugh. 'Just this morning, I ran into Bloomingdale's to buy clean clothes for work. I bought everything new. New suit, new blouse, panty hose, and bra.' My mother giggled. 'You don't have a boyfriend yet, do you, Chloe?'

'No,' I said, shaking my head.

'That's so surprising,' she said. 'Given how beautiful you are.'

I looked at Daisy, lying in the doorway, waiting with me for Sue. I absently touched my hair. The sweat from the game two nights ago had dried and hardened. Basketball was changing me in ways I did not like or understand. My hair was not soft and wavy like it was supposed to be; instead it was stiff and tangled and dirty, and as I sat on Sue's bed, clutching the phone, I worried that if I was not careful, I could turn into Sue. I would wake up one morning to find that we had switched places.

'Maybe,' my mother said, 'it's this basketball thing. I know it sounds terrible, but boys can be put off by a girl athlete. They want their women feminine.'

'I *am* feminine,' I said. My voice sounded shrill. It scared me that my mother was thinking the same thing.

'Of course you are, Chloe, honey,' my mother said. 'I don't know what I am saying.' She laughed to herself. 'It is so wonderful that you called.'

'When are you coming home?'

I knew what I must have sounded like to her, like a whiny little girl, a bother, but I did not want to spend another night alone in the house. I wanted my parents to bring home Sue. I wanted my parents to sit me down with their tape recorder and the yellow notepad and advise me that it was not in my best interest to neglect my studies for sports. But I knew that these things were not going to happen. Sue had been right all along. Our parents had not contributed to our lives in any significant way for as long as I could remember. Instead, I had taken care of my mother when I'd gotten back from Hawaii. She lay in bed, watching public television, and I made sure that she ate her meals.

There was silence on the other end of the phone.

'If you and Daddy are back together,' I said, 'maybe you can both come home, and help take care of the house a little.' My throat was dry. 'It's a lot for me to handle on my own.'

I wanted to tell my mother about Sue. Sue was missing, I knew that she really and truly had disappeared, but a voice in my head wondered what, exactly, that had to do with my parents.

'Oh, baby,' my mother said. I could hear other voices in the background. 'When did everything get so complicated? Things are so busy at the office. Can I put you on hold?'

Before I could respond, I heard classical music piping through the receiver. Priorities, I thought, a word I might find on the PSATs. I looked out the window as I waited. The sun had set, and it was turning dark outside. I had missed another day, waiting for Sue. I had not eaten or washed my hair. I hadn't taken Daisy out for a walk. She looked at me expectantly. I had to pull myself together. I was an athlete, a strong and gifted young woman. After I got off the phone, I would feed her. I would walk her. Maybe, like magic, when I got off the phone, my ankle would no longer hurt.

'Soon,' I said to Daisy. 'I'll be off the phone soon.'

Daisy pounded her tail on the floor, but she was also too listless to get up. The receptionist picked up the line.

'Chloe?' she said. 'Your mother had an appointment she couldn't be late for. She wanted me to tell you that both she and your father will be coming home this evening. You can expect them around nine o'clock.'

I looked at my hands.

My head was throbbing. I knew that I should eat. When I first started playing basketball with Mr Markman, my headaches had gone away. He explained that proper diet and exercise had cured my problem, but I knew it wasn't as simple as that. It was Mr Markman, being near him, that had made me well. He had never left one of my games early before.

Maybe Sue would be back by the time my parents came home. Maybe she had spent the last two nights camping in our backyard, spying on me through the window. My head hurt more than ever, my hair was dirty, and I smelled terrible. Daisy's constant whining made me want to scream. Sue would be thrilled to see me this way, practically out of my mind.

Sue

'You look punk rock,' Yumiko said.

She loved that my head was shaved. I was god-awful ugly with-out my hair. I couldn't understand why Yumiko was so pleased. But I was glad, anyway. I didn't know what Yumiko would think when I showed up at her door. I hadn't called before I got on a Greyhound bus. A homeless man at Penn Station gave me half of his tuna fish sandwich. 'You look totally insane,' Yumiko said.

I smiled, though I was not sure what she meant.

Yumiko was wearing the same outfit she wore on Christmas, the white lace dress over jeans. She twirled the end of her braid around her finger, taking her time checking me out. She wasn't a psych major anymore.

'I'm studying art,' she said. 'I couldn't take the classes. It was nothing about the mind, just day after day of insidious lab work and statistics. You can't believe how tedious it was. Look at you.' Yumiko held up my arms and then let them drop to the sides. 'I can't believe how tragic you look. I have to finish my portfolio for the semester. You'll be the perfect subject. I feel as if I dialed you up. Like 1-800-Mattress.'

twins

'Here I am,' I said, feeling a little bit better. Yumiko had liked me from the start.

She reached up to put her hand on my head. I had forgotten how little she was.

'It's so soft,' she said. 'Like peach fuzz. I'm going to have such a great time with your head. You can stay for a couple of days, can't you? You absolutely have to ride your unicycle for Smita,' she said. 'In India, the streets are filled with circus performers.'

Yumiko opened her door wide, and I followed her in, relieved, carrying my things with me.

'I've got the best room on campus,' she said. She walked me to the window, which was actually a door that stretched from the ceiling to the floor. It opened to a small balcony overlooking a big, grassy lawn.

'You know I dumped your brother?' she said.

I had not talked to Daniel. He would laugh if he saw me.

'You haven't seen him yet?' Yumiko tilted her head. She looked at the knapsack I'd dropped on her floor, my unicycle leaning against the wall. 'He fell in love with me. I could see it coming from the start. Poor boy. He wanted to see me all the time. He wanted to sleep over every night. He had no understanding of my friendship with Smita. He always thought he could join us for dinner. Just because he wanted to.'

I stood at the window and looked across the lawn. There was a small pond at the far end. I saw a couple feeding ducks. I knew Yumiko was talking about Daniel, but everything she said made me feel sad.

'Is that so bad?' I said.

'That kind of devotion will kill any relationship,' Yumiko said.

'It shouldn't,' I said. 'Not if it's real.'

Yumiko was describing what it was like to be in love. To be

part of another person. It made sense that Yumiko would not want Daniel's love. He was not good enough for her. But I was good enough for Chloe. I was the only person for Chloe.

'Do your parents know you're here?'

'Yes,' I said. 'Absolutely.'

It had never occurred to me to call them.

'I want to sculpt you.' Yumiko put her finger on my breastbone, pressing hard. I tried to stand up straight. I didn't like the way she touched me.

'No problem,' I said.

'Will you pose nude?'

'Do you want me to?'

I felt myself blushing, remembering how Lisa Markman would use any excuse to get my clothes off.

'It's essential,' Yumiko said. 'I'll draw you right now. I'd like to see your line. I'd love to do a series of nudes. Flat-chested will be a new challenge.' Yumiko pointed to her desk chair. 'You can sit there. We can talk while I draw you.'

I sat in the chair in front of Yumiko's desk. I took off my coat and the sweater beneath it and, when Yumiko nodded, the T-shirt.

Yumiko sucked in air through her teeth.

'I think you are actually concave,' she said.

She was looking at my chest.

'That's bad?' I said.

Yumiko reached for her pencil.

'You are an incredible subject. I can't believe you just showed up on my doorstep. Smita will have to come see you.'

'How should I pose?' I asked. 'How do you want me?'

I grabbed a hairbrush and a stapler and held them over my chest.

'No.' Yumiko shook her head. 'No props. I need to see your figure. Clean lines.'

twins

I could hear her pencil scratch against the paper.

'My adviser was distraught when I dropped out of the psych program. He didn't understand.' Yumiko paused from her drawing. 'But it wasn't just the lab work. I realized I don't want to give myself to others. I want to study the mind, but I don't want to fix it. I don't have the patience to sit and fix other people's problems. That's not me.'

I nodded, as if I understood what Yumiko was talking about.

'Don't move your head,' she said.

She squinted her already squinty eyes.

I was good at holding still. My posture was good from riding the unicycle. From my seat in front of Yumiko's desk, I could look out the window onto the lawn. I could see students walking by. Anyone who looked up could see me half naked. Yumiko told me to take off my pants.

I bit my lip. I was hungry and tired. I slid out of my jeans.

'Terrific,' she said, biting the end of her pencil.

Yumiko looked down at her sketch pad, spit on her finger, and rubbed the spit around on her drawing.

I posed for three long hours. Yumiko had started with drawing exercises. She drew fast to improve her technique. A drawing a minute. The stopwatch went off, and I would strike a new pose. I couldn't move during that minute or Yumiko would get mad. It was hard. My nose would itch. There was a draft from the window. My nipples were stiff from the cold. Yumiko didn't look at me like I was something she wanted to touch. It was not like with Lisa. I knew it was because of my hair. I was ugly. Yumiko didn't like me the way she used to.

'You look so terrible.' She said *terrible* as if it was the best thing in the world. She made drawing after drawing until I could not hold myself still any longer. The room had turned cold. I was shivering.

189

'You're cold?' Yumiko sounded annoyed. 'I guess we better stop. I did some great work tonight.'

We got ready for bed. Yumiko wore a pair of blue flannel pajamas with white clouds and yellow and pink bunnies. I had not brought anything to sleep in. Yumiko gave me a pair of pink silk pajamas. I recognized them instantly as Chloe's. She'd come back from Hawaii and, the very next day, accused me of stealing them. Chloe had put her hand on her forehead, looking at me like her head might explode, and demanded that I give them back.

'You take the wall,' Yumiko said.

Yumiko was so little, we fit perfectly in her little bed. She crawled in after me, and I could feel her breath on my neck. I started to breathe faster. I was beginning to feel a little better. Yumiko had once told me she liked me best. She liked me more than Daniel. She smelled nice, like grape bubble gum. For a long time, we pretended to sleep. I turned over, as gently as I could. Yumiko's eyes were closed. I kissed her mouth, a quick butterfly kiss, but Yumiko didn't respond. I put my hand on her shoulder, but soon she flipped over the other way and her breathing became more even.

We met Smita in an art studio on campus. She looked distressed when I took off the black knit hat that Yumiko had lent me.

'Wow,' Smita said, biting her lip.

'I told you,' Yumiko said.

'You did not give me an accurate idea.' Smita looked at the floor, as if she was embarrassed for me. 'Actually.'

Smita looked like she came from a royal family. She seemed stuck up somehow. Her skin was dark, and she had dark, heavy shadows under her eyes. Her accent sounded English. She wore long, dangling earrings that you could see past her hair, which was cut even with her chin.

'How old are you?' she asked.

'Sixteen,' I said. 'Almost seventeen.'

Smita lit a cigarette.

I started to take off my clothes.

'You don't have to undress. If you're not comfortable,' Smita said.

Yumiko shook her head.

'Sue posed for me all of last night,' she said. 'I told you. She doesn't mind. You can't get a sense of her line with the clothes.'

Smita frowned. Worse than Yumiko, who didn't seem to connect me to my naked body, Smita looked at me like I was something disgusting. I saw her wince when I took off my underwear. I pretended I didn't care. This was what Yumiko wanted. She quickly set up her easel and her sketch pad and charcoals, but Smita took a long time taking the lens cover off her camera.

'I'm not sure about this,' she said.

'I made the best drawings last night,' Yumiko said, waving her arm at Smita. 'Maybe the best I've ever done. There's so this fantastic quality about her. It's like her skin is actually translucent.'

'About Sue, you mean,' Smita said. 'She's not an object. And by translucent, you mean that you can see her veins.'

Yumiko nodded. In the studio, she had a drawing pad three times as big as the one in her dorm room.

'I want to take my drawing to another level,' Yumiko said. 'With every one I do, I can feel them getting better.'

I took off my socks.

'Why don't you lay on the blanket?' Yumiko said.

But before I could sit down, Smita walked around me. She held the camera up to her face. 'You have a tattoo?' she said.

Yumiko stopped drawing. 'I told you about the tattoo. I told you. Sue is an original piece of work.'

'Yes,' I said. 'It's a tattoo.'

'Chloe is your twin sister?' Smita asked. She squatted down to get a closer look. It was hard to believe that I was running away from Chloe so I could be asked such idiotic questions.

'Yes,' I said.

'Her identical twin sister,' Yumiko said. 'I told you.'

I closed my eyes. I had to will myself to stay still. Part of me wanted to kick Yumiko's easel over. But I couldn't do that. She had taken me in. I had remembered liking Yumiko better than this.

Smita got on her knees.

'Do you mind?' she asked. 'If I photograph your tattoo?'

'Go ahead,' Yumiko said. 'Sue will do anything!'

'No,' I said. 'That's not true.'

'What won't you do?'

I shrugged.

'She broke a girl's nose,' Yumiko said.

I looked at Yumiko's tiny face. She wasn't the way I remembered.

Smita circled around me. She took pictures of the tattoo from different angles.

'Don't you want to get her from the front?' Yumiko chewed on the end of her pencil. 'She has the best pelvis.'

Yumiko flipped her page over and started the next sketch. She was a frantic drawer, the pencil scratching loud on the page, her arm moving like crazy. She seemed all over the place, totally unlike Chloe when she played basketball, who always seemed like she was floating on a cloud.

Smita set up a light fixture behind me. She finished one roll of film and put another into her camera. 'Would you mind stretching your arms over your head?' she said.

Smita took two more rolls of film. I concentrated on the click of her camera. When we were done, she shook my hand.

twins

'I would like to thank you,' she said. I felt as if I should curtsy, grateful for her kindness, but I felt funny shaking her hand without any clothes on. I was sick of posing nude.

'You're welcome,' I said.

Yumiko looked bored. I turned away from them, got dressed quickly.

'Do you feel all right?' Smita asked me. She handed me my coat, helped me to put it on. 'Do you eat proper meals? Perhaps we should head straight to lunch.'

She opened a red beaded purse and handed me a bottle of multivitamins. 'Take two.'

I swallowed two of Smita's vitamins. They were big green pills, but I was used to big pills. Mr Markman's Percodans were about the same size.

I put Yumiko's knit cap over my head. My head got cold without any hair.

'It would be terrific,' Yumiko said, 'if we could get Chloe up here. Sue's twin sister. Do a study of contrasts.' Yumiko looked at me. 'Chloe hasn't cut her hair, has she?' Her voice was worried.

I shook my head.

'Sue used to have long, luxurious blond hair.'

'I don't know if this is okay.' Smita wrapped a black scarf around her neck. She spoke to Yumiko as if I wasn't standing right there. 'Have you spoken to her brother?'

'You're such a hypocrite, Smita. You know you got great pictures.'

Smita pursed her lips.

Yumiko laughed. 'Sue is tough as nails. She takes care of herself.'

Yumiko and Smita glared at each other. I had thought they were best friends. Yumiko told Smita we were too busy to go to lunch.

Smita kissed me on both cheeks.

'You should come to my house for dinner,' she said.

'I'd like that,' I said.

I really was hungry. Yumiko had not offered me anything to eat since I'd shown up the day before. I had bought a Snickers bar from the candy machine down the hall when she went off to the dining center for breakfast, but I threw it up so that I wouldn't look fat for the modeling session.

Yumiko lent me a lace dress to wear over my jeans and we went to a party.

'I hate parties,' I said.

Yumiko didn't care. She wanted to show me off. I could tell that Smita hadn't given her the reaction she wanted. She brushed thick mascara onto my lashes, lined my eyelids black. 'You look Goth,' she said.

There was a guy Yumiko liked at this party. He had short blond hair and blue eyes and wore a green silk shirt that was unbuttoned so I could see the curly hair on his chest. He was vile. His name was Matthias.

'Don't you know anyone with regular names?' I said to Yumiko.

'It's a common German name,' Matthias said. He had a strong German accent. He sounded stupid. He poured me a shot of tequila. 'You're a runaway,' he said, handing me the drink. 'I've seen it in the movies. Runaways always end up trashed in the dumpster. They'll do weird shit for money. Subject themselves to the worst humiliation.'

I didn't like Matthias. I reached for Yumiko's hand, but she brushed mine away.

'Have you ever run away?' I said. 'What the fuck do you know?'

Matthias cut me a slice of lime. He taught me how to lick my hand, shake some salt, shoot the tequila, bite the lime.

twins

'I don't need to get wasted,' I said.

I choked swallowing the tequila down.

Yumiko laughed. She was wearing her hair loose. She wore gold eye shadow, gold glitter on her cheeks. A real glamour girl. The second we walked into the party, guys started flocking around us.

'Where is Smita?' I asked.

Yumiko snorted. 'Smita hates parties. She thinks that if you go to a party you're going to get raped. She thinks that if you drink too much at a party, you instantly turn into an alcoholic.'

Matthias handed me another shot.

'Go ahead,' Yumiko said.

Yumiko had no idea. She thought I was a baby innocent, but I had spent the last few months wasted on pills. One time Mr Markman found Lisa and me on the couch in a blissed out stupor, not watching the TV that was on at full volume, our fingers touching. Without asking us any questions, he took us into the kitchen and made us hamburgers on his George Foreman grill. They were the best thing I had eaten in forever. I was jealous because I knew that Mr Markman must cook delicious hamburgers for Chloe all the time.

Yumiko put Matthias's hand on my scalp.

'She used to have perfect yellow hair,' she said. Yumiko shook out her beautiful, shiny black hair. 'Spun like gold.'

All of Yumiko's friends touched my scalp.

'She looks like a baby bird,' one guy said. 'The way they come out of the shell with big eyes and no feathers.'

I drank three more tequila shots. One two three. Boom boom boom.

Yumiko laughed, watching me.

'Tomorrow, I'll draw you hungover,' she said. 'The circles under your eyes will deepen.'

She put her arm around my waist. She does like me, I thought, closing my eyes. I knew that she liked me. I felt Yumiko's fingers at my side. I felt the floor swaying under me. Yumiko let me go. I could feel her move away. I opened my eyes, and there was my brother, Daniel, staring straight at me. I had almost forgotten he went to this college. I waved at him. I was drunk. Daniel didn't wave back. I figured, Why not say hello? I was drunk. He was my brother. I walked over to him.

'Look at you,' he said. 'Bald.'

It was impossible to look at me and not notice my head. I felt horrible. I remembered why I never wanted to talk to Daniel.

'I am ruined,' I said sadly.

'It's just hair,' he said.

I felt my head. It had been touched all night. I wondered why I had let them touch me. I looked like a sick baby bird.

'You look stupid in this,' he said, touching Yumiko's dress.

'I do?'

'You definitely do.'

Daniel and I stared at each other. I was supposed to have something to say. Why I was there. What I was doing. But all I could think about were baby birds. How the bird mothers chewed their food and then threw it up so that the baby birds could eat their vomit. I knew some things. I wasn't stupid just because Chloe thought so.

Daniel put his hand on my back. I wondered if I was passing out.

'What are you doing here?' he asked.

'You'd never mistake me for Chloe, would you?' I said. 'Not now.'

'No chance of that.' Daniel shook his head. 'What are you doing here? You came here with Yumiko? When did you get here?'

twins

I remembered everything. I had come to Daniel's college to see Yumiko. Yumiko, who had taught me that perfect was pus and guts. That terrible was extraordinary.

'I came here with Yumiko,' I said.

'She won't talk to me.' Daniel sipped his beer. 'She hates me. I thought she would be here tonight. I wasn't expecting to find you.'

'I'm staying with her for a while.'

'You're what?' Daniel said. 'You're staying where?'

I knew I couldn't trust Daniel. I had to keep far away from him. Gripping the wall, I made my way back to Yumiko. She was my friend, she was like no one else. We had been arrested together. She was sitting on a futon with the shiny, sexy shirt guy. Matthias, the slimeball. Mr Big Head. He had his hand on Yumiko's silky black hair.

'Are all Germans Nazis?' I asked him. 'I've never met a German before.'

He looked at me, speechless.

'Are you trashed?' Yumiko said. 'Do I need to get you out of here?'

I looked across the room at Daniel. I wasn't surprised he was watching me. I hated that he always watched me.

'You can't talk to people that way,' Yumiko said.

'Why not?' I said. 'They did experiments on twins, you know. Nazis. They tortured them for science.'

Matthias put his feet on the table.

'She's something else, Yumiko,' he said. 'You're right about that. But I wouldn't want her hanging around me for too long.'

'I want to leave,' I said, pulling on Yumiko's sleeve.

Yumiko noticed Daniel.

'He's a real creep, your brother,' she said. 'He comes to these parties and watches me.'

'No,' I said. 'He's watching me.'

'Wrong. Daniel doesn't want to sleep with his sister.'

'Ha,' I said. Sometimes Yumiko didn't know what she was talking about. She was just a pretty doll. She said something to Matthias, and then she grabbed my hand. We left the party. I could walk straight by using her head like a crutch. I took a handful of her hair and pulled it hard.

Yumiko slapped me away from her. I fell on the pavement. 'Are you crazy?' she said.

'Do you like me,' I said. 'Even a little bit?'

I got back up but then I tripped over a curb. Walking drunk was like learning how to ride a unicycle.

'You are not as interesting as I once thought,' Yumiko said.

In the morning, she shook me awake.

'All right, you have to go,' she said. She dumped my knapsack on the bed. 'You know you can't be a runaway in today's society. It's so Holden Caulfield, Sue, and the world is a much crueler place these days. It's not an economically feasible plan. I can't take care of you forever.'

Yumiko went to her bookshelf, got a book, and threw it at me. *Catcher in the Rye.* It was always that same stupid book. The murder handbook. Teachers at school insisted we read it. There was that guy who had killed John Lennon because of it. I wasn't interested.

'You should read it, Sue,' Yumiko said. 'You won't be interesting if you're not well-read. You're only interesting for now, because you are so young and tragic. But dejected twin will only take you so far.'

I threw Yumiko's book back at her. It hit her on the shoulder. She looked at me.

'Don't throw my things,' Yumiko said.

twins

We glared at each other. Yumiko had those slanted, almond eyes. They were hard eyes, dark and mean. The braids and the bunny rabbits and the lace dresses were a trick. Yumiko was not sweet or nice or easy to push around. Suddenly, I wanted Chloe. As much as I had ever wanted her. I felt a wave of nausea.

Yumiko got my unicycle from out of the closet.

'Hey, Sue,' she said. 'Your problems are too big for me. Go say hello to your big brother.'

'Daniel doesn't care about me,' I said.

I looked at my feet. Yumiko was waiting, tapping her fingers on her desk. I put on my shoes, Chloe's first pair of basketball sneakers; the rubber soles were almost worn through.

'You have no idea,' Yumiko said. 'Daniel is crazy about you.'

Her voice sounded almost sad. Even Yumiko wasn't happy like she used to be. She had seemed so self-assured last Christmas, talking to my mother about her divorce. Yumiko wasn't happy at college the way she was when we got arrested. She had leaned her head against mine in the jail cell. That had been one of the best days of my life.

'Don't you need me to stay?' I said. 'Don't you want to sculpt me?'

Yumiko hadn't finished her art project, but she was still kicking me out. From her big picture window, I could see that it was pouring. I didn't have an umbrella. I didn't have a raincoat.

Yumiko handed me my unicycle.

'Matthias is going to pose for me,' she said.

And that was it. Yumiko was done with me. She opened her sketch pad and handed me a drawing. I glanced at it quickly, taking in my flat chest, my pelvis bones, my head too big for the rest of my body. I crumpled the drawing, let it fall to the floor. Once upon a time, not long ago, I had looked like Chloe. I washed my hair and wore clean clothes. I had been almost perfect.

I'd left home without thinking. I hadn't even searched my parents' room one final time. I raided through Chloe's things and then I took off for the bus station. I barely had any money to start with. My dad had canceled all the stolen credit cards. My mother never kept cash in her wallet. I hadn't swiped any of Lisa Markman's pain pills. Instead, I had a useless leather jump rope and a pair of basketball sneakers. A stuffed polar bear. Chloe's things.

I couldn't go back home. Chloe didn't want me. She hadn't tried to find me.

I rode my unicycle around the main quad of the school in the rain. I couldn't show up at Daniel's door crushed and defeated. I didn't even know which dorm was his. I couldn't go home to Chloe with my bald head. I had to let my hair grow. The quad made a perfect lap, and I rode it again and again and again and again. The pavement was slick, a maze of wet leaves. I rode through puddles, hard and fast, going for the biggest possible splash. My bald head was freezing cold.

Why had I let that bitch Lisa cut off my hair? I was ruined. Why had I done it? I had been blessed to look like Chloe. Now I was a lonely, skinny, sad sack, ugly girl. I was the ugliest girl on the planet. I slipped on a patch of wet leaves and fell, ripping the knee of Chloe's favorite jeans. I looked at the blood on the fabric and did the thing I was best at. I started to cry. But I also got up and kept riding. I had nowhere to go. I could feel the muscles in my calves. I could ride with a torn-up knee. I could ride in the rain. I could ride with tears streaming down my face. I was a fucking marvel, the way I could ride. I hopped up a curb and jumped back down. The campus was deserted, a quiet morning in the rain. I saw a woman under a big black umbrella. I watched her approach me from a distance, coming steadily my way.

It was Smita.

When she saw me, she lifted her hand to wave. She called out my name, and I rode to her, pedaling as fast as I could. So fast that I couldn't stop. I crashed right into Smita, knocking her down on the grass. I was breathless from crying, from riding freezing in the rain. I started to laugh. I felt like maybe I had finally gone crazy.

'I was looking for you,' Smita said. She dropped her umbrella and put her hands on my cheeks. 'Yumiko told me you went to your brother's. I was going there now. You've got eyes like a wild animal.'

I couldn't say anything. I was still trying to catch my breath.

'Drama queen,' I could hear Chloe say.

But it wasn't true. That wasn't me. I didn't want drama. I wanted me and Chloe, together forever. I didn't mean to knock Smita down. I never wanted to hurt anyone.

Chloe

They looked like they were dressed for a party. My mother was wearing red: red lipstick and a red dress, a red silk scarf wrapped around her neck. My father's red tie stood out from his gray suit. He wore a red-and-white polka-dot scarf draped around his neck. They seemed almost giddy, bounding into the house, carrying a stack of gift-wrapped boxes. 'Presents for my baby,' my father said.

I stayed on the couch, icing my ankle. Mr Markman had never answered the phone.

'Does the house smell?' my father said, wrinkling his nose. I was lying on the couch, covered in a blanket, my hair was dirty, and for a second, at least, he looked concerned. 'Should we start with the presents?'

I did not get up, so my mother knelt down. She gave my head a meaningful pat. 'We are here now, baby,' she said, but then, to my surprise, she headed straight upstairs. She was looking, I supposed, for Sue, only Sue had not come home, and she hadn't called either. I did not understand how Sue could leave like that. We hadn't even had a disagreement.

twins

I sat up on the couch, and my father sat down next to me. He seemed eager that I open my gifts, so I started with the first box. It was a red silk scarf, just like my mother's. I touched it with my finger. I had never worn red before. My father draped it round my neck. 'Gorgeous,' he said. 'You look like a movie star.' Then he asked me to help unload the trunk, which he said was loaded with groceries.

'I can't,' I said.

'Are you sick?' My father put his hand on my forehead.

'I twisted my ankle,' I said. 'I can't help you carry anything.'

'Oh, no,' he said. 'You poor thing.'

His voice was far too jovial, a tone that was not familiar to me. 'We can't have you outside then, can we, carrying heavy packages on a sore ankle? No worries. I'll take care of the bags.'

I hopped upstairs, looking for my mother. I found her in the bathroom, taking notes in her legal pad.

'Does it smell mildewed to you?' she asked.

I shrugged. Not only was my ankle sprained; my entire body felt sore. It was already nighttime, but I felt as if I had never properly woken up. I had not showered or washed my hair or made myself anything to eat. I had only changed out of my basketball uniform and put on Sue's clothes, an oversize T-shirt and a pair of baggy carpenter pants.

'We will have to get the carpets professionally cleaned,' my mother said as we left the bedroom and started down the hall toward the bedrooms. 'And if that doesn't work, we can always replace them.' She gave me a quick, spontaneous hug. 'You did the right thing asking for help. With Daniel away at college, and the way you've always been so self-sufficient, I sometimes forget that you are not all grown up.'

'I'm not,' I said.

My mother squeezed my hand. Then she continued to inspect

the house. I made my way back downstairs, back to my spot on the couch, and waited until my parents were ready to talk to me. My mother examined the state of the curtains. She checked the paint on the walls and knocked on the wooden banister. My father brought the groceries into the kitchen; I could hear him unpacking. I stared out the living-room window, still looking for Sue. I wondered if I could ask my parents to cook me dinner. I put my hand on my forehead. I was not sick. I had a headache but no fever.

Finally, my parents stopped moving and joined me in the living room. They sat down in opposite armchairs. My father put the tape recorder on the coffee table, and my mother had her yellow legal pad on her lap. I still had a pile of presents to open: three more boxes and a brown bag from Bloomingdale's, my mother's favorite store.

'We have a lot to talk about, princess,' my father said.

I blinked. My mother had opened the linen closet and noticed the lack of clean sheets and towels, but she never said, Is this house missing something, perhaps our other twin daughter? Maybe my parents were confused. They had not been home for a while. Maybe they had noticed my dirty hair and the clothes I was wearing and my parents had mistaken me for Sue. Their minds were playing sinister tricks on them.

'We can't have a meeting without Sue,' I said. 'She hasn't been home in days. I guess we have to call the police, but I kept putting it off hoping she would come home. I should have told you earlier, but Mom was asking me about boyfriends, and then she put me on hold. I didn't want to tell the receptionist. But it's been almost three days. Sue always comes home. She always does. You wouldn't know it, because you don't know us, you're never here, but this is not like her at all.'

I listened to myself talk and could tell that I might sound

hysterical to my parents. It might sound to them like I was babbling out of control – the way Sue would go on and on when she got excited – but I could not make myself stop. I felt somehow that when I did, I was going to break out in tears, and I did not want to do that in front of my parents. I felt that something was very wrong with me. Suddenly, it occurred to me that I desperately needed to wash my hair.

My father smiled at me. It was the smile he used at trials, when he focused on female members of the jury. Phony and insincere. This smile gave me chills down my spine. *Cocksucker*, Sue would say. I had begun hearing Sue's voice in my head. She spoke to me when I least expected it; she put me down at the moments I felt most vulnerable. 'Who's a moron?' she'd say to me when I would sit down to take a test and stare blankly at the questions.

My father looked confused. 'We've been home for almost an hour,' he said to my mother. 'You didn't tell her?'

My mother shook her head. 'I thought you would talk to her about it,' she said. 'While you were putting away the groceries.'

'Ah.' My father nodded. 'There lies the confusion.'

'My ankle is hurt,' I said, in case my mother had not noticed.

'We know where Sue is,' my father said to me. He spoke slowly, as if he were talking to a child. 'Your sister, Sue, is fine. Your brother, Daniel, called. He says that he spoke to Sue at a party.'

'She went to see Daniel?' I said.

My mother snorted.

My father laughed.

'Unfortunately no,' he said. 'Sue is staying with the girlfriend, that little Asian girl.'

'Yumiko,' my mother said. 'She's a very intelligent young woman.'

My father sighed. 'Apparently, your brother and Yumiko are no longer seeing each other.'

'Then what is Sue doing with her?' I said. 'I don't understand.'

Sue had stopped talking about Yumiko a while ago. I had forgotten all about her.

'He says that Sue has shaved her head.' My father laughed.

I looked at both of my parents.

'Sue ran away from home?' I said. 'Why would she do that?'

How, I wondered, could she do that? Why didn't she take me with her? I was her identical twin sister and she had left me behind. My head was spinning. But I knew I would have laughed in Sue's face if she had asked me to go with her. I wouldn't consider going anywhere with her. I would have stayed, hoping that one day Mr Markman might call, wanting to take me to another Knicks game. Sue had left without me because she hated me, but I was the one who had hated her first. For so long now, Sue had been steadily trying to drive me mad. She was always there, right behind me, watching every little thing I did. Now that Sue was gone, there was Daisy, wagging her tail, expectant. My parents were staring at me. The tape recorder was running.

'Are you feeling okay, Chloe, honey?' my mother said.

I shook my head.

'I need to take a shower.' My hair was the dirtiest it had ever been.

'We're having a meeting, Chloe,' my father said. He straightened his red tie. 'You can take your shower when we're done.'

'After,' my mother repeated. She twisted her red scarf between her fingers. 'There are just a couple of things we need to talk about. Perhaps you'd like to open another present,' she said, handing me the Bloomingdale's bag.

I stood up from the couch.

twins

'No,' I said. 'You can wait for me. I have waited almost three days for you.'

I walked slowly out of the living room, careful not to put too much weight on my ankle, careful to maintain my dignity. It was amazing, the way my parents watched me go, startled into silence. They were used to this behavior only from Sue.

At the top of the stairs, I turned to look at them.

'I have been waiting for you all my life,' I said.

My mother's jaw dropped.

'Drama queen,' I could hear Sue tell me.

I sat on my bed for a long time before getting dressed. I sat there, combing my wet hair, contemplating the damage. It had never occurred to me to check my room while I waited for Sue. My dresser drawers were wide open, clothes thrown all over the floor. My new jeans were gone. She had also taken the first pair of basketball sneakers Mr Markman had ever given me, my leather jump rope, and my fluffy white polar bear, also from Mr Markman. Somehow, the bear struck me as the very worst thing.

I didn't know what I had done, but I must have done something terribly wrong to make my twin sister want to rob me of my favorite things. I felt so tired even though I hadn't left the house for days. I slid my comb through my clean hair and leaned down to kiss my knee. My skin was warm, and I smelled nice, like lavender soap.

Downstairs, I knew, my parents were waiting, impatient. They did not seem the least bit concerned that Sue had run away. Perhaps they were glad Sue was Daniel's problem now. I had handled her all these years. I hugged a pillow to my chest, wishing it was my polar bear. I wanted to put off going downstairs as long as I could. I got out the cell phone I never used and tried to call Mr Markman, even though I no longer had a reason to call.

I expected no answer; instead Todd picked up. I hung up. My legs started to shake. A moment later, the phone rang.

'Hello,' I said.

'Who is this?'

I recognized Todd Markman's voice. I didn't know what to say. I had nothing to say to Todd.

'Who is this?' he repeated.

'Hey, Todd,' I said. 'It's Chloe.'

'Did you call to ask me out on a date?' he said. 'Do you want to give me a blow job?'

I shook my head. I did not know why Todd was still so angry.

'Chloe,' he said, laughing into the phone. 'My dad is not home. You're out of luck.'

Then he hung up. I listened to the dial tone. My father was knocking on my door.

'Are you ready to come downstairs, princess?' he said.

I put my head on my knees and breathed.

'Focus on the ball,' Mr Markman would say. 'Quiet your mind.'

I didn't know what to do. I could challenge my father to a game of one on one.

My parents were not going to do a thing about Sue. They wouldn't lift a finger to bring her back home. My father stated what I already knew, that Sue had been stealing from him for years. He said he understood that Sue was an angry young woman. Guidance counselors had recently informed my parents that she was failing out of school. 'I appreciate,' my father said, 'that Sue is too much for you to handle.'

'So it's your turn?' I said.

'Some people are not meant to be parents,' my mother said, her voice quiet. 'You have grown up. Your characters are formed.'

twins

'We're only sixteen,' I said quietly. But our birthdays were coming up soon. Sue and I were actually closer to seventeen, old enough to drive. I did not have my learner's permit or a car or a parent to practice my driving with.

'Sue hasn't listened to us in years. You were the only one she listened to,' my father said. 'That's over, so now it's time to put our faith in Sue. Let's see what she can do for herself. She's already taken the first step.'

My parents were afraid of Sue. Perhaps they always had been.

My father slid a manila folder between my fingers. Inside was an article about teenagers who had legally emancipated themselves from their parents. I recognized several of the examples: Drew Barrymore and Macaulay Culkin, child actors who had earned millions of dollars. The next document was a bank statement in my name. The numbers swam before me. From a distance, I could hear that my parents were still talking. It turned out they liked New York. My parents found that it was much more convenient for them to commute from my father's apartment. They had chosen the suburbs as a wholesome place to raise their children, and now we were grown. These documents however, were not binding. Our family was merely on a trial separation.

'For now, Daniel is going to watch out for Sue,' my father said. 'He'll contact us if he believes she is in trouble. If she chooses to remain with Yumiko, at his school, we will send the appropriate allowance that Daniel will then pass along to Sue.'

'You are divorcing us,' I said quietly.

My mother sat back in her armchair.

'You misunderstand us,' she said. 'This is difficult, but we are trying to be practical. We are trying to respect your rights as grown-ups. Sue is allowed to live her life. She is angry and she is acting out. Let her act out in a safe environment.'

'With Yumiko,' I said.

My mother smiled.

'I was impressed with her,' she said. 'She took a considerable interest in your sister.'

'Oh,' I said. They had been arrested for shoplifting.

But what I understood more clearly than anything else was that my parents wanted to sell the house in New Jersey and live permanently in Manhattan. They were finished with us.

'I have one more year of school,' I said.

My mother frowned. 'It might be possible,' she said, 'to delay the sale of the house so as not to disrupt your education.'

'I wouldn't want to start again on a new basketball team.'

'Basketball,' my mother said. She looked at my father.

'You haven't finished opening your presents, princess,' he said. I nodded. There were enough gift-wrapped packages on the table that I was certain they would not feel the need to see me on my birthday.

'Open a present, Chloe,' my mother said, eagerly. 'You will like them, I think.'

I opened another box. Inside was a pink linen sundress. I knew that I would have once thought the dress lovely and been excited to wear it. But somehow it seemed too young for me now. I opened more boxes: there was a makeup kit, bubble bath, and a necklace, a thin gold chain with a pearl pendant. These were pretty and expensive items, and for the first time in my life, they would be safe. Sue was far away. She could not steal my things or destroy them when the mood struck her. I gathered my clean hair in one hand, and dropped the necklace over my head. I touched the pendant with my finger. It was the most beautiful thing I had ever owned.

'Thank you,' I said. I smiled, trying to remove the frown from my face. I wanted to appear grateful. It was possible, because I was not difficult, because I bathed regularly and did well in school, that my parents might not want to divorce me. Perhaps they did not realize that Sue and I were not a package deal. We had the same DNA, but our limbs were not connected.

'Have you seen much of Rodney Markman lately?' my father asked.

'No,' I said, surprised. 'Not lately.'

I watched my mother take note of the fact in her yellow pad. I noticed the small, but unmistakable smile that passed between my parents.

'Why?'

'It was a wonderful thing for Lisa's father to take an interest in you,' my mother said. 'Your father called him to thank him for his time. Mr Markman says that you are a talented athlete.'

'You talked to him?'

Mr Markman never told me that my father had called him. For what seemed like no reason at all, he had practically cut off all contact from me. He had left my last game of the season early, without a good-bye. I took off the beautiful necklace and gently lay it back in the black jewelry case.

'What else did you say to him?'

My father shut his briefcase. I knew this meant that our meeting was coming to an end, but I still did not understand why my parents were leaving or where they were going. They lived somewhere else, in a fancy apartment in Manhattan I had never seen. It did not make sense to me. This was their house and I was their daughter.

'Do you know why he's staying away from me?' I said. 'Did you say something to him?'

I could not believe what my father calmly proceeded to tell me. Not only had he talked with Mr Markman but they had met for lunch several weeks ago. 'I felt that it was my duty to clarify the terms of your friendship. He is an adult, a wealthy man, and in a position to take advantage of your trust. That photo in *People* had implications that I was not comfortable with.'

'You told this to Mr Markman?'

I watched in disbelief as my father put on his coat.

'One day you'll know why I did this, Chloe,' my father said. 'I wanted to make sure Mr Markman understood what was appropriate. I felt it was a necessary precaution to inform Mr Markman of the legal definition of statutory rape and the minimum mandatory sentence.'

'You didn't do that?' I said. My face had turned hot.

'It had to be done. You are still naïve in so many ways.'

I could feel the blood rush to my head. I could not believe my father would have suggested such a thing to Mr Markman. There was no person on the planet more honorable than Rodney Markman. But for weeks and weeks he had kept this conversation secret. He had stayed with me through the end of the season, and now it was over. Knowing what I now knew, I could not imagine seeing him again. I did not know how anything would ever be the same after such horrible words had been spoken. I pulled my knees to my chest and hugged them close.

'How could you do that to me?'

My father kissed me on the forehead.

'Don't have any wild parties,' he said.

My parents looked at me, rocking on the couch, hugging my knees.

My mother gave me an awkward hug. 'The kitchen,' she said, 'is stocked. You'll come see us this weekend.'

I watched them leave, their hands clasped.

'Gone,' I said out loud.

I used to think it was Sue that drove my parents away. Only now she was gone, and so were they.

twins

Daisy jumped onto the couch. She put her head on my lap and looked at me.

'Who is going to take care of you now?' I said.

I had always thought that I would have to wait until college to be free from Sue. Before high school started, I had counted the days. The only thing I thought I knew for certain was that Sue and I would split up after high school. Now, I had an extra year. Only it wasn't just a year. It was much more than that. It was the rest of my life.

Sue

Smita lived by herself in a two-story house off campus. She had graduated the year before and never left.

'I love my house,' she said.

Her house was an insane mess. Smita opened the door to the living room; the couch was covered with clothes and empty cheese doodle bags. I could see a path Smita had made through papers and magazines, more clothes, used tea bags. Newspapers were scattered in front of the fireplace, there were loose twigs all over the floor. The coffee table was covered with books and overflowing ashtrays and a small, neat pile of orange peel.

'I fired the maid,' she said apologetically. 'I think she was stealing.'

Smita showed me around her house. Each room seemed more crowded with her things than the last. The kitchen was overflowing with dirty dishes. There was a laptop computer and stacks of papers on her bed, wet towels and empty shampoo bottles on the floor of her bathroom, and finally, a surprisingly clean, small room. Her office, Smita said. There was a typewriter on the desk. The walls were covered with posters of Indian movies, pinups of an Indian actor with dark, oily hair, the same man who was in all of the movie posters. There were magazine covers with this actor's face tacked onto a bulletin board. He had a mustache in some of the pictures, in some he didn't. His shirt was always open. He had a hairy, muscular chest and a fake, plastic smile. He was revolting.

'My father,' she said, waving her arm toward the pictures.

'Your father?' I repeated.

He seemed even more outrageous than a six-foot-ten-inch-tall professional basketball player.

'Total macho man,' she said. 'Mr Bollywood incarnate.'

We stood in front of a poster where Smita's father stood shirtless, with a purple turban on his head, wearing billowing purple pants. He had his arm around a beautiful Indian woman wearing a purple-and-gold sari.

I looked at Smita.

'It's a totally different world out there,' she said. 'My father is the equivalent to royalty in India. If he sets foot in public, the people go berserk. Women actually faint. They hold out their arms for him to sign.' Smita shook her head. 'The pictures help me remember my childhood. Where and what I come from. Now that I am a modern young woman, educated first in England and then the United States, it's easy to forget. It's all for my book. I'm writing my autobiography.'

I loved the way Smita talked. She was the smartest person I had ever met. Much smarter than Chloe, who did well at school but learned only what she was supposed to. Smita was different. She puffed on her cigarette. 'I know that it might seem outlandish to you as I have only acquired twenty-one years. Eudora Welty wrote that we've experienced enough life material by the time we are three. And there are days when I feel like I am older than the planet.'

'A lot has happened to you?' I said.

Smita nodded.

'That woman, Sarita,' she said, pointing to the movie star in the sari. 'She was kind to me. She used to give me sweets when I visited my father on the set. She once hennaed my hands.'

'Where is your mother?'

'Dead. Run over,' Smita said. 'Flat like a pancake. The roads in India are filled with maniacs. The curbs are lined with squashed peasants who fall asleep on the streets. The country is a strange and grotesque place. I was raised by a nanny and then sent to boarding school in England.'

'That sounds like a story from a book,' I said.

'Exactly,' she said. 'Only I am real. So it should be, I hope, an interesting book. I've got all sorts of hooks: gender identity and class, sexual exploitation, coming of age in a foreign land. Self-realization.'

Smita looked at me. 'If you were older,' she said, 'I'd offer you a cigarette. But it looks to me as if your development has been stunted enough.'

We sat down on the futon in front of Smita's father.

'Raj Khan,' she said. She held up her middle finger to the poster. I held up mine. Both hands. I crossed my eyes.

Smita laughed. 'You are funny,' she said. 'I like you.'

Smita smoked and I watched her. We listened to the rain. My clothes were almost dry. There was crusted blood on the knee of Chloe's jeans. Across from the wall of posters, there was a big bookshelf, filled with books. There was a skinny clay vase holding dried flowers, a little blue box painted with white stars. I liked Smita's house. It was messy, but I had always liked messy. Smita's house didn't feel sad or doomed. There was no sad poodle following your every step, making you feel guilty for being alive. No twin sister who ignored you, laughed at your misery. Smita's

twins

house was full of pretty and interesting things. Her shirt had little round mirrors stitched into the bottom.

'I was going to cook you dinner,' she said. 'I came looking for you this morning, to invite you over for some aloo saag. But now that you are here, it has occurred to me that the kitchen is filthy. I keep putting off cleaning that dreadful room. Some people say writing is the hardest thing to do in the world, but I can write and write and write. The words come streaming out. But get me to do the dishes, oh no. Anything but that.'

'I can be your maid,' I said. I wanted to stay with Smita. 'I can sleep here on this futon. I'll clean your whole house.'

Smita looked surprised. 'You don't understand. I need someone to do my laundry and fold my clothes. I need someone to pick up my papers, and stack them into orderly piles. I need someone to vacuum the floors and do the dishes. I love to cook, but I make a ton of dishes.'

'I can do that,' I said. 'I'm great at cleaning. I can clean like you wouldn't believe. I'm the fastest cleaner. I once won a contest for vacuuming. I clocked two floors in less than eleven minutes.'

I had watched Chloe clean the house for years.

Smita smiled at me. She had two rows of perfect white teeth. Smita was much more beautiful than Yumiko. She was nicer than Lisa Markman. Wherever I went, there was someone new.

'Have you run away from home, then?' she said.

Smita looked at me with concern: not like I was an art project or a pain in the ass. I touched my head. I was still bald. I had left home. I had left Chloe behind.

'You need a maid,' I repeated.

Smita leaned forward. She pulled her knees to her chest, staring at me. She stared so hard I started to blush.

'I am a terrible pig,' she said.

Even then, Smita did not stop staring at me. Finally I looked

217

away from her. I pretended to be interested in a black-and-white photo of her father. He was winking at the camera. It felt like he was winking at me. Cocksucker, I thought.

'You cannot interfere with my book if you were to stay here,' Smita said.

She touched my chin, gently turning my face so that we looked each other in the eye once again.

'I would never,' I said.

Every day, I wanted not to miss Chloe.

Smita and I went to the supermarket. She bought cleaning supplies, potatoes, yogurt, and spinach. She decided that I would start in the kitchen.

'I'll cook for you when you are done,' she said.

I looked at the Ajax, the Fantastik, and the Windex. The green and yellow sponges, the steel wool. A big bottle of yellow Joy lemon fresh dish liquid. Bleach. A new mop and bucket. A roll of garbage bags. Mousetraps. I could not believe how many cleaning products existed. 'We need it all,' Smita said. She bought baking soda for the refrigerator. 'I must confess,' she said. 'I fired the maid quite some time ago. She used to bring her own supplies.'

The sink was stacked full of dishes. The counters were covered with dishes. On the table there were plates of unfinished food. There was dried, crusted food on the floor. The garbage spilled over the trash can. I couldn't possibly clean this. 'Do I use hot water?' I asked.

Smita shrugged her shoulders.

'You're all right then?' she said.

I stood with my arms at my sides. I wanted to be Smita's maid, but I had no idea how to clean. Smita went upstairs to write. I filled the sink with hot water, poured in the Joy. 'You soak,' I said to the dishes. I pretended to be Chloe. I remembered her scraping scrambled eggs into the trash. I took out the full trash bag, put in a new one. 'I can clean,' I said out loud. There was a dead roach floating in a cup of cold coffee. I screamed. Then I covered my mouth with my hand. Smita was writing. She would hate me. But Smita didn't hear. I put spices into the cupboards. I took a deep breath and started doing the dishes. I dropped a blue teacup, watched it smash to pieces. I found the broom. Swept it up. I shoved the broken pieces into the trash can. 'Be careful, Sue,' I said.

After a couple of hours, Smita came downstairs.

'Brilliant,' she said, smiling, taking it in. 'You've got the whole counter cleared.'

Smita walked to the table and started bringing over fresh dishes for me to wash. 'It had gotten so bad in here,' she said. 'I was scared to come into the kitchen. I used to go see Yumiko just to get out of the house.'

She stood at my side, whistling to herself, drying as I washed.

'It goes quite quickly, doesn't it?' she said. She looked at her nails. They were painted gold. 'It's quite shameful, I know, but until I came to college, I always had servants looking after me.'

I emptied a big pot full of red goo. Green mold was growing on top.

'Curry. With chickpeas,' Smita said, holding her nose. 'You did the cleaning at home? Like Cinderella?'

I shrugged. I was proud of how well I had done.

Chloe wouldn't believe it. Chloe had always thought I was useless.

When we had finished in the kitchen, Smita wanted to do laundry. 'This is so fantastic,' she said.

Smita sorted the clothes into piles. She lent me a pair of jeans and a shirt so I could wash my own dirty clothes. I carried everything down to the basement, where there was a washer and a dryer. There were instructions on the bottle of laundry detergent. When I came upstairs, Smita was stretched out on the couch in the living room, reading a book. 'I might never ever leave this house,' she said. 'Once it's clean.'

Later, she hummed to herself as we folded her clothes.

For dinner, Smita cooked aloo saag. It was made with the potatoes and spinach we'd bought at the supermarket, plus some onions and Indian spices I had never tasted before. There was a yogurt sauce to put over it. Raita, she called it. I tried to eat slowly.

'This tastes delicious,' I said.

'I'm glad,' Smita said. 'It's important to enjoy your food. For as long as you stay here, I'll cook and you can clean up. Okay?'

I nodded.

'Spinach,' Smita said, 'is loaded with protein.'

Yumiko hadn't fed me anything. She had gone to the dining center, and I'd waited for her in her room. When I got hungry, I ate candy bars from the machine down the hall. I told myself I was glad Yumiko didn't feed me. Two candy bars a day was an easy way to diet. But now I was eating, real food, a delicious meal. Chloe had never gotten fat from all that eating. Three meals a day, and instead of gaining weight, she made muscle.

I never could keep up with her.

I locked the door to Smita's bathroom. I wanted to look at myself. Really look and see. I had stopped looking at myself, turned away when I passed my reflection in a window. Crumpled Yumiko's drawing before I could see how awful I looked. Smita seemed to like me. Without my hair, without Chloe. Smita was not like Lisa Markman, who wanted me for a Chloe replacement. My entire life, when I looked in the mirror, I saw Chloe. And when I looked at Chloe, I saw a better version of myself. But now, I'd become some strange, sick, weird girl. I wasn't beautiful Chloe anymore.

twins

My head was a stubbly mess. My pretty blue eyes were buggy, too big for my face. I had a pimple on the tip of my nose. I had bones popping out of my chest. I didn't know how Smita could look at me and smile. When I felt done looking at my face, I lifted my pajama top, twisting around so that I could see my tattoo in the mirror: Chloe's name in pink block letters. The tattoo was still there. Our DNA was still the same.

I washed my ugly face clean. I washed the bloody cut on my knee, remembering how Chloe took care of me when I fell off my unicycle. I rubbed on antibiotic cream I found in Smita's medicine cabinet. I put on a Band-Aid. There were no pain pills. I sat down on the floor in front of the toilet. I put my finger in my mouth but didn't go through with it. I felt sad about throwing up the delicious food Smita had cooked just for me. The light was on in her room. Plus, the toilet in Smita's bathroom didn't smell very good. I decided I would start with the bathroom tomorrow. I could wait another day.

I fell asleep on the futon beneath the poster of Raj Khan in a bright purple turban. Smita's father was creepy. Smita had given him the finger. Lisa Markman also hated her father, but I thought that maybe he was all right. I wanted him to be. For Chloe. He seemed kind, the way he had smiled at me at Chloe's games. I never forgot the hamburgers he'd made for me and Lisa. Smita was a vegetarian. 'Hindus don't eat cows,' she said. 'Cows are considered holy creatures.'

'What about dogs?' I said, thinking of Daisy.

'No,' Smita said. 'Dogs are like trash. Children beat them over the head with sticks.'

I was the best maid ever. I cleaned places that had not been cleaned since Smita moved into the house. I dusted the tops of her books. I vacuumed beneath the beds. I pulled the stove away from the wall and swept up old food. I defrosted her freezer. Everything was dirty. The bottom of Smita's toilet needed to be scrubbed. I watered her plants, I fluffed her pillows, I brought her cups of tea, which I left outside her office door. Smita could never drink enough tea. I went up and down the steps.

'You are the best maid ever,' Smita said.

She liked to open her refrigerator just to admire the neatly packed produce drawer. I had refilled her spices, pouring turmeric and cumin and fennel seeds from messy plastic bags into glass jars. Sometimes Smita took breaks from her writing, just to watch me work.

'To tell the truth,' she said once, in response to nothing, 'the maid quit. She complained that I was too slovenly. But I bloody well paid her to work. She charged me a fortune. Certainly, I should not have to clean in order so that the maid could clean. For instance, she would do my laundry only if it was in the hamper. She picked nothing up off the floor. The truth is, the woman didn't like me. I am certain she hated Indians. She could not accept the fact that she worked for an Indian woman, even though she had the intelligence of a flea.'

In exchange for my cleaning, Smita cooked wonderful things. When Smita wasn't writing, she was cooking. She made vegetable curries and Indian breads. She made banana fritters and vegetable samosas, rice biryani, and vegetable korma, which was creamy and mild, with little slivers of almonds. I could only guess at the calories. Smita insisted that I eat. It was part of the deal we had made.

'Besides the food,' Smita told me, 'I miss nothing about India. Nothing. Not the bloody weather, not the people or the starvation or the culture or the fighting or the AIDS, not even the landscape. Nothing. Let the people kill themselves testing their bloody missiles. Most Indians are like children. Don't let anyone tell you otherwise.'

twins

Days went by, and then a week, and Smita never once talked about sending me home.

I could never throw up my meals because Smita was always around. She stayed up late, reading in bed. One night, after gorging on three vegetable samosas and two plates of korma, I set the alarm for four in the morning. I dragged myself out of bed, into the bathroom I had cleaned, and threw up as quietly as I could.

'I know all too well about the purge cycle,' Smita said the next morning. She opened my mouth and looked at my teeth. 'I forbid you to defile your body,' she said. 'Ruin your teeth.' She lit a cigarette. 'Weaken your bones, stunt your development.'

Smita puffed hard on her cigarette. She never ate breakfast. She smoked and drank dark tea.

'When you start eating properly,' she said, 'you can take up smoking. When is the last time you got your period?'

I shook my head.

'Not once?' Smita bit her lip, staring at her lit cigarette.

I shook my head.

'Brilliant,' she said, still angry. 'What about your twin? Has she gotten her period?'

I tried not to lie to Smita. She'd seen me at my worst, head shaved, riding my unicycle in the rain with nowhere to go. She had seen the tattoo on my naked back. She had seen me naked.

'Almost three years ago,' I said. Our birthday was in a week. We would be seventeen. I had never wanted to get so old. Everything had turned awful when we started middle school. We had been beautiful children. Our lives used to be golden. 'Maybe I have cancer,' I said.

I had believed my period would come the day after Chloe's. DNA was supposed to mean something. Our insides were supposed to be as alike as our outsides. Our hearts and livers and kidneys, the same. But I had not bled. Maybe I really did have cancer. The chemotherapy wouldn't be a problem because I didn't have any hair to lose. I bit my lip, wishing for a drag on Smita's cigarette. I was crazy about Smita, but I didn't want to die in her house, without Chloe or my dog or a stash of pain pills. I stared at my feet, confused. I didn't want to be dying.

Tears sprang to Smita's eyes. 'No,' she said. 'No, you don't have cancer.'

Smita hugged me. Rocked me in her arms the way Chloe used to rock me. I buried my head in her chest and started to cry with her. I loved to cry. It felt so good. 'You don't have cancer,' Smita repeated. 'It's plain old malnutrition. Just like in the third world. Except in this country of plenty, girls starve as a matter of choice. You are all bones, Sue.'

'Chloe was always the one on a diet,' I said. 'Not me. I love to eat. Lasagna used to be my favorite food.'

That afternoon, while I vacuumed the floors and dusted the bookcases, Smita cooked me her first non-Indian meal. A spinach lasagna. We sat the in Smita's sparkling clean kitchen, slowly eating her delicious food. She lit candles. Her dangling earrings shimmered in the glow of the candlelight. She took a bite, and I took a bite. First Smita, then me. I smiled at her. 'I love eating this way,' I said.

Smita sipped her wine. She took a bite of lasagna. I lifted my fork.

'I can't much imagine the point of a day,' Smita said, 'if there was no dinner to look forward to.'

'I haven't been living,' I said.

When we were done eating, Smita asked me if I wanted dessert as well. I knew that she had made brownies. I had seen the mix box in the trash. Smita, I knew, didn't like sweets. She had made brownies just for me. That is how much she liked me. Smita

smoked, finishing her glass of wine. She looked happy to watch
me eat. I felt like her little girl.

'No more diets,' Smita said. 'Ever.'

I got my period the very next morning.

Five days later I turned seventeen. I was old enough to drive. I'd
gained six pounds. Smita sent me out in the morning for blue-
cheese cheese puffs from the local health food store. I brought her
jasmine tea and some cheese puffs in a blue bowl, and then I went
outside to wash the windows. It was a bright, sunny day. I was
the best maid ever. I had a bucket, I had cleaner. I had rags and a
ladder.

I was up on the ladder, scrubbing the top windows, when I saw
Daniel's car pull up to the curb. He honked the horn. I watched
him get out of the car and open the door to the backseat. Daisy
came leaping out. She ran straight to the ladder and jumped on
it, barking. Daisy. I almost fell. My heart started beating fast. I
had a past. I had a family. Chloe hadn't found me, but there was
Daisy. My dog. My good poodle, wagging her tail like crazy. I
rushed down the ladder and wrapped my arms around her.

'Happy birthday,' Daniel said.

He was holding a bunch of yellow tulips.

For a second, I was happy. My brother had remembered my
birthday. The flowers were bright and pretty, and they would
look nice in Smita's house in one of her ceramic vases. Smita loved
flowers. She wanted us to grow a garden in her backyard.

I felt myself grinning at Daniel. My birthday, my poodle. My
brother. I hadn't told Smita I had turned seventeen. I was afraid
she would feel that she had to do something. I did not want to
become too much work for Smita.

I knelt down to pet Daisy.

'Hey, girl,' I said. 'Look at you. Beautiful poodle.'

'I worried about you, you know,' Daniel said. 'Yumiko called me to tell me you were coming, and you never came. I didn't know what happened to you.'

I didn't want to think about Yumiko. I looked at Daniel with the dog, and I realized that he had been back to the house. He must have seen Chloe. I didn't want to think about Chloe. I didn't want to know how she was. I didn't want her to know how I was. It was all over. Ruined. We weren't identical. It occurred to me that while I was cleaning the windows, Smita might have run out of tea. It was my job to bring her fresh cups of tea. My mouth had gone dry. I wanted Daniel to go away.

'I can't keep Daisy, you know,' I whispered. 'This isn't my house. You have to leave.'

'Sue?' Daniel said. 'Slow down. Say, Hello, Daniel. Take these flowers I brought you. They're for you. For your birthday.'

I willed him to lower his voice, but already it was too late. I could hear Smita coming downstairs. Smita hated dogs. She would hate Daisy. In India, she said, kids beat them with sticks. It was already too much that I was there.

I wanted to reach for the yellow tulips and rip them apart. Daniel had to leave.

Smita stepped out of the house, barefoot, wearing a red tank top and an orange skirt with blue flowers. This time of day, she was supposed to be writing.

'Dan,' she said. 'Hello. It's good to see you.'

Smita didn't know my brother.

'Were you washing the windows?' Smita squinted into the sun. 'That's brilliant. Sue,' she said to Daniel, 'has been doing a bit of cleaning for me. She's absolutely brilliant.'

'You've talked to each other?' I was stunned. I kicked over the sudsy bucket of water. Smita had conspired behind my back. It was conspiracy. Betrayal. As bad as Chloe betraying me for a basketball.

twins

'Let's have some tea,' Smita said. 'Let's go inside and we can have a civilized chat. Come inside, Dan, and Sue will make us some tea. I've never had you over to my house before, have I?'

'No,' I said. 'He can't stay.'

Smita gave me a cold look. We had never disagreed about anything before. My life with Smita had been perfect. 'We have an agreement, Sue,' she said. 'You don't stay here on my simple charity. You provide me with a valuable service.'

Again, she invited Daniel to come inside.

'Please, Sue,' Smita said. 'Go make us a pot of tea and put those flowers into a vase.'

She had never talked to me this way. I looked at Daniel, who was looking at the grass. Smita bit her lip. 'I'm handling this badly,' she said. 'I had a feeling you would be upset. Make us some tea, Sue, and I will explain.'

Smita smiled at me, pleading.

'You didn't tell me you were bringing a dog,' she said to Daniel. 'Hello, doggie.' Smita got down on her knees and looked Daisy in the eye. 'Hello, lovely girl.'

It was beginning to make sense. Daniel had come to take me away. Smita's house was clean. She didn't need me anymore. She didn't want me. She didn't know how to ask me to leave, so she called my brother. I had thought she liked me. I wouldn't make the bloody tea. I would smash all of her favorite blue ceramic bowls. I'd stomp on the wineglasses. I'd spit in the pot of chickpeas soaking on the stove.

This felt like the start of one of my parents' meetings. I would not be sent home. I couldn't go back. I had been the best maid ever. There had never been a better maid than me. I hated Smita. I hated Daniel. I hated Daisy, who wagged her tail at me, expectant.

'Sue,' Smita said. 'I thought you were tough.'

'No,' Daniel said. 'Not Sue. She cries all the time.'

I didn't even know that I was crying.

'Fuck you,' I said to Daniel. 'I hate you.'

I was standing on the lawn, crying. Daniel and Smita just stood there, watching me.

'She gets so angry,' Daniel said. 'I don't know what I ever did.'

I grabbed the flowers, my birthday tulips, from Daniel's hand and threw them to the ground. Daisy whimpered, her tail had stopped wagging. She hated it when I cried.

'Oh, Sue,' Smita said. She walked over to me and put her arm around my shoulder. 'You're not going anywhere. Nothing bad is happening, I just thought you might want to talk to your brother because he is a nice person and he is part of your family.'

'You hate your father,' I said.

Smita shook her head.

'Your brother didn't start masturbating you when you were six years old, did he?' Smita said quietly, only to me. 'I like Dan. Yumiko treated him shabbily. Just like you are doing now. There are so few good men on the planet, and they are invariably treated badly. I can't fathom it.' Smita put her hands on my shoulders and steered me into the house. 'Go wash your face and then make us some tea, angel. No one is going to hurt you.'

Smita had never said anything like that before. Every night, I slept beneath all of those pictures. Raj Khan with his smooth, brown chest, rippling with muscles. The ridiculous purple turban.

Daniel followed us inside. Smita nodded, and he sat down on the couch I had cleaned. Daisy jumped up next to him.

'I'm on your side, moron,' he said.

Smita lit a cigarette.

'Make the tea, Sue,' she said. 'Make the tea.'

* * *

twins

My parents knew where I was. They had given Daniel money to keep me clothed and fed and educated. Daniel had with him a copy of my transcripts and a suitcase full of my clothes in the trunk of his car. He gave me a one-hundred-dollar bill. 'From Dad,' he said. 'For your birthday.'

'Bloody wankers,' Smita said.

I put the money in my pocket. My hands were shaking.

According to the document Daniel gave me, my parents had set up a trust. I couldn't touch the money until I was eighteen.

'For now,' Daniel said. 'For one year, I guess, I'm sort of your guardian.'

'They don't want to talk to me?' I said.

'Dad said you were a cold child.' Daniel looked at his cup of tea. 'If you want them, they're a phone call away. That's a quote.'

I held the manila folder on my lap. My name had been printed on a laser label on the tab. A secretary had prepared these documents. On TV, when a young girl ran away from home, the family always tried to find her. The mother wept. Usually, she fell into a consoling police officer's arms. There was a lot of waiting by the telephone. Frantic moments. Prayers. The parents always worried. Even if I did hate their sorry asses, they were my parents and they should have worried.

'They've known you were here from the start,' Daniel said. 'I called them.'

'Chloe?' I said.

Daniel nodded.

Chloe knew. All this time, Chloe knew where I was.

'Chloe seems totally out of her mind,' Daniel said. 'She went on about training for the Olympics. Having no time. A year and a half until the next one, almost impossible, she'd never be ready. She said Daisy was peeing in the house and barking at her shadow,

I tried talking to her for a while. She never stopped moving. Sit-ups, push-ups, pull-ups. I got tired watching her.'

'She's a basketball star,' I said, looking at my teacup. I hated tea. 'She'll make the Olympics.'

Smita rubbed my shoulder.

'So this is our dog?' she said.

She held out her hand to Daisy. Daisy sniffed Smita. Then she licked her hand. I watched them together, curious. Daisy was my dog. I opened the folder, and looked at the document again. It was six pages, typed, stapled. Printed on letterhead paper. I nodded to myself. It was more than that I was ugly. I had been officially kicked out.

'I can't go home?' I said.

'Actually,' Daniel said, 'I think Chloe might be better off if you did go home.'

'She told you?' I said. 'She said that to you?'

For a second I felt almost ecstatic. Chloe needed me. It didn't make sense, when for so long, everything she had ever wanted excluded me.

Daniel shook his head.

'No,' he said. 'But she's there all by herself, exercising. She's in pretty bad shape, I think. Not that she would tell me. She said something about everyone abandoning her.'

'Where is our mother?' I said. 'Why is Chloe all alone?'

'Mom is living in New York.' He shrugged. 'With Dad. They're having an extended second honeymoon or something.'

'Chloe's *alone*?' I said.

I was surprised. I looked at Smita, but her face didn't show any reaction. I couldn't imagine Chloe all alone in the house, even though she almost deserved it. She had abandoned *me*. Jogging to school, learning to play basketball.

Daniel looked at Smita.

twins

'We don't really know each other,' he said. 'Except through Yumiko.'

Smita snorted.

Daniel turned to me.

'Do you want to hear the very best thing about Yumiko?' he said. 'The very best thing?'

Daisy was still licking Smita's hand.

'What?' I said. I had forgotten about Yumiko. I was watching Smita. In less than an hour, she had stolen my dog.

'Her parents aren't dead,' he said. 'They have a camera store in Lincoln, Nebraska.'

I shook my head. 'No. They died in a riptide. In Kyoto. She told me. When Yumiko was five. She has an inheritance.'

Smita laughed. 'Yumiko,' she said, 'is a compulsive liar.'

Daniel slapped his hand against his forehead.

'Oh, man,' he said. 'Does she tell lies.'

'It was the way she treated Sue,' Smita said to Daniel. 'Like an object, an oddity. That's when I knew that I had had it with her.'

I looked at Daniel and Smita, talking, drinking their tea. They knew each other. They had mutual professors. They were adults. I was a child. Daisy laid her head in Smita's lap. Smita smiled at me. I ran my finger over the top of the stapled document, my name in boldface. Daniel put his feet up on the table.

'I love standard poodles,' Smita said. 'They are the smartest dogs.'

Chloe

This guy named James called to ask me on a date. He had called me once after the article in *People*. I vaguely remembered him as being tall. Ever since I had started playing basketball, I noticed tall people.

'I've never even talked to you before,' I said. 'I'm not sure if I know who you are.' I held the phone too tightly. It was my birthday. I had turned seventeen.

'Sure you do,' he said. 'I couldn't believe you, that last game. Fifty-six points. I have never seen a girl move like that before. What are you doing right now?'

'Crunches,' I said. My forehead was covered in sweat.

The week after Sue left, all I could do was watch television. I propped my ankle on the table and watched soap operas and nature programs and reality TV. My ankle was still tender. The basketball season was over. I didn't care about finals. I had pizza delivered. I ate an entire cheese pizza by myself. Then, one night, I found a special about Sarah Hughes, the figure skater who won the Olympic Gold medal. She seemed ordinary. Her hair, at least, was nothing special. She talked about how normal her life was,

twins

how she was just a regular person who did chores and homework and went to school like everybody else. But I knew, and she knew, and the interviewer knew, that this slight girl was anything but normal. She was a national champion, a hero. There were six kids in her family, and I had no doubt in my mind which child her parents loved best. She was the one on the Wheaties box. She had her pick of Ivy League schools. I spit out my pizza, deciding then and there that I would go to the Olympics. Mr Markman had said that I could take my talent as far as I wanted to go. Mr Markman couldn't possibly ignore me if I were an Olympic champion. He would have to laugh off my father's ridiculous accusations.

'And then,' I said to James, not sure of what to say. 'Then, I'm going to do some weight training.'

I did not know how to talk to boys.

'Why don't I come over?' James said. 'I can spot you. For the heavy weights.'

'Okay,' I said.

I gave him my address. I was not entirely sure who he was, but it didn't matter. I was lonely. I didn't like living alone. I had trouble sleeping, hearing noises when there were no noises. I was convinced that someone was breaking into the house. I didn't even have Daisy to protect me. Daniel had come home the day before and taken her away. He had come to the house for Sue's clothes. He asked me how I was doing, but I did not know how to begin, and I knew that there was no reason for Daniel to care. Neither of us mentioned my birthday, even though he usually remembered stuff like that. He had once given us a book about a Nazi doctor that had given me nightmares. But he didn't care about me, he cared only about Sue, so I did push-ups while we talked. It was my fault he took Daisy. I told Daniel that I was training for the Olympics and that I did not have time for a dog, but as soon as she was gone, I wanted her back.

Sue got her. Sue always got everything she wanted.

I could not believe that someone had called to talk to me. 'James,' I said. I closed my eyes, hoping that he would be who I thought he was. It occurred to me that I couldn't do exercises with a boy like I had agreed to on the phone. I could not be wearing sweat-pants. I didn't know how long it would take for him to show up, but I risked taking a quick shower. I had to wash my hair. I wanted to be pretty and clean. If I was still pretty.

James showed up half an hour later. He was tall, not like Mr Markman but at least a head taller than me. His dark hair hung in his eyes. He was the one who came to my games. One time I'd seen him hold up a cardboard sign that read 'Chloe Is Awesome'. He held it over his head every time I scored a basket.

'You're done with your workout,' he said.

My hair was still wet. I had put on a pink T-shirt and a pair of tight, low-waisted jeans Lisa Markman once made me buy that miraculously still fit. I stood at the door, looking at James, amazed that he was standing there in front of me. He was cute. He smiled, and I could see two even rows of gleaming, white teeth. He kept his hands in his pockets, and we stood staring at each other on opposite sites of the door. He was wearing baggy jeans and a gray sweatshirt.

'Can I come inside, Chloe?' he said.

I laughed, embarrassed. That should have been obvious. I opened the door.

James kept his hands in his pockets, his head swirling around in all directions as I led him through the house. I took him into the kitchen, where I offered him something to drink.

He said, 'No, thank you.'

I took him back around through the living room and up the stairs. I showed him my parents' empty office.

'Nice,' he said.

Then I showed him Sue's messy bedroom.

'What a mess,' he said.

I took him into my parents' bedroom.

'Very nice,' he said.

I showed him my parents' bathroom.

James nodded. 'That is a big bathtub,' he said.

I ended the tour in my own room. I sat down on the bed, watching James take in my bedroom.

'Where is everybody?' he asked finally.

I shrugged. 'It's just me.'

James picked up the framed picture of Mr Markman I had on my desk. It was a photo I had taken in Hawaii: Mr Markman was wearing a Hawaiian shirt and a pair of khaki shorts, sitting on the couch where we had first watched basketball together. James put the photo back without commenting on it. He sat down on the bed next to me.

I understood that I had led this practical stranger into my bedroom. I knew that my belly button was showing.

'So you're an orphan?' James said. His voice had gone soft, almost with awe. He really knew nothing about me. My heart was beating fast.

'No,' I said. 'I have a mother and a father and a brother and a sister and a dog and all of them are alive and healthy. They just don't live here anymore.'

I had been alone in the house for almost three weeks, but I was starting to go crazy from loneliness. I had started talking to Sue. I would think of something, and I would get angry, and I would talk to her. 'It's your fault they are gone,' I'd say, falling asleep in my parents' king-size bed. I had started sleeping in all of the bedrooms. I felt like I was getting away with something. Sometimes, I wore Sue's combat boots. She had taken my sneakers but left her own black, bulky shoes at home.

James looked at me. He was confused. He didn't know when he came over that I would be by myself. Probably, he thought that he would have to meet my parents, that they would offer him lemonade and ask him about school, like it was in the fifties, like it probably still was in regular homes.

'But you live here all alone?' James said.

James stared at me, waiting for an answer.

I wasn't sure how a guy was supposed to respond to this situation. We were alone in the house and I had taken him to my bedroom. He would probably expect sex. In the matter of rape, my father would tell me, it would be a difficult case to win. The defense could maintain that, by luring James to my room and showing him my belly button, I was asking for whatever I got. James looked straight ahead. His hands were flat on the tops of his legs.

'They all left to do their own thing,' I said.

'That's cold,' James said.

I looked down, and then I look straight at him. I bit my lip. I hoped that my hair looked sexy, the way it fell forward, blocking my face. I tucked a strand behind my ear and tilted my head toward him. He put his hand on the back of my head, and we kissed. I kept my eyes open. I felt so proud of the ease with which this kiss happened. Like the simple footwork for a layup, the left, right, left that brought me under the basket for the easy shot. I slid my tongue into James's mouth. I had remembered how to kiss from Lisa's party, way back in the eighth grade. I had liked kissing then too. Every time my name was called to go into the closet, my heart would start to pound. I put my hand on the back of James's head. I pulled too hard, and our teeth knocked together. I broke away. I looked at James, his brown eyes, his dark, swoopy hair, his even, white teeth. He wore a gold hoop earring in his left ear. He tasted like toothpaste.

twins

'Hey, Chloe,' he said.

James still seemed nervous, but I knew just what I was doing. I could tell right away that James was sweet, the way Mr Markman had seemed kind from the first time I met him, and I leaned in to kiss him again. This time, with my hand on his shoulder, I held him tightly and pulled us back onto the bed. Again, it was easy. James lay halfway on top of me, kissing me gently, as if he was afraid to kiss too hard. I put his hand on my breast. I could hear him moan softly, and then, because I had given him permission, James stopped being nervous. He put his hand under my T-shirt.

I closed my eyes, trying to imagine how James must look when he played basketball. I felt his hand move down to my stomach, and I imagined that he would be good with a basketball. I wished that I had seen him play. I wrapped my arms around him, and then I slid my hands down the gap between his baggy jeans and his skin, and I could feel James shiver. But then, I heard a noise, the door opening downstairs, and I opened my eyes.

I put my hand on James's hand.

'Wait,' I said. 'Stop.'

I could hear the floorboards creak. I was certain that any second Sue would barge into my room. I looked at my closet, afraid she was hiding behind the door.

'You have to go,' I said. My shirt was pulled up over my chest. I pulled it back down. I kept listening for Sue's footsteps. My parents had said that she was at Daniel's college, but I always heard her lurking outside my door. She had broken Lisa Markman's nose because we had gone to the mall together. There was no telling what she would do if she found a guy in my bedroom.

James got up. He looked around the room, nervously, as if he too expected someone to walk in.

'Go?' he said. 'Okay? No problem.'

James held his hands out in front of him, as if I had accused him of attacking me. He walked out of the bedroom, straightening his clothes as he went, and headed down the steps. He walked quickly. I didn't think he was going to look back. I had offended him. I followed him downstairs and checked the front door while James went to the closet where I had hung up his jacket. The front door was still locked.

'Will you check to see if anyone is in the kitchen?' I said. 'Please?'

James looked at me funny, but he went into the kitchen like I asked him to.

'No,' he said, shaking his head. 'Nobody's in there. Did you hear something?'

From the clock on the wall, I could see that James had been in my house for less than half an hour. He was busy putting on his jacket; he seemed like he could not wait to leave. I wanted to cry. I had messed up. There was no one in the house, and I didn't want him to leave. I had done so well, getting him to come upstairs to my bedroom. I could still feel my lips tingling from the pressure of his kisses. I sat on the couch, waiting for him to leave. But James sat down next to me.

'This is a big house,' he said, 'to be in all by yourself.'

'I get a little nervous sometimes.'

James reached over and held my hand.

'I always think that someone is breaking in,' I said. 'Or that there's an intruder hiding in the closet. At night I think I can see my sister perched on the branches of the trees, staring at me through the window.'

James had started to caress the top of my hand with one of his fingers. I looked down at his hand. I felt myself shiver. I was staring at him, and he was staring right back at me. He looked nothing like me.

'There's no one here,' he said. 'You are safe.'

twins

'Can you check in my bedroom?'

James shook his head. 'I had an idea that you were a shy girl. I've never seen you talk to anyone before. And I mean anyone. I thought I was going to have to woo you. Take you to the movies and dinner and buy you flowers. I thought you would be expensive.'

'I like flowers,' I said.

'You have never said boo to me before,' James said.

'Boo,' I said.

We kissed again.

'So you want me to go up to your bedroom?' he said.

I shrugged.

'Maybe you could live here. You could move in, if you want to.'

'Everyone thinks I must be good at basketball,' James said.

We lay in the bed naked, under the covers, our bodies entwined. I wondered if I was in love. I didn't know if it was possible for it to happen so quickly. I knew nothing about James. I thought maybe, because he came to my games, because he was tall, because his body was muscular and lean, he might also play. He laughed when I asked him, and I was afraid that I might have offended him. I wanted to love James, and I wanted him to love me.

'But I dig watching you play,' he said. He stroked the top of my head. 'Didn't you notice me? Waving my sign? I only came to look at you.'

I had noticed James Patterson's sign, but not him. Not really. I kept my eyes on the ball and Mr Markman, tall and proud, sitting in the front row. Otherwise I made an effort not to look in the stands, pretending not to know that Sue was sitting in one of the upper rows, staring at me with hate in her eyes. I had never really looked at James. Now he was my lover, my very first.

I shook my head. I wondered why I felt disappointed.

'I can't believe I'm here with you like this,' James said. He kissed me again, and I smiled, closed my eyes, thinking that we would fall asleep together. Instead, James leaned down to the floor and reached for his sweatshirt.

'You're not staying?'

I put my hand on James's thigh. There were two more condoms in the top dresser drawer that were left over from the Christmas Daniel had spent at the house with Yumiko. It did not matter that James didn't play basketball, if only he would stay here, with me.

'You're serious?' he said.

He put his hand on top of my hand and smiled. I nodded. I kissed him again, happy, proud. His hands were exploring my body, and I knew that I had found something else I was good at.

James let his shirt fall back to the floor. He gasped when I touched his penis. 'I'll have to call my mother,' he said.

I liked that. James Patterson was a responsible boy. He slid his arms beneath my back, and he pulled me over, so that I was on top of him, my hair hanging down past my shoulders, my breasts exposed. I hoped that he would not be disgusted when he discovered my tattoo. He was going to spend the night. I hoped he would never want to leave.

'It's my birthday,' I told him.

Once I convinced James to play a game of one on one. I beat him soundly. He was not a good player, but even worse, he didn't care. He applauded when I passed him for a layup. As a form of defense, he tried to make me laugh, waving his arms wildly, jumping up and down like a spastic monkey.

'Who cares, Chloe?' he said. 'Who cares who wins? We're just goofing around. Having a good time.'

James and I were different. He was a year older than me, but he didn't act it. He thought life was all about having a good time. I was disappointed when I found out that James had been a mediocre student at best. I wondered if I was supposed to have asked him some more questions before I took him to my bedroom. James had never even taken the SATs. He laughed when I told him that everyone went to college. 'Not me,' he said.

James was in no way an ambitious person, but he was funny and sweet. He made me laugh. And he had a car and drove me to all the places I couldn't get to on my own: the mall and the super-market and the multiplex movie theater. He had a friend named Jamal, who hung out with us most of the time. Jamal's name was also James, but he had changed it when he started hanging out with James to avoid confusion. He was white but wore his hair in long dreadlocks, and like James, he dressed like the black kids in school with the baggy pants and gold chains and basketball sneakers. James and Jamal liked to cut classes together, get stoned and play Nintendo. They had a part-time job together, painting houses after school.

'I know you,' Jamal said, excited, the first time James brought him over to the house. 'We were in detention together, like ages ago. You sat at your desk and scowled. You juggled shit.'

'Detention?' James shook his head. 'Not Chloe.'

'It was Sue,' I said. 'I have an identical twin.'

Jamal shook his head. 'Pencils, erasers, staplers, textbooks. That girl could juggle anything. Are you sure that's not you?'

I gave Jamal a tour of the house, taking him into Sue's old room, showing him the pictures of us on the wall. I hated it that he could have mistaken me for Sue.

'And she's gone?' Jamal said.

'Jamal is slow on the uptake,' James said, slapping the back of Jamal's head.

'She's not dead,' I told him. 'She just doesn't live here anymore.'

'Damn,' he said. 'We could have double-dated. This house could have been like that reality dating show with the twins. The four of us swilling champagne in a hot tub.'

'This house doesn't have a hot tub,' I said.

'Double damn,' Jamal said. 'But we could have still drank champagne. Can you juggle?'

'I can ride a unicycle,' I said.

James looked at me in admiration. 'You keep secrets from me,' he said, grabbing my waist.

'I can ride one,' I said. 'But I don't.'

Jamal stared at the pictures of me and Sue.

'That must be some freaky shit,' he said. 'Growing up with someone who looks just like you.'

I wondered what Sue would have thought of him, or James, who had his hand firmly in my back pocket, and for the first time, I was glad she had left home. I did not want to talk to Jamal about being a twin, and I would have been mortified to have Sue there, looking down on me for having an ordinary boyfriend. Jamal stood in front of the picture of me and Sue, naked in a sandbox. I felt my skin turning red.

'Do you play basketball?' I asked Jamal, though I already knew the answer. Jamal was about an inch taller than James. They were big guys.

'Holy shit, no.' Jamal shook his head. 'All those practices. Coaches yelling at you, blowing their whistles in your face. It's like the army. I believe in recreational sports.'

'So is she coming back?' Jamal said, sitting down on Sue's bed. 'Your twin sister?'

I shrugged. 'Probably not.'

I looked at James and Jamal, eyeing each other.

'An empty room,' Jamal said. 'No parents.'

James was moving in at the end of the week. His mother had

been heartbroken when she found out about my offer. She had
pleaded with him to wait until he graduated. She threatened to
stop making his car payments.

'You want Jamal to live here too?' I said.

I thought it would be romantic, living in the house alone with
James, almost as if we had just gotten married.

Jamal lay back on Sue's bed.

'Firm,' he said. 'Nice.'

'Chloe,' James told Jamal, 'takes life very seriously.'

'Whatever you want to do, Chloe,' Jamal said. He sat up, smiling at me, his open face framed by dreadlocks 'If it's a problem,
if you're uncomfortable, it's no big deal.'

James put his arm around me. 'We could have such an awesome
summer. Kick back, fill the pool. Grill steaks, drink beer.'

'Would you be okay,' I said to Jamal, 'with the room down
the hall instead?'

I couldn't give away Sue's room. It would be too awful if she
were to come home and find out that she was not wanted. But I
didn't mind the idea of Jamal in Daniel's room, which had never
felt like it belonged to me. James and I were going to move into
my parents' bedroom. James had always wanted to sleep in a king-
size bed.

'Awesome,' Jamal said.

James and Jamal high-fived each other, and I laughed. It was so
easy to make James happy.

'Man will we party,' Jamal said.

He jumped up and down, like he was a kangaroo. His head
banged the ceiling light fixture. I thought of Mr Markman and the
little house in Hawaii, the way he often bumped his head on the
low-hanging chandelier.

I met James's mother at the dentist's office where she worked as a dental hygienist. I was surprised to discover that the office was in the same strip mall where Sue and I had gotten our tattoos. The area had gotten nicer, and the tattoo shop had been replaced by a café. Louise Patterson had scheduled an appointment for me.

'Some parents make you dinner,' James had told me. 'My mother cleans my girlfriends' teeth. It's her way of checking them out.'

Louise was younger than my parents. She'd dropped out of college when she'd gotten pregnant with James. He had told me that she had a history of picking lousy, abusive boyfriends and that, five years ago, she had given up on men altogether. 'She hates them all,' he said. 'She even thinks I'm a dog.'

Louise gave me a hug when she came to get me in the waiting room. She was gentle putting on the heavy apron I need to wear to have my X-rays taken.

'When is the last time that you've been to the dentist, honey?' she asked.

I shrugged.

'I'm not sure,' I said.

'One year, two years? Three?'

'A while, I guess.'

'Well, consider this my gift to you,' she said.

I did not know how to respond. Her son was moving in with me the next day. I supposed she could have bought us some kind of housewarming gift, even though the house was furnished with all of my parents' things.

First Louise took X-rays, and then she brought me to another room, where she cleaned my teeth.

'You are extremely lucky you don't have cavities,' she said, jabbing a small metal pick into my gums. 'This is why children need parents.'

Louise tsk-tsked when she looked into my mouth. She told me

that I was on the road to gingivitis. She scraped and prodded, and occasionally she handed me a small plastic cup to rinse my mouth. I spit out blood. When she finally was done, and my teeth were polished clean, I had a sensational headache. She filled another small plastic cup with water and told me to rinse. She gave me a new toothbrush and mint dental floss.

'Don't let my son move into your house,' she said.

The overhead fluorescent lights buzzed.

All week long, James had been moving in his things, and Jamal had already stayed over twice. I felt better when they were in the house. When I was alone my head filled up with thoughts and worries. I got angry at Sue. I started talking to myself.

'We'll be fine,' I said.

Louise shook her head.

'You're too young,' she said. 'You kids are going to run wild.'

'We're not,' I said. 'We won't.'

'I hate to say so, because he's my son and I raised him, but I don't trust the boy. He doesn't respect women. He takes things for granted. He's a taker, my boy.'

I rubbed my tongue along my teeth. One tooth still felt gritty with the pink powder she had used to polish them. I was surprised Louise would say such nasty things about her son. She was his mother. Parents were supposed to love their children.

'How much do I owe you? For the appointment?'

Louise shook her head. 'I wanted to do this for you,' she said. 'You had a nasty case of tartar buildup.'

It started to rain when I left the office. The sky had gotten dark. I slipped into the café where I had once gotten a tattoo and bought myself a cup of coffee.

I sat next to Louise the next day at James's graduation. She clutched her program, tears in her eyes as James stepped onto the podium to accept his diploma. She stood up to snap his picture when he threw his cap into the air. The day before, she had only bad things to say about him, so I felt reassured to see that she loved him anyway. It occurred to me that if Louise were my mother, she would have come to all of my basketball games. I wondered if my parents would come to my high school graduation. I wondered if Sue would graduate from high school.

Louise came back with us to my house. She walked up the stairs, running her hand along the banister, poking her head into the rooms. She and James had lived in a small, two-bedroom garden apartment.

'Who will cook James dinner?' Louise said.

'I will?' I said, giving the answer I thought she expected.

'Don't you dare.' Louise's voice turned surprisingly fierce. 'You make my son toe the line. You make him pay his own way or he will suck you dry.' She made her way back into the living room, examining the big-screen television and the stereo. 'I told you he was a taker. I bought that boy anything he wanted, hundred-dollar sneakers, a Game Boy, a Tommy Hilfiger jacket, I made sure he got it. When he was ten years old he wanted a trumpet, so I scrimped and I saved until I had enough money to buy James a trumpet. The boy played it one time and decided to quit. He said it hurt his lips.'

'Please, not the trumpet story,' James said, leaning against the wall, taking off his tie. 'You always go on and on about the trumpet.'

He put his hands on her shoulders and began to steer her downstairs toward the door. 'I've done good, Mom. I made it through high school, I'm living with my girlfriend. It's time for you to go home.'

Louise pointed to the kitchen. 'I thought we would have a quiet dinner,' she said. 'To celebrate. I brought us a casserole.'

twins

'Not another casserole,' he said. 'Sweet Jesus. I'm starting my new life with Chloe, here. We want to celebrate.'

I had told James he had been lucky to grow up with a mother who loved him and looked after his teeth, but he did not see it that way. His father had died skydiving when James was only six months old. When James had enough money, he wanted for us to try it.

'We will call you,' I told Louise.

I was surprised when she came over to me, giving me a hug. I was certain that she must hate me.

'You can call me any time,' she whispered into my ear. 'In the middle of the night. At work. You can call me any time.'

James slammed the door triumphantly behind her.

I looked at him, his eyes shining.

James was my prize, but I wasn't feeling the sort of happiness that I should have. I had hoped that Louise might stay with us, that we could have sat at the dining-room table and eaten her casserole. She could have made a toast to James's graduation, and then another to our future happiness. But maybe I didn't want happiness with James. Really, I still wanted more than that. I heard Louise's car pull away and was tempted to run after it.

James pulled me to him.

'Did you think she would ever leave?' he said. He slid his hand up my dress. 'You can call me night or day.' James mimicked her voice. 'My God, what does she think is going to happen?'

'Don't you want to eat the casserole?' I said.

'Are you insane?' James pulled the flowered dress I wore for his graduation up over my head and threw it on the couch. We were standing in the middle of the living room. I knew that I looked sexy to him, but I was no longer amazed by this fact.

'I love this bra,' James said. He could open the clasp with his teeth. This trick used to make me laugh, but now I was worried about the open curtains, the neighbors who could see us. He leaned over and popped it open.

'That's so awesome,' he said. 'I wish Sue were here so that I could watch you pop open her bra with your teeth.'

'That's disgusting,' I said.

'It is, isn't it?' James grinned at me. Sometimes I wasn't sure if James was sweet or a little bit brain-damaged. I wished that I could just love him completely, never think any critical thoughts. I also wished that he wanted to have sex a little less often.

'Not here,' I said, and I ran up the stairs for the bedroom, knowing that he would chase after me. We had been together for almost a month, but I still felt self-conscious naked.

I jumped under the covers of my parents' bed.

'You have to let me see you naked now,' he said, pounding on his chest, pulling off his white graduation shirt. 'I am the man of this house.'

The bright sunlight shone in through the windows. I laughed. James could always make me laugh. He jumped under the covers and made a loud, smacking fart sound with his mouth on my stomach. I would laugh at the stupidest things when I was with him.

James pulled the covers off the bed.

'No,' I screamed, covering myself with my arms.

'Yes,' he said.

James jumped on top of me. 'I command you to uncross your arms.' I shook my head. We wrestled on the bed, until James had my arms pinned over my head and we were kissing.

'I am crazy about you,' James said, putting his hands in my hair.

'You are?'

I felt serious all of a sudden. I often wondered what James thought of me. There had been so many times when I thought he might tell me that he loved me.

twins

I held my breath while he unwrapped the condom.

'I am crazy about you,' he repeated, putting himself inside me.

After we were done, James fell asleep. He could do that, close his eyes and fall asleep. I had never known him to worry about anything. I quietly got out of bed and went to the bathroom. I took a long, hot shower, and when I was done, I wandered into Daniel's old room. Jamal's things were strewn all over the floor. His bong was on the dresser, his Nike sneakers on the bed. He'd hung a poster of Bob Marley over the bed.

This was my life now. James and Jamal. They were a package deal, more like twins in spirit than Sue and I had ever been. I backed out of the doorway and went next door, into Sue's room. I lay on her bed, staring at the pictures on the walls. Chloe and Sue. In Sue's favorite picture, we were at the beach, wearing matching pink bikinis, our tongues sticking out toward the camera. We had our hair up in matching pigtails. We really did look like such happy little girls. According to Sue, we had always been happy. Deliriously happy.

Sue

My status had changed. I wasn't a runaway. I wasn't broke either. Even so, Smita said that if I wanted, we could keep things the same. I loved being Smita's maid. Making her tea, bringing her an afternoon snack.

'This is comfortable,' Smita said. 'Our arrangement.'

'You're happy that I'm here?' I said.

'I am happy that you are here,' Smita said.

It seemed like she was, but I could never really believe it. I often woke up thinking, Today she will make me go home.

I was gaining weight. That was my job, Smita said, more important than the cleaning. Smita wanted me to eat. She wanted me to change my relationship with food. I also had to take good care of Daisy and be nice to my brother, Daniel. Those were Smita's rules. By the middle of the summer, I'd gained twelve pounds. I couldn't fit into my clothes; my jeans wouldn't zip. Sucking in my stomach, I started to cry.

'No,' Smita said. 'Not that. Look at yourself. Really look.'

I looked at myself closely for the first time since I had moved into Smita's house. I was amazed by how much I had changed. I'd lost that tragic, cancer girl look. My eyes didn't bug out of my face. My hair had begun to grow in; white-blond strands that came down to my ears. I stared in the mirror, and I thought maybe I was even a little bit pretty. Not Chloe beautiful, but nice.

Smita dressed me in her own pretty clothes. The flowing white shirt with little mirrors sewn on the bottom and a pair of baggy black pants.

'How is this?' she said, fastening a choker around my neck.

It was the most wonderful necklace, silver elephants holding each other's tails. I bounced up and down as Smita fastened the necklace, looking at myself in the mirror. Grinning like a moron. I could see Smita in the mirror, standing behind me, smiling at my smiling face.

'Are you happy?' she said.

'Oh, Smita.'

I touched a silver elephant. I couldn't begin to tell her. I couldn't begin to tell Smita how much I loved her. How I loved her food and her house and all of her pretty things, her ceramic bowls and her wooden boxes and the colorful baskets and the tapestries on the walls. I loved Smita's small college town, where I was known at the bike store and the bookstore and the library and the health food store where I bought Smita's fancy blue cheese cheese puffs. Where everyone smiled at me and said, 'Hi, Sue,' as if the town had been created as a place to please me.

I couldn't get over how fast I had gotten over Chloe. I didn't think about her. Ever. Thinking about Chloe was against the rules. Like throwing up. She was an unmentionable. She was a bad dream. A previous life.

But I knew that, as much as I wanted to, I couldn't forget Chloe entirely. Smita worked so hard *not* to forget her horrifying father. She had a room full of pictures, just so she wouldn't forget. I hung a newspaper clipping next to the poster of Raj Khan in the purple

251

turban. 'She Shoots, She Scores' read the headline. There was a picture of Chloe, in her ugly uniform, her cheeks puffed out, jumping toward the basket.

My whole life, Chloe had been the reason for my misery. Now I knew it had been Chloe's fault. Because I was not a miserable person. That wasn't me. I had been happy as a child; we had been happy, but Chloe had turned on me. She'd turned my love for her into poison. She couldn't blame me now if she was all alone. With Smita, I was happy again. Crazy happy.

'I love this necklace more than anything else,' I said.

Smita kissed my forehead.

'It's yours,' she said.

Smita was like that. What I didn't understand, more than anything else, was why Smita chose to like me. She didn't talk to Yumiko anymore, though I knew that Smita had once liked her too.

My favorite part of the day was going to bed. Before I went to sleep, Smita came into my room to tuck me in. She told me bedtime stories. They were different every night. She told real stories from her life: the time she had ridden on an elephant at her fifth birthday party. Her first math class at Hampshire College, where she had asked to borrow a rubber, which she told me means eraser in England, and how the whole class had laughed at her. But the best stories were the ones Smita made up, about a duck named Salman, who could not fly or swim because of a bullet wound to his wing. Instead he traveled through India by rail. Salman was named after an Indian writer whose early novels Smita said she admired.

Some nights, Daniel came over for dinner. One time, he stayed late to watch a movie, and when I asked Smita to come tuck me in, he tried to come with her into my room. 'You are off-limits,' I said.

twins

'I want to hear about the duck,' he said.

'You are out of your mind.'

At first, I was nice to Daniel only because Smita insisted. Smita liked Daniel, and she wanted me to like him. We started spending more time together. He was my source of money; if I wanted cash for anything – clothes, books, a rubber chicken at the toy store – I asked Daniel and he gave it to me. He was taking a squash class, so we practiced together at his gym on campus. I liked to smash the ball as hard as I could. Sometimes, we would run into Yumiko, and together, we jubilantly ignored her. One time Yumiko saw us and dodged behind a soda machine.

When we were done with squash, Daniel would drive back to Smita's. He always wanted to stay for dinner. I liked the aloo saag; Daniel liked Smita's vindaloos. Smita could make curries so spicy they made my eyes water. Daniel and Smita would wash the food down with beer, but not me. I didn't even ask to try. I wanted to be a good girl for Smita. I didn't want to drink or smoke or do anything that Smita might say was bad for my development.

'This is nothing like home,' Daniel said, sopping up his sauce with a piece of nan, Indian bread Smita made herself. We had escaped. We both knew it. Daniel loved Smita's cooking as much as I did. He also loved Smita; I never said anything, but I could tell from the way he looked at her. From the way he checked himself out in the car mirror before we went into the house. We became vegetarians just to be like Smita. She said that such heroic gestures were unnecessary. 'You tell that to the cow,' Daniel said.

I learned to like cauliflower. Chloe could eat all the grilled hamburgers with Mr Markman she wanted.

After our dinners, I washed the dishes and Daniel dried them. Then I walked Daisy. When I got back to the house, Smita would have put on some music in the living room. We played board games and watched movies, or sometimes we just sat around and read. Smita gave me books to read, so that I would feel ready for school in the fall. One night, I watched as Smita put her feet on Daniel's lap, and he started to rub them. Smita looked at me, and I looked back down at my book. I would gladly have massaged Smita's feet. I would have rubbed her shoulders, brushed her hair. Smita shrugged her feet away from Daniel's lap. He kept reading as if nothing had happened. I got down on the floor and rubbed Daisy's tummy.

Later, they both came into my room for my tuck-in. Daisy came in too, jumping on the bed. Smita sat on the edge. She pulled the quilt up to my chin. Daniel leaned against the door.

'You're a couple,' I said to Smita. 'It's fine.'

Smita bit her lip and I knew it was true. They probably hadn't told me sooner because of Daniel. He would have told Smita that I was a violent monster, that I had crying fits, threw temper tantrums, and when that didn't work, I'd hit the dog. But that wasn't me anymore. I was a new Sue. I wasn't mad. I wasn't even jealous that Daniel had started spending so much time with Smita.

'Really?' Smita said. She laughed. 'I don't know why I was so bloody nervous.'

I nodded. Smita was nervous because she was Smita. Because she was good. Because she was the best person on the planet. Better than Chloe could ever be. 'I love you, Smita,' I whispered.

Smita blinked. Then she kissed my forehead. We looked at each other, our faces serious. 'I love you too,' she said.

I bit my lip.

Smita loved me. It was not a given. Our DNA was one hundred percent not the same. Smita was not obligated to love me.

'Wow,' Daniel said. 'That's it? That's all you girls have to say? Where's the violence? Where's the drama?'

I gave Daniel the finger. If Smita wanted to sleep with my

brother, that was fine. That was what Smita wanted. I was not a drama queen. But only Smita got to tuck me in. Daniel could not listen to our stories about Salman, the traveling duck.

Smita seemed to understand without my saying a word.

'I'll tell you a story tomorrow then,' she said.

'Tomorrow,' I said.

Chloe

A call came from an administrator at the basketball camp I had
enrolled in wondering about my absence. I was supposed to have
spent six weeks at a university in North Carolina. Jamal spit up
his beer looking through the glossy pamphlet I showed him. 'You
were going to spend your summer playing *basketball*,' he said.
'You *paid* for this?'

Coaches from the best women's college teams taught at this
program. Players from the WNBA gave demonstrations. Mr
Markman had said that many top players attended such summer
programs. But the more time I spent with James and Jamal, the
sillier it had seemed for me to care so much about basketball.
James first started to like me watching me play, but he never knew
how hard I worked or how important it was. Nobody understood
besides Mr Markman, and he had stopped caring. I would never
make the Olympic team.

I had a new project, something to take as seriously as the SATs
or basketball. I was determined to become a new and improved
Chloe, the kind of free-spirited girl who got drunk and high with
her boyfriend, always willing do to anything for a good time. It

was hard work. I was afraid taking hits from Jamal's bong. The thick smoke that came through the tube made me cough so hard I couldn't breathe.

I spent the summer in our backyard by the pool, working on my tan. Every day I settled out on a lounge chair in the sun, glistening with coconut oil, reading glossy magazines. I thought spitefully of Sue and her stupid unicycle. I wondered what she would think if she saw me in one of my new bikinis, James and Jamal dunking each other in the deep end, James spreading lotion on my back. I had stopped playing basketball just in time. I had a beautiful body, James told me, and he was glad that I wanted to show it off.

'You look hot, baby,' he said.

James even thought that my tattoo was hot. He told me to show Jamal, as if he were proud.

Jamal said that my tattoo was the most boring thing he had ever seen.

'If I didn't know about your twin,' he said, 'I'd think that you were into lawsuits or something.'

Jamal had a koala bear on his shoulder.

'Why,' I asked him. 'Why a koala bear?'

'Fuck,' he said. 'I went to Australia last year and got shitfaced drunk. I wanted something Australian, so the tattoo artist made a koala. They really are the cutest fuckers you've ever seen.'

'I hate my tattoo,' I said. 'I always hated it.'

'You can get it removed,' James said. He seemed surprised that I felt so strongly. I had never explained to him about how things had been between me and Sue. After Jamal had become part of our daily lives, I never really talked to James about anything.

'I couldn't do that.'

When I was thirteen, I had never heard of laser surgery. I believed I was branding myself for life, imprinting Sue's name into my

body. I had been willing to do that for her. I was never sure why.
I had been frightened by her desperation, how she had sat on the
floor, weeping. Now that she was gone, I hoped that maybe I had
gotten the tattoo because I really and truly loved her more than
anyone else and wanted her to believe me. Removing it now would
be almost like murder. Sue had been right; I did not want to forget
her. Maybe there were times when Sue looked at her tattoo and
she remembered me.

'You are scowling,' James said.

I nodded.

'I can't see it anyway,' I said, ending the conversation. I
leaned over and kissed James on the lips. He pulled me toward
him, untying the string that held up my bikini top. I still loved
kissing James, his face and his lips and the way that he held me.
I wanted us to take off our clothes and skinny-dip in the pool.
Carefree Chloe would do wild and crazy things just like that. I
imagined the two of us making out in the sunshine, my wet
hair, James's hand on my bare back, the picture that would
make.

'Hey, kids,' Jamal said. 'Get a room.'

James and Jamal came home from shopping with bags and bags
of food and a pretty black girl named Tashika. 'We've got steak,'
James said, holding up a package of bloody meat. 'We've got rum.'
Tashika's short hair was frosted blond. Her red fingernails were
so long they curled under. She leaned over and touched my hair.
'I would kill to have this hair. Is this your house? I like it.'
Tashika grabbed Jamal's hand, and they went upstairs. I noticed
a suitcase leaning against the wall in the hallway. I felt my head
starting to hurt.

'What's going on?' I asked James.

I followed James into the living room, where he put on some

reggae music. I followed him into the kitchen, watching silently as he made strawberry daiquiris in the blender.

'You are scowling again, Chloe,' James said. 'Nothing's going on. We're having dinner. It's like a dinner party. A double date. Did your parents leave some fancy dishes in some hidden cabinet we can eat on?'

I shook my head. I had grown tired of doing all of James's and Jamal's dishes. They were messier than Sue. The dishwasher had broken, and we had started to use paper plates.

'Ah, who cares?' James shrugged.

I followed him out to the grill and stood next to him as he cooked the steak. He kept his arm around me, humming to himself while poking the meat with his free hand. I concentrated on drinking my tall, pink drink, trying not to think about Jamal and Tashika upstairs in Daniel's bedroom. I wanted them to leave and never come back. The ice was cold against my teeth, making my head ache. I knew that I was failing miserably at being carefree Chloe. I knew, even though he never said so, that James was disappointed in me. He did not like it when I got quiet.

When I finished my drink, I poured myself another.

'I'm going to get drunk tonight,' I told James.

'Way to go,' he said, smiling. 'I knew you'd love these girlie drinks. I made them just for you.'

Later, I lay in the grass while James and Jamal and Jamal's new girlfriend, Tashika, ate steak. I had drunk four strawberry daiquiris. My head was spinning, my teeth were numb, and my stomach felt bloated. I didn't come when James called me over to eat. From the grass, I watched them eat. I watched them pass around the bottle of rum and take long swigs. It was my house, which almost made it my party, but I felt like I didn't belong there, with these people. They were taking advantage of me. I closed my eyes, and when I opened them, James was sitting in the grass beside me.

259

'Are you okay?' he asked me.

'Great time,' I said, nodding. 'I am having a great time.'

Tears were streaming down my cheeks. James leaned over. He lifted his T-shirt, rubbed it across my face, drying the tears.

'I think I am drunk,' I said.

I had passed over the fun part of being drunk and gone straight to feeling sick. 'Is Tashika going to live here now too?'

James shrugged.

'This is your house, Chloe. You make the rules.'

'Do you love me?' I said.

James seemed surprised.

'You don't know?' He held my face in his hands. 'You are the most gorgeous, smartest, most serious girl.'

'You love me?' I said.

'Sure, I love you.' For a second, James looked upset. Then he kissed my forehead. 'You've had too much to drink,' he said.

I figured that this was when I was supposed to tell James that I loved him back.

'I'm drunk,' I repeated.

I got up, unsteady, and walked to the bushes. I knelt down in the grass, put my finger down my throat the way Sue once taught me, and threw up. James pulled my hair back from my face.

'Poor Chloe,' I could hear Jamal say as if from a great distance. He was laughing. Tashika came and stood next to me, watching me vomit.

'The girl has got to learn to hold her liquor,' she said.

'It happens to the best of us,' James said.

I woke up in the bedroom with James leaning over me, running his hand up and down my leg. 'Hey, girlfriend,' he said. He bit my shoulder.

'No.' I shook my head. 'I'm sick.' I closed my eyes, falling back asleep.

James shook me gently awake. 'Please, Chloe,' he said. I could see his clean white teeth, feel his hands on my body, and I was reminded of Sue, always relentlessly needing me. I gave Sue everything she wanted and it was never enough.

'I want you so bad,' James whispered.

I closed my eyes, thinking of all of the things I had done for Sue.

'Please, Chloe,' James said.

I must have nodded my head, though, because James climbed on top of me, and I moaned because he was heavy, but James didn't seem to understand, and then we were having sex. My head ached, and I knew that I smelled bad. I could smell the vomit in my hair, and James's breath tasted terrible, like rum and cigarette smoke, and it hurt having him inside me. I tried to move beneath him so that he would finish faster. I kept thinking about Sue, wondering where she was now.

Sue never had any interest in boys.

Sue

Daisy loved me. I walked her every day. I petted her hard, scratching beneath her chin the way she liked, and I gave her treats, dog biscuits and chocolate chip cookies. Smita said standard poodles were smart dogs; Daisy had forgiven me for hitting her. I found an empty field not far from Smita's house where I could let Daisy off her leash. We'd run, we'd wrestle, I'd throw her tennis balls and she'd chase them down. Daisy would run at my side while I rode my unicycle. We would fall into a perfect rhythm. I never fell, not even when Daisy tugged at the leash when she saw something, a squirrel or a cat or a car to chase after. I'd hop off of the unicycle and still be in perfect control of my dog.

On a beautiful day toward the end of summer, for no reason at all, I pedaled back to Smita's as fast as I possibly could. We wove through traffic, the wind whipping my face, ignoring the waves and cheers of admiring onlookers, as Daisy pulled me faster and faster. When we reached Smita's house, I fell off my unicycle onto the lawn. I was panting, out of breath. Daisy jumped on top of me. She licked my face.

twins

'You crazy Daisy,' I told her. She would not stop licking my face. I laughed and laughed, and then suddenly I could see us, like a picture framed on the wall. Me, Sue, pretty, healthy, happy Sue and her dog, Daisy, a standard poodle, on the front lawn of Smita's magical house. I could see my short hair, my denim jacket, and Daisy, wagging her tail. I decided right then that I would call Chloe. I would call Chloe, and I would explain things to her. I would tell Chloe that it was all her fault. Everything. The way I used to be. Those years when I ate nothing but Häagen-Dazs bars. The depraved sexual things I did with Lisa Markman when Chloe was at basketball practice. The constant misery from years of wearing pink.

It was all Chloe's fault. I had to let her know.

I rushed inside the house. I felt great. I was going to tell Chloe everything straight. Only a stranger answered the phone. At my house. It wasn't Chloe. The voice wasn't even female.

'I told you,' he said. 'Jamal's not here.'

I hung up the phone. My legs started to shake.

I dialed again. Slowly, making sure I got the number right.

'Have some dignity, girl,' the same strange male voice said. 'I'll tell him to call you when he gets home.'

I hugged my knees to my chest. I didn't know who Jamal was. Chloe didn't know any guys. She knew Mr Markman, but he was not the voice on the telephone. I looked up the stairs toward Smita's room. Her door was closed. I could hear Smita's laugh. Daniel's car was parked outside. Daisy had gone into the kitchen, I could hear her lapping up water from her bowl. I didn't know what I wanted to do. I wanted to know who'd answered the phone. I needed to know where Chloe was. Where was she? I was still holding the phone, my legs were still shaking. I dialed Lisa Markman's number. She picked up on the first ring.

'Bonjour,' she said.

I said nothing. I had not meant to call Lisa Markman.

'Is this Marcus?' she said.

I had nothing to say to Lisa Markman.

'Marcus? Hello? Is anyone there? Is this a sick and twisted stranger? A pervert? Do you want to know what I am wearing? I am wearing tight leather pants. These pants are so tight that I have to hold my breath just to put them on they are so tight. Does that turn you on? Do you want to know what kind of underwear I'm wearing?'

'Okay, sure,' I said. 'Tell me about your underwear.'

'Oh, my God,' Lisa said. 'It's the psychopath. It's you. Where the fuck are you?'

'Far away,' I said. 'Amherst.'

I looked back upstairs. If Smita and Daniel were in the bedroom, they probably wouldn't be listening to this phone call. Smita did not need to know about Lisa Markman. She would not like Lisa Markman, who was vain and boring and stupid. I wanted to hang up the phone. I wondered if Lisa knew the guys who were staying at my house.

'I give you one bad haircut and you disappear.'

'It wasn't just a haircut,' I said.

I hadn't planned on calling Lisa Markman. She was part of the misery that came with being Chloe's identical twin. That was ancient history. It was stupid to call. Chloe could rot away with Jamal and the girl who was after him. I had my own life. It was Chloe's fault I had called Lisa Markman.

'You know, I didn't mean to laugh at you the way I did,' she said.

I remembered. She had held the shaver over my head, holding long strands of my hair in each hand, and she had laughed at me. I was ruined, and Lisa laughed.

twins

'You didn't?' I said.

But I didn't care if Lisa was sorry. Fuck her. I had three inches of soft, pretty, wispy blond hair. I rubbed the pretty silver elephant necklace around my neck. I wore it every day.

'I was nervous, you know? I felt horrible after I cut off your hair. Right away, I wished that I could take it back. I didn't mean to laugh. I didn't know what else to do.'

Lisa Markman had never apologized to me before. Not for anything.

'You disappeared,' she said.

I kissed my knee. I didn't know I could feel guilty about Lisa Markman. We were never friends. I never even liked her.

'So what are you doing wherever you are?'

I shrugged. 'I don't know. I live here now.'

'Give me your address,' she said. 'Where's Amherst? Is that in New Hampshire?'

'Massachusetts,' I said, and without thinking, I told Lisa my address. 'Are you going to write me a letter?'

Lisa laughed, but it was a nice laugh. I remembered Lisa's laugh. We would take hydrocodone and lie on the rug in her room, and just about anything I said would make Lisa giggle.

'No, psychopath,' she said. 'I got a car for my birthday.'

Smita and Daniel came downstairs, flushed, their hair wet. They had sex all the time. I hung up the phone while Lisa was still talking.

Lisa Markman showed up the next day, driving a red convertible.

I was vacuuming the living room when I saw her from the window. She parked in front of Smita's house. I watched her look at herself in the dashboard mirror, put on lipstick. I hurried outside before she could get out of her car. I had given Lisa an address, the name of a street and a number, and there she was. She was wearing leather pants.

'This is the farthest I have ever driven,' she said. 'Four hours and twenty-two minutes. I was speeding like crazy. I was going like eighty-five miles an hour for this long stretch of road. I was freaked out that I was going to get a ticket. I love to drive fast.'

Lisa's cheeks were red. Her new nose looked just right on her face. I opened the door to the car, and sat down next to her. It was a fancy, shiny car. Lisa smiled at me. I touched the creamy leather interior.

'Do you know how many cows sacrificed their lives to fulfill your selfish needs?'

'What?' Lisa Markman looked at me like I was out of my mind.

'Leather,' I said. 'Your pants. The inside of this car. They kill cows for this stuff.'

'So?' Lisa said. She shook her head at me. 'You're still a psycho. You look good, though. I like your necklace.'

She reached out to touch my hair. 'It's gotten so much longer,' she said.

'What are you doing here?' I said.

Lisa slapped the side of my head. 'Is this where you live?' She pointed to Smita's pretty house.

'Show me where you live already,' Lisa said.

Lisa could not go inside. Smita and Daniel were home, upstairs. The door to Smita's room was closed, but that would only last so long. I put my feet up on the dashboard. Daniel would remember Lisa Markman. He would remember the day when I broke her nose with a tennis ball. He would remember, and worse, he would tell Smita. Lisa frowned at me.

'I got engaged,' she said.

She held out her hand, showed me an enormous diamond ring

on her finger. 'I told you about Marcus. I could not say no to this ring. I had to have it. My father wants to kill me. Listen to this, Sue, my father wants me to go to *college*. The deal was I finish high school and then I could start working again. I'm already past my pre-pubescent look.'

Lisa sighed.

'Asshole,' she said, and then she leaned toward me, and I looked at her, and I saw that she was going to kiss me. I was not going to start that over again, I thought, but she put her hand in my hair, her tongue in my mouth; we were kissing. We were kissing, slow and nice. We hadn't taken any pain pills. Chloe was not downstairs in Mr Markman's gym, practicing her jump shot.

I pulled away.

'Why are you here?' I said.

'Stupid psychopath,' Lisa said. Her voice was tender. 'I missed you.'

'Bullshit,' I said.

Nobody missed me. Chloe didn't miss me. She had never tried to find me. She never called. My parents certainly couldn't give a shit. They sent Daniel money, and I spent it. I wasn't missed. For all I knew, Chloe could be dead. That strange man who answered the phone could have killed her, buried her body in the backyard, and moved into the house. Maybe it didn't mean a goddamned thing to me anyway. I had tried calling the house a couple more times, and no one had answered. I didn't care. I was a brand-new person. Smita had saved me from myself. I ate regular meals. I had regular periods. I never threw up. I had learned how to defrost a refrigerator.

'You drove all the way here?'

Lisa nodded her head.

'Have you gotten stupid?'

'Fuck you,' I said.

'Fuck you.' Lisa gripped the steering wheel. We sat in her car, looking straight ahead. I wished that we were still kissing. Smita wore canvas sneakers. She might not talk to a person who wore leather pants.

'That was all bullshit,' Lisa said, looking straight ahead. 'My saying that I hung out with you because I was bored. Or because you looked like Chloe. I was messing with your head. You practically saved my life. I felt horrible after you left. I drove more than four hours to get here. I almost got into an accident with an enormous truck. I've never driven on a highway by myself. I risked my life to get here. I got into these insane fights with my father when I was learning how to drive. I'm surprised we didn't kill each other. Do this, check that, look both ways, slow down. One time he reached for the wheel and I tried to hit him. I jumped a curb and crashed into a tree.'

I had no idea Lisa Markman could get unhappy. I wanted to look at her. I was amazed. She twisted the diamond ring on her finger.

'Is he still with Chloe all the time?' I asked. 'Your father?'

'I wish.' Lisa sighed. 'No, he doesn't see Chloe anymore. His career is over, so now he wants to be a father. That's why I got this car. Emotional bribery. We go to family therapy. He makes me and Todd talk about our dead mother.'

Lisa rolled her eyes.

'You can't believe how bad it sucks at home.'

'Therapy?'

'I used to be this model, Sue. In Milan? You can't believe the time I had. Walking the runways, wearing these clothes you could not believe, everyone always fussing over me. Telling me that I was gorgeous, that I was sexy. I went to parties in villas. I went sailing on Lake Como. Now my life is bullshit. I do homework and I eat turkey sandwiches my father packs me for lunch. You just fucking left, you bitch.'

'You wanted Chloe,' I said. 'Not me.'

Lisa looked straight ahead.

'That was just a game,' she said.

But I hated Lisa Markman. I had hated her for years and years, long before the day I broke her nose. I reached for her face. I turned her head, kissed her again. I didn't know what I was doing. I looked up at Smita's house. Her blinds were still pulled.

'I like your nose,' I said.

Lisa touched the tip of her nose. She closed her eyes and smiled.

'I love my nose,' she said.

We made out on the couch.

Lisa slid her hand up my shirt.

'More than your hair is growing,' she whispered, and suddenly, I felt shy. I needed a pill or at least a blanket. I was glad when I heard Smita's door open upstairs. We jumped up from the couch, straightening our clothes. We were both breathing fast. Lisa looked pleased, smiling at me, as if this was the reason she had driven all this way.

'Hey, I remember you,' Daniel said, coming down the stairs 'You're Chloe's little friend.'

Daniel sat down on the edge of the armchair, grinning at Lisa.

'No,' Lisa said. 'Negative. I'm Sue's little friend.'

There it was. I felt myself blush. Lisa Markman liked me. She preferred me over Chloe. She had driven more than four hours to see me. Just me. She liked my hair, my necklace, my chest that had finally started to grow. I introduced Lisa to Smita, hoping that she could see beyond Lisa's pants.

'Gosh,' Smita said.

Right away, Smita took in the clothes. It wasn't only the leather pants. Lisa was wearing high-heeled boots, and a sheer red shirt with a black camisole underneath. 'You are so stylish. You look like you stepped out of the pages of a magazine.'

'I am a model,' Lisa said. 'Or, I used to model before my father went parental and decided to ruin my life.'

'Fathers,' Smita said. She shook her head. 'I wish women could reproduce without the bother of sperm. There are so many bad fathers.'

'Well,' Daniel said, scratching his face. 'Men are okay.'

But we were three to one. Smita seemed to like Lisa.

'I am starving hungry,' Smita announced.

'So am I,' Lisa said. 'I have been driving all day.'

Lisa drove us to a restaurant in her red convertible. I sat in the front seat, Smita and Daniel in the back. At the restaurant, Lisa reached for my hand under the table. I felt her press a pill into the palm of my hand. I swallowed it with my water while Smita and Daniel looked at their menus. Lisa winked at me. We were the kids; Smita and Daniel were the adults. This was what dinner out with your parents was supposed to feel like. Daniel and Smita and Lisa talked and talked, and I gazed at them through a happy haze.

'You are quiet tonight,' Smita said.

I smiled at her.

Lisa and I shared a chocolate mousse for dessert. I let the chocolate sit on my tongue. I swirled it round the top of my mouth. I had never quite tasted chocolate like this before.

Smita was asking Lisa questions about modeling.

'Tell me about the gaze,' she said. 'Did you enjoy being the object of so much attention?'

'Absolutely,' Lisa said.

'Did it bother you that your image was being used to sell merchandise?'

'That never bothered me,' Lisa said. 'I got a lot of free stuff.'

Smita nodded. 'Free stuff,' she said.

Daniel, I noticed, wasn't talking either. He was staring at Smita like a lovesick puppy.

'Hey, Daniel,' I said.

'Sue,' Daniel said. 'Hello.'

This was my life without Chloe. I had never wanted Chloe to leave me, but instead I had arrived someplace on my own. I was all right by myself. I had my own hair. My own clothes. I had my own face.

I looked at Daniel, and somehow he knew. We smiled at each other in the dim, candlelit restaurant.

'You're great, Sue,' he said. 'You're terrific.'

Lisa and Smita were still going back and forth.

I heard Smita break out into laughter.

Lisa was showing Smita her diamond ring.

'You'll have to give it back,' she said. 'When you break the engagement.'

'No way,' Lisa said. 'The ring is mine.'

'You sound just like Gollum,' Daniel said.

'What?' Lisa said.

Smita sipped her coffee.

'You are giving our gender a bad name,' she told Lisa.

I loved the way Smita flat-out ignored Daniel when she felt like it. 'Women shouldn't accept gifts from men they do not love,' she told Lisa. 'Women should not engage in relationships for profit's sake. It gives the wrong message.'

'Isn't that what marriage is all about?' Lisa said.

'Is it?' Smita said. 'I think the rules of partnership have changed in recent years.'

Lisa shook her head. 'But look at this ring,' she said. 'Have you looked at it?'

I decided to look. It was a big ring. A large rock. Larger than my mother's. I had forgotten that Lisa said she was engaged. 'Who are you engaged to?' I said. 'Do you have a boyfriend?'

Lisa patted my head like I was her pet dog.

'I have some books you need to read,' Smita said. 'Back at the house.'

'No way,' Lisa said. 'I'm not interested.'

I took another spoonful of mousse. I did not have to worry about Lisa's faraway fiancé. I just had to taste the chocolate in my mouth.

'You have to try it on,' Lisa told Smita.

Smita held out her hand. She had long, graceful fingers. Her skin was darker than Lisa's.

Daniel and I watched as Lisa slipped the diamond ring on Smita's finger.

'It sparkles,' Smita said.

'Is this an engagement I am watching?' Daniel said.

Smita was studying the diamond.

'Fascinating,' she said.

'Take off the ring,' Daniel said. 'I can sense its evil powers.'

Smita gave Lisa back her ring.

'You can't keep it,' she said. 'Unless you marry the man.'

'Of course I can,' Lisa said. 'Feminists are hopeless. Angry man-haters who don't shave their armpits.'

'These are outdated ideas,' Smita said. 'Stereotypes all of them. Look at me.'

'You're not a feminist,' Lisa said. 'You're much too pretty.'

Smita moved her head up and down.

'Holy shit,' Lisa said.

I wondered who Chloe ate dinner with. I hoped she did not eat all alone. I was her other half, but I had left her behind. I'd left her to be murdered by strange men who answered our telephone. It had been years since I had seen Chloe laugh. Suddenly I felt sick with guilt. I would die if something had happened to Chloe.

I went to the bathroom and threw up.

Chloe

I felt much too old, tired, walking back to high school to start my senior year. Sue did not have to go confront the same faces. James and Jamal had graduated. Only I had to walk those horrible halls: one more year of passing Lisa Markman and her brother, Todd, Melanie and Brittany, all of the friends I had never made and no longer wanted. On my way, I recognized the corner where I had once broken into a jog, running to get away from Sue when I could not stand her for another second. I remembered the exhilaration I felt as I picked up the pace, sprinting the last quarter of a mile until I reached the front steps of the school. I no longer had any reason to run.

It burned when I peed.

I put my head on the desk during my classes. Official basketball practice wouldn't start for several months, but the coach had arranged some early sessions for returning players. He had even called the house to confirm my attendance, but Tashika answered the phone. I dodged him in the hall and cut gym class. Kendra, the center of the team, once tried to talk to me, but I brushed her off. 'I've got better things to do,' I told her. I saw the surprise on her face and realized that I was doing a terrible thing. I was the star of the team, and Kendra had been nice, always passing the ball to me.

But I felt like I was finished with basketball. Mr Markman would not be in the stands to watch me play. I came home from school and locked myself in the bathroom, forcing myself to pee. I did not know why it stung. There was the chance that James had given me some horrible disease. He had taken me to the beach at the end of the summer. I could see that he was trying to be sweet to me, and we spent the day swimming in the waves, but I got sunburned, and by the time we got back to the house I felt sick with fever. My skin was so hot I sweated through the sheets, and I made him go sleep on the couch.

'We're not having so much fun, are we, Chloe?' James had said.

He could not make me laugh like he used to. Most days, he came home tired from painting houses. He and Jamal crashed on the couch, playing Nintendo. Tashika took classes at the community college. She had started keeping the house a little cleaner. She often brought home chicken from Popeyes for us to eat.

James was disappointed when I told him I didn't want to play anymore. He smiled his sweet smile at me, flashing those two rows of perfect teeth. 'Running down the court in those cute, shiny shorts, that's what got me interested in you in the first place. You have to go back. You have to play. I want to go to your games.'

'Really?' I said, feeling tears well up in my eyes. 'Really?'

I had become just like Sue. There wasn't a day when something did not make me cry. But I put on my running sneakers and headed to the track, thinking, Yes, I will go to practice, yes, I can start again. I can start again. I ran laps and remembered how good it felt to move my body. I enjoyed working out, pushing myself, even the sheen of sweat from the exertion. But the next day, I woke up feeling tired and defeated all over again, and I slipped quietly out of bed to get dressed for school, leaving my basketball sneakers in the back of the closet.

It all made sense to me now: why my parents had left, why Sue decided that I was not her sole purpose in life. I was not an exceptional person. I had given up my dog without a fight, I had surrendered my family, lost my virginity, misplaced my confidence, and now, it seemed only logical that I give up basketball, a game that had once given me joy. It was a stupid sport, and I was probably mistaken about the joy part. It had always been Mr Markman who took pleasure in my success.

Rodney Markman had no reason in the world to be afraid of my father. My absent father had no idea what I did every day. Mr Markman could have raped me every day and my father would never have had any idea. It was all so sad and ridiculous, because Mr Markman would never have done anything to hurt me. He was too good. But for what were supposed to be my own best interests, I had been forsaken. I had seen him once at the movies, standing in line at the popcorn counter with Lisa and Todd. Mr Markman did not see me, and I made James and Jamal take me home before the movie started.

Now Kendra also ignored me at school. I was a true social outcast, like Hester Prynne in *The Scarlet Letter,* the book I was reading for English class. I no longer talked in my classes. Teachers looked at me hopefully, but I raised my hand only to be excused to the bathroom. I constantly felt like I needed to pee, though when I tried, nothing happened. Only the burning, stinging sensation between my legs. I'd sit in the bathroom stall and cry quietly into my hands.

In December, I started to pee blood.

I decided, finally, to call James's mother.

She took the afternoon off and we went to her gynecologist.

twins

Louise, still dressed in her uniform, sat with me in the waiting room reading *People* magazine, and it seemed fantastic that my picture was once in those pages. Louise promised to wait for me while I was examined by her doctor. I was instructed to change into a paper robe, and then wearing just the robe, walk through the hall to a bathroom, where I had to pee into a paper cup. In the examining room, I started to cry when the doctor had me scoot down to the end of the table and lift my legs for a Pap smear. She gave me a tissue to wipe my face, and I answered her questions about my sexual history. I did not know the right answers. I hung my head in shame. I was grateful that she did not ask me about my parents.

The doctor told me I had a urinary tract infection. She gave me a prescription for antibiotics.

'That's it?' I said.

For the first time in a long time, I found myself grinning. The doctor looked at me, concerned.

Louise drove me to the drugstore, and she sat with me in blue plastic chairs as we waited for my prescription to be filled. She kept her lips pursed, as if she was dying to say something. When the prescription was ready, Louise asked me if I wanted her to take me back home, and when I shook my head, she took me back to her apartment. I loved Louise's tiny apartment, the slipcover on the couch, the cheerful welcome mat and the crocheted pillows.

Louise treated me as if I were sick. I sat at her kitchen table while she made me chicken soup with stars. She poured me a glass of cold milk to drink. When the soup was ready, Louise sat across from me, watching me as I ate. The canned soup was delicious, better than anything I had tasted in weeks.

'You tell that boy to keep his hands off you,' Louise said.

I did not want to talk about James. I just wanted to eat my soup. I wondered if I had made a bad choice, coming to her. I had knowingly gotten myself into this mess. I was the one who had seduced her son. I had let his friend Jamal move into the house. I had let Tashika stay. I had introduced them to my father's case of Irish whiskey in the basement. I had paid for the food and the electricity and for the neighborhood boy who mowed the lawn. James liked steak, and Jamal liked French cheeses, Brie and Camembert and Port Salut, and even though they both had jobs, I paid. I saw everything go wrong as it was happening. My life was my own fault.

'Well, what are you going to do?' Louise said.

I looked at the cute little stars floating in the bowl. I could not remember my mother ever making me soup from a can. She was above such small domestic activities. She made far too much money to eat processed food from a can. She would look down on every single part of Louise's life, from her small apartment to her lavender headband, which matched her uniform.

'What are you going to do, honey?' Louise repeated. 'This can't go on. You could get a kidney infection if you are not careful.'

I shook my head. I gulped down my milk. After handing me my prescription, the doctor had warned me about kidney infections. Almost all teenage girls, everyone but Sue, had sex. I was the only one who got a urinary tract infection.

I felt my eyes growing wet.

'Thank you for the soup,' I said.

'Tell me, Chloe,' Louise said. 'Do you love my son?'

Love? I looked at Louise, who was tall like James, who had the same eyes. I wasn't sure. I wanted to love James, but almost from the start, he had seemed inconsequential. He could not live up to the comparison of Mr Markman. James and Jamal spent hours and

twins

hours stoned in front of the TV playing video games. They took it for granted that I did their laundry.

'That's a personal question,' I said.

Louise nodded. 'Okay. Tell me this. Do you like living with my son?'

I took a deep breath. I could answer that question honestly.

'No,' I said. 'I really don't.'

I felt my heart beating fast. I had never flat-out admitted this fact. I hated Tashika, even though she brought home food and made James and Jamal turn down the music at night. She borrowed my clothes without asking. She wore my makeup. Jamal left his bong on the living-room table for the neighbors to see. The tub in the bathroom was filled with strange hairs.

'You don't like it?' Louise said. 'The experience has not been everything that you expected it to be?'

I could see what an effort it was for Louise to keep her expression even. It was not possible, I told myself, that she would be gloating over my failure. She was a kind person, and she was worried about me; she'd taken time off work to take me to the doctor. She had cleaned my teeth.

'You don't want to continue living with my son, do you, sweetheart?'

I shook my head, looking down into my bowl of soup. My leg had started to shake. I did not want to go on as I was, and that, I understood, was the real reason I had called Louise. I could have found a doctor on my own, but I had no idea how I could make them all leave. James and Jamal and Tashika. They were more comfortable in my house than I was.

'Do you need my help?' Louise said.

Louise was watching me. I had begun to cry steadily into my soup, and she started to cry with me. I felt strangely happy because we were crying together.

'Of course, Louise Patterson, that is why the girl came to you. Because she needs your help.' She touched my hand. 'I let this happen. This is my fault. I foresaw this. I can bring James home if that's what you want.'

I looked up at her. I wiped the tears from my face.

'Can I stay here instead?' I asked. 'With you?'

Louise looked surprised. 'Sweetheart,' she said. 'You have a lovely house. You go wash your face, and then I'll take you home. I will stand beside you when you tell my son that he has to pack his things and go.'

Louise, of course, did not know about the others.

'We have to break up?' I said.

I felt panicked at the idea. James was my boyfriend, the only person in the entire world who loved me. He really did care about me. He told me to play basketball. All the other stuff, his friends and the noise and the mess, that didn't matter. I would take my antibiotics and work at being happier.

'You have to call your parents,' Louise said.

She patted my hand, and I understood. This was the end of my relationship with both Louise and James Patterson. If things went her way, she would have her son back by the end of the night. My problems were my problems.

But I would not call my parents. We had gotten our divorce. I had visited their Manhattan apartment. I had admired their elegant furniture, the view from the thirty-fourth floor. We had eaten dinner together in an expensive French restaurant and made conversation. My mother worried that I was gaining weight. My father asked me which Ivy League college was I shooting for. We did not talk about Sue. At the end of the meal, my mother sprayed my wrist with her new perfume and we agreed to skip dessert. The moment we stepped outside, a cab pulled up in front of the restaurant to let out another couple, and my father put me inside the empty taxi. He handed me a one-hundred-dollar bill and kissed both of my cheeks as my mother blew kisses from the sidewalk. I never told them about James.

'You have to call your parents,' Louise repeated. 'You need them.'

But it was Sue I wanted to call. She had been gone for so long. I wanted to know how she did it. I had been so afraid for her for so long. Afraid when I left for Hawaii that she would kill herself. Afraid that when I left for college she would come after me and sleep on the floor outside my dorm room until I let her in. Instead, Sue had left before I did. For the first time in our lives, Sue had gone first.

Louise fumbled in her purse for her car keys. I just looked at her and kept crying. Sue was gone. I could cry enough for two identical twins. James was going to leave me, not a single person in the world cared if I lived or died, so I did not care if I was making Louise uncomfortable. I would cry and cry if I wanted to. I was surprised when Louise came to me, wrapping her arms around me. I hated Louise Patterson with all of my heart, but I let my head fall into her chest.

'Shhh, shhh,' she said. 'You'll be fine.'

'Do you have any aspirin?' I asked.

'In the bathroom,' Louise said. 'You go wash your face. Take your time.'

I went to Louise's bathroom and I washed my face. I took a deep breath, looking at myself in the mirror. My eyes were puffy and red, with dark circles underneath. I swallowed two aspirin, still staring at myself in the mirror. My hair was long and blond. I took my comb out of my purse and combed until it fell straight and shiny. Sue used to stare at me, dumbstruck, when I brushed my hair.

I found Louise at her desk in the living room, sorting through a pile of catalogs.

'James can start taking classes in the spring,' she said. 'He'll have only missed a term. It's not too late for you children to get a fresh start.'

'No,' I said. 'Of course not.'

I was certain that James would not come back home after I told him to leave. I couldn't see him attending classes at a community college, wearing a clean shirt, and taking communications courses. James and Jamal would start again, somewhere else. I had heard them talk about Florida.

I put on my coat, smiled a fake smile, and walked to her car. I buckled the seat belt and smoothed my hair.

Sue

Smita wanted me to go to school, so I went.

It was a private school. It was expensive. Daniel sent my parents the bill, and they paid it. They sent a letter that said, 'Good for you, Sue.' I did not write back. I was a senior, the new girl in town, the only new student in my grade. I was practically a celebrity. I would come home from school and tell Smita about all the girls who talked to me, which ones invited me to do things with them on the weekends, who sat with me at lunch. A girl named Carrie Lind had baked me mint brownies. She lent me CDs and her favorite book of poems. She laughed, amused when I called her a moron.

'I don't know why,' I said, showing Smita the things she had lent me.

'Because she likes you,' she said. Smita put the CD in the stereo, and we listened to the band that neither of us had ever heard of.

'Everyone always liked Chloe,' I tried to explain. 'Not me.'

But Smita had never met Chloe. She said she often forgot that I was a twin. 'You are weird enough on your own,' she told me.

At my new school, riding my unicycle was considered a form of expression. For an elective period, I co-taught a circus class with another student, who was also a gymnast. I wasn't the bad twin anymore. There were no standardized tests, no grades either, just teacher recommendations. Even the teachers liked me. 'Relax,' they said. 'Relax.' No one seemed to worry about the classes I had failed in my former life. 'What can you do now?' they wanted to know.

The new Sue loved going to school. I got my ears pierced so I could wear Smita's dangling earrings. Smita said they looked good with my boyish haircut. Two girls at school cut their hair short like mine. I woke up early to go over my homework. For the first time, I wanted my teachers to love me – the way teachers used to love Chloe. I loved mornings in Smita's house, sitting at the kitchen table, reading for school while Smita drank her dark tea. When she finished her tea, she would go into her room and find something for me to wear.

Before long, Smita started talking about my going to college. She was fairly certain I could get into Hampshire, even though I had only one year of respectable academic activity.

'It's an alternative school,' she explained. 'They make exceptions.'

It was hard to believe Smita could be right about this. I wasn't the kind of person who could do well on my own. I had always figured I would go wherever Chloe went.

Lisa came to see us every weekend. She stayed with me in Smita's office, the two of us spooned together on the single futon, safe and warm beneath the poster of Raj Khan and the newspaper story about Chloe. Lisa and I had used up her father's supply of pain pills, but we were more alert without them, giddy when the time came for Smita's tuck-ins.

twins

In the latest episode of Salman the Duck, Salman had to travel third class because there was only one seat left in first class, and the Indian princess in the car was allergic to duck feathers.

'Salman's lucky the princess didn't eat him,' Lisa said.

'Fantastically lucky,' Smita answered. 'The girl was not Hindi, and I've heard it said that duck curries are very delicious when served with mango chutney.'

Lisa was wearing a red silk slip. She always brought something sexy to sleep in. Not me. I had on a Hampshire T-shirt and Chloe's pink silk pajama bottoms.

'What happened to Salman in third class?' Lisa said.

In third class, Salman found a pregnant bride hiding under a pile of coats who was traveling to Bombay to meet her husband. The girl was afraid that she might be in labor, but she was ashamed to have her baby in a train car full of people.

'Did Salman help the girl deliver her baby?' I asked.

Smita shook her head. 'Salman had dropped out of medical school. He knew nothing about delivering babies.'

Instead Salman read to the young woman from a fairly recent Rushdie novel about a rock star who could shake the earth with her music. The pregnant girl was so engrossed in the duck's narration that she could not be bothered to have her baby.

'Books are that powerful,' Smita said.

Smita's stories often came packed with a lesson.

When the pregnant bride and Salman arrived at the station, they were met by the young woman's husband, a computer programmer who wore aviator glasses.

'Isn't that a stereotype?' I asked.

Smita nodded.

'Some stereotypes,' she said, 'exist for a reason.'

The nerdy husband, who had four ballpoint pens in his shirt

pocket, thanked Salman repeatedly. He called Salman 'Sahib', which is a form of master in India. He also gave him several juicy oranges to eat. He offered to upgrade Salman's computer, but as Salman was a traveling duck, he did not have a computer, not even a laptop, and he said his good-byes. He did not want to be around when the labor pains began.

'Is that a feminist story?' Lisa asked.

'Why not?' Smita said. 'Young women get married. After the baby was born, they moved to England, where the girl got her degree in social work.'

'To help improve conditions on the railways?' I asked.

'Quite possibly,' said Smita. 'Salman went on to the sea to relax after all the excitement. Salman loved to look at the stars, and where he went, a beautiful coastal town called Mamallapuram, the sky was jammed full of them.'

Lisa and I both giggled.

'It sure is exciting being a duck,' Lisa said.

'It certainly is,' said Smita.

She kissed us both on the forehead, pulled the covers up to our chins, and said good night. 'Be good, children,' she said, and we giggled some more.

Smita paused in the doorway for a moment. 'That is quite a nightgown,' she said to Lisa, and then she flipped off the light. We knew that Daniel was waiting for her in her bedroom. He was only allowed to sleep over on weekends. It was a new rule. Smita wanted Daniel to study, but mainly, I knew, Smita wanted her privacy.

'You have to fight against life's distractions,' she had told me. 'Good and bad.'

Weekends were marked by huge meals and hushed sexual activity behind closed doors. Smita and Daniel never said anything, but they knew that Lisa and I did not lie together chaste and innocent like sisters. Except that Chloe, my sister, would have never, ever let Lisa crawl into bed with her.

Maybe Chloe had always known I was funny about girls.

Most of the time, it was just me and Smita and Daisy. Lisa finished her senior year back home. If she saw Chloe at school, she didn't tell me about it. I tried not to ask.

We were the perfect combination. Daisy was wild about Smita. She followed her around the house with her tennis balls, wagging her tail whenever Smita approached, licking Smita's face, licking Smita's hand. Smita cooked dinners for just the two of us. I would ask her to make aloo saag, the first dish she had ever cooked for me. Sometimes, we would eat it five nights in a row.

'It's the new macaroni and cheese,' I said.

'I like having you here so much,' Smita said.

I dropped my fork on the floor. I didn't want Smita to see my face if I started to cry.

'I'd been alone for too long,' Smita said. 'I think perhaps I was turning a bit odd.'

I remembered how Smita's house used to be. The roaches in the kitchen, the piles of clothes on the floor, her fear of the refrigerator. Maybe it was true. Maybe Smita had been unhappy before me. Maybe I made Smita a little happy too. All those dinners Smita cooked for me, she got to eat them too. We had made it through the winter.

'You think it's bad to be alone?' I said.

Smita shrugged. I caught my breath. Smita didn't shrug. It was Chloe's shrug. Chloe.

'It wasn't a good thing for me,' she said.

I had started calling Chloe regularly, riding my unicycle to town, dialing from a pay phone. The strange male voice never picked up again. Chloe always answered. She would say hello. I hung up every time.

I thought about Chloe living alone in our house. The upstairs and the downstairs, all those empty rooms, the backyard and the front yard. No one to clean up after her the way I did for Smita. No Mr Markman to grill her hamburgers or help her with basketball. No one to ask about her homework or edit her essays. No one to eat dinners with. Maybe Chloe did not even eat at all. Maybe she was back on a diet with no one wonderful like Smita to tell her about the medicinal power of spinach.

Sometimes, Lisa would run her hands up and down my back, her fingers passing over my tattoo, and I would think about Chloe. I would clean the toilet bowl with Lysol disinfectant and I'd think about Chloe. How I'd made her throw up. How I made Chloe eat. I looked at Daisy licking Smita's face and remembered how angry I'd gotten when Daisy licked Chloe. Daisy used to shit and pee in the house, and Chloe had cleaned that up too. I'd look at Lisa Markman, who drove all the way to Massachusetts to see me, and think about how much I liked her. I hadn't let Chloe have her own friend. Lisa had told me that they did not even have a good time together in Hawaii.

Still, I was happy. Crazy happy. Smita loved me, I was doing well in school, I had a girlfriend. I was pretty. I was smart. But if I relaxed for even a second, my stomach started to hurt. What about Chloe? My other half. The better part of me. I didn't want to think about Chloe. I tried to remind myself that she had been the reason for my misery. She had wanted me gone. She went to Hawaii. She joined a basketball team. Anything to get away from me. Only now I was the one who was gone. Chloe could do whatever she wanted, wear whatever she wanted, be whoever she wanted. I didn't care. I was having dinner, alone with Smita.

twins

I pushed my aloo saag back and forth on my plate.

I wasn't hungry, and it was my favorite dinner. I couldn't eat, and it was Chloe's fault. Chloe was still making me crazy. I smashed a potato flat on my plate with Smita's blue ceramic saltshaker.

'Do you think,' I asked Smita, 'that it's bad for all people to be alone?'

'I do,' Smita said. 'Even monks who take a vow of silence don't live alone. But tell me. What people do you mean?'

I smashed another potato. Then I wiped the bottom of the salt-shaker clean with my napkin.

'Chloe,' I said.

'Chloe,' Smita repeated.

I had lived with Smita for almost a year, and never once had I talked to her about Chloe. Smita made me eat, she made me go to school and be nice to Daniel, but she had never once asked me about my identical twin sister.

'I think,' I said, slowly, twisting a longish lock of hair around my finger, 'I think that I was mean to Chloe.'

'You think you were mean?' Smita said.

She was repeating after me like she was a retard. She smashed a potato on her plate and then ate the mashed potato with her fingers.

'Yes,' I said.

All the cruel things I had ever done were coming back to me. Stealing Chloe's clothes, calling Chloe stupid, following Chloe through school, making Chloe get a tattoo.

'How were you mean to your sister?'

'I wasn't mean on purpose.'

'That's beside the point,' Smita said. 'Intention is irrelevant.' She lit a cigarette. Smita never smoked with dinner. She was breaking her own rule. 'My father thought he loved me when he molested me in my bed every night when I was six years old. He called me his little princess and gave me sweets and pretty dresses to wear.'

I smashed the pieces of yellow potato on my plate, one by one. The spinach was already flat. 'That's not fair.'

'No.' Smita blew smoke into the air. She took the saltshaker from my hand. 'It's probably not. I just want you to know that cruelty is cruelty.'

'I said I was mean. Not cruel.'

Smita smiled. 'You think there is a difference?'

Of course there was a difference. There had to be.

'You hate me?' I said.

'You are not like my father,' she said. 'I don't know why I said that. Obviously there are varying degrees of cruelty.'

But I wondered if maybe I was as bad as Smita's father. Maybe I was a monster.

Smita smoked quietly, and I waited for whatever it was she would say next. I could see her thinking. I wished I hadn't mentioned the name. Chloe. Now Smita and I could not go back like we were before. I watched Smita inhale her cigarette, the puff of smoke that she blew from her mouth.

'I never showed you the photos,' she said. 'The ones I took the day I first met you, with Yumiko. I developed them right away, but I didn't think you were ready to see them. Would you like to see them now?'

'No,' I said.

Smita went upstairs and came back with the pictures.

'I don't want to see them,' I said.

Smita handed them to me anyway.

'I am naked,' I said.

The bones of my pelvis stuck out from the rest of my body. I could hear Yumiko, so fucking pleased, telling me what a great pelvis I had. There were dark, dark circles under my eyes. I was bald. My arms were crossed over my skinny chest. I was staring past Smita's camera way off into the distance. I flipped to the next picture. It was my back. The picture started at the base of my neck, a big, knobby bump, and then, one by one, all of the little bones that made up my spine, and finally, where the bones stopped, the small of my back. My tattoo. The simple pink block letters: C H L O E.

I knew the tattoo was there. I didn't have to see it to remember. I had made Chloe get the tattoo so she would never be able to forget me. I gently touched the tattoo on the photo with my finger. I had trained myself to stop rubbing my back.

Smita watched me.

'I look much better now,' I said.

'You do,' Smita said. 'It used to hurt just to look at you.'

Smita had hennaed my hair red. It had grown in, wispy and soft. I looked like a different person.

'I like my hair,' I said.

There was one more photo in the stack.

'Go on,' Smita said.

It was of a younger Smita, sitting on a park bench, wearing a green hospital gown.

'I was eighteen,' she said. 'My weight was down to seventy-two pounds. They had to feed me intravenously.'

I looked across the table at Smita, pretty Smita, her dark hair shining, the dangling earrings, her confident face.

'You were anorexic?'

I never knew why it mattered to Smita that I ate. I thought it was because Smita was good, because she was the kind of person who did good things for no reason at all.

'For a long time, I couldn't swallow food,' Smita said. 'I was in therapy, and I started to remember things about my childhood. About my father. Things that I had made myself forget. My father forcing his penis into my mouth. And after that, I couldn't eat. I would gag on my food.'

'I didn't know,' I said.

'I never told you.'

I stared at Smita's picture. Her hair hung down to her waist. She looked hollow, small. If you'd kicked her, she would have shattered into a million, billion tiny pieces. Smita had told me before that her father had molested her, but what that meant had never registered with me. She had never told me how he hurt her, damaged her. I could not believe this girl in the picture. I looked at it, and I looked at the pictures of me. I touched my hair, and I looked at Smita, in front of me, beautiful. Smita laughed all the time, and sometimes, she danced while she cooked. She loved blue-cheese cheese puffs and jasmine tea. Smita was fine.

Smita touched my hand, and I started to cry. I didn't want to cry anymore. I had never meant to be cruel. I did not want to be a cruel, awful person like Smita's father. I didn't know I was being horrible. I had only wanted Chloe to love me. I wanted Chloe to love me the way I loved her.

'Chloe was always on a diet,' I said. 'I started throwing up so that I could stay the same as her. No matter what, I would not let Chloe get thinner. And then, she started to eat again, but I couldn't. I just couldn't. It wasn't even that she ignored me. Chloe didn't care that I was alive. So I shaved my head.'

'And you weren't identical,' Smita said.

I reached around, touched my tattoo on my back. I could almost feel the letters raised on my skin, even thought the spot was smooth. We had never been identical. Chloe would always be an eighth of an inch taller.

'Would you take my picture now?' I said.

Smita nodded. 'I would love to.'

'Why did you never ask me about Chloe before?' I asked.

twins

'It's your story to tell.'

'I don't have a story.' I took the saltshaker from Smita. The potatoes were all smashed. I salted them. 'I'm boring.'

Smita laughed. I liked to hear Smita laugh. She ground some pepper over my mashed potatoes. 'You've got to meet some more people, Sue,' she said. 'If you want to know about boring.'

'Boring,' Smita repeated, her eyes shining. 'That's brilliant.'

My eyes were still wet with tears. Smita had never been mad at me before. I had felt my whole world collapsing around me, but just as quickly, everything went back to being fine.

'I want to see Chloe,' I said.

'You should see her,' Smita said.

'I don't want to be a cruel person.'

Smita shook her head. 'I never actually said you were cruel.'

'I was mean,' I said. 'I once broke Lisa Markman's nose with a tennis ball.'

Smita smiled at me. 'I'd like to take your picture, right now.'

I leaned back in my chair, closing my eyes. I would go see Chloe. Smita would take me to her. Smita could take our picture, together. Chloe could wear anything she wanted. Smita went upstairs to get her camera.

'That was the best thing,' I said to myself. 'Smashing Lisa's nose.'

Chloe

The house was quiet after James left. Jamal and Tashika went with him. James had kissed me on the forehead. 'You can call me, too,' he said, leaning forward at the last minute, whispering into my ear. 'I'll be staying at Jamal's cousin's for a while.'

He wrote the telephone number on the back of a pizza box.

I was not sure if I was happy. I had wanted them gone. Louise Patterson had come into the house and taken control of the situation like she had promised. James didn't even seem surprised. It had been so easy. They packed their things that same night. I let them take the stereo, the blender, and a camel hair coat my father had left in the closet. I had thought that James might try to fight for me. I had even thought, if he really wanted to stay, I might change my mind.

I poured myself a tumbler of whiskey and sat on the kitchen floor, surveying the mess they had left me. My ears were ringing from the quiet. I did not feel like I was any happier. I swallowed four aspirin with my whiskey, resting my hand on my stomach. My period was late. I had always been careful about using condoms, and I had recently peed into a cup at the doctor's office. But it was late nevertheless. I already shared my DNA with one other person, and I didn't know how to be myself.

I took a sip of whiskey.

I could feel it in the pit of my stomach right away. James and Jamal had said all of my father's booze was top of the line. I thought how funny it was that my father had always believed Sue was the problem twin. After Sue got arrested for shoplifting, he assumed that the drinking and the drugs and the sex would all come later. Instead, she learned how to juggle. It was my life that had turned to shambles. My father was not the smartest of men. He was not the most impressive of fathers. I would never go to Harvard Law School. I would have to find something else to do.

The telephone rang.

'The phone,' I said.

I realized that I could talk to myself if I wanted to. I was all alone in a three-story house.

'The phone, the phone, the phone,' I said in a singsong voice.

I could not remember the word for telephone in French. Maybe I had never learned it. Maybe it was something easy, like le téléphone. Once Tashika moved in, the phone had never stopped ringing, but it was never for me. I had a feeling this call could be for me. I took another large gulp of my drink and crawled across the kitchen floor, steadily making my way, but the phone stopped ringing before I could answer it.

'Quel dommage,' I said.

I was surprised that I still remembered any of the French I had learned. I was pleased. I did not want to be stupid. I had almost liked being smart.

'Je m'appelle Chloe,' I said.

The phone started to ring again. I sprang to my feet, answering it right away this time. The caller hung up.

I slunk back to the floor and waited. When the phone rang again, I grabbed the cord, pulling the receiver down to me so that I would not have to get back up.

'Hello?' I said. 'Sue?'

The caller hung up. My heart was beating fast. I knew it was Sue. It had to be her. I realized that I wanted nothing more than to talk to Sue. Where had she gone? What was she doing? Why didn't she miss me? How was it possible that she could survive without me? Still off the hook, the phone started to buzz in my lap. I made my own buzzing sound to go with it. I could not hear the noise in my head. I considered lying down on the floor, but I had a feeling that I would not have been able to get back up. This is what it had all come down to. I could fall asleep on the floor, and when I woke up, I would be that much closer to the refrigerator. I could have been a star on a television sitcom. Sue and I could have gone on double dates with James and Jamal.

I could feel the whiskey, warm and angry in my stomach.

'Here we go,' I said.

It seemed fitting that I finished my first night alone in the house down on my knees, in front of the toilet, throwing up. I was certain I was purging my system of the alcohol. I hoped it was not the side effects of alien cells multiplying in my body. I wanted to believe that I was throwing up the last year of my life. The next day, I would let myself start all over again. I would wake up and I would wash and condition my hair.

The next time Sue called, I talked before she hung up. 'I think about you,' I said. 'At the weirdest times I wonder, What is Sue doing right now, where is she? Where does she sleep? Is she sleeping in my pink pajamas?'

I held the phone, listening to the silence, listening to Sue breathe.

twins

I had no doubt that it was her. 'You used to drive me crazy. I used to count the days until I could go to college so that I could get away from you, but now I just miss you.'

I held the phone, wondering what to do next.

'You don't,' Sue said.

I took a deep breath. I had not talked to her in so long. Her voice sounded so much like mine.

'I do,' I said.

'No,' Sue said.

And then I smiled to myself. Because it was never easy with Sue. She would not believe me. She would not be nice, for example, and say something sweet, like, I missed you too, Chloe. She was still the younger sister.

'I do,' I said.

'What are you doing home now?' Sue said. 'You're supposed to be at basketball practice.'

I pressed the phone between my shoulder and my ear, laying my hands on my flat belly, closing my eyes.

'I think,' I said, nodding to myself, 'I think I quit the team.' The coach had stopped calling. 'I did,' I said to Sue. 'I quit.'

I remembered that I used to be ambitious. I had once been a talented athlete. I had once been a good student. But I had done all of these things to distance myself from Sue, and now, I simply wanted her back.

'That's impossible,' Sue said. 'You love to play basketball.'

'I do?'

It seemed so silly, when I thought about it, to actually care about sinking a ball through a hoop, to get pleasure from the stupid sound it made when it fell through the net.

'You're such a fucking moron,' Sue said. 'You are crazy about the game.'

'I am?' I said.

Sue sighed. 'You love it,' she said. 'Your face gets all aglow.'
'It does?'

I tried to picture Sue. My parents had told me she had shaved her head. They said she was going to private school.

'Where are you?' I said, but Sue had hung up on me.

But I knew where she was. In a college town in Massachusetts with my brother, Daniel, and his newest girlfriend. How, I wondered, would Sue know what I love? She knew nothing about me, my life. She did not know about James or Jamal. She had no idea who I was. The last thing that I wanted to do was play basketball.

I would show them all: my father, who thought I had law school potential; Mr Markman, who thought I'd play in the WNBA; Sue, who always thought I was a Goody Two-shoes. I would be an unwed mother. I would start smoking crack. I would be the bad girl Sue had always threatened to become.

But Sue called again at the same time the very next day. 'You're not at practice,' she said.

'I told you. I quit the team.'

'Retard,' Sue said. 'Go to practice.'

'Why do you care?'

A long silence followed. It was only our second phone call, and already I was exasperated.

'Chloe,' Sue said. 'You have to. You have to.'

Something about the way she said my name, a familiar longing, a plea, broke my heart. I wished that she was with me, sitting on the floor next to me, so that I could comb the tangles out of her hair.

I told her I would start the next day.

It all came back to me.

The basketball's arc and fall, the mesmerizing swish the ball made as it passed through the net. I took my place at the foul line and shot continuous free throws; I felt that familiar thrill as the ball sailed from my fingers and sank into the basket. I remembered Mr Markman telling me that I had a gift.

I loved to play basketball.

I had forgotten how much I loved it.

I wondered how Sue had known this. She had always glared at me from the stands.

The coach said, 'Chloe, thank God you've come to your senses.' He surprised me by giving me a hug. 'We missed you here.'

Kendra smiled at me like we were old friends. 'Hey, girl,' she said. 'You're back. I've seen you walking through the halls, looking like a zombie. I figured you must be pregnant.'

'My period,' I said, 'is two weeks late.'

Kendra's mouth opened wide. She had been joking, but I wasn't. She touched my arm.

'It could be nothing,' she said. 'Stress can make you late.' She spun the basketball around on her finger, slowly, as if she was thinking. 'Do you have three hundred dollars?'

I nodded.

'Then either way, it's no big thing,' Kendra said. 'A simple medical procedure.'

Kendra, I would find out, was a terrifically practical person. 'I will go with you to the clinic if you want me to.'

I looked at Kendra in amazement. She was almost a full head taller than me, and according to Mr Markman I was plenty tall for women's basketball. It was easy to talk to her, and I wondered why I had not tried before.

'Are you going to play in college?' I asked.

'Of course.' Kendra nodded. 'Aren't you?'

Kendra had started dribbling as we talked, moving the ball back and forth between her right hand and her left. I was back on the team. I had stepped out of my world, and now, I was stepping back in. I had not ruined my life. 'I think so,' I said.

Then I remembered I had not applied to any schools.

Kendra stopped dribbling. She rolled her eyes at me. 'You think so?' she said. 'You're the best player on the team.'

'Okay,' I said. 'Why not?'

'You can write your own ticket,' Kendra said.

I nodded. The coach blew his whistle, and we lined up midcourt for a layup drill. I was first in line. I drove to the basket, making my first layup of the season. I hadn't lost a thing. I had the footwork; I had control of the ball. I sank the ball through the net, again and again. I felt right with a basketball in my hand, my skin slick with sweat, my heart beating fast. Nothing else mattered, just putting the ball to the hoop. I could not believe how good it felt.

I had found my first real friend in Kendra. I was careful not to talk about her when Sue called. I didn't want to make Sue angry. She seemed pleased that I was back on the team. She kept track of my schedule. She asked me how many points I scored during my games. I thanked her for making me go back to practice.

'I am not an awful person,' Sue said.

'I know,' I said.

'I don't want you to hate me,' she said.

Sue had started calling late at night. Sometimes we would just listen to each other breathe. I would lie curled on my side in the bed, holding the phone to my ear. She did not call on the weekends.

Kendra was nothing like Lisa Markman. She was both practical and kind, and though she was only eighteen, she already had the entire course of her life planned out. She thought of basketball as a means to an end, a full college scholarship. Kendra wanted

to be an investment banker. She wanted to get married to a professional black man, have two children and a Labrador retriever she
would name Happy. Kendra wanted to drive a Lexus. She loved
her mother and father; she had never gotten drunk. She had never
had sex. She was going to wait until she got married.

'No one ever told you James Patterson was a fool?' she said.
'It's common knowledge. Why didn't you ask me?'

It was Kendra who bought me flowers after I got my period.

'You are one lucky girl,' she said, watching me as I put them
into a tall crystal vase.

And for the first time, I started to think of myself in a brand-
new light: lucky. I was blessed with an enormous talent, and I was
not going to waste it. I had my whole life in front of me. If I
wanted to, I could still hope for the Olympics, and I would be
going not for Mr Markman but for myself. Kendra was a big
believer in female empowerment. I had missed the deadlines for
college applications, but Kendra assured me that I could apply the
following year. All the best schools, she said, had women's basketball teams, all of them would want me. A year wouldn't matter.
Kendra often came to my house after practice, to do her homework on the new laptop computer my parents had sent me out
of the blue.

Kendra sat at my desk, teaching herself to use Excel.

'It is always good,' she said, 'to get ahead of the game.'

I sat on the bed, with a notebook propped on my knees, writing a letter to Mr Markman. Now that James was gone, now that
I was almost talking to Sue, it was strange how Mr Markman had
begun to reclaim his place in my mind; he was with me at practice,
he was watching me play, admiring my new technique. In my letter,
I did not tell him that he meant more to me than my own parents
or that Sue had stolen all of the presents he had given me. I wrote
those sentences and then I crossed them out, started on a clean sheet

of paper. Instead, I thanked him for the interest he had taken in my life. I apologized for my father's rudeness and assured him that I had never doubted his intentions. I wrote that he would approve of my coach at school, who was transforming me into a power player. I told Mr Markman that the coach said my shooting skills were out of this world, and so we were focusing on my being more aggressive. He wanted me to draw fouls and move in hard for rebounds. My new motto was 'Be aggressive', though every time I said the words in my head, I started to laugh. I wished Mr Markman the best in life. The very, very best. I folded the letter, sealed the envelope, and Kendra and I walked together to the mailbox.

'That was something when I saw you on TV with him,' she said. 'No one on the team thought you were sleeping with him. You seemed much too mousy to do something like that. His daughter, Lisa, now she's a real bitch.'

I saw Lisa at school. She would sit in the cafeteria by herself, eating a sandwich and reading: first it was *Midnight's Children* by Salman Rushdie, then *The Color Purple* by Alice Walker. She studiously avoided making eye contact with me, but I found myself wanting to talk to her. I wanted to know what had happened to her. How she had become a different person. I imagined Sue had also transformed herself, living so far away for such a long time, living without me.

Sometimes I walked through my clean, empty house and thought that I had made up James Patterson, that he had never existed.

Between the two of us, we had a championship team. First we won our division, then the county. The state championship was next.

'You should see the trophy,' Kendra said, cutting a tall space in the air with her hands.

twins

I felt calmer on the court than I ever had. Sue was not in the top row, watching with her cold, hard stare. James never showed up with his funny cardboard signs. And Mr Markman was not in his regular seat, sitting upright at the end of the row. Winning did not matter; I did not tally how many baskets I had scored in my head like I had the previous season. I simply played for every shot.

Kendra said my technique was very Zen. I was scoring between twenty and thirty points a game. The other girls on my team, Gabrielle and Patrice and Tiffany and Jessie and Eliza, they all liked to win, and because I was friends with Kendra, they liked me too. We went out for pizza after the games. I ate extra-cheese pizza. Sometimes, I would eat three slices.

'You can write your ticket, girl,' Kendra said. 'Anything you want. Look at you with your blond hair. You are blessed.'

Sue

Chloe told me about the state championships.

I didn't know if it was an invitation. She mentioned the day
and told me where she was playing before I hung up the phone.
I felt bad. I felt terrible. I looked at the faded newspaper clipping
on the wall. 'She Shoots, She Scores.' I had always liked watching Chloe play basketball. She was the best player on the court,
serious and self-assured, running, passing, dribbling, shooting. She
never laughed or cracked a smile. In between points, she smoothed
her hair and looked at Mr Markman. I used to be so jealous, watching the way her face changed when he smiled at her. I had been
jealous of Chloe my entire life.

I called right back.

'I'm sorry,' I said, breathless, 'for hanging up on you.'

'It doesn't matter,' she said. I could picture Chloe shrug. 'You
called back.'

She told me, again, where her game was being played. Chloe's
voice sounded different from when I first started calling. She had
sounded flat and tired; she had scared me when she said she quit
playing basketball. I knew that somehow, unknowingly, I had

done her harm. But I was not like Smita's father; I wanted to be good. I wanted Chloe to love me the way I loved her. She made me cry when she told me about her high scores because she was feeling better. I wiped away my tears, grateful that she couldn't see them. I had expected Chloe to get angry with me, but she didn't. Instead, she thanked me. Our whole life, I could not remember Chloe thanking me for anything. I told her about my hair, which was red and came down almost to my chin.

'Red?' Chloe said, laughing. 'Really?'

I had been accepted to Hampshire. I would start college in the fall. Out of the blue, my useless parents had sent me a laptop computer. I was typing my memoirs, beginning from the moment I was born, four minutes behind, smaller, louder, and cheated from the start, when my parents gave Chloe the better name. I could type fast, without looking at my fingers.

At school, I hung around with my new friend, Carrie Lind. She had long, curly hair. We played footsie under the desk during classes, and once we made out in the janitor's closet.

Lisa Markman still visited every weekend. She taught me how to drive in her red convertible. She let her tongue linger longer and longer in my mouth when she kissed me good-bye. She had stopped wearing her diamond engagement ring and started calling during the week. She got jealous when I talked about Carrie. This made me ridiculously happy.

For days I wandered around nervous, excited, thinking about Chloe's game. And then, finally, I told Smita. She flung a cheese puff at my head. 'Ding-dong,' she said. 'Are we going or what?'

'We are going,' I said.

I was going to see Chloe.

Chloe

I could hear the crowd yelling my name.

I had gotten fouled as the buzzer rang, marking the end of the fourth and final quarter just as I scored a layup to tie the game. If I made the free throw, I'd win the championship for the team. Kendra stood beneath the basket, sweat dripping off her face, her hands clenched into fists as she watched me. Kendra had already gotten into college and been awarded a four-year scholarship, and still, she wanted to win.

'This is your shot.' She mouthed the words.

I felt as if I had entered a scene from one of Mr Markman's basketball videos, except that I was actually on the court, and the crowd was cheering for me. There was no gentle song of tropical birds in the distance.

I needed to focus.

I had spent the entire week in a nervous state, unable to fall asleep, cursing myself for inviting Sue. I was certain she would not show up, and I felt humiliated knowing how much I wanted her to be there. Kendra had also instructed me to invite my parents. She had learned forgiveness long ago in Sunday school; she said that my parents were in dire need of redemption. I had shrugged, telling Kendra that my parents were busy people.

'They will come,' Kendra said. 'It's the championships.'

She was right.

Everyone I had ever known was in the stands.

My parents, sitting upright in their bleacher seats, wearing matching sweaters and clapping politely whenever my team scored a basket.

James and Jamal, who I had not spoken to since the day they had left. They sat in the rafters, waving an enormous red and white banner that read, 'Go, Chloe, Go.' I could tell from one quick glance that they had a smoked a joint before the game, and that James still enjoyed looking at my legs. I was happy they did not hate me.

Mr Markman was there, tall and amazing, in the very front row with his children, both Lisa and Todd. Before the opening whistle had been blown, I looked into his deep, dark eyes, and he held my gaze. We stared at each other, and then he smiled, blowing me a kiss. 'Be aggressive,' he yelled, and I knew that he had read my letter.

Before the game had begun, I was in the locker room lacing my sneakers extra tight, taking a long, deep breath, when I heard a loud burst of applause. The coach came up to me. 'Rodney Markman is in the house.' He patted my back with a kind smile, and I realized that the coach, for one, had never believed the rumors. He had always liked me. Everyone on the team liked me. Kendra told me I was not a difficult person to like.

All through the game, I felt my legs solid on the court, my hands on the ball, fielding rebounds, scoring baskets, but really I was floating through the stands. I saw my mother mark something down on her legal notepad. I saw my father nod in approval when the ref blew the whistle after I'd been fouled. I saw Todd staring at the clock, and Lisa whispering into the ear of my beautiful twin sister, Sue.

My twin sister, Sue, who was no longer identical to me. She had chin-length red hair, long bangs that hung in her eyes. Sue! She sat between Lisa Markman and a beautiful Indian woman who smiled at me as if she knew who I was. My brother, Daniel, was there too, his arm around the Indian woman's shoulder.

Sue never clapped when I scored. She sat on her hands, biting her lip. After I scored the layup that tied the game, I looked for her. I smiled at Sue, and nobody else, and she grinned back at me, tears spilling down her cheeks.

Drama queen, I thought, bouncing the ball to calm myself down.

I was ridiculously pleased that I could still make Sue cry. I stood at the foul line and I stared at the basket. I could feel all of their eyes on me as the ball rolled off my fingertips and sailed up toward the basket. I could sense a hush in the stadium. I closed my eyes, and I listened.

Acknowledgements

I'd like to thank my agent Alex Glass, my editor Joelle Yudin at William Morrow, Charlotte Mendelson and Leah Woodburn at Review, the Writers Room in NYC, the Soaring Gardens Artists' Retreat, the wonderful Dermanskys – Ann, Ira, Michael and Julie – and especially, Jürgen Fauth.